A Shadow in Love

A BADGER BLISS BOOK

By

Karen D. Badger

DEDICATION

My mom, Ellie Atherton, left us at the age of eighty-six, on January 2, 2021 after fighting a fifteen year battle with kidney failure. She was feisty and strong, and she taught me everything I know about being a warrior and about being the best mom I could be to my own kids. She was my best friend, and my hero, and she loved her lesbian daughter unconditionally. I've often said she would shout from the rooftops how proud she was of me, if only she could climb the ladder!

Shortly after I finished this book, I put it into the capable hands of my beta readers, one of whom was my mom. She has been a beta reader for every one of my books. She used to love to rub it in whenever she found an error, and it used to irk me to no end. How I would now love for her to needle me just one more time. She got through the first five chapters of this book before she was hospitalized, and finally left us. I hope she has the chance to read the rest of it in heaven.

I struggle to see through tears as I write this dedication. My heart is fighting a battle between sadness that she is gone, and joy that she is now free of pain and sickness, and finally reunited with my stepdad, Boone and my older brother, Steve.

I miss you, Mom, and I will love you forever.

Karen

ALSO WRITTEN BY KAREN D. BADGER AND
AVAILABLE FROM BADGER BLISS BOOKS:

ON A WING AND A PRAYER
YESTERDAY ONCE MORE (*Award Winner!*)
THE BLUE FEATHER
ALL MY TOMORROWS
1140 RUE ROYALE (*Award Winner!*)
OVER THE CRESCENT MOON (*2X Award Winner!*)
A SHADOW IN LOVE

<u>The Billie/Cat Commitment Series:</u>
  IN A FAMILY WAY
  UNCHAINED MEMORIES
  HAPPY CAMPERS
  COLLECTIVE IDENTITY
  SWEET ANGEL
  RELATIVE-LY SPEAKIN
  TAILSPIN
  FLASHPOINT
  IN THE BLINK OF AN EYE (*YA - Award Finalist!*)
  UDDER NONSENSE

www.badgerblissbooks.com

A Shadow in Love

$\mathcal{B}$

A BADGER BLISS BOOK

By

Karen D. Badger

This is a work of fiction. All characters, locales, and events are either products of the author's imagination or are used fictitiously.

A SHADOW IN LOVE

Cover image: Karen D. Badger
Cover design by Karen D. Badger

A Badger Bliss Book
Published by Badger Bliss Books
Georgia, VT 05468

www.badgerblissbooks.com

Print book ISBN 13: 978-1-945761-32-4
Ebook ISBN 13: 978-1-945761-33-1

First Edition, February 2021

Printed in the United States of America and in the United Kingdom

ACKNOWLEDGMENTS

This is my first attempt at writing science fiction. I have never been much of a sci-fi fan, except for 'Seven of Nine' (wink, wink), and as such, I had to rely heavily on my wonderfully sci-fi geeky wife, Barb Sawyer for advice and counsel. Thank you, sweetie!

I want thank those who worked to find my typos and fix my literary errors. A mere thank you is not enough to acknowledge the contribution of these wonderful women.

My literary squad includes:

Ellie Atherton, my eight-six year old mom and number one fan, Carol 'Chief Eagle Eye' Poynor, Sallyanne Monti, my 'Sedona Connection', 'Downtown' Donna Brown and last but not least, Barb Sawyer, AKA, 'Bliss', my better half and keeper of my soul. A special thank you to Nat Burns, amazing editor and sister from another mother, who worked tirelessly to make this story the best that it could be.

A Shadow in Love

Prologue

Zangendar made the final adjustments to the vortex coordinates while an older individual looked over her shoulder.

"Tell me again why you chose this particular location," her companion asked.

Zangendar displayed the image of a planet on her screen and pointed to a specific spot. "This planet has several locations with concentrations of vortex energy, but the intensity appears to be strong at this one particular spot. The atmospheric analysis indicates this will be the easiest point of entry."

"Are you certain your mission will be successful, daughter?"

"As certain as I can be, Molinder. My research indicates a compatible atmosphere. I am, however, somewhat concerned about the passage of time there."

"Concerned how?"

"It appears to move slower than we are accustomed to—by a factor of ten to be precise. It could have an adverse affect on our life spans."

"That does not give me comfort, daughter."

Zangendar turned to her mother. "Molinder, you know how important this mission is. It is the season for procreation for my generation, and soon there will be insufficient sustenance for our people in our current habitat. We need to find other ways to insure the future of our species. If we do not do this, it will be only a matter of time before there is no one left. It may already be, too late."

"Belander will not be pleased."

Zangendar sighed and lowered her chin to her chest. "Molinder, I realize she gave birth to me, but that alone is not reason enough for me to desert my mission. I realize that every generation is expected to contribute to the proliferation of our species, and I realize that we have to travel to other planets to accomplish this since Vakillia is dying, but it is up to my generation to solve this problem or there may not *be* a next generation. We not only need to procreate, but we need to find a new homeland as well.

"There certainly are risks. I could encounter hostility. I could be exterminated, but I must do this. You and Belander will have one another in the event I am unable to return." Zangendar looked around. "Where is she, by the way?"

"Belander refused to join me to wish you safe travels. She said it pains her too much to know it could be the last time we may see you."

Zangendar turned her attention to the console. "She never did have much confidence in my abilities. I have been working with Tredoran for nearly a birth year. The academy has enough trust in this project, and in us, to have provided funding from the beginning. Our research indicates the atmosphere is compatible. We know the resources are plentiful."

"And the natives? Will they have us?" Molinder asked.

"That is yet to be determined. That is the primary objective of this pilot trip. That is the very reason I am going alone—to minimize our exposure."

"And if they reject us? What then?"

"Then we move on and explore further."

The door to the lab slid open suddenly, admitting Zangendar's best friend and fellow scientist.

"Tredoran, you are here," Zangendar said.

Tredoran embraced her friend. "You could not keep me away. And besides, who will operate the controls to get you back?"

"If you survive this mission to come back," Molinder said below her breath.

Tredoran looked at the older woman. "We would not be doing this if we did not have confidence in our chances for success. I know we are a peaceful race, but Zangendar will have the means to defend herself if necessary."

"Tredoran is correct, Molinder." Zangendar reached for her mother's hand and placed it on the side of her own face. "My fondness for you and Belander knows no bounds. Have faith in your only offspring. I know I have not always fit the mold of our people, but I will not risk the mission. I will return. You have my word."

"Do you have your medication with you, Zangendar? In the event you cannot return immediately, you will need to have it with you," Molinder said.

"I have it in my pouch, Molinder."

"Do not forget to take it."

"I will not forget."

Molinder nodded and took a step back.

Tredoran immediately filled the void. The two friends placed their right hands on the other's left shoulder and then lowered their foreheads to touch.

"My soul travels with you. Be safe," Tredoran said.

"My trust is in your hands. I will return soon," Zangendar replied.

Chapter 1

Mackenzie Caldwell slid into the booth at the paleo restaurant and immediately ordered a green tea smoothie. She was parched. While she waited for her drink, she searched the social media sites on her phone for the latest status on her friends and family. Almost against her will, she went to Jessie's home page. As she searched, she hoped this particular site didn't share search history with its page owners. The last thing she wanted was for Jessie to know she had yet to move on. She didn't need Jessie to know her heart was still bruised and tender from the way things ended between them.

Kenzie thought back to six months ago. Life with Jessie had been exciting with never a dull moment. Jessie Cole was a freelance artist, specializing in oil portraits. She had an amazing talent and the ability to transfer what her eye saw to a canvas in a remarkably short amount of time, and in such realistic detail that many commented that her portraits looked more like photographs than paintings. In addition to her artistic talents, Jessie was a true people person. She knew no stranger.

Jessie was quite literally a throwback to the hippie generation. She was the epitome of the nineteen-sixty's flowerchild with long blonde hair parted in the middle, and a headband or bandanna tied around her head. Frayed blue-jeans, oversized T-shirts that always seemed to be stained with paint and the obligatory sandals were her typical wardrobe. Her demeanor and approach to people immediately drew them to her and contributed greatly to her popularity as an artist.

Jessie had come into Kenzie's life at a time when she desperately needed affirmation of her worth. At the age of twenty-six, Kenzie came out to her parents and was immediately rejected by them and by the deeply religious community she had been raised in. The fact that she was gay was not the issue. The fact that she acted on it, was. She was ordered to ignore her feelings or be subject to ecclesiastical discipline, including probation, termination of fellowship and finally excommunication. So engrossed was her family in the teachings of the church, that excommunication meant they were required to shun her as well. Sadly, they were prepared to do just that. The church literally demanded she choose between acknowledging who she was and never seeing her family again.

She chose herself.

Kenzie cut off her long red hair and had it styled in a short, boy-cut. She packed her belongings and put in her notice at the hospital where she was a registered nurse with a specialty in genetics. Two weeks later, she moved away from her Utah hometown and signed a lease on a cozy one-bedroom flat in Sedona, Arizona. Within days, she bought a case of sunscreen to protect her freckled, Irish complexion and sunglasses to shield her green eyes from the bright sun. She also found employment at the urgent care center within walking distance of her apartment. The new job did not make full use of her genetics skills and training, but Kenzie welcomed the change and the chance to escape the prison she had found herself in, back in Utah. Here in Sedona, she was free to be who she was and to celebrate all that life had in store for her.

Before long, Kenzie allowed the peaceful spirituality of Sedona to captivate her, and she soon became intimately familiar with the beautiful red rock formations, hiking trails and spiritual centers throughout the area. Three times a week, she practiced solitary yoga off the hiking paths of Bell Rock, Cathedral Rock and Boynton Canyon. In these environments, she found peace and self-love.

Then, along came Jessie.

Kenzie remembered the day she met Jessie. She had been working at the urgent care center for all of two weeks when this cute hippie-chick limped in. She had fallen down a short flight of stairs while carrying a huge portrait. Kenzie was immediately smitten. Her hands shook as she wrapped the ace bandage around the blonde's ankle. Jessie left with Kenzie's cellphone number tucked safely in her pocket. Three weeks later, Jessie moved in with her.

That was two years ago.

Kenzie picked up her smoothie and took a long, cool sip. She flicked the screen upward on her phone and revealed a picture of Jessie with her latest conquest. This was a new one— not the one Kenzie found her with six months ago—in their bed, no less.

Her heart broke again.

"Hey, there!"

Kenzie was startled by the perky, blue-eyed, raven-haired beauty that slid into the booth across from her. She immediately put her phone face down on the table.

"Bree, you scared me!" Kenzie said.

"I'm not surprised. You looked like you were in a daze when I spotted you from the doorway." Bree looked at Kenzie's phone and grabbed it before Kenzie could stop her. "Please don't tell me you've been pining after Jessie again."

Bree flipped the phone and was greeted by a picture of Jessie with her newest flame. "Geeze, Kenzie. Why do you torture yourself like this?"

Kenzie sat back and cradled her smoothie in her hands. "I can't help it, Bree. She was my first, you know? I loved her with everything I am. She broke my heart."

Bree closed the social media app on Kenzie's phone and slid it across the table toward her. "You need to do something to get yourself out of this funk."

"I do yoga," Kenzie said lamely.

"You can't cuddle with yoga at night," Bree said. "I tell you what…Jimmy and I are going clubbing this weekend. Wanna join us?"

"I'm not sure a honky-tonk bar is the best place to meet lesbians, Bree."

"Well, it's better than sitting at home and feeling sorry for yourself, girlfriend."

"You might be right. Hit me up again as we get closer to the weekend. I might be ready for a night out by then."

"It's a deal," Bree said. She picked up the menu. "Now, what looks good? I'm starved."

"Don't eat so much that I need to nudge you awake in the crossover meeting this afternoon," Kenzie said.

Bree put the menu down quickly. "Ugh! I hate that meeting."

"I do too, but the urgent care administration insists on a review of all the cases at the end of each day. I guess there was some kind of malpractice suit a few years ago and the admins weren't informed enough to deal with it."

"So, we get to pay for someone else's negligence."

"Pretty much. Oh, here comes the waiter. The green smoothies are awesome here. I recommend you start with one," Kenzie said.

***

Kenzie walked Bree to her car after work.

"Do you want a ride home?" Bree asked.

"No. I'm just a few blocks away."

"But it's really, really hot out here. You'll be scorched by the time you get there."

"I'll be fine. You get on home to Jimmy."

"I hate knowing you're going home to an empty house, Kenzie."

"Actually, I'm going to grab my yoga mat and some water, and head to Little Horse to meditate. I was going to go to The Chapel of the Holy Cross, but the crossover meeting went a little later than I'd hoped, so I'll save that for another day."

"Considering where you've come from, I'm surprised you want anything to do with a church."

"The Chapel is different. I don't go there to religion. You're right—I've pretty much given up on all of that. I go there because it's so beautiful. The chapel is built right into the red rock. When I'm there, I feel like I'm inside a protective bubble that's full of energy. It's like the energy pulses through me. I've done most of my healing there. It's a place I can feel safe and secure. It's an amazing experience. You should try it some time."

"Do you really believe in all that vortex stuff?" Bree asked.

"During the past two years, I've visited all the places in Sedona that vortexes are reported to be, and I have to admit that I do feel things when I visit some of the sites. Not all of them, mind you, but definitely at some of them."

"What kinds of *things*?"

"Well, like at the chapel, I feel safe and loved. At other sites, I feel this intense energy that is really hard to explain. When I do yoga at these sites, my mind is more open to my surroundings, so I tend to be more aware of the sounds and smells around me. Sometimes, I feel a tingling in my body, and sometimes, I have such intense emotions that it makes me cry, or yell, or even laugh.

"I was doing yoga at Bell Rock once and suddenly I got dizzy and fell down. I literally couldn't move. All I could do was lie on my mat and stare at the sky. I had absolutely no strength in my body. It was both scary and reflective. And then, there are times when I'm troubled or confused about something and meditating at a vortex site helps to bring clarity to whatever it is that's bothering me.

"In any case, without fail, whenever I visit one of the vortexes—and especially when I meditate there—I always come away more inspired, recharged and more peaceful than when I arrived. For me, they are truly places of healing. They were a godsend during the Jessie stuff."

"Have you always been open to all that New Age, metaphysical stuff?" Bree asked.

"I think being raised in a religious immersion environment as I was made me more open to things like that. You should try it some time."

"Maybe I will."

Bree climbed into her car and reached her hand through the open window.

Kenzie grasped it.

"I'll see you at work tomorrow," Bree said.

"Give Jimmy a hug for me."

"I will."

Kenzie waved as Bree backed out of her parking space and then watched her friend drive away.

***

Kenzie changed into spandex hiking shorts and a T-shirt, and hiking shoes to tackle the Little Horse Trail. Then she donned a wide-brimmed hat, grabbed her sunscreen, phone, earbuds, water and yoga mat; the latter strapped onto the bottom of her backpack. She hefted her bike off the rack she installed in her vestibule and headed across town toward the trail. When she arrived, she locked her bike to the fence in the visitor parking lot, and entered the trailhead.

Kenzie felt the tension from the day ease the moment she stepped foot on the trail. Little Horse Trail was a moderate trail, however, relatively easy to maneuver, with limited climbing. Parts of the trail led her through tree shaded areas, and some of it was wide open with red rock formations on both sides of the path. Partway down the trail, she encountered a relatively flat area that overlooked a valley. Kenzie walked to the edge of the cliff. In the distance, she could see Cathedral Rock.

She admired the beautiful scene before her for a few more minutes and then turned to head back up the trail. As she turned, she noticed something interesting. Her shadow was projected over the edge of the cliff onto the valley and low shrubs below her. With Cathedral Rock in the distance, Kenzie decided it would make a really good picture, so she fished her phone out of her backpack, captured the scene before her, and then slipped the phone back into her pack.

She picked up her pack and swung it onto her left shoulder. The movement caused her upper body to sway a bit to the right, and she felt a slight push on her shoulder, followed almost immediately by a sudden tingling that caused the hair to stand up on her arms.

Kenzie looked around but couldn't see anything that might cause goose bumps on such a warm day. A chill ran down her spine and she shivered. It passed as soon as it had come, and she attributed it to the spiritual vortex in the area. She had experienced similar encounters several times in the past.

Kenzie glanced at her watch. Her original plan was to follow the trail to where it ended at Chicken Point, but because of her late start, she would not have time for yoga before it became too dark to make it back to the parking lot, and then to ride her bike home safely. She decided instead to stay where she was and to roll out her mat. She placed her sunglasses and two bottles of water—one she had opened at home, and a new bottle that had yet to be opened—next to the mat.

Kenzie lay flat on her back and stretched her arms above her head, and at the same time, pressed her heels downward to lengthen her spine. She then sat and spread her legs wide and alternately reached for her toes to stretch her hamstrings, glutes and quadriceps.

For the next hour, she ran through the yoga routines she had learned while taking hot yoga classes in Utah. At the end of her routine, she sat cross-legged on her mat and placed the backs of her hands on her knees. She sat with her spine and neck as straight as possible, and with her eyes closed, she cleared her mind of all the tension that had accumulated throughout the day.

And then it happened again. The sudden tingling, followed by goose bumps, a shiver and a chill that ran down her spine. Without moving, she opened her eyes and looked around, but saw nothing out of the ordinary. She relaxed once more and continued to meditate. She didn't know how long she sat there, but after a time, her eyes snapped open and she realized she had fallen asleep sitting up, and dusk was approaching.

Kenzie knew she would have to hurry to have enough daylight to make it home on her bike, so she quickly rolled up her mat and strapped it to her backpack. She then pulled her phone out of her bag and was surprised to find it was dead. Odd, since it had nearly a full charge before she left home.

Kenzie shrugged and stuffed the phone back into her bag. She also grabbed the two water bottles she had placed next to her mat when she began her meditation. She was confused. She didn't remember drinking the water.

With no time to worry about these oddities, she made her way quickly down the path toward the parking lot. Once there, she unlocked her bike and rode it home in the fading daylight.

***

Kenzie made it home with little daylight to spare. She took care of her bike and then pulled her phone out of her bag and plugged it in to charge. She also removed the empty water bottles and threw them into the recycling bin in her kitchen. She stripped off her hiking clothes and showered the trail dirt and sweat from her body before she considered what to have for dinner. After the big lunch at the paleo restaurant with Bree, she didn't need much. Finally, she settled on a bag of microwave popcorn and a couple hours of television before she retired for the night.

Chapter 2

Zangendar stood on the transference pad with her arms straight down by her sides. "I am ready," she said.

"Do not forget to cloak your visibility as soon as the transfer is complete," Tredoran reminded her.

She nodded and waited for the burst of adrenalin she knew she would feel when her molecules became excited and separated during transference, only to be reassembled when she reached her destination.

Zangendar stumbled and nearly fell once the transfer was complete. Her breath came in short, shallow pants and she felt lightheaded and nauseous. She was so consumed with how she felt that she nearly forgot to cloak herself. A sense of relief filled her as the cloak fell into place. She did a quick visual check, and relaxed when she realized there were no natives in the immediate area to witness her arrival. While on their long trek during the past year, they had been fooled more than once when the ship's scanners reported faulty readings. She would report when she returned to the ship that the accuracy of the surface scanners had been rectified.

Zangendar reached out to touch a nearby wall of red rock to steady herself and to establish her bearings. Her heart was beating wildly in her chest. A momentary panic filled her mind at the thought that her data had been wrong and that the atmosphere would not support her needs after all. She pulled her omni-spectrometer from her belt and verified the research she had done to assure she hadn't missed anything. As suspected, the data indicated environmental compatibility.

Zangendar felt a thirst more intense than anything she had ever experienced in her two hundred and seventy-two years. The situation was compounded by the extremely arid feel to the air at this place where she had chosen to enter the atmosphere. She held the omni-spectrometer to her wrist to collect her own biometrics for analysis when she returned to the ship. Based on how rapidly her heart was beating, she surmised her difficulty breathing was due to her excitement and anxiety about this mission.

Zangendar forced her metabolism to slow down to conserve energy while she determined how to address the situation. She leaned her body against the red rock wall she was standing by and took several deep breaths. Before long, the sound of her heart beating in her ears subsided and her respiration became more regular. She realized that her elevated state of excitement contributed to her tenuous state, and that by forcing herself to calm down, she would buy some time to deal with the problem of thirst. She also realized that her choice of clothing was not appropriate for the combination of temperature and low humidity at this location. She surmised that her current outfit of a one-piece, long sleeved jumpsuit, tucked into shin-high boots, as well as protective headgear, would prove to be too warm in a short amount of time.

Zangendar looked around at her surroundings while she waited for her metabolism to equalize. It was hot...and very bright—so bright, in fact, she had to squint to reduce the pain that had taken up residence at the back of her eyes. This was so much brighter than what she was used to, and she feared it might be a detriment to accomplishing her mission. She realized that if they were to inhabit this planet, they would have to develop shields of some sort to protect themselves from the light.

She wondered if it was this bright all the time, or did the light source abate with the rotation of the planet as her research had suggested?

Zangendar knew of other worlds that did not rotate, and as a result, one side of the world was oppressively hot and bright, and barely able to sustain life, while the other side was a dark, frozen wasteland. She had done research on this planet, and was sure it moved on a rotational axis, but the intensity of the heat and light at this very moment made her anxious.

Zangendar used her omni-spectrometer to scan the area for life forms and potential danger, but none were noted in her immediate vicinity, thus giving her the opportunity to safely assess the environmental conditions she had transferred into.

She quickly collected data on the heat and humidity levels in the area, as well as oxygen content in the air. She also scanned to determine if there were toxic substances in the air that might have been missed during her research. She quickly determined that although the environment was warmer and significantly more arid than what she was used to, the atmosphere was safe and compatible with her species.

Zangendar visually scanned the area around her. The plant life fell into two categories—a spattering of short, dry, spiny structures, and dense areas of very tall plants with relatively large diameters at the base, topped by foliage of some sort at the top. She noted the diameter of these tall plants varied in size from something similar to that of her arm…to some larger than she could wrap her appendages around. The ground covering was, for the most part, a finely granular substance as well as many larger rocks. She reached into her memory of research information, and grasped the words brown, orange and green as descriptive terms for the hues around her. It was in sharp contrast with the blue shade of the sky above her.

In the distance, Zangendar saw towering structures that she estimated to be hundreds of time times larger than she was in both height and width. They were deep orange in color and appeared to have horizontal striations of color, as though they had been created in layers.

In many ways, this world was similar to her own Vakillia—hence the reason for choosing it—but the dry, arid environment and extremely bright light above made her wonder if life here would be any less difficult, and longevity any more assured, than on her current planet. As she looked around, she was most concerned about the absence of any visible water sources. Her people required water, not only to sustain life, but as a vital requirement for reproduction. She wondered if the entire planet was as arid as this particular location was. Research had suggested otherwise.

Thirst once again reminded Zangendar that she was on a mission. She took one final account of her physical state and decided she was ready to begin her investigation. She pushed off the wall behind her and immediately fell forward when she attempted to take a step. Her legs felt extremely heavy.

"I forgot to compensate for the difference in gravity! How could I be so careless?" she whispered to herself.

Zangendar struggled to her feet and held her arms out to the sides until she adjusted to the gravitational pull on her body. Very slowly, she lifted one foot and moved it forward. Her foot slammed down hard on the ground in front of her, and again, she counterbalanced herself with her arms. For the next several minutes, Zangendar practiced walking, until she could move forward without the help of her arms to maintain her balance.

Her gait felt awkward and clumsy and she knew she would need to compensate for this before the next transfer.

Zangendar activated the omni-spectrometer on her wrist and walked slowly down the path. She stopped to collect samples of dirt, rocks and plant life on the way that she would bring back to the lab for analysis. To conceal her samples, she had to deactivate her invisibility shield and then reactivate it after she placed the samples inside the collection bag strapped to her side. Before collecting each sample, she had to carefully verify the absence of natives who might see her.

Zangendar continued down the path after collecting her samples. Her progress was hindered by an abundance of caution while she adjusted to her new gait. Several moments later, she rounded a bend and stopped short when her monitor indicated a large life form ahead. Zangendar drew her weapon and quickly checked to see that her cloak of invisibility was in place before moving on.

Zangendar rounded the bend and stopped as soon as she made visual contact with the life form that was moving toward her along the worn path. Based on scans with her omni-spectrometer, she determined the life form was a human female, with hair nearly the same color as the red rock surrounding them. She was slim in stature, but not as tall as Zangendar herself. She wore clothing that exposed the lower parts of her legs and arms while covering the rest of her body. Her footwear only came to her ankle and she wore a wide-brimmed head covering that was tilted back enough to expose her orange-hued hair. Dark lenses covered her eyes, and Zangendar realized that even the natives had an aversion to the bright light above them. On her back was a pack that Zangendar speculated was some sort of life support.

Zangendar sensed no danger from this human, but kept her weapon trained on her as a precaution. She set her omni-spectrometer to collect the native's vital signs. They would later be used to determine any commonality between this species and her own.

The native walked off the path, to the edge of a cliff. Zangendar inhaled sharply when the native took the pack off and dropped it to the ground. So much for it being life support.

She took several steps forward to afford herself a closer look.

The native turned away from the edge of the cliff, but then stopped and turned back. She then squatted beside the pack and retrieved something from it and turned toward the cliff once more. She appeared to be looking at the large structures in the distance.

Confident that her invisibility cloak would shield her, Zangendar again dared to approach the native, close enough that she was nearly standing beside her. She stood there for what seemed like an eternity and watched this female scan the scenery before her. She was close enough to smell the sweat on the female's skin.

Zangendar watched her raise the flat, rectangular device she had retrieved from her pack. She held it in front of her and then lowered it again after the device made a clicking sound. She then tucked the device securely inside her pack once more. The native rose to her feet and swung the pack over her shoulder. The gesture caused her upper body to sway to the side, and she momentarily made contact with Zangendar's arm.

Zangendar froze—her weapon at the ready.

The female stopped and looked around. After a few seconds, she shrugged and looked at a device she had strapped to the left wrist. She seemed to make a decision.

Zangendar watched the native walk back toward the path but stop just short of it to spread a long narrow mat out on the ground. Beside it, she placed her pack and two containers with clear liquid in them. Finally, she sat on the mat and removed the dark lenses she had covering her eyes and placed them on the ground beside the containers. She lifted one of the containers, drank some of the contents and then placed it back on the ground beside the other container.

Zangendar used her omni-spectrometer to scan the containers, and nearly exclaimed out loud when the readings indicated the containers held water. She had all she could do to resist lunging forward to take the containers from the native. She had to find another way to obtain them without scaring the female. She understood that a peaceful relationship with the people of this world would not be possible if it started with an act of theft or assault, so she patiently waited and watched while the female contorted her body into several poses.

Finally, after a time, the female sat in the center of the mat with her legs crossed and her hands resting on her knees. Zangendar watched her for a few moments and realized the female was practicing a mental trance, something she herself did often when she needed to relax.

Zangendar took this opportunity to approach the native. She returned her weapon to its holster and retrieved her omni-spectrometer from her belt. She circled the mat and collected additional bio-metric data on the female.

During her analysis, her monitor once again alerted her to the presence of additional large life forms. She retrieved her weapon once more and waited patiently for them to come into view. She heard the two life forms long before she could see them. She trained her omni-spectrometer on the path and collected data on them as they approached. They appeared to notice the female subject who still sat on her mat in a meditative trance. They looked directly at her, but they did not stop, nor did they attempt to engage the female.

Zangendar noted that they appeared to be different from one another. One was verifiably female, but her companion was larger, not only in body size, but also in shape and physical features. Her scan results confirmed that the companion was the male of the species that she had learned about in her research. She continued to scan them until they moved out of her range of sight.

Zangendar returned her weapon to her belt and looked again at the female sitting on her mat. She found it interesting that she appeared to be unaware that two others of her species had just passed by. Feeling secure in that knowledge, she moved behind the female as quietly as she could, and knelt down on the mat behind her. She then reached forward and placed her hands on both sides of the female's head. Zangendar froze when the female opened her eyes and looked around. She remained as still as possible until the female relaxed and closed her eyes once more, and then waited for several more moments until she was sure her subject had returned to a state of meditation.

The first observation Zangendar made was how soft the native's skin was and how supple it felt beneath her hands.

Zangendar closed her eyes and concentrated on the alpha-theta border between the native's conscious and subconscious minds where electrical brain waves are the strongest during such introspection. She delved deep into the female's subconscious and nearly removed her hands from the native's head when an intense wave of emotion rushed through her.

For the next several moments, Zangendar searched through the female's short-term and long-term memories. The language was difficult to pick up at first, but she was able to discern the meaning from the emotions, as well as from the words spoken by the female and others she had interacted with in her memories.

In the female's memory, she saw a young child who was repressed in the name of a higher power, simply because she was female. She saw the native as an older female who struggled with her feelings for another female. Zangendar felt an intense stab of emotional pain rip through her when she realized the native was forced to choose between a life of love—and a family who poorly judged her for *who* she loved.

Zangendar almost broke contact with the native as she struggled with the physical pain this revelation caused to her own soul. She was not used to intense levels of emotion. This was something her people thought of as weak, and she had been discouraged when young, from expressing feelings of any kind. She sat back on her heels to regain control of her emotions but maintained contact with the native. She closed her eyes again and delved deeper.

Zangendar saw her native with another female. One with long yellow hair. They were laughing and touching their lips together. She heard the native call out the name Jessie with such passion, it brought moisture to her eyes and a strange and intense feeling in the pit of her being. She was unaware that such depths of feeling were even possible.

Zangendar suddenly felt she had violated this female's inner being and had trespassed in places she should not have gone. She released her grasp and sat back. Her hands shook and she struggled to control the emotions she felt after delving into the memories of this female. On some level, she realized this native had already lived a life full of intense emotion, more than Zangendar had ever known. Part of her was envious, and part of her was fearful that she may never have that opportunity. She had read about the emotions of the natives during her research of this place, but she had resisted discussing it with others for fear of being ridiculed. Yet, she was curious.

Zangendar knew the aftereffects of the mind probe would continue for the next several minutes. She took the opportunity to search the female's pack. She found the flat, rectangular device inside and examined it. She realized it was an electronic device of some sort when she pushed the round button at the bottom and it came to life. Zangendar wondered why the female held it in front of her at the edge of the cliff. Within moments, the device shut off by itself and she shoved it back into the pack.

The female stirred. Zangendar realized she would risk disclosure if she stayed much longer. She reached for the two containers of liquid and overcome by thirst, she consumed both in seconds, and then returned the empty containers to the ground beside the pack.

She looked into the sky to determine how much time had passed and was immediately struck by an intense headache from the bright light that entered her light-sensitive eyes. Zangendar grabbed her head until the pain subsided. It was then she noticed the female's dark lenses were still on the ground beside her mat. She quickly grabbed them, and realized that although she was invisible, the lenses would not be. Unless she wore them before she cloaked herself.

Zangendar glanced briefly at the female, who was becoming more and more aware of her surroundings and made the quick decision to uncloak just long enough to don the lenses. She then stepped back and watched the female return to full awareness.

The female looked at the sky and seemed alarmed. She moved quickly to gather her belongings and then opened her pack. She removed the electronic device and was distressed when it did not react. She also seemed confused that her containers were now both empty. With a sense of expediency, the female shoved all of her belongings into her bag and then hurried down the path.

Zangendar followed as close behind the native as she dared until they reached a common area where there were several other natives, as well as several machines. Although still protected by her invisibility shield, Zangendar drew her weapon in the event she needed it to defend herself against these natives.

She observed a native enter one of the machines and then leave the common area. Zangendar surmised these machines were transportation devices and she wondered which one *her* female would enter. She was surprised to see the female mount a two-wheeled vehicle that appeared to propel under her own power.

Zangendar felt a foreign sense of heaviness in her chest as she watched her female disappear into the distance and finally fade away.

With more work to do, Zangendar returned to the trailhead to resume her scientific analysis before she returned to the ship.

Chapter 3

After her human left on the two-wheeled vehicle, Zangendar collected additional environmental samples and then returned to her ship. Later that evening, her friend Tredoran entered her quarters while she prepared to take samples of soil, rocks and plants to the lab for analysis.

"Welcome back. Molinder was pleased that Dartan was able to retrieve you from the surface," Tredoran said.

"I never had any doubt," Zangendar replied. "My apologies that I lingered on the surface beyond the end of your shift, but Dartan executed her role as your stand-in perfectly."

"Did you contact any natives?" Tredoran asked.

"I did. In fact, I had ample opportunity to study one."

"Please explain."

"I encountered a female about this tall." Zangendar raised her hand to about her own chin level. "She had hair the color of the red rocks in the area. In some ways, she was very similar to us."

"Similar, how?"

"As I have said, she was shorter in stature than I. In fact, all the humans I encountered were. Their biometric data will be able to quantify that for us. Besides my superior height and some facial differences, our physical appearances are very much the same."

"What kinds of facial differences?"

"The humans' respiratory organ is in the middle of their face rather than on their necks as ours are."

"One would think that might impede their ability to breathe under water," Tredoran observed.

"I have had that thought as well," Zangendar replied. "Oh, and the hair on their heads comes in many different hues, unlike ours, which is what the humans might call green. I found that interesting. Other than that, we are very much the same as these humans. If we could change our hair and add a prosthetic respiratory organ in the center of our faces, we might likely pass as human."

"Did you communicate with her?"

"I did, but not directly. I didn't think that was wise until we determine how receptive they will be to our presence. I always kept my invisibility shield in place. I did, however, find her to be interesting."

"How so?"

"It was apparent she came to that place with the intent to go into a trance state. She laid a mat on the ground and then proceeded to perform a set of poses. When she was finished, she sat with her legs crossed and her back very straight. She closed her eyes and was very still for an extended time, so much so that I began to think she was renewing. I took that opportunity to search her thoughts."

"You actually touched her?" Tredoran asked excitedly.

"I did. She was very soft."

Zangendar paused to recall the mind probing exercise with her human. A small smile formed on her lips.

Tredoran folded her arms. "Do I detect underlying emotion for this human?"

Zangendar looked at her friend. "I do admit that she caused a feeling deep inside me that was quite foreign."

"What do you mean?"

"I think the word empathy best describes it. When our minds met, I learned that she had been raised in a strict and judgmental environment and was made to feel inferior, simply because she is female."

Tredoran's head snapped back. "So, the research is correct...they have more than one gender."

"Yes. Unlike us, there are males and females on this planet. I collected biometrics data on a male while I was on the surface. He was in the company of another female who was similar in size and shape to the first female I encountered. I will submit that data for analysis along with the soil and plant specimens. From what I interpreted through the female's memories, men dominated her world when she was a child."

"We have encountered the males of many species, and I must say, there is not one of them that I would allow to dominate me," Tredoran said. "I for one am glad we are a race of females."

"I agree with you, Tredoran. It is fortunate that our race has determined how to reproduce without the involvement of male biology. Had our physical environment not betrayed us, the development of parthenogenesis techniques would have ensured the proliferation of our species for generations to come. Unfortunately, with diminished water supplies, there is no future for us or our species on Vakillia."

"What else did you learn from this female life form?" Tredoran asked.

"It became apparent during our mind probe that this human is also attracted to females, and consequently, she was rejected by her family unit. It was very painful for her, and empathically, very painful for me as well."

"Please describe what painful means."

Zangendar fell silent for a moment before she addressed her friend again.

"It is a feeling of intense emotion that is similar to a broken limb, but felt within one's chest. I find my explanation to be inadequate, but the best comparison I can make is that something is broken inside one's mind, causing pain that extends to the heart."

"I see."

"Tredoran, my encounter with the human made me realize how emotionless our lives are. I feel a fondness for Molinder and Belander, and I feel a fondness for you, but through the mind probe with the human, I now realize that in our world, there is little distinction between the level and degree of fondness we feel for all of the individuals in our lives.

"I learned from this human that in their world, fondness can range from indifference, to mild satisfaction with another being, to one of intense attraction and emotion. On the negative side, it could also mean intense disappointment and hatred. I also found their way of expressing affection for one another to be very…interesting."

"How do you mean?"

"During the probe, I saw the female touching lips with another female."

"Touching lips?" Tredoran asked. "That sounds quite unsanitary."

"Perhaps, but both females appeared to enjoy it immensely."

Tredoran frowned and then stepped forward. She touched her lips to Zangendar's and then broke away abruptly. "Is that how the females touched lips?" she asked.

"Not exactly," Zangendar replied. "It was more intense than that. Let me demonstrate."

Zangendar touched her lips to Tredoran's and opened her mouth. Her tongue sought entry into Tredoran's mouth.

Tredoran immediately broke away and wiped the back of her mouth with her hand.

"That was quite unpleasant," Tredoran said.

"I do not disagree," Zangendar replied. "It is possible that you need to be human to enjoy it. In any case, it appeared to evoke intense emotion in the humans."

Tredoran frowned. "It sounds like a complication we do not need in our lives, Zangendar. It could prove to be a distraction."

"I thought so as well, Tredoran, however, although empathizing with the human was painful for me, it made me feel an intensity of emotion I did not think I was capable of. I think I liked it."

Tredoran placed her hand on Zangendar's shoulder. "Be careful, my friend. We both know that emotions make us weak. We need to remain strong to complete this mission."

Zangendar nodded. "I will not fail in this mission," she said out loud. *However, I will not turn away from the chance to feel, either,* she added silently to herself.

"What are your plans for returning to the planet?" Tredoran asked.

"I will return at first light. I need to spend a significant amount of time observing their behavior and interactions with one another. We need to determine how to emulate the natives if we have any hope of living with them stealthily. As I indicated, they are similar to us. However, an abundance of physical data will be helpful in the emulation process."

"I will take these specimens to the lab for you then. You have had an exciting day, and you should take time to renew," Tredoran offered.

"Thank you, my friend," Zangendar said. "Oh, wait, Tredoran."

Tredoran stopped in the doorway and turned around. "Yes?"

Zangendar pulled Kenzie's sunglasses out of her pouch. "These are the human's eye lenses. They protect her eyes from the light."

Tredoran tilted her head and examined the glasses. "Primitive," she said.

"I agree, but I find them interesting. They looked very appealing on the face of the human."

Tredoran tilted her head to one side and looked at her friend for several long moments before she excused herself and left Zangendar to her rest.

***

Zangendar watched her friend leave. She placed the glasses on a nearby table and then removed her clothing. She climbed into her renewal unit and lay on her back. She knew she should be tired, but instead, her body felt alive with excitement.

Zangendar looked at the glasses on the table and decided to try them on in the darkness. She felt a tinge of foolishness with light blocking lenses covering her eyes in the darkened room, but the knowledge that they belonged to the human overrode her common sense.

She lay motionless with the lenses on and her eyes closed. Finally, she felt herself relax and decided to remove the lenses before they fell off and became damaged while she renewed.

She reached to remove them, while at the same time, she opened her eyes. There, on the lenses, Zangendar could see images. Zangendar lowered her hand.

What was this?

Zangendar watched images of a woman with yellow hair run across her vision. She was nearly naked, with a scant amount of cloth covering her breasts and private areas. She could see water in the distance, massive amounts of water. The woman ran toward the water and entered it to her knees. She reached a hand toward the wearer of the lenses. Zangendar assumed the woman was reaching out for the human female she had mind probed that afternoon.

Was she seeing a memory? Could this be Jessie? She was similar to an image she had seen in the female's memories.

Zangendar felt an intense emotion fill her. It was an emotion she was completely unfamiliar with and it made her feel uneasy. She quickly removed the lenses and placed them on the table once more.

It was a long time before she succumbed to renewal.

***

Kenzie woke the next morning feeling refreshed and full of energy. She attributed this good fortune to her spiritual experiences on the Little Horse Trail the day before. She had felt tingles and chills before on the vortex trails, but what she felt on yesterday's hike was far more intense than anything she had previously experienced.

Kenzie put a pod in the coffee maker. While it brewed, she verified that her phone was fully charged. She was still confused as to how the battery had died so quickly. While she waited for her coffee, she opened her pictures to review the new snapshots she had taken on her hike. She opened the picture she took of her shadow on the cliff and nearly dropped the phone.

"Oh, my God! What the fuck?"

There were two shadows in the picture.

"What the fuck?" she said again. Kenzie zoomed into the picture for a closer look. "Where on earth did that other person come from? There was no one beside me when I took this."

The shadow in the picture was taller than she was, and its head appeared proportionally larger than it should be. She scanned the remaining pictures she had taken on the hike, but none of them seemed out of the ordinary.

"I need to show this to Bree."

Kenzie was thankful that she had showered the night before. After donning clean scrubs, she grabbed her backpack and set out on foot for the short walk to work.

The morning was bright and sunny. Kenzie stopped on her front porch and looked through her bag for her sunglasses.

"Damn! Where are they?" she murmured.

Kenzie thought back to the last time she had seen them. It was on Little Horse Trail when she put them next to her yoga mat.

She didn't remember picking them up when she hurriedly packed to make it home before dark.

Damn it! She had either forgotten them there or lost them on the trail. Now she would have to go back to look for them, or she knew she'd never see them again.

Kenzie took a few moments to go back into her apartment to retrieve her backup pair of sunglasses, and set out once more for work.

***

"Good morning, Kenzie," Bree said. "How was yoga last night?"

Kenzie grabbed her lab coat from the hook and pulled it on. "It was good, although I think I lost my sunglasses on the trail. I couldn't find them this morning."

"Well, that sucks!"

"I agree. I must have fallen asleep while meditating. One minute I was sitting on the mat, working on my breathing, and the next thing I knew, I snapped awake and realized dusk was falling. I had to rush to get packed up and home before dark. I either left them where I was meditating, or I dropped them on the trail. I'll go look for them after work, although with my luck, someone else has picked them up."

"Want some company?" Bree asked. "Jimmy is getting together with guys after work, and I'm at loose ends."

"That would be awesome. Thanks!"

"We'll take my car since I'm sure you don't have two bikes."

"Okay. That's actually better, since it's a little overcast right now and it might rain."

"Remind me to stop at a store for water on the way. I don't want to be caught on the trail without it."

"I have water at my place. I can bring enough for both of us. I'll need to go home first to change anyway. I don't think hiking in our work clothes is a good idea."

"You're right. I'll run home during lunch for a change of clothes as well."

"That sounds like a plan. Oh, speaking of water, I brought two bottles with me yesterday and somehow, I must have drunk both without remembering I did. They were nearly full when I began meditating, but when I packed up to leave, they were empty. Weird!"

"Maybe it was some psychic energy from one of your vortexes that drained them."

Kenzie pushed on Bree's shoulder. "Get out! You're such a kook!"

"You're the one who believes in that voodoo-hoodoo shit, not me, girlfriend," Bree said in her own defense.

"It's not voodoo or hoodoo, Bree, but it certainly is odd. Oh, by the way, something else strange happened yesterday."

Kenzie fished her phone from her pocket and opened the photo folder. "Take a look at this."

Bree took the phone from Kenzie and studied the picture. "Who's in the picture with you?"

"Nobody."

"What? There is clearly a second person in this picture."

"It looks that way, but I was alone when I took the picture. I stood at the end of the cliff. I noticed my shadow reflecting on the ground below and thought it would be a cool picture, so I took it. I was alone. I swear it."

***

Zangendar transferred through the vortex that morning just as the sun rose above the horizon. The temperature of the air was cooler than she expected, but she soon realized that the atmosphere would warm significantly once the light source rose higher into the sky. Before she collected the data, she walked back and forth across the terrain to test the modifications made to compensate for the gravity differential on this planet. She also tested the light-reactive corneal contact lenses she had inserted before transferring to the planet's surface. She looked directly into the light and as expected, the lenses darkened and protected her eyes from the bright light.

Zangendar's mission was to develop an extensive scientific database about the planet to determine if her people would be able to thrive in its environment. It was also her personal goal to determine if relationships between her people and the natives of this planet could be possible.

In the early hours of this morning, Zangendar found herself alone and she took advantage of that time for her environmental analysis. It was several hours later, when the light was high in the sky, that she became aware of native life forces.

She spent the rest of the day observing the natives, save several intervals when she returned to the ship for water and nourishment. She found it difficult to take in sustenance while remaining invisible and she soon realized she would have to find a way to remedy that situation if she hoped to spend longer periods of time on the planet's surface.

Zangendar collected countless videos, images and biometrics of the natives. How they looked, moved, and how they spoke. Many of them came in pairs, mostly male-female pairs, who openly displayed affection for one another. Zangendar was fascinated by the way they interacted, with the way they offered a hand to help their partner step over a rock, or how they constantly touched one another, hand in hand, arm in arm. Contrary to what she had been taught, they did not look weak. She recorded all this information to analyze when she returned to the ship.

The displays of affection she witnessed between her human subjects made Zangendar think about her encounter from the day before. It also made her realize that she felt more for the human than she should. It was a feeling that scared yet exhilarated her. It was a totally irrational feeling, and she knew that Tredoran was probably right. She didn't need this complication in her life—especially when she was in the middle of such an important mission. She felt heaviness in her chest when she realized the likelihood of encountering her human again was remote.

Zangendar focused her thoughts on the task before her—studying the environment, and its inhabitants. Still, she could not help but speculate about the possible source of attraction between these humans. Having little experience with emotion, she assumed the attraction was based on physical appearance.

Zangendar couldn't help but compare herself to these natives and she wondered if her human would find her lacking.

She looked somewhat different from the males and females of this planet. She looked very different from Jessie with the yellow hair.

Zangendar recalled what she had said to Tredoran the night before. They needed to determine how to emulate and interact with the natives without alarming them.

Zangendar stopped walking and looked around. She immediately recognized the area as the exact spot she had probed the human's mind the day before. She smiled and wondered to herself if she somehow had subconsciously made her way to familiar ground.

Her thoughts were suddenly interrupted by the approach of new, large life forces. Out of habit, she drew her weapon and aimed her omni-spectrometer on the path. She focused on the data displayed on her device's small screen. Two forms, female. Zangendar gasped when familiar biometric readings appeared on the screen.

It was her!

Zangendar held her breath. She turned her attention away from her spectrometer, to the path before her. She could feel her heart pounding in her chest as the two forms came into view.

The first thing she saw was hair the color of the red rock structures around them. It indeed was her human, and she was accompanied by another female, similar in size and build, but with hair the color of night. They both wore clothing similar to the other humans she had seen that day, lightweight coverings that left their arms and legs exposed, wide-brimmed hats, and sturdy foot coverings.

"Have you been scanning the path, Bree?" her human said.

The dark-haired human had a name…Bree.

"Yes, I have. I'm guessing you either didn't drop them on the path, or someone picked them up," Bree replied.

Her red-hair human stopped and placed her hands on her hips. She looked around. "This is where I was doing yoga yesterday. I took my glasses off and put them on the ground beside my mat."

Zangendar realized she was standing in almost the exact spot that the mat had been laid out on the day before. As quietly as possible, she took several steps sideways. During this maneuver, she stepped partially on a rock and it skidded away.

"What was that?" her human said.

"What was what?" Bree asked.

Zangendar froze when her human pointed directly at her. She quickly checked to see that her invisibility cloak was still in place. It was.

"I could have sworn that rock moved. Odd."

"I don't see anything, Kenzie. It must have been your imagination."

Kenzie.

"Maybe," Kenzie said. "Anyway, I laid my mat right here. My sunglasses must be around here somewhere. I have to find them. They're my favorite pair."

Zangendar suddenly realized that Kenzie was referring to the lenses she had taken the previous day. An odd feeling came across her, a feeling that she had done something unacceptable by taking Kenzie's lenses. She reached into her pouch and retrieved them.

How could she return them without making herself visible?

***

"I don't see them anywhere, Kenz. Did you go anywhere else?" Bree asked.

Kenzie wiped the sweat from her brow and looked around once more. "Yeah. Remember the picture I showed to you yesterday? I took it there—on the edge of the cliff."

"Well, let's go take a look," Bree suggested.

Kenzie pointed to the ground. "But I'm sure I took them off right here."

"What have you got to lose by looking?"

"Ahhh! I guess you're right, but it seems like a waste of time."

Bree approached Kenzie and slipped her hand in hers. "Come on, girlfriend. Humor me. And if we don't find them, at least you can show me how you captured that awesome picture. Maybe we can even get one of me and you."

"All right, all right, but the sun isn't shining right now, so good luck seeing shadows," Kenzie relented.

***

Zangendar watched the two females turn their backs to her and walk toward the cliff. She was frozen by an emotion she was totally unfamiliar with. She found herself resenting the human named Bree. She resented the way she behaved with Kenzie.

What is this new emotion? It is not one I like very much, she pondered silently.

The sense of urgency quickly returned. Zangendar disabled her invisibility cloak, bent down, and gently placed Kenzie's lenses on the ground, near a low growing shrub close to where her mat had been laid the day before. She stood and saw that Kenzie was once more holding the rectangular device from the day before, with it pointed toward the valley below. The human named Bree stood close to her with her arm around Kenzie. Their heads were tilted toward one another and touching.

Zangendar was filled with sudden dismay.

"Great picture, Kenz, but I'd still like to know who the other person is in the one you took yesterday," Bree said.

Kenzie slipped her phone into her pocket. "I'd like to know that as well, Bree, but right now, we're looking for my sunglasses. As I suspected, they are not here."

Bree continued to look at Cathedral Rock in the distance. "This is such a beautiful area."

Kenzie picked up her pack and swung it over her shoulder, and just as the day before, the motion caused her upper body to swing around. "Oh, my fucking God!"

Zangendar panicked when she realized she had failed to reengage the invisibility cloak as soon as she stood. She quickly veiled herself and hoped that Kenzie had not seen her. She quickly moved several yards away to the far side of the path.

Kenzie grabbed Bree's arm. "Oh, my God, Bree. Did you see that?"

"I didn't see anything. I was looking at Cathedral Rock," Bree replied. "What did you see?"

Kenzie scanned the entire area before her. "I...I don't know. It's not there now."

"What was it?"

"I...a figure, a shape, maybe? It was just a flash."

"Maybe it was some voodoo coming through the vortex," Bree teased.

Kenzie tilted her head. "Ha, ha. Very funny," she said sarcastically.

"Hey! What's that?" Bree asked.

"What?"

"Look on the ground. There by the bush. Something reflective."

Kenzie and Bree ran to the bush.

"My sunglasses! Awesome! I must've kicked them here when I packed up my stuff yesterday. I'm so glad we found them."

"Mission accomplished," Bree exclaimed.

Kenzie tucked her sunglasses into her pocket and locked arms with Bree. "Cool beans! How about I take you to dinner?"

"The green smoothies at the paleo place *were* pretty awesome."

"Sounds great. Let's go!"

***

Zangendar leaned against the red rock wall and watched Kenzie and Bree walk away, arm in arm. Heaviness filled her chest, which she didn't understand. She would have the medical personnel scan her when she returned to the ship.

She looked at the sky and realized she had limited time left before she would lose her light.

There were several more samples to collect before returning to the ship. She needed to complete her tasks with more expediency than she had during the past and needed to be aware that the mission came first. Tredoran was right. Emotions make you weak. Zangendar needed to remain strong to complete this mission.

Chapter 4

The next morning, Zangendar stared at the dome of her renewal unit and thought about her encounter with Bree and Kenzie the day before. She struggled to understand why this human had such an effect on her. She also struggled to understand why she had dark thoughts about the friend, Bree.

Zangendar's thoughts were interrupted by her call buzzer. She looked at the device on her wrist and noted her caller was Tredoran.

"Enter."

Zangendar sat up in her unit as Tredoran entered the room and stood stiffly, her hands clasped behind her back.

"You are not yet ready," Tredoran said.

"I am not ready. I fear I am not well," Zangendar replied.

Tredoran removed a device from her belt and held it above Zangendar. "Your vitals are within acceptance range."

"My vitals are not what are causing my illness."

"Explain."

Zangendar swung her legs over the side of the renewal unit and lowered her head into her hands. She rubbed her face vigorously. "I don't know how to explain this to you, Tredoran. My illness is not in my body. It is within the depths of my brain."

Tredoran sat beside her. "Do not say that, Zangendar. Do you remember Aldorant?"

"Aldorant? Yes, I remember her. She struggled with a disease of the mind. Wait! You don't believe…"

"I don't know what to believe. You tell me your sickness is in your brain. Aldorant was permanently retired. Do you remember that? She was eliminated after the council determined her unfit and unable to contribute."

Zangendar touched her forehead to Tredoran's. "Tredoran, I am not at all like Aldorant."

Tredoran abruptly stood and walked a few feet away. She turned sharply to face Zangendar. "Explain yourself."

Zangendar looked at her hands in her lap. "This is difficult to explain. I say it is in my brain, but it is actually in my thoughts and my heart."

Tredoran folded her arms across her chest. "This is about the human."

"I think she saw me yesterday."

"She saw you? What was her reaction?"

"It was very brief. I uncloaked to return her lenses and she saw me briefly before I could cloak again. I am not sure she realizes what she saw."

Tredoran rushed across the room and stopped in front of Zangendar. She leaned in close. "Do you realize you are putting the mission at risk with this obsession?" She stood and regained her composure. "I am sorry, Zangendar, but I feel I must report this. We cannot risk the mission." Tredoran turned to go.

Zangendar jumped to her feet and grabbed Tredoran's arm. "No! Tredoran, you are more my sister than my friend. I implore you not to take action."

Tredoran looked at the hand on her arm. "Release me."

Zangendar lowered her hand and sat back down. She looked at her friend. "I need you to understand. I need your help." Try as hard as she could to stop them, tears came to her eyes.

Tredoran frowned and sat beside Zangendar once more. "Those are tears," she said. "How is this happening?"

Zangendar wiped the moisture from her eyes. "I do not know. It is like emotion that is spilling out of my body."

"Is it painful?"

"On the inside, yes. It is painful, but not in a physical way."

Tredoran shook her head. "I do not understand."

"Mind-blend with me, Tredoran."

Tredoran sat back. "You know mind probing is discouraged by the elders. It is a tool to communicate with other species, not with one another."

"Tredoran, emotion is a critical component of human life. If we do not understand it, how can we expect to live among them? I cannot be the only one of us to be aware of this."

Tredoran sat for several moments in silence. Finally, she turned to her friend. "I understand your argument, and I will help you."

***

Kenzie looked forward to her yoga session just off the Little Horse Trail that afternoon. She chose this particular site for its strong energy center, and located at the intersection of two of the ley lines that covered the earth, lines through which energy moves easily. It was here that Kenzie was best able to give up her consciousness to the energy of the earth.

She spread a long narrow mat out on the ground. Beside it, she placed her pack and two containers of water. Finally, she sat on the mat, removed her sunglasses and placed them on the ground beside her water. She drank from one of the bottles and then returned it to the ground beside her mat. She spent the next half hour contorting her body into several poses.

Finally, Kenzie sat in the center of the mat with her legs crossed and her hands resting on her knees. She closed her eyes and allowed the spiritual energy of the vortex to spread through her. Just as she drifted off, she felt a presence around her. This was nothing new. She regularly experienced the presence of Native American spirits while she meditated.

But this time was different.

This time, the touch felt real.

She opened her eyes and looked around, but she was alone, so she once again allowed herself to succumb to the spiritual energy of the vortex.

Suddenly, she felt the spirit enter her mind. This had never happened before. Not like this. It felt almost like a caress. It felt like the spirit was delving deep into her memories. She relived the memories of her restrictive childhood. She relived the memories of suppressed sexuality and rejection when suppression was simply no longer an option. She relived the memories of having to give up everything she had known in life, simply to be true to herself. She relived the memories of the love and passion that were so much a part of her relationship with Jessie.

And then suddenly, it stopped. Suddenly the spirit released her.

She was unable to move.

She was unable to speak.

She was barely able to open her eyes.

But she *was* aware.

She could feel the spirit move around her. Through slitted eyes, she saw it open her pack, remove and then return her phone. She saw it drink her water. And then suddenly, she was alone.

Kenzie sat up suddenly in bed and looked around. The time on the clock was seven-fifteen.

"Shit! I've slept through the alarm!"

Kenzie threw off the blankets and climbed quickly out of bed. She grabbed a clean set of scrubs from her closet, socks, bra and panties from her bureau, and ran into the bathroom. Twenty minutes later, she emerged fully showered and dressed and threw her cellphone, water bottle and a change of hiking clothes and shoes into her backpack while the coffee brewed. She would have to skip breakfast, as she had just enough time to ride her bike several blocks to the clinic.

Kenzie arrived at work without a moment to spare.

Bree met her at the door. "Hey girl! You're late,"

"I am not. Look, it's exactly eight o'clock."

"Yes, it is, but you're normally early."

"Sorry, I slept through my alarm this morning."

"Rough night?"

Kenzie paused as she poured herself a new cup of coffee. "Rough? Not really, but it *was* odd."

"Whaddaya mean?"

She sipped the coffee. "I had this really weird dream."

"Well, maybe you can fill me in during lunch. The boss called an eight-fifteen status meeting."

"Ugh! I really don't need to start my day off with one of those boring status meetings," Kenzie complained. "Especially when I haven't had breakfast!"

***

Zangendar and Tredoran sat facing one another, cross-legged, on the floor of Zangendar's quarters. Tredoran was clearly nervous.

"Before we start, tell me how emotion feels," Tredoran said.

"It is difficult to explain. It feels like a build-up of pressure inside your head and in your chest. Did you ever worry about your acceptance exams into the research program?" Zangendar asked.

Tredoran tilted her head. "I was well prepared for the entrance exam."

"Yes, but did you worry about it? Did you have any feelings of anxiety or doubt while you waited for the acceptance?"

"*That* was emotion?" Tredoran asked.

Zangendar nodded. "Yes. Anything that makes you veer from the logical thinking path is emotion."

"Then, yes. I have experienced emotion. Several times, in fact."

"Give me an example," Zangendar insisted.

Tredoran tried hard to hide a small smile. "Do you know who Cadantor is?"

"She is the chief engineer on the ship."

"Yes. She makes me veer from the logical thinking path."

"I find that curious. She is the closest we have to the male species on board, yet you have been very clear that you would not allow yourself to be dominated by a male."

Tredoran raised her eyebrows. "She is not a male."

"You are correct. She is not, but her mannerisms and attitudes are very close to those of the male species we have encountered on other planets. She would be a male, except that she is missing certain male parts. I am curious that she has an effect on you."

"Let me correct you on one thing, my sister. I said I would not allow a male to *dominate* me. Cadantor does not dominate me," Tredoran explained. "And to be truthful, you are not far from that male model yourself, Zangendar."

"Logical reasoning," Zangendar said. "And I cannot argue with you when you speak truth about my own attitudes and mannerisms. Are you ready to receive the mind probe?"

"Will we join with one another, or will you only join with me?"

"If we join with one another, I will be able to guide you through the experience of feeling human emotion rather than just transmitting those emotions to you."

"I agree," Tredoran said. "Let us begin."

***

Sometime later, Tredoran stood by the window in Zangendar's room and stared into the darkness of space. "I was totally unaware such things as emotions existed, Zangendar. How have we survived as a race for so long without *feeling* anything?"

"Emotion often leads to destruction, Tredoran. The logical part of my mind understands why emotion was eliminated from our world. It wasn't until I felt Kenzie's emotions that I realized what I was missing."

"I am forever changed. After our mind probe, I will not be able to return to what I once was, nor do I want to." Tredoran turned around to face Zangendar. "Sister, I want to join you on the planet. I want to experience this for myself."

Zangendar held her hand out for Tredoran, who crossed the room and joined her on the renewal unit. She took Tredoran's hand in her own. "I would like for you to join me, but not until I have established where the safety margins are and have determined what the expectations would be for blending into human society. I will bring back what I learn, and I will willingly share it with you. Until then, we must present a consistent and *expected* behavioral front to the others on the ship."

Tredoran looked down and remained silent.

Zangendar squeezed her friend's hand. "I know you are disappointed—another new emotion for you, by the way, but I need you here to help me prepare. To help *us* prepare. We will need to practice human behaviors together. We will need to physically emulate how they look. We are not all that different from them, but it will take some work to make us undetectable. I promise it will not be long before you can join me on the surface. Are you willing to work with me on this?"

Tredoran looked up and grinned. "I am looking forward to transforming your appearance."

Zangendar narrowed her eyes. "You are making me worry about your intentions! Do I detect a level of mischief?"

Tredoran nodded. "This emotion thing may be better than I originally thought!"

***

Kenzie and Bree slid into a booth at the local diner after placing their orders at the counter.

"I am famished!" Kenzie said.

"I'm not surprised, considering you missed breakfast," Bree replied. "So, tell me about the dream."

"It was really odd. It was almost like I was reliving my yoga session from two days ago—the day I lost my sunglasses—except while I was meditating, it felt like the vortex spirits were actually invading my body."

"Well, *that's* creepy!"

"I'm serious. I mean, I've had spiritual encounters before at the vortex sites, but they were clearly meditative events. During my dream last night, it was more physical than meditative."

"Are you sure it didn't *really* happen?"

"Are you suggesting that someone physically violated me while I was meditating?"

"That's exactly what I'm suggesting. I mean, there's that odd picture you took with the second shadow in it."

"But I took that picture *before* my yoga and meditation session. And besides, I opened my eyes in the middle of meditating and there was no one around me."

"Wait—what? Are you saying you *felt* something while you were meditating? The possibility that it was real may not be that far off the mark."

"Bree, I opened my eyes and there was no one there. And besides, I feel the spirits quite often while meditating. I've never worried about it, and I don't plan to start worrying now."

"Well, it sounds pretty creepy to me. Do you plan to go back there?"

"Absolutely. In fact, I'm heading there after work."

"Oh, good, here comes our food."

A thought crossed Kenzie's mind as she watched the waitress walk toward them with their food.

But my phone was dead…and I saw it touch my phone.

Chapter 5

Kenzie locked her bike to the fence at the parking lot at the Little Horse trailhead and made her way down the path to her meditation area. Bree had tried to talk her out of going on her own, but Kenzie assured her that she would be okay, that she had never felt threatened or unsafe on the trails.

When Kenzie reached her usual stop, she looked at her watch and realized she had time for a hike to the Chapel of the Holy Cross. It was located at one of the stronger vortexes in Sedona.

She loved spending time in the chapel. Bree thought it was odd that she would willingly spend time in a church after her traumatic experiences as a child, but Kenzie felt peace and safety there. For her, it was more of a spiritual experience than a religious one.

Decision made, Kenzie continued down Little Horse Trail until she reached the turnoff to the Chapel Trail. The trail was moderately difficult, and the day was warm and sunny, so she took her time and even stopped a few times to chat with other hikers returning from a visit to the chapel. She took these opportunities to rehydrate, and when she stopped, she looked around carefully to see if she was being followed. Each time, there was no one there.

As often as she had visited the chapel during the past two years, Kenzie was never completely prepared for the impact the chapel had on her. It was a concrete, monolithic structure built into the red rock butte formations that surrounded it. Believed to be one of the more intense vortex sites in Sedona, there were almost always crowds of tourists visiting; brought in by the busloads by local businesses that depended on the beauty and the vortexes of Sedona for their livelihoods.

Chapel of the Holy Cross

Kenzie emerged from the trail to see the glory of the chapel, awash in sunlight. She stopped and closed her eyes to absorb the aura of peace and serenity she always felt just by being near the structure. A few moments later, she opened her eyes and surveyed the area around the chapel. As expected, there were several busses in the parking lot, and dozens of tourists dotting the walkway leading to the chapel doors.

She realized Sedona's economy was largely dependent on tourism, yet it was an annoyance to Kenzie to not have unencumbered access to her beloved spiritual sites after a long day at work. She glanced at her watch and realized that as the dinner hour approached, the horde would thin, and there would still be time for a short meditation. She actively pushed her annoyance to the back of her mind and ascended the long winding ramp to the tall, glass front doors of the chapel. She shimmied between two tourists standing in the doorway, made her way into the chapel, and found a seat in a pew near the back of the church.

Kenzie looked around the chapel while she waited. The three-story ceiling made the structure feel lofty and larger than it was. The most dramatic features by far, were the floor to ceiling windows at the front of the church, in front of which hung a gigantic crucifix, complete with the body of Jesus Christ. The chapel had been commissioned by a local sculptor in nineteen thirty-two, and was owned and operated by the Roman Catholic Diocese of Phoenix.

Kenzie looked around at the people currently perusing the church. It always amazed her that people suddenly became reverent and quiet while inside such a building. She could hear whispers all around her, whispers that bounced off the walls of the concrete structure. There were several tourists lighting votive candles at the back of the church, and nearly everyone genuflected and crossed themselves when entering and leaving the church. She wondered to herself if they practiced their piety in day-to-day encounters outside the church. She suspected that for the most part, it was not so.

One by one, the tourists left, some directly, and others after visiting the gift shop in the basement that was run by Catholic nuns, offering artifacts of the Roman Catholic faith, such as bibles, rosary beads and religious statues.

Kenzie found herself nearly alone as the sun slowly lowered on the horizon. She moved to a pew in the front of the church to take full advantage of the setting sun flooding the structure with bright orange beams. She sat there with her head tilted back and her eyes closed. A feeling of inner peace filled her heart, and she opened her mind to the spirituality around her. Once more, she sensed that she was not alone, that something was touching her mind, and she welcomed the invasion of spirituality around her.

Soon, a flood of emotions filled her, emotions so intimate they brought tears to her eyes. She had experienced intense emotions before during vortex experiences, but this time, her entire being was held captive to the touch she swore was real. This time she was powerless to resist the force consuming her body and soul. Her entire body felt like it was on fire as her mind opened to the almost sensual sensation.

A rush of memories flooded her mind, and the emotions became even more intense. She relived the prejudice, intolerance and rejection of the very people she should have been able to count on to make her feel safe and valued. Her body stiffened with anger and conviction when, in her mind, she literally and figuratively cut the ties that bound her to the prison that was her early life.

When it passed, her body molded limply to the pew on which she was sitting, and her mind was at peace. Kenzie was convinced more than ever, that she was where she belonged. She had given up on the notion that she would burn in hell for her sin of forbidden love. She had found the confirmation she sought when she came to this place, and she would not return to the darkness for anyone. Yet, she yearned to share her life with someone special, someone who wouldn't judge, someone who felt the way she did.

Bree had urged her to sit back and let love come to her. She said love would find her when she least expected it. Kenzie hoped that was true. As full as her life was with her friends and her job, she *was* lonely.

"Miss? Miss, we are closing the chapel. I'm sorry, but you must go."

Kenzie snapped to awareness and sat straight up. Suddenly the touch was gone, and she felt alone once more. There was an emptiness deep inside her, a coldness she didn't understand.

"Oh! I'm sorry, sister. I was so consumed with the serenity of this place, I think I fell asleep."

"No worries. It happens all the time. Did you hike here?" the nun asked.

Kenzie stood and pulled her backpack onto her shoulder. "Yes. Yes, I did. From the Little Horse trailhead."

The nun looked out the front windows. "I think you have time to get back before dark if you don't dally too much along the way. God be with you."

"Thank you, sister."

Kenzie exited the chapel and hurried down the winding ramp toward the trail. The nun was right. She could get back to the parking lot before dusk as long as she didn't waste too much time.

Kenzie made good progress along the trail. When she reached the area she normally used for her meditation sessions, she was awed by the sunset on Cathedral Rock in the distance. A quick glance at her watch confirmed that she had a few minutes to spare, so she pulled her phone out of her pack and walked to the edge of the cliff. She raised her phone and centered her viewfinder on the rock structure bathed in the orange glow of sunset, and then snapped several pictures. She flipped through the pictures and was pleased that she'd been able to capture the beauty of nature before it was lost in the sunset.

Just as Kenzie reached the last picture, she was distracted by a movement. She froze as she saw a shadow slowly approaching on her left side. She expected it was another hiker, also intent on taking a picture of the beautiful sunset, so she closed her photos and slipped the phone into her back pocket.

"Let me get out of your way," she said, but then stopped short.

No one was there.

She spun in a circle and looked all around her, but no one was standing close by.

Kenzie had all but convinced herself the shadow she had seen was caused by a bird flying by, when she realized it was still there, on the ground, beside her. It was clearly a shadow of a human-like form, projected on the ground by...by nothing at all. She gasped and took several steps backward.

"What the fuck?"

Suddenly, the shadow turned and moved quickly away from her—back toward the trail.

Kenzie realized immediately that whatever was causing the shadow was more afraid of her than she was of it, so she followed it.

"Wait! Wait! Stop. Please stop," she called out, but the shadow continued to move away from her. "Please stop. I won't hurt you!"

The shadow suddenly stopped about twenty feet ahead of her. Kenzie continued to move toward it, and when she was within six feet, she heard an odd electronic sound and then the shadow disappeared.

She walked into the space last occupied by the shadow and felt around the air with her hands. Nothing.

"What the actual fuck?" Kenzie said out loud. "What just happened here?" How can there be a shadow without something solid casting it? Could that have been a spirit?

She placed one hand on her hip and ran the other through her hair.

The second shadow in her earlier picture! Could it be?

Kenzie glanced at the horizon and realized anew that she had better get moving before she lost daylight.

She looked around once more before she left, knowing she would need to come back the next day to figure out what was happening here.

Chapter 6

Zangendar immediately fell to her knees as soon as she reappeared on the transference pad. Her respiration was rapid and she was sweating profusely.

Tredoran ran to her. "Zangendar, what happened? I received your urgent call and started the retrieval sequence as quickly as I could."

Zangendar took Tredoran's hand and pulled herself to her feet. "Come with me. We have much to discuss."

Tredoran sat on Zangendar's renewal unit and watched her pace back and forth across her quarters. Zangendar was in a highly agitated state, a behavior totally abnormal for a Vakillian.

"Zangendar, I can't help if you don't communicate with me. What happened on the surface to cause you such distress?"

Zangendar stopped and pulled a chair in front of Tredoran. She sat in the chair and looked directly at her friend. "Our invisibility cloaks are not totally effective," she said.

"What do you mean? Were you seen?"

"Yes, and no."

Tredoran's head snapped back. "How can the same question be answered with a yes and a no?"

"Kenzie was aware of my presence without actually seeing me."

"Explain."

Zangendar sat back and ran a hand through her hair. "It might be best if I start from the beginning."

"I agree."

"I have detected a pattern by which Kenzie visits the trails. For the past three earth days, she has arrived a little more than halfway through the light cycle. With that in mind, I spend the first half of the cycle collecting additional environmental data, as well as biometric data from other humans that appear on a regular basis on the trails. When it becomes close to the time that Kenzie visits the trails, I go to her normal meditation site and wait."

"And did she come today?"

"She did, only on this day she did not stop to meditate. Instead, she continued to traverse the trail. I followed close behind, but at several intervals, she stopped to converse with others who were also on the trail. I have observed that humans in general openly approach one another, even if it is apparent that they are not acquainted. I find that odd."

"That *is* odd behavior," Tredoran agreed. "Do they not know that open, unsolicited communication can invite confrontation and hostility from others?"

"It occurs to me that they are unconcerned about that, Tredoran. It is as though hostility is not a normal first response in this world. I suspect that is a good thing. Where was I? Yes, interactions on the trail. I watched Kenzie closely each time she stopped and collected biometrics on her and the others she conversed with. Her biometrics indicated a heightened level of adrenaline, almost as though she was concerned or frightened about something."

"Did her conversations with the others indicate a crisis was at hand?"

"Quite the contrary. If I have deciphered the language enough to understand it clearly, their primary discussion was about the weather and what a nice day it was for hiking. Her words clearly did not relay any sense of danger, but each time she stopped, she looked around and appeared apprehensive about something."

"So, tell me how she was able to detect you."

"I am getting to that. At the end of the trail, there was a large structure that was surrounded by many other humans. Kenzie made her way slowly toward the structure and went inside. I sat behind her and continued to collect biometrics until all of the other humans left. By this time, the light was nearly finished its cycle and was dropping toward the horizon. The most colorful array of light emitted from the light source and filled the structure we were in. Kenzie moved to a seat closer to the front of the structure…and of course, I followed. She leaned her head back and closed her eyes and fell into a meditative state. I saw this as my chance to probe her mind."

"Is that when she became aware of you?" Tredoran asked.

"It is not."

"What happened next?"

"While probing her mind, I learned that she yearned for a presence to share her life with. I believe the humans call it, being lonely. Tears ran freely down her face and mine as well. The emotion in her mind was so intense it felt as though it would consume both of us. I never would have imagined emotion of that intensity was even possible. I thought at one point that the mind probe was causing the escalation of her emotions, but I was powerless to release her. It was painful for me. I can only imagine how it felt for her.

"The probe abruptly stopped when another human came to her and asked her to leave so the structure could be closed. That very moment when our connection ended felt like a deep stab wound to my chest. I could barely breathe and struggled to compose myself."

"What happened next?" Tredoran was totally captivated by Zangendar's encounter with the human.

"We left the structure and returned to the area she normally used for meditation. Even though the light was rapidly fading, she stopped to scan the scenery before her. I supposed she enjoyed the display of light on the formations in the distance."

"Humans seem to be very visual-centric," Tredoran observed.

"Yes. I agree. When she finished her scan, she suddenly froze and looked at the ground beside her." Zangendar paused and looked at her friend. "Tredoran, I was standing beside her."

"You were visible to her?" Tredoran asked.

"No. I was invisible, but my shadow was not."

"Your shadow was visible? But how is that possible?"

"It is possible because we failed to take into account how the wavelengths of light on Earth would interact with non-solid entities. Think, Tredoran. We knew how to make a solid body invisible, but we never gave any consideration to intangible artifacts and how they might interact with spectrum of visible and invisible light on Earth."

"How did she react?"

"At first, she was alarmed, but then I turned and ran, and for some reason I fail to understand, she followed. That is when I began transmitting my call for help. You retrieved me when she was within am arm's length of me."

Tredoran stood and walked a few feet away. "How could we miss something as important as your shadow?" she said.

"We had a lot of think about, Tredoran. None of us thought of it. You and I both missed it, as well as the other engineers on the project."

Tredoran walked toward the door.

"Where are you going?" Zangendar asked.

"To engineering. They must work on a solution for this right away."

"No. We can't tell them I was discovered. They might report it to the academy. We cannot risk the mission being cancelled. There is too much at stake here."

Tredoran approached Zangendar and stopped within a few inches of her. She pushed Zangendar backward. "What you do not want to risk is losing Kenzie. I fear you are more interested in the human than in our mission."

"That is not true. The mission is my first priority. But it is so wrong of me to want more?"

"We cannot continue this secrecy, Zangendar. If we are found out, we could be convicted of treason. At the very least, we will be removed from the mission and incarcerated until we return to Vakillia."

Zangendar grasped Tredoran's shoulders. "Do you not see that the future of our race depends on more than just finding another homeland? The proliferation of our species will always be at risk if we continue our old ways. Even if we do manage to populate Earth, after knowing what emotion is, can you honestly say you want to return to what we had on Vakillia? Do you really think we can co-exist with the people of Earth without understanding and experiencing what they *feel*?"

Tredoran broke free of Zangendar's grasp and walked a few feet away. "I admit that I do not want to continue to live a life with no emotion, but we cannot go back and risk the entire mission, Zangendar."

"Yes, we can."

"You do not want to alert engineering of our failure to cloak your shadow. Unless we do something, the mission will be a failure. How do you propose to fix this, Zangendar?"

Zangendar pulled her omni-spectrometer from her belt.

"With this. I have biometrics data on this device for hundreds of humans. We need to move our timeline forward sooner than expected. We can use the data I have collected to model human-like biometrics for ourselves. You are correct—we cannot go back like we are. We need to go back in a state that will allow us to blend in. It is time to create our avatars."

Chapter 7

Kenzie arrived at work the next morning and immediately encountered Bree.

"Hey, girlfriend! It's Friday! Know what that means? Barhopping and karaoke! Are you up to it?" Bree asked.

Kenzie poured herself a cup of coffee. "I was going to go hiking after work, but after last night's meditation session and hike, I think I'd like to do something different tonight. Clubbing and karaoke sounds like fun."

Bree took Kenzie's arm and led her to a table in the break room. "Did something happen to you on the trails last night, Kenzie?" she asked in all seriousness.

Kenzie held her coffee cup between her hands and stared at the mocha-colored liquid for several moments.

"Kenzie, you're scaring me. Spill it!" Bree insisted.

Kenzie's glance met Bree's. "Something happened…but it wasn't hurtful in any way."

"Sooooo?"

"It was almost…paranormal."

Bree sat back abruptly. "What the hell does that mean?"

"Maybe paranormal is the wrong word. Maybe metaphysical is a better description."

Bree reached across the table and took Kenzie's hand. "Okay. Tell me exactly what happened. Are you okay?"

"I'm fine, Bree. I wasn't hurt in any way. I suppose I could have been in a little bit of danger, but it didn't feel that way at the time."

"Damn it, Kenzie. You really shouldn't go hiking by yourself. What happened?"

"I'm not sure. I don't know how to describe it. You probably wouldn't believe me anyway."

Bree glanced at her watch. "Shit! We've got a meeting in five minutes. We can talk about it during lunch. My treat today."

***

During her mid-morning coffee break, Kenzie contemplated how much she should tell Bree about her encounter on the trail the day before. She wasn't even sure how much of it really had happened. It was possible that it was just her imagination playing tricks on her, just like when she thought she saw the figure on the trail the day she and Bree went in search of her sunglasses.

Kenzie pulled her phone out of her pocket and went directly to her photos, where she pulled up the picture of the two shadows.

Was she losing her mind? This couldn't possibly be real. But she had seen the shadow on the ground next to her the day before. She was sure of it! What the hell was going on here?

"Hey, girl!"

Kenzie looked up to see Bree standing in the doorway of the break room.

"Your one o'clock appointment is here. Room three," Bree said.

"Oh! Okay. Thanks, Bree."

Kenzie shoved her phone into the pocket of her white coat, finished her coffee, and threw the paper cup into the recycle bin before seeing to her patient.

***

"I'll have the antipasto salad. Oh, and please bring us the bagel crisps and spinach artichoke dip as an appetizer." Bree handed the menu to the waiter. "How about you, Kenzie?" she added.

"The antipasto salad sounds good to me too, but, no olives, please. Thanks."

"Can I bring you ladies a beverage?" the waiter asked.

"Water is fine for me," Kenzie said.

"Make it two," Bree added. She turned to Kenzie once the waiter walked away. "Okay. So, what happened on the trail last night?"

"There is no way you are going to believe me," Kenzie replied.

"Try me."

"Well, I may have an explanation for the mysterious shadow picture."

"Pray tell!"

"I think it's a ghost, or maybe a spirit."

Bree reached across the table and placed her palm on Kenzie's forehead. "Hmm. You don't feel feverish."

Kenzie brushed Bree's hand away. "I'm serious, Bree."

"You really think it's a ghost? Do ghosts cast shadows?"

"I...I don't know! I just...I can't think of any other explanation."

"So, what exactly happened on the trail last night?"

"Well, I hiked all the way to the chapel, but on the way, it felt like I was being watched. I stopped several times to look around, but I couldn't see anyone following me. It was kind of creepy."

Bree shook her head. "I've told you several times not to hike alone, Kenzie. You never know what kind of crazy might be waiting for you."

"I didn't see anyone following me. Anyway, I went to the chapel, and while meditating, it felt like something was invading my mind. It was really intense, and almost sensual."

"A ghost was having sex with your brain? Seriously?"

"I know it sounds crazy, but that's what it felt like. Every emotion, every thought was super intense. Anyway, I must have been in a deep meditative state because a nun shook me back to consciousness to tell me the Chapel was closing."

"A ghost was having sex with your brain. In a church? Girl, you are going to hell for sure."

Kenzie couldn't help but grin. "Kind of sounds kinky when you put it that way."

Just then, the waiter returned with their water and salads.

Once the waiter left, Bree resumed her questioning.

"So, how does this explain the mysterious shadow picture?"

"I'm coming to that. So, after I left the chapel, I headed back down the path and on the way, I stopped again where I lost my sunglasses, and I walked to the edge of the cliff to get a picture of Cathedral Rock bathed in this gorgeous orange sunlight.

"I took a few pictures, and then I saw a shadow come up beside me. I moved aside to give that person room to take their own pictures, but there was no one there."

"What? There was a shadow, but nothing casting it?" Bree asked incredulously.

"Exactly."

"No way! Are you sure it wasn't *your* shadow? Or maybe a big-assed bird flying overhead, or maybe even a low hanging branch?"

"I would be inclined to believe any of those possibilities, except, it ran away from me."

"Get out of Dodge!"

"I'm not kidding. It ran away from me, and I chased it."

"You *chased* it? Are you out of your goddamned mind?"

"I figured it was more afraid of me than I was of it, and when I got really close, it suddenly disappeared. It was the oddest thing I've ever seen."

"And you were actually going to go back there after work today? Alone, I might add?"

"Yes."

"Do you have a death wish? Jesus, Kenzie. That isn't something to take lightly. You should call the police."

"And what do you propose I tell them? That a ghost is stalking me on the Little Horse Trail? Do you *want* to see me locked up in the loony bin?"

"Good point. What I *do* think is that you should avoid that trail for a while…unless you bring someone with you."

"Funny thing is, Bree, I wasn't afraid. Like I said earlier, I didn't feel like I was in danger. I'll give it a few days. I'll probably go back after work on Monday."

"I'm going with you."

"Bree, I'll be fine. That isn't necessary."

"I'm going with you—no argument. Capiché?"

"Okay! Okay! Sheesh!"

***

"Yay, Kenzie!" Bree clapped for her friend as she finished singing. "You rock!"

Kenzie sat at the table and took a swig of her beer. "You're making me blush," she said.

"Damn, girl! You have an amazing voice."

"Listen to her, Kenzie, she speaks the truth," Jimmy added.

"I've always enjoyed singing," Kenzie admitted. "I started singing in the church choir when I was around ten years old. Of course, the types of song we sang were *just* a little tamer than karaoke!"

"You should audition for one of those talent shows on television," Bree suggested.

"Not on your life! Singing in a karaoke bar is one thing. Singing in front of millions on national TV is something else all together!"

The next singer selected a slow, sultry song. Jimmy stood and extended his hand to Bree. "May I have the honors?" he asked.

Bree looked at Kenzie. "Will you be okay?"

"Go dance with Jimmy. I'll be fine!"

Kenzie watched her friends sway to and fro on the dance floor, cheek to cheek, and without a sliver of daylight between them. She felt a sense of nostalgic emotion for the days that she had been able to share similar moments with Jessie. Her mind went back to how lonely and vulnerable she had felt when the nun had awaked her from her meditation in the chapel. Her heart swelled with affection for her friends, but she yearned for a loving relationship of her own.

"You have an amazing voice, pretty lady."

Kenzie snapped out of her daydream and saw a handsome young man standing at her side, also watching Bree and Jimmy dance. He was slim, and a bit taller than she. At first glance, he

63

looked like a typical Arizonan cowboy with his blue jeans, button up plaid shirt, boots and worn cowboy hat, tilted back far enough on his head to expose a mop of brown hair. But if his appearance made him look like he just rode his steed across the desert plains, his demeanor was anything but cowboyish. He smiled brightly at Kenzie and exposed a row of straight, white teeth and dimples in both cheeks. Kenzie thought he was kind of cute—for a guy.

"They're cute together. Don't you think?"

"Huh?" Kenzie stammered.

"Bree and Jimmy. They're cute together."

"Yes! Yes, I agree. And you are…?"

"I'm sorry. Where are my manners? I'm Charlie. Charlie Cross." Charlie took his hat off and extended his hand to Kenzie.

Kenzie smiled. "It's nice to meet you, Charlie Cross. I'm Mackenzie Caldwell." Kenzie slipped her hand in his. "You can call me Kenzie. I take it you know Bree and Jimmy?"

"I work with Jimmy in the vortex tourism industry."

"So, you're a tour guide for the vortex sites?"

"Actually, I pilot the helicopter while Jimmy does the tour guide thing. I also work with the rescue squad on the side. You know, if hikers are stranded in hard-to-reach places."

"Wow! A pilot!"

"I have to confess that Jimmy works harder than I do. They paired us up a few years ago. We work pretty well as a team."

"That's a cool job! I am a registered nurse at the urgent care center."

"So, you must work with Bree?"

"Yes, that's where I met her. She's become a really good friend during the past two years."

"Maybe we can do dinner with them some night," Charlie said.

Kenzie grimaced. "Ah, if you are suggesting we double-date with Bree and Jimmy, I need you to know that I bat for the other team. Sorry!"

Charlie grinned. "I totally respect that, but the offer for dinner stands. Totally platonic. A guy can never have enough friends."

"I'd like that, Charlie. Thank you."

Bree and Jimmy sauntered back toward the table at the end of the song.

"Charlie!" Bree hugged her friend. "I see you've met Kenzie."

"I had to come to compliment her on her singing," Charlie said. "And it turns out we're both looking for new friends, so clear your calendars for tomorrow night. We're going to dinner." Charlie turned to Kenzie. "Does tomorrow work for you?"

Kenzie raised her hands. "Tomorrow is great. Let's do it!"

Chapter 8

"I believe your mammary masses need to be larger," Tredoran said.

"Larger? Truly, Tredoran? On what data do you base that observation?" Zangendar replied.

"I assume you want to present as female to the humans. Am I correct?"

"Yes, especially as I *am* female."

Tredoran looked at the computer screen on the wall. "Computer, display videos of the humans."

A continuous stream of videos appeared on the screen.

"Watch closely, Zangendar. What do you notice about the human females that distinguishes them from the males?"

Zangendar crossed her arms. "I know what distinguishes them from the males, they are smaller and…"

"And less muscular, and *non-linear*," Tredoran interrupted. "If you want to present as a human female, you need to soften your appearance."

"Are you implying that I more closely resemble a human male than female, Tredoran?"

"That is exactly what I am implying. Look at the females in these pictures. They all have far more mammary mass than you. Or I, for that matter."

Zangendar reached forward and wrapped her palms around Tredoran's breasts. "You have certainly made your mammary masses larger than I have. Do you believe the size you have chosen is adequate for me?"

"I was contemplating making mine larger as well. I suggest the same for you."

"This is a much more difficult task than I anticipated," Zangendar complained.

Tredoran tilted her head to the side as she continued to watch the videos on the screen. Suddenly, she grabbed

Zangendar's arm. "Computer, pause!" She turned to face Zangendar. "I have a thought."

"I am listening," Zangendar said.

Tredoran released Zangendar's arm and stepped up to the monitor. "Computer, assemble a composite of all the common features for the females in these videos."

Zangendar approached and stood beside Tredoran. While they waited for the results, she cupped the breasts she had manufactured for herself. "Do you really believe they are too small?"

Tredoran glanced at Zangendar's breasts and then pointed to the screen. "Pay heed, Zangendar. The composite is nearly finished. And yes, they are too small."

Zangendar and Tredoran stood captivated as the computer displayed the image. They were silent for several minutes. The composite image was significantly disproportionate.

"That is *not* a very appealing female," Zangendar commented. "In fact, she seems extremely distorted. Is it your plan to model our avatars after *that* image?"

"Not exactly." Tredoran pulled a scanner from her pouch. "I will scan you, and then you will scan me. I will upload our images to the computer, and then program the computer to compute a best-fit comparison for each of us. With this approach, our human avatars will closely resemble each of us, but without our distinct Vakillian features."

"So, the goal is to not *look* like the composite, but to use the composite to identify where our Vakillian features differ from the humans."

"And to suggest modifications that will create human-like renderings of our images," Tredoran said.

Zangendar placed her hand on Tredoran's shoulder. "This is why I recommended you for this mission, my sister. You have exceptional analytical and programming skills."

Tredoran uploaded their full body scans to the computer and quickly wrote a subtraction algorithm to identify unique features between the composite and each of their scanned images. Once identified, the algorithm would then remove those unique features from their scanned images and replace each with the corresponding feature from the human composite.

Zangendar studied the human composite image while Tredoran worked on the algorithm.

"I am finished. Now all we have to do is run the algorithm," Tredoran said.

"Wait." Zangendar pointed to the computer screen. "The composite's hair is an odd color that I do not think any of the humans really have. It is a combination of the gray, yellow, black, red and brown hair of the females in the images. I fear that will not be realistic."

Tredoran studied the composite image on the screen. "You are correct. The eye color is unnatural as well. That is a good observation, Zangendar. I will modify the algorithm to allow us to choose hair and eye color. Do you have any other observations before we begin?"

"Will we have the ability to adjust our avatars? Humans have traits that vary from human to human. Some have dots on their faces and arms. There are various shapes of eyes and noses. Some have peach-colored skin, while others have shades of tan and brown. There are so many variations. I don't want the two of us to appear *too* much alike."

"I believe I can allow for modifications in the algorithm," Tredoran said. She walked back toward the computer and then stopped to look at Zangendar. "If I am the analytical one, you are the one with a well developed sense of observation. I believe the humans would call that, 'having an eye for detail.' We are a good team, my sister."

Zangendar grinned. "Your emotions are showing, Tredoran—and that is a good thing."

***

Zangendar and Tredoran sat side by side on Zangendar's renewal unit, going through the various images they had optimized through the subtraction algorithm Tredoran created.

"What is your opinion?" Zangendar asked.

Tredoran did not reply right away. Instead, she studied the images for a few more minutes on the hand-held tablet.

"Tredoran?"

"I see a strong resemblance to you, Zangendar, in all of your images. It is unusual to see you with other than green hair, but it does look like a human version of the Vakillian Zangendar. The prosthetic breathing device in the middle of your face is distracting to me, but I assume it will seem normal to the humans."

"Then you approve?"

"I approve. And what is your opinion of my avatar?" Tredoran asked.

"It is distinctly female, but then your Vakillian self is also distinctly female. You were correct to go with larger mammary masses. They complement the rest of your human form. I am curious as to the length of hair you chose."

Tredoran nodded. "I was intrigued by the various ways human females arrange their hair. I assumed this length would allow me the opportunity to experiment. Do you approve?"

"Very much so. I am confident that we will present as human with little question."

Tredoran rose from the unit and paced the room. Zangendar watched her curiously.

"You seen concerned, Tredoran."

Tredoran stopped and faced her friend. "I *am* concerned. I am concerned that something will happen and the humans will reject us. I am concerned that the commander will discover what we are doing and we will face dire consequences. I can't help but calculate the risks, Zangendar. As you noted, I am analytical. Does this not concern you as well?"

"I will not deny that I have had moments of doubt, but unlike you, I have been on the surface. I have seen what Earth has to offer, or at least part of it. From Kenzie's memories, I know that there is so much more to be seen, and so many more places to explore."

Zangendar sat forward for emphasis.

"Tredoran, there are *massive* amounts of water on this planet. *Massive* amounts—enough to assure the proliferation of our race for hundreds if not thousands of years. We should easily be able to accomplish our mission. With the abundance of water, we will be able to procreate with one another on this planet, and instead of returning to Vakillia, we will be able to stay here and flourish. We won't fail. We *can't* fail."

Tredoran crossed the room in three long strides and took Zangendar's hand. "Come. We have little time for rest."

"What is your intention, Tredoran?"

Tredoran pointed at the tablet. "We might be able to transform our appearance to *look* human, but that will be of no use to us if we don't *act* like humans."

Tredoran pulled Zangendar to the computer screen on the wall where the videos continued to stream.

"Look at them. They move differently than we do. Their arms sway when they walk. Their entire bodies seem relaxed, where we have been taught since birth to stand straight and tall. They have countless facial expressions. They move their heads and raise their brows when they talk. They smile. A lot! Some of them touch one another when they talk. We have so much to learn about how to *be* them. And what do we know about their speech patterns? These videos contain little of that."

Zangendar put her hand on Tredoran's shoulder. "This is when analytics get in the way, sister. Yes, we need more information. Yes, we need to study them more, and it would be best if we could learn all of this before we engage, but we do not have time for that. We will need to learn by doing and we *will* make mistakes. We need to interact with the humans on a graduated basis. The more we learn, the more comfortable we will become, and the more we can interact. The alternative is to do nothing, and then our race will certainly die. Or we can take the planet by force, and our race may *still* die, and so will the humans. If you are uncomfortable with this plan, I release you from your obligations, but I am moving forward, with or without you."

Tredoran pushed Zangendar backward. "Is that what you think of me? You call me sister, yet you think I will abandon you. I have always stood by you, even when I knew it was unwise. Even when I risked my own advancement. And, why? Because I know your cause is noble, even if it *is* reckless. Because I have always wished I were brave enough to be like you. I reject your attempt to release me from this obligation, but I will *not* go into this unprepared."

Zangendar sat on the edge of her renewal unit and studied her hands folded in her lap. "I was unaware of your feelings, Tredoran. I owe you an apology."

"You are correct. You do owe me an apology, but not for your insolence. You owe me an apology for opening my mind to emotions. What I feel right now is not pleasant."

"But it *is* a feeling."

"Yes, it is, and it is too late and impossible to reverse."

"So, what do you propose we do?"

"We study. We practice. We visit the surface and begin to integrate. You are correct. We will learn as we go, but there is much we can do to prepare. We begin tonight by way of virtual, continuous loop immersion in the videos while we renew. Upon the new day, we will continue to study the videos, and then we will emulate the humans' mannerisms until we can no longer stand. I recommend you begin the renewal process immediately."

"How long do you believe this process will take?"

"It will take as much time as we need. We cannot risk discovery, Zangendar."

Zangendar looked down at her hands and her shoulders slumped.

Tredoran clasped her hands behind her back and tilted her head. Her brow furrowed. "What is this posture I am witnessing, Zangendar?"

Zangendar looked up at her friend. "I do not have a name for it, Tredoran. All I know is that I have a heavy feeling in the center of my chest, and my mind is filled with something similar to worry."

"Could it be fear? Do you fear we may fail in our venture?"

"It is not fear, Tredoran. I am determined that we will not fail. No, it is something else."

"What is the origin of this feeling?"

"It came to me during your assessment of how long it may take for the learning process. It came to me when I realized it may be a substantial number of cycles before I will see Kenzie again."

Tredoran placed one hand on Zangendar's shoulder. "It will take as long as it takes, sister. If we succeed, you may have your entire future to spend with Kenzie. If we fail, well, if we fail, you may never see her again. We must be prepared."

Zangendar nodded and then stood. She placed her own hand on Tredoran's shoulder. "I am fortunate that you are my Vakillian sister, Tredoran. You give me a sense of determination. We will not fail."

"We will not fail," Tredoran repeated. "Until morning, then."

"Until morning," Zangendar said to Tredoran's retreating form.

Chapter 9

"So, tell me about yourself," Charlie said. "I already know you learned to sing in your church's choir."

Kenzie picked up her napkin and wiped her mouth. "There's not much to tell. I was raised in a religious community in Utah. It was pretty restrictive, and based on my life experiences since I left, it was pretty boring as well."

"A religious community, huh? Was it one that believes a woman's place is in the home, barefoot, pregnant and chained to the stove?" Charlie asked.

"Something like that."

"Charlie spent some time in a seminary," Jimmy offered.

Kenzie's eyebrows rose to her forehead. "Really? You don't strike me as priest material."

"That was before he was a pilot in the Army," Bree offered.

"You were in the Army." Kenzie stated rather than asked.

"Yes. That's where I learned to fly. I did two tours in the sandbox," Charlie replied.

"The sandbox?"

"Yeah. That's what we called the Middle East."

"So, what made you leave the priesthood?"

"It wasn't actually the priesthood. It was more like the ministry. I left because I didn't quite fit their mold. But enough about me. What's your story?"

"That's a long one," Kenzie said.

"The night is young. We have time. Dinner hasn't even arrived yet," Charlie replied. "Really...I'd like to know."

"Don't say I didn't warn you," Kenzie joked.

For the next several minutes, Kenzie talked about her early life in the religious community, and about how women in general were treated as less than. As hard as she tried, she couldn't keep the hurt and anger from her voice.

"It must have taken a tremendous amount of courage to leave," Charlie observed.

"I didn't have a choice. It was either stay and suffer through an arranged marriage to a boy I had no feelings for or be true to myself and leave."

"Wait! Let me get this straight. They knew you were gay, but they still arranged a marriage for you…to a man?" Charlie asked.

"Yes. You see, the fact that I was gay wasn't the issue. The fact that I wouldn't renounce it was. I could have continued to live under their repressive rules for the rest of my life if I agreed to deny who I was."

Bree reached across the table and took Kenzie's hand. "I am so glad you chose to leave. I would never have met you if you had stayed."

Kenzie smiled and raised Bree's hand to her lips for a light kiss. "Ditto, sister," she said.

"Hey, none of that, Caldwell. Bree is *my* girl!" Jimmy joked.

Kenzie picked up a kernel of popcorn from the basket in the middle of their table and flicked it at Jimmy. It hit him on the end of the nose. "You snooze, you lose, Jimmy-boy!"

"I dare you to do that again," Jimmy said.

Kenzie tossed another kernel at Jimmy, who caught it in his mouth. He immediately stood and raised both fists into the air.

"She shoots! She scores! Yay!" Jimmy shouted.

Bree grabbed Jimmy's waistband and pulled him back into his seat. "Sit down, you goofball."

Charlie shook his head and laughed. "Are you guys always this crazy?"

"As often as we can be," Kenzie said.

"Judging by the environment you were raised in, it must be really freeing," Charlie said.

"Very much so," Kenzie admitted.

"So, have you seen your folks much since you left?" he asked.

"No. They aren't allowed to speak to me. In fact, they have completely disowned me. The whole community has. Rules are rules."

"Sheesh! That's kind of extreme, don't you think?"

"It is what it is. It was difficult living in a community where I was scorned for being different. My life has been so much better since I left. Sure, I miss them, but they made their choice and I made mine. I chose me."

Charlie covered Kenzie's hand with his own and squeezed. "I know all about being different. I chose me as well."

Their dinners arrived before Kenzie could ask Charlie to expand on his comment, and the four friends quickly fell into an enjoyable evening of good food and good company.

***

"Walk across the room again," Tredoran instructed.

Zangendar strode across the room as casually as she could.

"Move your buttocks more."

Zangendar looked at Tredoran with a surprised expression on her face. "More? Explain more."

Tredoran stood. "Like this." She walked across the room while swaying her hips back and forth dramatically.

"Surely, you jest," Zangendar said. "Humans don't walk like that naturally."

Tredoran took Zangendar's arm and pulled her to the video station on the wall. "Computer, run the videos demonstrating human movement on a loop."

For the next few moments, they watched videos of women walking toward them, and away from them. Tredoran paused the video and pointed to a woman's buttocks. "Watch how her posterior sways back and forth when she walks. Computer, resume."

After a few more moments, Zangendar tilted her head. "Computer, pause." She turned to Tredoran. "It seems to me that the way these females walk depends on their overall demeanor."

"How so?" Tredoran asked.

"Computer, resume. Watch this female here." Zangendar pointed to the screen. "As you noted, her buttocks sway back and forth, but a female is about to enter into the field of view who walks with much less movement. There she is. Observe as she walks."

Tredoran nodded. "Computer, pause. Yes. I see your point. Why is it that they walk so differently from one another?"

Zangendar put her hand on Tredoran's shoulder. "It occurs to me that, unlike Vakillians, humans are encouraged to be unique. It also occurs to me that the more female-like the earthling is, the more their buttocks sway when they walk. I believe if you were a human female, your buttocks would sway when you walk, and mine would not."

Tredoran turned back to the video screen. "Computer, resume." She watched for several more minutes. "I believe you are correct, sister. I believe I require more practice swaying my buttocks than you do."

"We must also learn to coordinate our arm movements. Opposite arm with opposite leg."

Tredoran walked across the room while swaying her hips and swinging her arms.

"Your movements appear to be quite stilted and awkward, Tredoran. Human movement is much smoother. I am afraid we have a lot of work to do."

"I agree, my sister. Perhaps if we practiced while cloaked in our avatars, it might feel more natural? Perhaps the human females' mammary masses and buttocks change their center of gravity?"

"You may be right, Tredoran. Perhaps we should remain cloaked in our avatars at all times, except when we are within view of our crewmates. We need to learn to be comfortable as humans, and an extended period of time cloaked in our avatars may help."

***

Zangendar lay on her back in her renewal unit and stared at the ceiling. She found it difficult to lie comfortably in this foreign body with its curves and non-linear dimensions. Lying on her front was nearly impossible with the mammary masses in the way. She was exhausted from countless hours of practicing human movement, yet she was unable to relax and succumb to the renewal process.

She closed her eyes and resorted to meditation in an attempt to relax. She was unable to clear her mind. Instead, she saw visions of Kenzie on the insides of her eyelids. In her mind's eye, she watched her walk down the trail toward the chapel. She watched her buttocks sway back and forth in a manner similar to what Tredoran was attempting to achieve. Kenzie was one of the more female-like humans. She was soft and curvy. She had attractive mammary masses. Her red hair and green eyes were difficult to look away from, especially her eyes.

Zangendar struggled with the unfamiliar stirring within her chest. Even though she was lying down, she felt light-headed and her stomach threatened to mutiny. She could feel her heart pounding in her ears, and a rush of heat rose into her neck and face. She tried to push Kenzie out of her mind, but she failed miserably.

She recalled when she had followed Kenzie to the chapel. She sat behind her in the pews. She touched her tenderly and entered her mind. Then, quite unexpectedly, Kenzie turned around and looked directly at her. She reached one hand up and gently trailed her fingertips across Zangendar's cheek and across her lips. Zangendar felt herself quiver in response.

Kenzie touched her lips to hers, gently at first, but then with more ferocity. Zangendar found it difficult to breathe and she squirmed under the unfamiliar spasms coming from deep within her abdomen. She felt like she might lose consciousness.

In that moment, she had felt her mind and body meld with Kenzie's.

In that moment, she wanted nothing more but to spend the rest of her life exactly where she was, regardless of the price.

"Miss? Miss, we are closing the chapel. I'm sorry, but you must go."

***

Zangendar's eyes flew open and she sat up abruptly on her renewal unit. She was drenched in sweat and breathing heavily. She felt an unfamiliar wetness between her avatar legs. She ran her hand over the nipples on the center of her mammary masses and was surprised to find them erect and tender. Another spasm passed through her abdomen and she pulled her knees into her chest to contain the warmth she felt spreading through her avatar body.

Was this what it felt like to be human?

Zangendar was not sure she liked being this vulnerable. She thought again about Kenzie pressing her lips to hers, and was immediately rewarded with increased throbbing and wetness between her legs.

What did it mean that she was having this reaction at the mere thought of Kenzie? She didn't recall her reaction to Kenzie being this intense while she was in her natural body. Could it be that she was actually feeling human reactions while cloaked in her avatar?

Zangendar ran her hand across her forehead. Her skin felt warm and clammy. She would have to learn how to control this human body's reaction to Kenzie. She instinctively knew it would not be socially acceptable behavior.

For the first time since this mission began, she doubted her ability to succeed.

Chapter 10

Kenzie awoke the next morning feeling refreshed. She had thoroughly enjoyed dinner the night before with Bree, Jimmy and Charlie. The conversation had been interesting, but she would have liked to learn more about Charlie's back story. All she knew was that he spent time in the seminary and in the Army as a chaplain, and that he currently flew helicopter for one of the vortex touring companies in Sedona. Her mind went back to something he'd said at dinner.

I know all about being different. I chose me as well.

She wanted to know what he'd meant by that, but the subject had been quickly changed, and soon the four of them were enjoying a satisfying dinner while chatting like they had been friends forever. By the time the evening finished, her curiosity about his comment had totally slipped her mind. Before they parted for the evening, Charlie promised to give her a helicopter tour of the entire town and all of the most popular vortex sites. She was looking forward to taking him up on that offer.

Kenzie had originally planned to spend Sunday doing housework and catching up on her reading list, but by noon, she became restless. She was tempted to call Bree, but then felt guilty about commandeering precious weekend time away from Jimmy. She suddenly felt sorry for herself. After more than two years in Sedona, Bree and Jimmy were her only friends, and she didn't feel she knew Charlie well enough to seek his company. She felt a sense of loneliness and homesickness fill her chest. Never in a million years did she think she'd ever miss her life in Utah, but she had to admit that as horrible and restrictive as it had been, it was far from lonely.

"Ugh! I've got to get out of this house before I lose my mind" she said out loud. "Maybe a nice walk or a movie would do the trick."

Kenzie dressed in shorts, a tank top and cross-trainers, threw on a baseball cap and grabbed her backpack into which she stuffed her wallet, a bottle of water and a few snacks, and then headed out for a walk.

***

Zangendar's communication device alerted her to a presence at the entrance of her quarters. The biometrics on her visitor identified them as Tredoran.

"Enter," Zangendar said.

The hatch to her quarters slid open and admitted Tredoran. Tredoran cloaked in her human avatar the moment she entered the room and the hatch closed. "Good morning, Zangendar."

"Good morning. Was your renewal restful?" Zangendar asked.

"To be truthful, no. I found it difficult to lie comfortably in this human form," Tredoran replied. "And you?"

"I also found it difficult. Difficult and disturbing."

"Disturbing in what way?"

"I found myself thinking of Kenzie and discovered that my avatar body reacts quite oddly to her in ways my natural body does not."

"Explain."

"Some of it is quite personal, so I will spare you the details, but I will say that I have concluded that my avatar appears to be more than just a cloaking device. I appear to *feel* things differently when I am cloaked."

"Were the feelings pleasant?"

Zangendar paused before answering. "That is difficult to answer. I suppose if it hadn't been the first time I experienced that level of emotion, it might have been pleasurable, but to be honest, it was somewhat uncomfortable."

"Are you reconsidering our plan to use avatars to integrate?"

"No. I still believe the avatars afford us the best chance to determine if we can live among the humans. In fact, I plan to visit the surface today."

"Do you think that is wise, Zangendar? We have practiced for only two days. We have much more to learn."

"I do not plan to interact on this first trip. I will simply observe. I thought I might bring a mat and feign meditation. I have seen many of the humans meditating on the trails. I do not believe it would draw any attention."

"I wish to go with you, Zangendar."

"I am not sure that is wise. I do not want to draw undue interest."

"Did you not say it was common for humans to walk these trails in pairs or even in groups?"

Zangendar looked at her friend for several moments. "As you wish. We will need to transfer while cloaked, in the event something unforeseen happens and we cannot cloak on the surface."

"To do that, we will need to reveal our avatars to the transference room technician."

"That is correct."

"But, Zangendar, we will most likely be arrested and brought before the council."

"That is exactly what I am counting on. Are you ready, Tredoran?"

"Do you recall when you asked me if I had ever felt feelings of anxiety or doubt?" Tredoran asked.

"Yes, I do recall asking you that question."

"That time is now."

"Are you reconsidering this trip to the surface?"

"Absolutely not. I will be your side, but I am beginning to understand how these human avatars make us more susceptible to human emotion."

Zangendar nodded. "I believe it is time to go."

***

"Halt!"

Zangendar and Tredoran made it halfway to the transference room before they were stopped by a fellow crewman, who now held them at bay with her phaser.

The crewman spoke into a communication device on her wrist. "Intruder alert. Deck four, section nine."

Zangendar and Tredoran stood with their hands in the air.

"Aucrud, it is Zangendar and Tredoran," Zangendar said.

"How did you get onto this ship, and how do you know my name?" Aucrud asked.

Tredoran stepped forward. "Aucrud…"

Aucrud stunned Tredoran with her phaser and watched her fall to the floor.

"Stop!" Zangendar said. "Aucrud, we are not who you think we are. We are Zangendar and Tredoran. We are disguised for our trip to the surface."

Aucrud pointed her phaser at Zangendar. "Silence!"

Just then, the security guards appeared at the end of the hall and quickly made their way toward them.

"Identify yourself," one of the security guards demanded.

"We are Zangendar and Tredoran. We were preparing for a trip to the surface. Our appearance has been altered in order to move among the natives unrestrained."

Tredoran recovered and pushed herself into a seated position.

"Allow me to help her," Zangendar asked.

"No!" The security guard motioned another guard toward Tredoran. "Help her up. We are taking you to the holding bay until we can determine who you are and how you got onto this ship."

Moments later, the guards pushed them into a holding bay with electronic bars holding them secure.

"I urge you to contact Molinder and Belander. They are my birth units," Zangendar called to the guards' retreating forms.

When the guards were out of sight, Zangendar joined Tredoran on the bench on the far side of the room. "I trust you will recover?" she asked.

"Explain to me *why* you wanted to be arrested?" Tredoran asked.

"Being arrested proves our disguises are effective. Aucrud and the guards did not know who we were. Molinder and Belander will know who we are."

"How can you be so sure?"

"Because I will uncloak to show them who I am."

***

Molinder paced back and forth in front of the holding bay while Belander rested her back against the opposite wall. Her arms were crossed, and a stern expression had taken up residence on her face. The electronic bars formed a barrier between Zangendar and her mothers.

"Molinder, I need you to look at me," Zangendar insisted.

Molinder stopped and faced her daughter. "Prove to me you are who you say you are."

Zangendar uncloaked and Molinder gasped. A chuckle could be heard coming from Belander, who still remained positioned against the wall. Molinder turned around sharply to look at her mate.

"I fail to see what is so amusing," Molinder said.

"It is ingenious. Don't you see? Even you weren't convinced until she uncloaked," Belander said. She looked at Zangendar. "I was unsure you would be successful in this venture, until now, daughter. I commend you."

Zangendar felt an unfamiliar emotion in her chest to finally gain the approval of her beloved Belander. "I am honored," was all she could manage in response.

Molinder approached Belander and stopped just inches away from her nose. "She is so much like you. It is infuriating at times."

Zangendar was sure she saw a hint of a smile on the corners of Belander's mouth. Her attention was drawn back to Molinder as she approached once more. "You will have your mission, daughter, but I implore you not to keep such important matters from us in the future."

Molinder motioned for the guard to release the electronic bars.

Zangendar stepped out of the room, followed by Tredoran.

"We will need our packs," Tredoran said to the guard.

"I will retrieve them for you," the guard said.

"Please have them brought to the transference room," Zangendar added. She re-cloaked and then approached Belander. "I appreciate your support, Mother. It means a great deal to me."

"Do the humans really dress like this?" Belander asked.

"They do."

"Not too different than we are, but apparently less modest these days," she replied.

"I agree. Not so different."

Belander nodded and then offered her arm to Molinder and they walked away.

*** *** ***

Zangendar glanced at Tredoran before they stepped onto the transference pads. "Considering our human forms react differently than what we are used to, we will wait to engage the gravity equalizers in our footwear until after we are on the surface."

Zangendar nodded to the transference technician once they were ready. Moments later, they materialized behind the red rocks on the Little Horse Trail. Zangendar watched Tredoran's reaction to her first time on the surface. Tredoran appeared to be frozen to the spot.

"Are you well?" Zangendar asked.

Tredoran looked at her, eyes wide. All she could do was nod.

Zangendar took a tentative step with little to no difficulty. It appeared the gravity on this planet had less hold on her in her human form. She took a moment to look around and was relieved that they appeared to be alone.

"Tredoran, take a few steps toward me."

Tredoran did as she was told and soon seemed to realize that movement would be relatively easy and stable in this new environment. She stopped next to Zangendar and placed a hand on her arm. "It is so bright," she said.

"Yes. It is good that we are wearing light blocking lenses in our eyes. It was a good idea to manufacture them in different colors. The blue ones are appealing with the hair color you have chosen," Zangendar said.

"And you have chosen green eye lenses," Tredoran replied.

"Yes. They are green, like Kenzie's eyes."

Tredoran walked a few feet away. "The light is warm on my skin. It is strange to expose so much of our bodies to the environment."

"This is how the natives dress. Nearly all of them wear clothing that leaves their arms and legs, and even their mid-sections exposed. I also found it odd at first."

"Is it always as warm as this?"

"The heat is less once the light has set. The natives call their light source, the sun. It is at its peak right now, and hence, the heat is as well. We should choose a spot to lay our mats so we can pretend to meditate and observe the behavior of the natives."

Tredoran followed Zangendar to an open spot on the other side of the trail. "When will we see natives?" she asked.

"It is my experience that they appear at random times."

"And Kenzie? Will we see her?"

"This is much earlier in the light cycle than I normally encounter her, so I do not expect to see her unless we are still here much later in the cycle. We will lay our mats here. This is where Kenzie normally meditates."

Zangendar and Tredoran laid their mats side by side and then sat on them, with their legs crossed and their hands resting on their knees.

"The humans close their eyes to meditate. It is similar to our renewal process. You will be able to open them when we hear humans approach."

"Are you sure the humans pose no danger? We are quite vulnerable sitting here without protection," Tredoran commented.

"It is my experience that the humans are not aggressive. As I have told you, they are quite friendly and readily talk to others, even if they are unfamiliar with one another. We have nothing to fear from humans passing by on the trail. We are not here to engage today. We are here to listen and to watch patterns of speech and behavior."

Zangendar and Tredoran sat in silence for a few moments.

"Where are the humans?" Tredoran whispered.

Zangendar ignored her.

A few more moments passed.

"This environment is very hot."

Zangendar looked at her friend. "Is this how you meditate on the ship?"

"It is not hot on the ship."

"Your body will adjust to the heat in time. Right now, you need to focus on the mission."

Tredoran reached for her backpack and retrieved a bottle of water. As she took a drink from it, they heard the sound of voices approaching from the wooded areas a few yards away. She quickly screwed the cap back on, shoved it into her pack, and resumed her position on the mat.

Zangendar sat as still as she could, and observed through slitted eyelids, two females approach them. Instead of walking by, they paused in front of where they sat on their mats.

"Wow! What a great shot of Cathedral Rock. Let's take some selfies," one of the females said.

Zangendar watched them run to the edge of the ledge and then hold a rectangular device in front of them for several moments as they stood with their backs facing the rock formation in the distance. She found it amusing that they contorted their faces into various expressions while performing this ritual, all the while laughing and touching on another. Finally, they were finished.

"Girlfriend, those are really good pictures. Send them to me, okay?"

"No problem. I'll post them to Facebook too."

"Awesome!"

Finally, the two women walked back onto the trail and moved on.

***

"I assume they were human females?" Tredoran asked.

"Yes. They were human females," Zangendar replied.

"They touch one another quite often, and they are very familiar with one another."

"Yes, they are."

"I am not sure I can adjust to that."

Just as Zangendar was about to reply, they heard more voices approaching on the trail.

Chapter 11

Kenzie walked from her apartment to the downtown shopping center, intent on browsing and passing time until the airtime for the movie she had decided to see approached. She strolled through the mall and ended up in the sporting goods store, where she decided to purchase new workout clothes and yoga pants. She pulled the yoga pants on and then came out of the stall to look at herself in the full-length mirror positioned in the common area of the dressing room.

"Wow! You look amazing!"

Kenzie swung around and came face to face with Charlie, who had just exited a stall on the men's side of the dressing rooms.

"Charlie! I didn't expect to see you here!"

Charlie held a pair of gym shorts and a T-shirt in his hand. "I needed new workout gear. Mine is getting a little threadbare."

"Same here. I've picked out some new hiking clothes, and of course, these yoga pants. I'm thinking about joining a hot yoga class I saw an ad for last week."

"I enjoyed dinner last night. Thank you for accepting my invite," Charlie said.

"I had a really good time too. We should do it again some time. Bree and Jimmy are a lot of fun to hang with."

"I agree. It's nice to go out with friends once in a while. It beats sitting at home alone."

"I know what you mean. That's one of the reasons I hike. It is definitely better than staring at the walls of my apartment."

"Do you hike often?"

"I do. Almost every day, in fact. The vortex sites in this town are amazing. They bring me peace, especially after a hard day."

"I'm so used to seeing the trails from the air that I don't think about what they would be like to hike."

"You should try it some time. It's really a spiritual experience. At least it is for me."

"I might just do that. Well, I should let you get back to shopping. I'll see you later, then?"

"Absolutely."

Kenzie watched Charlie walk away but stopped him before he got too far.

"Charlie!"

Charlie swung around. "Yeah?"

"Are you busy now?"

"Not really. I just gotta buy these clothes."

"I was going to go see a movie, but if you're interested, maybe we could go hiking together instead."

"Hiking? Like, now?"

"Sure. I just live a few blocks from here. We could go back to my place and change into our new clothes and then hit the trails. The day is still young. We could get a few hours of hiking in if you're up to it."

Charlie walked back toward her. "You know, that's the best offer I've had in a long time. Sounds like fun. I'd love to go."

***

Kenzie shoved four bottles of water into her backpack, along with a few snacks, her sunglasses and some sunscreen while Charlie used the bathroom to change into his new gym shorts and sleeveless T-shirt.

She felt excited at the thought of having a new friend. It was so refreshing to have a guy-friend without feeling like he had an ulterior motive. She truly felt safe and comfortable with Charlie. There was something about him that appealed to her psyche. It almost felt as though they connected on some higher level.

Charlie was a good-looking man. He was around five-foot-ten and slim, but he appealed to her more on a spiritual level than a physical one. More than anything else, she appreciated that he respected who she was, and he was willing to accept her friendship with no strings attached.

"All set," Charlie said as he came out of the bathroom. "I'm afraid my legs are a bit scrawny."

"They're perfect!" Kenzie said. "Ready to go?"

"Yup. Here, let me take that backpack." Charlie reached for the bag. "Wow, it's heavier than I expected."

"Water and snacks for both of us. Oh, and sunscreen. I'm afraid my Irish complexion objects to sunburn."

Ten minutes later, Charlie pulled his car into the parking lot of the Little Horse trailhead, and within moments they were on their way up the trail.

"So, you do this every day?" Charlie asked as they walked side by side on the trail.

"Nearly. It depends on the weather, and how late it is when I get out of work. Sometimes I have time for a longer walk, but on really busy days, I get a later start than I'd like, and I have to settle for a shorter walk and mediation. We have lots of time today, so a longer hike is in order."

"Which vortex site is our destination on this hike?"

"The Chapel of the Holy Cross. It's…"

"It's one of the strongest and most easily felt vortexes in all of Sedona. The feeling within the walls of the chapel is one of inspiration and joy. The energy of this vortex site also includes love, harmony, unity and oneness with all that is," Charlie said in his professional announcer voice. "Forgive me, but I've heard Jimmy recite that hundreds of times on our air tours."

Kenzie laughed. "You may have memorized the spiel, but have you ever actually been there?"

"I confess I have not."

Kenzie locked arms with Charlie. "Well, then, you're in for a treat."

***

Zangendar stiffened as she listened to the humans approach them on the trail. A wave of anxiety filled her chest when she recognized the voice. She glanced sideways at Tredoran, who also sat stiffly. "It is her. It is Kenzie," she said under her breath.

Zangendar tried hard to relax so that her meditation pose appeared normal when Kenzie approached, but she couldn't control the rapid beating of her heart, nor could she stop the bead of sweat forming at her hairline.

"How long have you lived in Sedona, Charlie?"

"Three years."

"Three years and you've never hiked the Chapel Trail? That's incredible."

The closer Kenzie came, the faster Zangendar's heart thumped. She could clearly hear that Kenzie was not alone, only this time it wasn't the female named Bree who was with her. This time, it was a male voice she heard, a male that Kenzie named Charlie. She could clearly hear their conversation as they approached, despite the pounding in her own ears.

"I came here for the work. I figured I could put my flying skills to good use. Like I said, I didn't really have any friends to hang with. Not until I met Jimmy and Bree, anyway."

"Well, you have me now too, so be prepared to hike more often."

"I look forward to it."

Tredoran took a moment to glance at Zangendar and noted that her friend was barely maintaining control of herself. She was visibly shaking and had sweat forming on her skin.

"Zangendar, breathe. You need to maintain control," she whispered hoarsely.

Zangendar inhaled deeply and nodded almost imperceptibly. She exhaled slowly and forced her body to relax.

***

Kenzie and Charlie finally reached a point on the trail where they came into full view of where Tredoran and Zangendar were sitting. They suddenly stopped.

"Is something wrong?" Charlie asked.

Kenzie couldn't stop looking at the two women who were sitting on the mats in front of them, directly in the spot that she normally meditated. There was something about the larger of the two women that felt familiar to her.

"Kenzie?"

Kenzie shook her head. "I'm sorry, Charlie. I guess I'm just surprised to see someone meditating in the exact spot I normally set up my mat. I'm fine. We should move on."

"Lead the way!"

Kenzie and Charlie moved forward once more, but Kenzie couldn't take her eyes off the women as they approached. She specifically couldn't look away from the taller woman.

Just as they were about to walk past them, the taller woman opened her eyes and looked directly at Kenzie. Kenzie's breath caught in her throat and she was struck by the most beautiful green eyes she had ever seen. The woman's gaze locked with hers until they were beyond their mats.

Charlie noticed the distraction and again asked Kenzie if she was all right.

"I'm fine, Charlie. Really. There was just something familiar about that woman. I feel like I know her from somewhere. Maybe if they're still there on our way back, I'll chat with her about it. But for now, let's enjoy this beautiful day and awesome hike!"

***

Zangendar was on her feet as soon as Kenzie and Charlie were out of sight.

Tredoran looked up at her from her mat. "What happened to you, Zangendar? You nearly lost control when she walked by. You made visual contact with her!"

Zangendar turned around sharply to face her friend. "I know. I know. I could not stop myself. She was with a male companion. Did you see that?"

"Yes, I did see that. Does it concern you?"

"It does, but I do not understand why."

"Did you not tell me that she prefers females?"

Zangendar ran her hand through her hair. "Yes. That is what I learned through the mind probe with her."

"Then why does it concern you that she had a male companion?"

Zangendar sat down again on her mat. "I do not know. There was something about the male that did not seem right."

"I thought the male was quite appealing," Tredoran said.

"You found him appealing?"

"Yes."

"I believe we have been here long enough for one day."

"But we have seen only four humans."

"We can return with the new light. Right now, I need to assess my reactions today. My performance was less than exceptional."

"You may be right about these avatars. They may be making us feel more human emotion than we would without them. You need to consider whether your Kenzie is worth this level of emotion." Tredoran stood and then offered her hand to her friend. "Come. We need to return to the ship. We have more work to do."

Chapter 12

Kenzie arrived at work on Monday morning with enough time to enjoy a cup of coffee and a stroll through her social media page before her status meeting. It was in the middle of this stroll that Bree found her. Bree fixed coffee for herself and sat at the table beside Kenzie.

"Good morning, girlfriend!"

Kenzie put her phone on the table and turned her attention to her friend. "'Morning, Bree."

"We had such a good time at dinner Saturday night," Bree said. "You and Charlie seemed to hit it off well."

"Yes. I really like him. He seems like a good guy. In fact, I ran into him in the sporting goods store on Sunday and we ended up hiking together."

"Seriously?"

"Yes. I was climbing the walls with boredom, so I decided to do a little shopping, and it turns out Charlie likes to shop when he's bored, too. We were both buying workout clothes, so that led to a discussion about hiking, and before we knew it, we had agreed to spend the rest of the day hiking together."

"Cool! So, tell me what you *really* think of him," Bree prompted.

"Like I said, he seems to be a really nice guy. I feel comfortable with him. We seemed to connect."

Bree sat back and grinned. "I was hoping for that."

"What do you mean?"

"Well, Charlie is not your typical guy. I was just hoping that you two would like one another."

Kenzie leaned forward and narrowed her eyes. "Bree, what exactly are you trying to do here? You know I'm gay."

"Yes, but like I said, Charlie is not your typical guy."

"I agree that he's not typical. I actually feel like I can let my guard down without him trying something stupid. I want nothing more from him except friendship, and I think he feels the same about me."

"But what if he *did* want something more?"

"Bree, you're freaking me out here. I'm not attracted to him in that way. Wait! Did he say he wanted more?"

"No! I mean, I don't know. He hasn't said anything to me, but I can't vouch for what he has or hasn't said to Jimmy."

"Jesus, Bree, now you're making me paranoid. Look, Charlie is a guy. I am not into guys. He seems really nice, and I look forward to developing a friendship with him, but he's a guy. I'm not attracted to him physically—not at all."

Bree threw her hands up. "Okay, okay. I get it. I'm just looking out for my girl."

Kenzie took Bree's hand and squeezed it. "I appreciate that, Bree. Really, I do. But if love is going to find me again, it isn't going to be because my best friend arranged for it to happen. Didn't you tell me that love would find me when I least expected it?"

"Yeah, I guess I did say that, didn't I?"

"Yes, you did."

"Okay, I'll let it go for now. So, how was your hike with Charlie yesterday?"

"It was great. We entered the Little Horse trailhead a little after noon, and hiked to the chapel, and then circled back to Chicken Point before returning to Little Horse. Do you know that before yesterday, Charlie had never hiked any of the trails? Can you believe it? He's flown tours over all of them for the past three years, but he's never set foot on any of them. It was an awesome hike."

"It was a long hike! Did you take time out to meditate like you usually do?" Bree asked.

"No. We didn't bring our mats, but speaking of meditating, on our way to the chapel, we passed the spot where I usually set up my mat and there were two women there meditating."

"Well then, it's a good thing you didn't bring your mats. Otherwise, you would've had to find a new spot."

"Exactly. When I saw them, it made me pause. Don't ask me why, but I was a little shocked to find someone in my spot. I mean, it *is* my spot, after all!" Kenzie chuckled.

"The nerve of them!" Bree added with mock injustice.

"Seriously though, it threw me off a little. That, and there was something about one of the women that felt familiar. I must know her from somewhere, but I couldn't place it. Anyway, they were gone by the time we hiked back to Little Horse."

"What did she look like?"

"Well, I could tell from the length of her legs that she was tall. She was kind of butch looking with short dark hair, slim, and with the most amazing green eyes."

"Green eyes? I thought they were meditating."

"They were, but as Charlie and I approached their mats, she opened her eyes and looked right at me, and she continued to look at me until we had walked past. It was odd."

"Sounds creepy to me. What did the other one look like?"

"She was smaller and curvier, and she had long blonde hair pulled into a ponytail."

"Would you know them if you saw them again?"

"I'm pretty sure I would."

"Well, maybe you'll run into them again sometime."

"Maybe."

"Speaking of hiking, I told you last Friday that I would go with you today," Bree said. "Unless of course, you're too tired to hike after yesterday."

"No, I'm still going after work, but you really don't have to come with me."

"I said I would go, and I'm going."

"Okay. That would be great!"

Bree glanced at the clock on the wall. "Oops, our meeting starts in about three minutes and I gotta pee first. We'd better get going."

***

Zangendar and Tredoran sat, cloaked in their avatars, at the table inside Zangendar's quarters. An electronic tablet lay on the table between them.

"Read the list to me again, Tredoran."

Tredoran picked up the tablet. "Focus on the mission. Fluid movements. Smile. Take special note of human expressions. Emulate human speech patterns. Emulate behavior and mannerisms."

"That does not appear to be a very scientific list," Zangendar observed.

"I surmise it is not supposed to be scientific, Zangendar. I surmise it is supposed to reflect human behavior."

"You are correct, as usual, my sister. I am just distracted by my poor performance yesterday. I will strive to do better today."

"We will both do better today. I found myself to be impatient with the environment and the circumstances. I do question, however, how you will react if we encounter Kenzie again."

"I have been thinking about that myself. I will need to focus on suppressing my reaction to her."

"You have been to the surface several times, and you have observed human interaction on many occasions. How do they interact?" Tredoran asked.

"They appear to encourage interaction between themselves. They smile. They clasp hands. Their movements are animated. They speak in an agreeable manner toward one another."

"I suggest then that we emulate that behavior if we encounter humans and they engage with us."

"That is a good idea, Tredoran. I recommend we allow them to engage us first until we learn their ways, and then at some point, when we have experienced enough engagements, we can make first contact."

"I am concerned about engaging in actual conversation with the humans," Tredoran said.

"How so?" Zangendar asked.

"It appears conversation is based on common knowledge or shared experiences. For example, Kenzie and Charlie engaged in two-way conversation about hiking, and the two females we saw earlier conversed about pictures. They both appeared to be familiar with the topics they were conversing about. In our case, we have no familiarity with their world, and I fear we will not know how to respond."

Zangendar inhaled deeply and then put her hand on Tredoran's shoulder. She released her breath slowly. "My sister, we may be over thinking this situation. I recommend we engage as best we can and see how things progress. We have studied the language. We can speak it, and we can certainly understand when it is spoken to us. What we lack is context.

"When I have followed Kenzie on previous visits, she would encounter others she was unfamiliar with, and she talked to them about the weather. Maybe we can do the same. I suspect conversation will progress naturally. We just need to be careful not to talk in our native language when in the presence of the humans."

***

"I am so glad this day is done," Kenzie said as she hung her white coat inside her locker and then grabbed her backpack. She and Bree walked toward the locker room to change into their hiking clothes.

"I'm sorry you had to deal with that combative patient," Bree said. "It could have been worse. Before you moved here, we had a patient pull a knife on one of the nurses. Luckily, no one was hurt, but it could have been bad."

"I miss the days when I worked in the genetics lab. Things were relatively safe there."

"I almost forgot you had a degree in genetics. What I want to know is how you were allowed to get such a good education when your community didn't believe women should hold important positions."

"They had their ulterior motives. My job was to do the research necessary to improve the genetic superiority of our leadership. I had a knack for science, and that outweighed the fact that I was female when it came to achieving their goals, and even though I have a doctorate degree, they still only allowed me to perform at a technician level. Heaven forbid that a woman should have a position that was more important than any man in the community."

"Sheesh! I'm surprised you stood it for as long as you did."

"Like I said at dinner on Saturday night, I'm happy to be away from it. It was the best decision I've ever made for myself."

"It's too bad you're not using your degree here."

"I'm enjoying what I do. At least for now. I've thought about applying at one of the medical universities in Flagstaff, but for now, I'm in no hurry to go anywhere. Flagstaff is only thirty miles away, so if I decide to leave the health center, I could still live here and commute to Flagstaff if I wanted to."

"Well, I'd hate to see you leave, but it's a pity not to be using your degree. And besides, if you still live in Sedona, we can continue to be best buds."

Kenzie hugged Bree. "Best buds forever, Bree. Nothing will ever change that. Now let's get changed and hit the trails."

Kenzie and Bree entered side by side stalls and changed their clothes.

"Which trail are we hiking today?" Bree asked.

"Little Horse," Kenzie replied.

"You hike that one almost every day. Don't you get bored with it?"

"I like it because it has some of the strongest vortex vibes…and it's close enough to the chapel for an impromptu visit when I have time. The chapel is one of the strongest vortex sites in the area."

"I get all that, but if I hiked as much as you do, I'd get bored with the same trail, unless, of course, there is some other reason you want to go there today."

"Some other reason?"

"Yeah, like maybe you'll run into that woman who stole your meditation site?"

"Ha, ha! Am I that transparent, Bree?" Kenzie asked.

"Clear as glass."

"Busted! I admit that I am curious about her. I want to figure out where I know her from."

"Fair enough. I'm dressed." Bree stepped out of her stall, followed closely by Kenzie.

"Me too. Let's go!"

***

Zangendar and Tredoran walked slowly up the trail toward the chapel. As they walked, they passed several hikers walking in both directions. Nearly every hiker greeted them pleasantly with casual salutations, which they returned readily with the same response.

"This is not as difficult as I thought it would be," Tredoran said.

"As long as we do not have to engage in lengthy conversation with these humans, we should be able to obtain the learning and observations we came for," Zangendar replied.

"Are you aware of where we are going?"

"We are going to the spiritual building that Kenzie led me to on one of my visits. If I am correct, there will be many humans there to be observed and to converse with."

Sometime later, they came to the end of the trail and stepped onto the concrete walkway that led to the Chapel of the Holy Cross.

Tredoran stopped short when the chapel came into view. She looked back and forth between the chapel and Zangendar. "It looks very similar to the structures on Vakillia."

"Yes it does. Belander implied that there might be some connection between Vakillians and these humans. We must research the Vakillian archives to determine if that is true. The fact that we resemble one another physically, and that this planet is compatible to our species may not be a coincidence. And now we have this example of architecture to further support that possibility."

"I am interested in exploring this structure."

Zangendar motioned Tredoran forward with her hand. "Proceed, and do not forget to observe and engage."

***

"Hold up for a minute. I need some water," Bree said.
"Not a bad idea."

Both women retrieved water bottles from their backpacks and quenched their thirst.

"Do you always move at this pace?" Bree asked.

"Pretty much, except on the weekends. We have limited daylight after work—especially in the fall—so I try to hike at a steady pace."

"That makes sense."

"The junction for the Chapel Trail is just ahead."

Bree took another drink of water and then shoved the bottle back into her pack. "Okay. I'm ready when you are."

Kenzie and Bree reached the end of the trail about twenty minutes later and emerged onto the walkway leading to the chapel.

"I never get tired of seeing this," Kenzie said. "It is an amazing building. I feel such a sense of serenity here."

"I've been here a few times during the years, but I have yet to feel any emotional connection to it. I envy you in a way," Bree said.

"You need to open your mind to it, Bree. Maybe I can help you. Come on. Let's go inside."

Kenzie and Bree maneuvered their way up the winding walk and around the crowds of tourists taking pictures of the building and surrounding grounds. Kenzie grabbed Bree's hand so they wouldn't become separated as they made their way through the throng of people. When they were halfway up the ramp, Kenzie stopped short, causing Bree to run into the back of her.

"What the fuck?" Bree exclaimed. She covered her mouth quickly with her hand. "Oops! Why did you stop?"

Kenzie pointed into the crowd. "Do you see those two women?"

"Where?"

"Right there, against the wall. One tall with dark hair, and the other one, shorter with blonde hair. Their backs are to us."

"Okay, I see them now."

"It's them. They're the ones who were meditating in my space yesterday. I'm going to go talk to them."

Bree grabbed her arm. "Are you serious? You're just going to walk up to them and start talking?"

"Why not? That's how you and I became friends."

"Yes, but we work together. We *had* to talk to one another."

"Look, Bree, I had this intense feeling like I knew the taller one when I saw them on the trail yesterday. Don't ask me how I know that. I just do."

"Well, I'm not leaving your side, just in case she tries something funny."

"You are such a mother hen!" Kenzie complained.

"Cluck, cluck!" Bree replied.

Kenzie and Bree made their way through the crowd and stopped in front of the two women. Kenzie tapped the taller one on the shoulder.

***

Zangendar swung around, and immediately grabbed Tredoran's arm when she realized who had touched her shoulder. Tredoran also turned around and froze. Zangendar looked directly into Kenzie's eyes and barely acknowledged Bree at her side. Try as she might, she could not look away.

"I'm sorry! I've startled you," Kenzie said. Kenzie had to look up into Zangendar's face, as Zangendar was at least six inches taller than she was.

Bree interrupted when no response was forthcoming from Zangendar. "Let me apologize for my friend. She has a way of going up to strangers without warning them first." Bree grabbed Kenzie's arm and started to pull her away.

Zangendar reached out. "No. Please stay. I am Zangendar, and this is Tredoran."

"Those are unusual names. You're not from around here, are you?" Bree asked.

"No, we are not from here."

"I saw you on the trail yesterday. You were both meditating. I remember feeling like I knew you from somewhere. Sheesh! Where are my manners? I'm Kenzie Caldwell."

Kenzie extended her hand to Zangendar, who looked at it before reaching forward with her own hand. She felt a surge of warmth fill her chest as Kenzie's hand disappeared inside her larger one. She followed Kenzie's lead and shook her hand gently up and down. She felt a sense of loss when Kenzie pulled her hand from hers and offered it to Tredoran.

Bree declined to shake hands, and opted instead to wave. "Hi! I'm Bree Johnson."

"It's so nice to meet you both," Kenzie said. "Is this your first time visiting Sedona?"

"Yes, it is," Zangendar replied.

"Are you staying long?" Bree asked.

"We are considering it," Tredoran replied. "We are evaluating whether it meets our needs."

"You can take it from me that Sedona is a beautiful place to live. It's so spiritual, and there are so many places to hike. It's truly a magical place." Kenzie gushed with excitement.

"Have you lived here long?" Zangendar asked.

"I moved to Sedona a little more than two years ago. Bree, on the other hand, grew up here. How long are you visiting for?"

"As Tredoran said, we are here to evaluate the area. We have no real timeline to leave," Zangendar explained.

"Are you staying in town?"

"Geez, Kenzie. Ask them their life history while you're at it. I have to apologize for my friend. She just loves to meet new people." Bree exclaimed.

Zangendar smiled. "No worries." She looked directly into Kenzie's eyes. "We are staying outside of town."

Kenzie shook her head. "I swear I know you from somewhere. I just can't remember where."

Zangendar touched Kenzie's forehead with the tip of her finger. "I have heard that Sedona has vortexes and spiritual centers. Maybe we have known one another in a different dimension."

Tredoran put her hand on Zangendar's shoulder. "I believe we will need to go soon. We are losing light."

Tredoran's voice broke Zangendar's focus and she finally looked away from Kenzie's eyes. She glanced at the sky. "You are right. We should go."

"I want to get a look inside the church before we go, then we'll need to head back, too. It'll be nearly dark by the time we get to the parking lot," Bree pointed out.

Kenzie shoved both her hands into her pockets. "It was so nice to meet you. Maybe we'll see you again on the trails?"

Again, Zangendar smiled. "I'm sure we will meet again."

"Have a great evening," Kenzie said.

"You have a great evening as well," Zangendar replied and then she and Tredoran walked down the concrete walkway toward the trail.

***

Bree stood beside Kenzie and wrapped an arm around her shoulder as they watched Zangendar and Tredoran disappear onto the trail.

"Wow, Bree. What happened there?" Kenzie asked. "I felt captured. I couldn't look away, even if I wanted to. I felt this amazing energy when she shook my hand."

"She certainly is attractive," Bree said. "And her friend is pretty cute too. I wonder if they're a couple."

Kenzie looked alarmed. "A couple? Do you think so?"

"I don't know. Maybe."

Chapter 13

Zangendar stopped on the trail and braced one hand on a tree while grasping her chest with her other fist. She lowered her chin to her chest and closed her eyes.

"What is it, Zangendar? Are you ill?" Tredoran asked.

"I…I have this pain in my chest. No, it is more than a pain. It is a tightness. It is difficult to breathe and to think. I need to regain control."

"There is a large rock just a short way down the trail. Let me guide you to it so you can rest," Tredoran suggested.

Once Zangendar was seated, Tredoran squatted in front of her. "I am concerned for you, sister."

Zangendar leaned forward with her forearms resting on her thighs. "I will be well soon, Tredoran." She glanced back down the trail toward the chapel.

Tredoran noticed the direction of her friend's gaze. "Do you think your illness may be connected to Kenzie and Bree?"

"I know it is."

"Explain yourself."

"When I touched her, when I held her hand in mine, it was like my entire body woke up. I could *feel* her in a way I have never felt another being. I do not know if my reaction is due to this human avatar, or if it is due to Kenzie. She is the only human I have touched while cloaked in the avatar. I did not have this reaction to her when I probed her mind. I was not cloaked in my avatar during those contacts."

"How are you feeling now?" Tredoran asked.

"My condition is improving."

"Unless you want to encounter Kenzie and Bree again, we must continue to the transference site. They will be approaching us soon."

Zangendar glanced down the trail once more. Part of her wanted to stay right where she was, but the other part of her knew they needed to reach the transference site before dark. She needed to gather biometric data on herself and to study it thoroughly to understand this reaction she'd had to Kenzie. She sat up straight and inhaled deeply. "I believe I am well enough to continue," she said.

Zangendar and Tredoran reached the transference site at dusk. They stepped off the trail and waited for other hikers to pass by so they could be transferred without witnesses. They had to wait for several minutes before they felt they had clearance to transfer. Just as the transfer was to begin, they heard more voices coming down the trail.

***

"Do you really think they might be a couple, Bree?"

"I don't know, Kenzie. The shorter one, Traydon, or whatever the hell her name was, seemed to be really familiar with Zan."

"That doesn't necessarily mean they're a couple. I mean, you boss me around all the time!" Kenzie laughed for emphasis.

Bree pushed Kenzie's shoulder. "Well, someone's gotta look after you!"

Kenzie suddenly stopped. "Look. There they are! They're standing off the trail."

"I wonder if they're lost," Bree said.

Bree's attention was suddenly diverted to the vibration coming from her pocket. She grabbed Kenzie's arm to prevent her from approaching the women. "Hold on. My phone is ringing." She pulled the phone out of her pocket and held it to her ear. "Hey, Jimmy. Yes. I'm hiking with Kenzie. Okay. Okay, that works. I'll see you later at home." She shoved the phone back into her pocket. "That was Jimmy. He and Charlie are going to play pool for the next few hours."

"Cool! So, there's no rush to get home then. Let's go see if they need help."

Kenzie and Bree approached the two women standing beside the trail.

"Hi, again!" Kenzie said. "Are you lost? Do you need help finding your way back to the trailhead?"

"No. We are just resting. We are not used to this environment. I'm afraid I have a bit of heat exhaustion," Zangendar said.

Kenzie slipped her backpack off her shoulders and unzipped it. She reached inside and pulled out her spare bottle of water and handed it to Zangendar. "Here. This might help. I was caught on the trail once without enough water and I became really dehydrated and nearly passed out."

"You can have my spare bottle too." Bree handed a bottle of water to Tredoran.

Both women drank from the water bottles and then gestured to hand them back.

"No, keep it. You need to drink all of it to really feel better. Trust me, I've been there," Kenzie insisted.

"Do you need a ride somewhere?" Bree offered. "I have room in my car for two more."

A momentary look of panic passed between Zangendar and Tredoran before Tredoran replied. "No. We are fine. We will be on our way soon."

"Well, don't wait too much longer. It will be dark soon and the path is pretty hard to see, especially through the forested parts," Kenzie said.

"As Tredoran said, we will be on our way soon. Thank you for your concern," Zangendar replied.

Kenzie smiled. "Will you be back tomorrow? Maybe we could hook up with you and hike another trail, or maybe meditate?"

Bree touched Kenzie's arm. "Sorry, Kenzie, I can't do tomorrow. I promised Jimmy we'd do a bike ride after work."

"That's okay, Bree. I'll probably still hike anyway."

"I would like that very much," Zangendar said.

Tredoran shot her a stern look.

Kenzie threw her backpack over her shoulder once more. "Awesome! We can meet in the parking lot if you'd like, say, five o'clock? That will give us a couple of hours to hike, and maybe even do a short meditation before dark."

"Five o'clock is an acceptable time," Zangendar replied.

"Great! I'll see you tomorrow, then. Bye."

Bree grabbed Kenzie's arm after they had walked several feet away. "Are you insane? Do you really think it's wise to hike with a total stranger?"

"Zan isn't a stranger. Not really. I'll be fine, Bree. There will be other hikers around, and besides, it will give me a chance to get to know her."

"I wonder if the other one will be with her tomorrow."

"I guess if she is, that will shed light on whether they are a couple or not."

"Promise me you'll have your cellphone handy at all times and that you'll call for help if something happens."

Kenzie stopped and looked at her friend. "I love you for worrying about me, but nothing will happen. If she felt unsafe to me, I wouldn't have suggested hiking with her."

"I'm sure Jeffrey Dahmer felt safe to his victims, too."

Kenzie interlocked her arm in Bree's. "Come on. It's getting dark." She glanced back up the trail. "I hope they head out soon. Or at least have a flashlight with them, or there may not *be* a hike tomorrow."

"They'll be fine. Let's go back to my place. Jimmy won't be home for a while yet, so we can throw together a quick dinner and watch a chick flick before I take you home."

"Sounds great!"

***

Zangendar and Tredoran watched the two women walk away.

"Why did you agree to return tomorrow to hike with her?" Tredoran asked.

"I need to know why I had this reaction to her. Was it really dehydration? Or was it something else? I have to admit that I feel better after drinking the water. If we fall ill every time we touch a human, then this environment may not be right for our species."

Tredoran tilted her head. "I suspect your reasons include much more than scientific research, sister."

Zangendar stared at her friend for several seconds before replying. "I will not tell you an untruth, Tredoran. I feel things for Kenzie that I do not feel for Bree, nor for any other human we have encountered thus far. I need to understand why that is. I think I need to return alone tomorrow."

"I am not comfortable with you being here by yourself, Zangendar."

"I have been here by myself several times before we created our avatars. It was more dangerous then, than it is now. At least now, we can blend in. No, I believe it is best that I return alone tomorrow."

"I do not agree, but I will respect your wishes. For now, we must return to the ship. There are no other hikers nearby. I believe it is safe now to do so."

***

Later that evening, Tredoran found Zangendar in the lab, working on a small rectangular box.

"Greetings, Zangendar. Molinder said I would find you here. You are still cloaked in your avatar."

"Yes. I believe the more I am cloaked, the more human-like I will feel. I recommend you do the same."

"I have removed the avatar to avoid the odd looks I get from our crewmates. I assume you are correct, however. If we determine this planet is best for our survival, we may all have to adjust to human avatars when in public."

Zangendar turned her attention to testing the rectangular device on the table in front of her.

"May I ask what you are working on, sister?" Tredoran said.

"I have adapted an omni-spectrometer into a smaller footprint to emulate the communication devices the humans carry."

"How do you know they are communication devices? We witnessed two human females use one to take selfies, whatever that means."

"I suspect they serve many purposes. On the trail today, we saw Bree communicate with someone called, Jimmy on her device. I want to be able to collect biometric data on humans and on the environment without drawing suspicion to myself, and I surmised this to be a good way to do that in stealth mode."

"I see. Speaking of biometric data, did you evaluate your own readings to determine the cause of your illness on the surface earlier today?" Tredoran asked.

"I did. The data indicated there was no underlying medical reason for the illness. It did indicate a low level of dehydration, but the condition was not severe enough to have caused illness."

"Then you can conclude the illness was caused by physical contact with Kenzie while cloaked in your avatar?"

"That would be the logical conclusion, but like any hypothesis, it will require repeated testing to verify."

"I understand. I assume you will engage in that testing tomorrow when you meet Kenzie at the trailhead?"

"Yes, that is my intention." Zangendar picked up the rectangular box from the table. It had a solid backing and what appeared to be a glass front. She pointed the device at Tredoran and tapped the screen. A graphical user interface was displayed on which Zangendar selected an icon. The device immediately collected biometric data on Tredoran. Zangendar nodded. "It works. I am pleased."

"It is late, sister. I recommend you renew as soon as possible to be well rested for your hike tomorrow," Tredoran recommended.

"Yes. I will take nourishment in my quarters, and then I will renew. I feel lightness in my chest when I think of the hike tomorrow. I am hoping I will be able to renew successfully."

"I question whether you should be going alone tomorrow, Zangendar, but I will respect your choice. I urge you to arm yourself in the event you need protection."

"I do not fear danger from Kenzie, Tredoran."

"I agree. However, danger could come from others on the surface. You should at least carry a weapon in your pack."

Zangendar nodded, and the corner of her mouth lifted in a half-smile. "I will *have* to carry it in my pack. There is very little room in this clothing to conceal a weapon. I am not used to being among others while wearing so little clothing."

"I will admit the humans are appealing with so little clothing," Tredoran said.

"They are indeed."

Especially, Kenzie, she thought.

Chapter 14

Kenzie looked at her watch several times in the few minutes she had left before the end of her workday, a gesture that did not go unnoticed by Bree.

"Chill, girlfriend. I'm sure Zan will wait for you if you're late."

Kenzie grimaced. "I have really got to learn how to hide my emotions. You can read me like a book."

"Yes, I can. Look, Kenzie, I know you're excited, but don't invest your heart too soon. You don't even know if she's going to hang around. Didn't they both say they were just checking the area out to see if it would work for them? And oh, by the way, they *still* might be a couple. It almost felt like they were on a house-hunting expedition *together*."

Kenzie sighed. "I know. You would think I'd have learned not to jump in with both feet after what happened with Jess."

"Not everyone is like Jess, Kenzie, but after what that cheating bitch did, I'd be extra cautious if I were you."

"I know." She looked at her watch again. "Will this day *ever* end?"

Just then the receptionist poked her head into the break area. "Sorry for the short notice, but the boss just called a four o'clock staff meeting."

"You're kidding me!" Kenzie exclaimed.

"Nope! Mandatory attendance," the receptionist said before she disappeared into the hallway.

"Shit!" Kenzie exclaimed. "I'll never make it there by five o'clock, now! My car is in the shop, not that I need one most of the time since I tend to ride my bike everywhere, but I walked to work today. By the time I go home to get it and then bike to the trailhead, she'll think I'm not coming, and she'll be gone."

Bree reached into her pocket and pulled her car keys out. She placed them on the table in front of Kenzie. "Yes, you will. Take my car."

"How will you get home if I take your car?"

"I'll call Jimmy to come get me. You can return my car in the morning when you come to pick me up for work."

Kenzie wrapped her arms around Bree's neck and hugged her close. "Thank you, Bree. What would I ever do without you?"

"I want to see you happy, my friend, and if you have that chance with Zan, I'm all for it, but if she hurts you, I'll be on her ass in a heartbeat."

"Don't worry. I'm not going to rent a U-Haul yet. Like you said, they may not even stay here, or she may already be involved with Trey."

***

Kenzie pulled into the parking lot of Little Horse Trail just before five. Zan was leaning against the split-rail fence that served as a barrier between the parking places and the trailhead. Zan pushed off the fence and waited for Kenzie to exit the car. Instead, Kenzie lowered the window and leaned out.

"Get in. I thought we'd hike the Bell Rock Pathway today," Kenzie called.

Zan stood there with a look of trepidation on her face.

Kenzie frowned and threw her door open. She climbed out of the car and approached Zan. "Are you okay?" she asked.

"I am fine. I just assume we would hike this trail." Zan pointed to the Little Horse trailhead.

"I had planned to hike Little Horse with you today, but since Bree loaned me her car, I thought we'd try something new today."

"But I told Trey to collect me here when it became dark."

"Don't worry. I won't kidnap you. I can get you back here by dark." Kenzie grabbed Zan's arm and started to pull her toward the car.

Zan flinched.

Kenzie immediately released her arm. "Are you sure you're okay?"

"I am fine. Please lead the way."

Zan followed her to the passenger side of the car where Kenzie pulled up on the handle and opened the car door. Zan slipped her pack off her shoulder, and climbed into the car. She placed the pack on the floor between her feet.

Kenzie closed the door and walked around the front of the car to climb into the driver's seat. She pulled her door closed and reached for her seat belt. She then turned the key in the ignition and the car came to life. A beeping sound came from the dashboard at the moment Kenzie put her foot on the brake and slipped the car into reverse.

"Oops! You need to put on your seatbelt," Kenzie said.

Zan frowned.

Kenzie grabbed the strap that was lay diagonally across her chest to show Zan. "Seatbelt. You need to put on your seatbelt."

Zan looked back toward her door and pulled the belt across her chest and latched it into the buckle on the left side of her seat, in the same manner than Kenzie's belt was fastened.

"I take it they don't require seatbelts where you come from," Kenzie observed.

"You are correct. They do not," Zan replied.

Kenzie tilted her head. "I am also guessing that English is not your native language. Your speech is very formal."

Zan blushed. "Correct again. My apologies."

Kenzie placed her hand on Zan's leg. Again, Zan flinched.

"There's nothing to apologize for. You're doing great! If I were in a strange land, I'd be totally making a fool of myself. No worries!"

With Zan's seatbelt in place, Kenzie backed out of the parking space and headed down Route 179 toward the Bell Rock parking area. She glanced at Zan as she drove. Zan appeared wide-eyed and very nervous.

"Hey. Don't look so terrified. I'm not such a bad driver!"

Zan sighed. "I am sorry."

"Relax, Zan. You're safe with me. We're almost there."

"You call me Zan. Is it customary for your people to shorten names?"

"Actually, yes it is. Especially if your name is long or unusual. For example, Bree's name is really Breanna, and my full name is Mackenzie, or Kenzie for short. Do you mind that I've shortened your name?"

"No. I like it."

"Good! You know, I don't even know your last name."

"Last name?"

"Yes, like Caldwell is my last name."

"Tafadon. My name is Zangendar Tafadon."

"What about Trey?"

"Tredoran Harlax."

"Those are definitely unusual names. Look, there's the parking lot for Bell Rock."

Kenzie pulled into a parking space and turned off the ignition. "I think you'll like this hike. It's relatively easy. I thought it would give us an opportunity to get to know one another without having to gasp for breath." Kenzie chuckled as she grasped the door handle and pushed the door open.

Zan followed her lead and opened her own door.

Zan stood beside the car and waited while Kenzie retrieved her pack from the back seat. She reached for the car with her left hand to steady herself as she fought back a lightheaded feeling that threatened to overcome her.

"Hey, are you okay? You look a little pale. Maybe we should skip the hike," Kenzie said from the other side of the car.

"No. No, I will be fine. I think I just need a little water." Zan picked her pack up that she had put on the ground beside the car and retrieved her water bottle. After two long gulps, she returned it to the pack. "That's better. Are you ready to go?" she asked Kenzie.

"Absolutely! The trailhead is right there."

Zan followed Kenzie for the first part of the trail, which was narrow. From her vantage point behind her, Zan was mesmerized by the way Kenzie's hips swayed back and forth as she walked, and how her calf muscles flexed when she climbed the steeper part of the trail.

Kenzie suddenly stopped, causing Zan to nearly run into her. "Sorry! I should have warned you that I was stopping. The trail will become wider in just a bit, then we can actually have a conversation without me having to look back over my shoulder."

"That will be good," Zan said, relieved that Kenzie didn't realize she was staring at her backside while they hiked.

Within the next few yards, the trail widened, and the magnificent splendor of Bell Rock made itself visible.

"Why is this formation called Bell Rock?" Zan asked.

"Because it's shaped like a bell, silly!" Kenzie replied.

Zan took a mental note to research what a bell was when she returned to the ship.

Kenzie locked arms with Zan. "Finally, we can walk side by side!" she exclaimed. "So, tell me about yourself."

"What do you want to know?" Zan asked, thoroughly distracted by the feel of Kenzie's skin on hers.

"The usual stuff. You know, where are you from? What do you do?" Kenzie replied.

"I am from a place called Vakillia," Zan said.

"Vakillia? I've never heard of it," Kenzie replied.

"I am not surprised. It's quite far from here. What else do you want to know?"

"How old are you?"

Zan did the mental calculation, dividing her age by a factor of ten. "I am twenty-seven years old." She had to consciously remember not to say 'in earth years.'

"Really? I'm twenty-eight! Cool!"

"Anything else?" Zan asked.

"Ah, what do you do for a living?" Kenzie asked.

"For a living?" Zan appeared confused.

"Yeah. What is your job? What do you do all day?"

"I am doing research in this area."

Kenzie released Zan's arm and gently shoved her. "Duh! I know that! You said as much on the trail the other day, but what do you do when you're not researching a new place to live?"

Zan realized that she needed to be clearer. "I'm sorry, Kenzie. What I meant to say is that I am an environmental scientist. My people need to resettle, and I am using my training to determine if this environment will work for us."

"What is so wrong with Vakillia that you have to leave?"

"The environment is becoming inhospitable. Our water supply is diminishing."

"Well, you picked an odd place to research, then. Arizona has a lot of desert."

Zan suddenly became alarmed. "But there *is* water here. Is that correct?"

"Yes, of course. Arizona has several bodies of water, but large parts of it are also hot and dry. Global warming isn't helping things, but then you should know that if you are an environmental scientist."

Zan mentally added global warming to her list of research terms before replying. "As you say, it is warm here, but the conditions are worse on Vakillia."

"*On* Vakillia? Don't you mean *in* Vakillia?" Kenzie asked.

"Yes! Yes, of course. I am sorry. The language here is very different and sometimes confusing," Zan said quickly.

"I can certainly understand that. I've heard that English is one the hardest languages to learn."

"I can confirm that. So, now it is your turn. Have you always lived here?" Zan asked.

Kenzie once again linked arms with Zan as they continued down the level path. "I moved here more than two years ago. I used to live in Utah."

Zan's insides felt like they were flip-flopping, and an odd sensation was forming deep within her abdomen. The place where Kenzie's skin touched her arm felt like it was on fire with electrical pulses. She struggled to focus her attention on what Kenzie was saying. "Ah…why did you relocate?"

"Let's just say I did it for personal reasons. Next question?"

"Where did you meet Bree?" Zan asked.

"We work together. Before I moved here, I was a genetic researcher, but now I am a nurse at the local urgent care center. Bree is a nurse as well."

"So, you are a healer?"

"You could say that."

"That is a noble profession."

"I'd like to think so."

Their conversation was suddenly interrupted by a rumbling noise coming from Kenzie's stomach.

"What is that sound?" Zan said.

Kenzie grinned. "I'm afraid my stomach is demanding food. I didn't have time for lunch today. How about we cut our hike short and get some dinner. My treat?"

***

Kenzie sat across the table from Zan and watched her peruse the menu again.

"Do you have any questions about the menu?" Kenzie asked.

"There are so many choices," Zan said.

"Well, are you a vegetarian? Do you eat meat?"

Zan frowned.

It was apparent to Kenzie that Zan was struggling to understand. She wondered to herself how Zan could speak such good English, yet failed to understand simple concept words such as vegetarian. "Let me try it this way, do you eat only plant-based foods, or do you eat flesh based foods as well?"

Zan's eyes opened wide. "Flesh? People actually eat flesh here?"

"Yes. We call it meat. You know, beef, pork, chicken."

"A chicken is an animal."

"Yes it is, and beef comes from cows and pork comes from pigs. Oh, and there's also fish and seafood. Surely, there are meat eaters in your community?"

"I'm sure there are, but I am not aware of any."

"So, I assume you would like a plant-based meal, then?"

"I think that would be good, but I might want to try your meat some time."

And I wouldn't mind trying your meat as well, Kenzie thought. She felt the heat rise into her face when she realized the direction her thoughts were going in. She quickly scanned through the menu. "Okay, then, let's look at their vegetarian dishes."

Kenzie handed the menus to the waiter. "Two vegetable stir-fries on rice, please. Thank you."

"Can I interest you in a beverage?" the waiter asked.

Kenzie raised her brows. "Hmm, I'd like a piña colada. How about you, Zan?"

"I will have the same."

Kenzie reached across the table and placed her hand on Zan's. "You need to know that it has alcohol in it."

"Alcohol? I am not familiar with that word."

"Alcohol is the word we use to mean intoxicant."

"I see. I think I would still like that."

Kenzie looked at the waiter. "Two it is, then."

"Thank you for making that easy for me," Zan said after the waiter walked away."

Kenzie pulled her hand back. "I think you will enjoy the stir-fry. It has a sesame-like Asian flavor. It's one of my favorites."

Zan sat back in her seat. "Do you mind if we continue our discussion from this afternoon?"

"Not at all. What else would you like to know about me?" Kenzie asked.

"You said that you left your home two years ago for personal reasons. Do you mind telling me more about that?"

"My family didn't approve of my orientation."

"You are talking about your preference for females?"

Kenzie tilted her head to one side, while maintaining eye contact with Zan. She reached across the table once more and placed her hand on Zan's.

Zan's stomach was in her throat.

"Yes," Kenzie replied. "I'm glad you realized that for yourself and that I didn't have to tell you."

Zan couldn't look away from Kenzie's eyes, and in that moment, it felt like Kenzie's hand was reaching straight into her core.

"Is it safe to assume you are the same?" Kenzie asked.

"You have assumed correctly," Zan replied.

Just then, their drinks arrived, and Kenzie pulled her hand back yet again.

Kenzie picked up her drink and held it toward Zan. She nodded toward Zan's drink. Zan followed course and picked her drink up as well. Kenzie clinked their glasses together.

"Cheers!"

"Cheers!" Zan repeated and they both drank.

Zan's eyebrows rose high onto her forehead. "This is very pleasing!" she said.

"Yes it is. I love the coconut flavor."

Kenzie watched Zan take another sip from her drink. "Are you in a relationship?" she asked.

"Are you asking if I have a partner?"

"Yes."

"No. I do not."

"What about Trey?"

"Tredoran? She is my sister."

"Your sister? I would never have guessed. There doesn't seem to be any family resemblance."

"To be truthful, she is my sister in my heart. In our community, there is only ever one offspring."

"So, she is like your best friend then. Like me and Bree."

"Yes. Like you and Bree."

"I am an only child, too. My parents were unable to have any more children after I was born."

"Do *you* have a partner?" Zan asked.

"Not anymore. I had a partner for almost two years. Her name was Jessie, but it ended poorly about six months ago."

"What about the person you were hiking with several days ago?"

"Do you mean, Charlie? Charlie is a dude. I'm not into men."

Their dinners arrived before the conversation could continue.

"Okay, ladies, two orders of vegetable stir-fry. Enjoy your meals."

Chapter 15

"Have I told you yet that you are very pleasing to look at?" Zan asked.

Kenzie motioned to get the waiter's attention. "Check, please?" She turned to Zan. "Yes, you have, about five times."

Zan picked up her drink and sucked the now diluted icy water out of the bottom of it. "Could I have another of these?"

"I think three is your limit, Zan. And besides, it's beginning to get dark. We have to get you back to the trailhead."

Zan sat up quickly. "Yes! Trey will be waiting for me. We must go!" She made a move to slide out of the booth.

"Whoa, hold on. I need to pay the bill. Just sit for a minute. You won't turn into a pumpkin if we're a few minutes late."

Zan frowned. "How would a person turn into a pumpkin?"

"Sorry. That was a reference to Cinderella getting home late from the ball."

"Cinnerella? Who is Cinnerella?"

"Cin-der-ella. Never mind. Here comes the check." Kenzie handed a debit card to the waiter and then sat back to wait for the receipt.

"I had a really enjoyable time tonight," Zan said. "The food was very good, and the beverages were good, too."

"I'm glad you enjoyed it. Maybe we can do it again sometime soon?"

Zan belched and quickly covered her mouth. Her face turned a bright shade of red. "My apologies. I am not used to this food and drink."

Kenzie chuckled. "No worries! It happens to the best of us. I enjoyed our time together as well, Zan."

The waiter returned Kenzie's card and receipt, on which she added a generous tip and then slipped the card into her wallet.

Zan frowned. "What is that card for?"

"It's a debit card. My paycheck is automatically deposited in my bank and I use this card to withdraw funds to pay for things I want and need. Don't you have something similar in Vakillia?"

"We have electronic currency, but we do not use cards. We have chips embedded in our fingertips."

"What? Are you serious? Let me see."

Zan extended her hand across the table, palm up. Kenzie traced the tips of Zan's fingers with her own index finger.

"I don't feel any chips," Kenzie said.

"They are far enough below the surface to not be damaged by ordinary wear."

Kenzie continued to trace the tips of Zan's fingers.

Zan closed her eyes. "I feel a tingle inside," she said.

Kenzie immediately withdrew her hand. "I'm sorry. I didn't mean to make you feel uncomfortable."

"It was pleasurable."

Kenzie had to admit that she felt a tingle, too, but Zan was inebriated, and there was no way she was going to take advantage of her. And besides, she had to get her back to the trailhead where Trey would be waiting for her.

Kenzie slipped out of the booth and extended her hand to Zan. "Okay, my friend, we need to get you back."

Zan took her hand and slid out of the booth. She needed to place her other hand on the back of the seat to steady herself. "Why do I feel like I will fall?" she asked.

"My guess is that you've had little experience drinking alcohol in Vakillia. Don't let go of my hand. I will help you to the car," Kenzie said.

Luckily, they had been seated close to the door, and it was a short walk through the restaurant and onto the sidewalk out front.

Zan held onto the building once they were outside. "I don't know if I can walk without falling," she said. "My head feels like it is spinning."

Kenzie wrapped her arm around Zan's waist and draped Zan's arm around her shoulders. "Okay, lean on me if you need to. The car is parked just across the street."

As luck would have it, there was little traffic and Kenzie was able to guide Zan across the street and into the car with relative ease. Within moments, they were on their way to the parking area of Little Horse Trail.

Zan was noticeably quiet on the drive to the trailhead.

"Are you okay?" Kenzie asked.

Zan nodded, but didn't say anything.

"Are you sure? You're awfully quiet."

"I am ashamed of myself."

"What? Why?"

"My behavior is inappropriate. I am not in control."

"Sweetie, it's okay to get a little tipsy. There is nothing wrong with that."

Zan looked curiously at Kenzie. "What is sweetie?"

"I'm sorry. It's a term of endearment. It just came out. Now I'm the one being inappropriate. There's the parking lot. I don't see Trey yet. It looks like we beat her here."

Kenzie pulled into the parking lot of the trailhead and into a parking place. She shut off the engine and turned to Zan. "Zan, give yourself a break. You're only human after all. We all kind of lose control every now and then. It's okay."

"But I am not," Zan said.

Kenzie frowned. "You're not what?"

"I am not human."

Kenzie sat back. "Get out of Dodge! You sure look human to me."

Zan stared at her hands without speaking for several long moments.

Kenzie unhooked her seatbelt and leaned toward Zan. She placed her left palm on the right side of Zan's face and turned it toward her. She was unprepared for the twinge of feeling deep inside her when Zan raised sad eyes in her direction. Emotion made her voice heavy.

"Zan, please don't berate yourself. I really had a good time tonight, and I am hoping we can do this again. I don't know what it is about you, but I feel something deep inside that I thought died two years ago when Jessie left."

"I feel it, too," Zan whispered.

"I want to kiss you," Kenzie said hoarsely.

Kenzie took Zan's silence as permission and leaned closer until her lips lightly brushed Zan's.

Zan shivered.

Kenzie pulled her face back. "Are you okay?"

"Do it again," Zan whispered.

Once again, Kenzie brushed her lips across Zan's, lightly at first, but with increasing ardor, stopping only when she heard Zan whimper.

Kenzie was alarmed and immediately broke the contact. "Oh, my God, Zan! Did I hurt you?"

Zan grabbed her hand. "No. I...I am overwhelmed. I have never felt—"

Kenzie sat back in the driver's seat. "Maybe you need a little more time." She leaned forward and looked around the dark parking lot. "I wonder where Trey is. Shouldn't she be here by now? Maybe you should call her on your cellphone."

Zan looked alarmed. "My cellphone?"

"Yes, you looked at it during dinner. I assumed you had a text message or something."

Zan felt in her pocket and found her omni-spectrometer. "Oh, yes, my cellphone." She pulled it out of her pocket and looked at it. "I will call her." Zan tapped the screen and then held it to her ear for several long moments. Finally, she slipped it back into her pocket. "There is no reply."

"Well, that sucks! Maybe she's on her way. We'll give her a few more minutes."

Zan reached for the door handle and pushed it open. "I will wait here so you can go home. I am sure Trey will be here soon."

Kenzie threw herself across Zan and reached for her door. She pulled it closed, decidedly. "No, you won't. I am not leaving you here all by yourself after dark. If Trey doesn't show up in the next few minutes, you're coming home with me."

***

Kenzie retrieved a fresh set of sheets from her linen closet. She hoped Zan would be comfortable sleeping on the pull-out bed. It had been ages since anyone had slept on it, and she hoped it wouldn't be too lumpy where the mattress had been folded in thirds inside the sofa frame.

They had waited for another hour for Trey to show up at the trailhead. Zan offered several times to wait alone, but Kenzie repeatedly turned her down and insisted on waiting with her. Finally, after two more failed attempts to contact Trey by phone, Kenzie decided to bring Zan home with her. They would try again to reach Trey in the morning and Zan would drop her off at the trailhead before going to pick Bree up at home.

Kenzie paused while making the bed to listen to the retching sounds coming from the bathroom. She realized then that she probably should have limited Zan to two drinks. It was obvious to her that Zan was not used to alcohol. She resolved to act like she didn't realize Zan had been sick. She sensed how embarrassed Zan would be if she knew Kenzie had heard the retching.

Zan sat on the bathroom floor with her back against the door and her head between her hands. Her head was pounding, and waves of spasms passed through her stomach as she fought further bouts of retching. It had been years since she had been this sick, and she had forgotten how horrible it was to reject the contents of one's stomach. After a time, the spasms subsided, and her thoughts moved on to what a fool she had been in front of Kenzie. She was sure Kenzie would dismiss her in the morning and would never want to see her again.

Zan ran her fingertips on her lips, the same lips Kenzie had kissed. The intensity of feeling that coursed through her when Kenzie's lips touched hers, terrified her. Never in her life had she felt so out of control. Was it always like this with humans? She had had encounters with her own kind, but none were as intense and all encompassing as what she felt when Kenzie kissed her. Yes, it terrified her, but she found herself wanting to do it again and again.

A short time later, Zan felt she had recovered enough to put some distance between her and the bathroom. She stood, rinsed her mouth with water from the bathroom sink, did her best to brush her teeth with her fingertips, and then opened the bathroom door. From the doorway, she could see Kenzie in the living area, preparing a place for her to renew.

Kenzie looked at Zan as she exited the bathroom. "I hope this pull-out bed will be comfortable enough for you. I'm sorry, I don't have another bedroom for you to use, but this will have to do." Kenzie noted the red rims around Zan's eyes, and the pale pallor of her skin and decided that the sooner she got to bed, the better she would feel in the morning.

"I'm sure it will be fine. I appreciate you providing me with a place to stay tonight," Zan replied.

"No problem. I feel better knowing you're safe. We'll need to get out early in the morning. I need to drop you off at the trailhead and then drive to Bree's house to pick her up before work and to return her car. I'll set my clock for six."

"I will do my best not to make you late."

Kenzie approached Zan and stopped just in front of her. She reached for Zan's hand and hugged it to her chest. "I really enjoyed your company tonight, Zan. Truly, I did. I hope I didn't scare you away with that kiss in the car. I would like to see you again."

Zan smiled and lowered her lips to Kenzie's for a light kiss, but a kiss that lingered for several seconds. She stood erect again and looked into Kenzie's eyes. "I would like that too."

Kenzie smiled. "Good night then. Sweet dreams."

Zan watched Kenzie walk into her bedroom and close the door. "Sweet dreams to you, too, Kenzie," she said under her breath.

She folded down the covers and climbed in. She lay on her back and pulled the blanket over her. "Lights out," she said out loud, and was surprised when the lights remained on. Zan examined at the lamp on the table beside the sofa and determined she had to turn the knob to extinguish the light source manually. Once that was accomplished, she lay on her back again and stared at the ceiling in the darkness.

Zan thought again about the kiss she'd shared with Kenzie in the car. She had never felt anything so intense in her life. She was completely overwhelmed by the emotions she felt when Kenzie's lips touched hers. Kenzie's very touch caused an intense response in her, but the kiss was nearly her undoing.

Between the tenderness at the back of her throat, and the intensity of desire that coursed through her body, Zan knew renewal would be beyond her grasp that night.

***

Kenzie climbed into bed and turned out the bedroom lamp. The digital readout on her clock said ten o'clock, just eight hours before the alarm would go off. Her eyes were wide open. She was too geared up to sleep.

Kenzie was intrigued by Zan's reaction to her kiss in the car. She wasn't sure if Zan was a virgin and had no experience at all, or if there was such an intense attraction between them that the simple intimacy of a kiss overwhelmed her. If a kiss alone could generate such a response, she found herself wondering how intense making love to her would be.

Kenzie moaned as an involuntary spasm coursed through her. "Oh, my God. I'm in trouble," she whispered into the darkness.

Her body was on fire. There would be little sleep for her tonight.

Chapter 16

Kenzie rolled onto her side and shut off the alarm. She remembered last looking at the clock around three in the morning. "Well, at least I got a few hours of sleep." She threw the covers back and swung her legs over the side of the bed. "Gotta pee…"

Kenzie pushed off the bed and shuffled through her bedroom and into the kitchen. She stopped dead when she saw Zan sitting in a living room chair.

"Ah, sorry. I thought you might still be asleep." Kenzie tugged at the bottom of her T-shirt to cover her near nakedness. "I just gotta pee real quick." Kenzie ran the rest of the way into the bathroom and quickly closed the door. "How stupid can you be, Kenzie?" she said under her breath. "At least you could have put some pants on!" Kenzie grabbed her bathrobe from the back of the bathroom door before she entered the living room again.

"Sorry about that. I'm used to being here by myself," she said to Zan. "I hope I didn't make you uncomfortable."

"Not at all. You are quite pleasant looking in the morning," Zan said.

"Oh, yeah. I must be really beautiful half dressed and with my hair sticking up in all directions." She walked to the kitchen. "Can I make you a cup of coffee before I get into the shower?"

"I can wait to take sustenance until after you are ready. I tried to organize my sleeping area, but I was unable to fold one of the coverings," Zan replied.

Kenzie walked to the sofa and looked down. Zan had folded the flat sheet and blanket, but the fitted sheet was in a ball in the middle of the mattress. "Oh, my God, that is so funny! Here, let me show you how to do it." Kenzie picked up the sheet and handed one end of it to Zan. "Okay, find the corners, then tuck one corner into the other, and I will do the same on this end. Then we'll tuck your corners into mine, just like that. Okay, let's put it on the bed now and square off the sides, and then fold it in half, and in half again. There. See how it makes a nice neat square?"

"It is much easier than it looked originally. How do you put the bed away?"

"Grab the frame at the foot of the bed and fold it in, and then lift the whole frame up and push it into the compartment inside the sofa. Just like that. Now put the cushions back on and it's a sofa again."

Zan looked at the finished result and nodded. "Simple, yet effective."

Kenzie shoved her hands into her bathrobe pockets. "Look, I need to jump in the shower. Make yourself at home and when I'm finished, I'll make us a quick breakfast before we go."

Kenzie ran into her bedroom for a change of clothes and then disappeared again into the bathroom.

***

While Kenzie showered, Zan occupied herself by looking at the various pictures that decorated Kenzie's walls. There were several pictures of her with Bree and another male, and several paintings. One of the paintings looked very much like Kenzie. The initials JC could be seen in the lower corner of the painting.

A short time later, the sound of running water stopped, and ten minutes after that, Kenzie emerged from the bathroom, dressed for work, although, her hair was still damp.

"God, what a shower can do to improve your attitude!" Kenzie said. "It feels good to be clean. It's too bad you don't have a clean change of clothes, or I'd offer you the use of the shower, too."

"I will refresh when I get back to the...er, when I get back to where we are staying," Zan replied.

Kenzie stopped and looked at Zan. "You know, I could just bring you back to your hotel instead of you having to meet Trey at the trailhead."

"No, that is all right. I have contacted Trey, and she will meet me there this morning. We may hike before we go back to the hotel."

"Did you ask her where she was last night?"

Zan hesitated. "Ah, she fell asleep and was unaware of my calls."

"Well, I hope she apologized to you. I'm so glad I didn't leave you there last night."

"I am glad as well."

Kenzie looked at the clock. "We have about a half-hour before we need to go. How about coffee and a bagel?"

"What can I do to help?" Zan asked.

Kenzie reached her hand forward. "Come with me. You can make the coffee while I toast the bagels."

Zan took Kenzie's hand and followed her to the kitchen. Before releasing her, she squeezed Kenzie's hand. "Do you feel that?" Zan asked.

"If you are talking about the incredible sensation running through our hands, then yes. I definitely feel it. I thought it was just me." Kenzie said.

"I felt it every time you touched me yesterday, when you put your arm through mine, when you helped me to the car last night. Your touch does something to me, Kenzie. I have never felt that from another living being."

"Does it bother you?"

"The only thing that bothers me is that we cannot stay this way."

Kenzie reached up and touched the side of Zan's face. Zan closed her eyes. "Zan, I definitely want to explore this thing between us further, but I am so afraid of having my heart broken again. If you don't find Sedona suitable, you will leave. I don't want to be hurt, and I don't want to hurt you."

"I thought about you all night. I did not sleep," Zan said.

"I didn't get much sleep myself. Same reason."

"Will I see you later today?"

"I can meet you at the trailhead after work if you'd like. I won't have a car today, or I'd pick you up."

"I will meet you there."

***

Kenzie pulled into the parking lot at Little Horse trailhead at seven. Trey was nowhere in sight.

"Where the hell *is* she? I don't feel good leaving you here alone, Zan."

Zan took Kenzie's hand. "She said she would get here early and meditate before I arrived. I will not be alone. Now you must go before you are late. I will see you later in the day."

Kenzie took Zan's face between her hands and kissed her tenderly. "I will see you after work then."

Zan opened the door and climbed out and then retrieved her pack from the back seat. She stood by the fence until Kenzie backed out of the parking space. Just as Kenzie pulled away, Trey exited the trailhead into the parking area. Kenzie noticed her and gave Zan a thumbs-up in acknowledgement before driving away.

***

Zangendar and Tredoran walked side by side up the trail in the direction of their usual transference site.

"You have much to answer for, Zangendar!" Tredoran was livid.

"I can explain," Zangendar replied.

"I waited for you at the transference site well after the light source was gone. I finally had to return to the ship."

"I was unable to return to the trailhead."

"Did you couple with her?" Tredoran asked angrily.

"What?"

"Did you couple with her? Is that why you could not return to the trailhead? I saw her touch lips with you before you exited that vehicle?"

"No, I did not. How can you even ask that question?"

"You have been careless ever since you met that human female."

"Her name is Kenzie."

"I know what her name is! That is all I've heard for the past two weeks."

"Does the council know of my absence last night?"

"Of course, they know. The transference records only show one transfer last night, not two. You will need to explain yourself to them when we return."

***

Kenzie pulled into Bree's driveway and honked the horn. She put the car in park and climbed out to walk around and get into the passenger seat. Bree came out of the house by the time she'd fastened her seatbelt.

"Good morning, girlfriend. So spill it," Bree said.

"First things first. Here's your coffee from Starbucks. Oh, and I filled your gas tank," Kenzie said.

Bree accepted the coffee. "You are an angel! Now, spill it!"

"Well, she spent the night."

"Get out! Are you serious?" Bree cried out. "You dog!"

"It's not what you think. We started our hike and partway through, we decided we were hungry, so we went to dinner. It turns out she's never had alcohol before. She had three piña coladas."

"Holy shit! Three? I bet she was shit-faced!"

"Let's just say that I had to help her to the car after dinner. I took her back to the trailhead just before dark where Trey was supposed to meet us, but she never showed up. I wasn't going to leave her there, so I brought her home with me."

"And…?"

"And nothing. She slept on the pull-out, and this morning, I dropped her off at the trailhead before coming to pick you up. Trey was there this time."

"So, nothing happened, then?"

Kenzie tried hard to hide her grin.

"I see that look on your face. Come on, spill the beans, girlfriend."

"I think she's a virgin."

"Get the fuck out! Are you serious?"

"I think so. She was really nervous. So much so, she was trembling. We kissed, and I swear electrical currents passed through us both when our lips touched. It was the most intense experience I have ever had with a woman."

"Well, all you really have to compare it to is Jessie the bitch."

"True, but kissing Jessie was nothing compared to kissing Zan. She was so affected by it that she actually cried. She has such innocence about her. I'm not sure how life is where she comes from, but she has curiosity about ordinary things, like what my debit card was. She seems to have a really good grasp of English, but I suspect it's not her native language because she struggles with the names for simple things."

"Like what?"

"Well, for example, she didn't know the English word for vegetarian. I'm sure it is called something else in her native language."

"So, she slept on the sofa, huh?"

"Yes. Neither of us slept well last night. From what she said this morning, she spent the night the same way I did, staring at the ceiling and thinking of one another."

"She definitely sounds like a virgin. Did you learn anything else about her?" Bree asked.

"I learned quite a few things. Like, she's an environmental researcher, an only child, and a vegetarian. She comes from a place called Vakillia, and she's researching other places to live for her community because Vakillia is running out of water. Oh, and she's twenty-seven."

"Vakillia. Vakillia. I've never heard of it. I'll have to look it up. At least she's close to your age."

"Yeah, just a year younger."

"So, what do you think? I mean, I don't want you to get hurt, so I'm not going to push you in her direction. I want you to be careful, but I don't want you to be alone either."

"My biggest concern is that she'll leave. I mean, if she's looking for a place with ample water, there are better choices than Arizona."

"So, what about Trey? Are they a couple?"

"I asked her about that. She said Trey was more like her sister and that their relationship is kind of like mine and yours."

"Well, that's good. Where is she staying?"

"I don't know. I didn't think to ask her. I assume it's at one of the local hotels. Like I said, I don't know how long she'll be here. Part of me hesitates to get involved, but there's something about her that grabs me, you know? I have never felt such a physical attraction to another person before. She is gorgeous. All I've got to say is, thank God for panti-liners!"

Bree nearly choked on her coffee. "Jesus, girlfriend! Warn me before you say something like that!"

"Sorry!"

"Are you planning to see her again?"

"On the trail after work today."

***

Zangendar stood before the council, still cloaked in her avatar; her arms clasped behind her back and her head held high. The council of eight was an imposing body, made even more intimidating by the fact that her mother, Belander, was among its members.

"Zangendar, it has come to our attention that you did not return from the surface last night."

"That is correct," Zangendar admitted.

"Explain yourself."

"I had a planned encounter with a human female. The purpose of that encounter was to determine if we could infiltrate into their society without them becoming aware that we are not human.

"We engaged in the popular recreational pastime of hiking, after which, we partook in nourishment. Afterward, the human transferred me back to our meeting point, where she believed Tredoran would be waiting for me. In truth, Tredoran was waiting at the transference site, rather than at the trailhead. The human refused to leave me alone after dark."

The council head leaned forward in her seat. "She refused to leave you alone? Why did you not simply insist?"

"I did not want to alarm the human. She was concerned for my safety, and I must admit that while taking nourishment, I had consumed a liquid substance that caused confusion and unsteadiness. Hence, I was concerned about my ability to traverse the irregular terrain between the trailhead and the transference site without causing injury to myself. All things considered, I thought it was best not to resist."

"Do you realize you could have put this mission at risk by consuming substances that affect your ability to remain in control?"

Zangendar sighed. "I was unaware when I consumed the substance that it had the ability to affect my judgment."

Another member of the council spoke up. "What else did you disclose to this human while you were incapacitated?"

"I do not believe I disclosed anything of concern. I did, however, learn several interesting things about the humans."

"Such as?" the head councilmember asked.

"I learned that some of them are flesh eaters, animal flesh to be exact, and that they use plastic currency that connects electronically to a financial institution in which they store their paychecks, which I assume is their source of income. While in the eating establishment, I was also able to witness a transfer of paper currency as a form of payment. It was very interesting. In addition, I spent time in the human's home. They are primitive, to say the least, but I found it to be comfortable. Oh, and their transportation vehicles are quite interesting."

The head councilwoman leaned back in her chair. A heavy silence filled the room for several moments. Zangendar felt uncomfortable under the scrutiny of the council.

Finally, the chair of the council leaned forward once more. "There are those of us on this council who believe you behaved recklessly by directly disobeying protocol and remaining on the surface beyond the designated return, Zangendar. You could have put yourself in grave danger, not to mention putting the mission at risk. For the remainder of this cycle, you will be restricted to your quarters, while we contemplate the future of your involvement in this mission."

Zangendar felt like she had been punched in the stomach and she struggled to maintain control in front of the council. She clasped her hands tightly together behind her back, so tightly as to cause pain to distract her thoughts from the agony of not seeing Kenzie again.

"You are dismissed, Zangendar. We will summon you upon the new day with our decision."

Zangendar pulled a sullen mask over her expression. "As you wish." She turned to leave.

"One more thing, Zangendar," the head councilwoman said.

Zangendar stopped but did not turn to face the council.

"When you are on this ship, you will not be cloaked in your avatar. Is that clear?"

"As you wish," Zangendar said before she left the room.

***

"Zangendar, please allow me entry."

"Go away!"

"I will not. I am concerned for you. Please allow me entry, sister."

The door slid open and Tredoran stepped into Zangendar's chambers. She looked around the room. "Your quarters are in a state of disarray, Zangendar."

Zangendar was lying on her renewal unit with her hands behind her head. "I was angry."

"We have been taught not to display anger," Tredoran replied.

Zangendar stood and began pacing across the room. "I have come to realize that suppressing our feelings only makes them intensify rather than diminish. To be truthful, it felt good to do this." She swept her arm around the room to make her point.

Tredoran approached Zangendar and put her hand on her friend's shoulder. "Tell me what happened on the surface, sister."

Zangendar looked directly into Tredoran's eyes and try as she might, she could not hold back the tears.

Tredoran reached up and wiped one tear from Zangendar's cheek. "Your eyes are leaking," she said.

Zangendar broke away from her friend's grasp and walked a few feet away. She placed her hand directly above her heart and responded in a shaky voice. "I have such intense emotion in my mind and in my chest. I will surely die if I cannot see Kenzie again. I cannot bear the thought. If that is my fate, then there is no reason for me to live."

"What happened to make you feel this way?"

"*Life* happened, Tredoran. Fate has brought Kenzie and me together. I feel with every part of my being that we are *supposed* to be part of one another's lives. When she touched her lips to mine, I felt like I was exploding inside. I never imagined I could feel this intensely toward another living being. I had planned to tell her how I feel when we were to meet later in this day. I fear she will believe me insincere when I am not there to meet her."

"I struggle to think of what I can do to help," Tredoran said.

Zangendar hung her head. "There is nothing you can do. It is up to the council now. If you do not mind, I would like to be alone."

Tredoran walked toward the door but paused before she left the room. "Will you be all right, sister?"

"I do not know. I just do not know."

Chapter 17

Kenzie rolled her yoga mat out on the ground in her usual spot and then sat cross-legged in the middle of it. She reached for her water and took a long drink before returning the bottle to her pack. Finally, she placed her hands on her knees and closed her eyes to concentrate on the sounds and smells of her surroundings. It wasn't long before she heard footsteps approaching her.

"Zan?"

She opened her eyes and was immediately concerned.

"Trey? I was expecting Zan. Where is she?" Kenzie quickly climbed to her feet and looked around.

"Zan is not with me. She was detained," Trey said.

"Detained? What do you mean? Is she okay?"

"She is fine, at least she is unharmed."

Kenzie frowned. "Unharmed. You're not making me feel any better here, Trey. What's wrong?"

Some passing hikers halted their discussion.

"Can we go somewhere more private to talk?" Trey asked.

"Yes. Yes, of course. Do you have a car? I'm on my bike."

"No, I do not have a car."

"Okay. I guess we'll have to ride double on my bike to my house to get my car. Luckily, I just got it back from the shop. How did you get here if you don't have transportation?" Kenzie knelt on the ground to roll up her yoga mat.

"I was dropped off today by a friend."

"You were dropped off specifically to meet me?" Kenzie said. "How did you know I'd be here?"

"Zan told me she was supposed to meet you here."

"Did she send you?"

"No. She does not know I am here."

Kenzie strapped her mat to the bottom of her pack and turned to face Trey. "Come on. My bike is locked to the fence in the parking area."

***

"Hop in. I'll take you to The Vortex. It's just around the corner. It's a local bar with great appetizers and I'm a little hungry. How about you?" Kenzie said after they arrived at her apartment.

Trey wasn't sure how she was supposed to respond, and she wasn't sure what an appetizer was, so she just agreed. "That sounds good."

"Seatbelt!" Kenzie said when the alarm beeped.

Trey looked at her questioningly.

"Sheesh! What is it about you Vakillians?" Kenzie said. She reached across Trey and pulled the seatbelt around her and secured it in the clasp. "Zan had no idea what a seatbelt was for either."

Trey was alarmed. "You know we are from Vakillia?" she asked.

"Yes. Zan told me, although I have no idea where Vakillia is. I assume it's somewhere on the other side of the world."

"What else did Zan tell you?"

"Not much. Only that you are searching for somewhere new for your community to live because Vakillia's water supplies are drying up."

"That is true. Water is essential for our future reproduction."

"Water is essential for life in general," Kenzie said. "Here we are!" She pulled into the parking lot of the bar and turned off the ignition. "Come on. We'll see if we can find a table before this place fills up. It's a popular watering hole at the end of the workday."

Kenzie and Trey managed to find a table at the back of the bar and ordered soft drinks and appetizers. While they waited, Kenzie confronted Trey about Zan.

"So, why are you here and Zan is not? Not that I mind spending time with you, but I was expecting Zan."

"Zan was detained," Trey said.

"You said that earlier, but detained by what, or by whom?"

Trey sat back and played with the napkin on the table in front of her as she thought about how to explain their situation to Kenzie. "Zan and I are here on behalf of our community. That community is led by a council, and the council is concerned that Zan may not be making decisions for the good of the community."

"What the hell does that mean? Does this have to do with her staying with me last night?"

"Yes. Zan confessed to ingesting substances that clouded her judgment and made it difficult for her to return last night."

Kenzie leaned forward. "Well, if *you* had been there to pick her up like you were supposed to be, she would have been able to go home with you. There was no way I was going to leave her alone in a dark parking lot last night."

Trey felt a small surge of emotion that was quite alien to her. She was tempted to react in an angry and defensive manner but decided to take a different course of action. "It appears we had confused our meeting place. I was waiting for her at the meditation site where you and I met today. When she did not come, I left. By then, I assumed she was still with you."

"But Zan said this morning that you had fallen asleep and didn't hear your cellphone."

Trey looked around nervously. "That is true to an extent. I was meditating while waiting for her, and yes, I fell asleep."

Kenzie made herself relax. "Well, I can see how that might have happened, but a little miscommunication should not be held against her. And by the way, doesn't she have the right to come and go as she pleases?"

"You need to understand that we are but a few in a foreign land. We must protect one another."

"I get that, but there is such a thing as personal freedom. At least in this country there is."

"We are accustomed to a much more rigid hierarchy. Please don't question our methods," Trey said sternly.

Their conversation was briefly interrupted by the waiter delivering their drinks.

As soon as the waiter walked away, Kenzie fired back.

"Look, Trey, I don't want to fight with you. It just upsets me that Zan is obviously being punished for something that is not her fault."

"I do not disagree with you, but it is not my place to enforce the rules," Trey responded.

A tense silence fell between them during which Trey noticed a tear roll down Kenzie's cheek.

"You care for Zan," Trey said. It was a statement more than a question.

Kenzie nodded. "I do. I don't know why, seeing as I've only known her for what, two weeks? But there is something about her that has touched me in a way no one else ever has. It pains me to know she is suffering because of me."

"How is it because of you?" Trey asked.

"I allowed her to have too much to drink. I could tell after her second one that she was becoming intoxicated, but she was enjoying it so much, I allowed her to have a third drink."

"The number of drinks she had would not have changed the outcome. The communication issue relative to our meeting location was not caused by how many drinks she had."

"I suppose you are right, but it breaks my heart anyway. I was really looking forward to seeing her tonight."

Trey instinctively reached forward to touch Kenzie's hand, and realized it too late to retrieve it gracefully. "She was looking forward to seeing you as well."

"So, she doesn't know you're here?" Kenzie asked.

"She does not."

"You are a good friend to her, Trey."

"She is my sister from a different birth unit."

Kenzie chuckled. "That's a funny way of putting it, but she said the same thing about you."

"We have been close since we were children."

"Tell me, Trey. Are you finding what you need here? I mean, I know you are looking for a place for your community to resettle. Do you think it will be here?"

"We are still collecting data. There are so many factors involved. Your world has ample resources, especially water, but we need to know that our people will be accepted here."

"My world? You make it sound like you're from another planet or something. Sheesh! Anyway, I really hope you find what you need here."

Trey tensed when Kenzie made reference to another planet, but her demeanor indicated she was not serious, so she tried her best to downplay the comment by changing the subject.

"I sense you are afraid of losing Zan if we do not stay."

"Am I really that transparent? I need to work on that."

***

"Well, if it isn't Kenzie Caldwell!"

Kenzie's attention was drawn to the sound of her name coming from across the room. A wide smile split her face when she recognized the person voicing it.

"Charlie Cross! Aren't you a sight for sore eyes?" Kenzie slipped out of the booth and stood to give Charlie a big hug. "It's so nice to see you! Come join us."

Trey's eyes grew large when Charlie slipped into the booth beside Kenzie.

Kenzie made the introductions. "Charlie, I'd like you to meet Trey Harlax. Trey, this is Charlie. Charlie is a mutual friend of mine with Bree and her boyfriend, Jimmy."

Charlie extended his hand across the table. "It's nice to meet you, Trey."

Following what was apparently the custom, Trey offered her hand back. She felt a flush rise to her cheeks the moment her hand contacted Charlie's. "It is nice to meet you as well," Trey said.

Charlie narrowed her eyes at Trey. "You look familiar. Where have I seen you before? Have you done any of the vortex tours in town?"

"No, I have not." Trey replied.

"I know I've seen you before. There is no way I could forget such a beautiful face."

149

Trey blushed again and felt lightheaded. "You are too kind," she said.

"I'm just speaking the truth," Charlie replied.

Trey was rescued by the waiter who chose that moment to deliver their appetizers.

Kenzie bumped Charlie's shoulder. "Help yourself, if you can spare a moment away from your flirting."

"Do you blame me?" Charlie said. "Look at her. She's beautiful!"

"Stop, please," Trey said. She covered her face with her hands to hide the blush.

"You're embarrassing her, Charlie," Kenzie warned.

"Okay, okay. I'll behave. Those appetizers look good."

"Dig in," Kenzie encouraged.

***

Trey took a long pull on her soft drink in hopes that it would cool the fire in her face. She was beginning to understand how Zan felt about Kenzie.

Charlie downed the rest of his beer and put the empty bottle on the table. "What are you ladies drinking?" he asked.

"Cokes," Kenzie replied.

"Wow, heavy drinkers tonight," Charlie teased. "I'll be right back."

The moment Charlie slipped out of the booth, Kenzie reached across the table for Trey's hand. "I'm sorry he embarrassed you. He's such a flirt."

"He is very pleasant to look at," Trey said.

"Oh, yes. He is very handsome, and he really is a good guy. I just met him a short time ago and we really hit it off. I like him a lot."

"But you prefer Zan to Charlie?" Trey asked.

"Yes, I do. Zan sends me over the moon with a simple touch, while Charlie, well, Charlie feels like my brother."

Trey nodded. "I think I understand. Look, he is coming back."

Charlie returned to the table with a new round of drinks for everyone, and smoothly slipped back into the booth.

"So, Trey, what brings you to Sedona?" he asked.

Trey looked nervously at Kenzie who jumped in to answer for her. "Trey is on a scouting trip, looking for a potential place to settle with her community. I met Trey and her friend Zan on the trails."

"Well, butter my butt and call me a biscuit. I just remembered where I've seen you before," Charlie said.

"Where?" Trey asked.

"On the trail." He turned to Kenzie. "Remember the day we went hiking after running into one another in the mall?"

"Of course!" Kenzie said. "I remember now. Trey and Zan were meditating in my usual spot."

"I *knew* you looked familiar!" Charlie said.

"Well, since then, I have gotten to know Zan and Trey better. Bree and I ran into them on a totally different hike, and I have had a hiking date with just Zan as well."

"Small world," Charlie said. "Hey, I have an idea. Why don't I take the four of us on a helicopter tour of the Sedona vortexes? I owe you a tour anyway, Kenzie."

Kenzie grabbed Charlie's arm. "Wow! Can you really do that?"

"Sure! Why not? I'll just tell the boss it's a chartered tour. No problem!"

Kenzie turned to Trey. "Do you think you and Zan could do that with us?"

Trey could feel the excitement radiating from Kenzie and Charlie. She looked back and forth between them. "I...I will discuss it with Zan."

"Awesome. Let me know when you're free and I'll arrange it." Charlie looked at his watch. "Jesus! I gotta go. I have a sunset tour scheduled in an hour." He reached across the table for Trey's hand. "It was a pleasure meeting you, beautiful lady, and I can't wait to see you again." Looking to Kenzie, he pointed to his cheek, "Plant one here, sweet thing."

Kenzie quickly complied.

Charlie downed the rest of his beer and once again, slipped out of the booth. He put his cowboy hat on and pointed to the appetizers. "I got that covered. Have a great evening, ladies!"

Trey couldn't take her eyes off Charlie's retreating backside.

"He's cute, isn't he?" Kenzie said.

All Trey could do was nod and think, *what is a helicopter?*

***

It was just before dusk when Kenzie pulled into the parking lot at the Little Horse trailhead. Trey unhooked her seatbelt and reached for the door handle.

"Are you sure your ride is coming soon? It's beginning to get dark," Kenzie said.

"They will be here soon. There is no cause for concern," Trey replied.

"Thank you for coming tonight, Trey. It was really nice to get to know you better. You mean a lot to Zan, so that is important to me too."

"Yes. I can see why Zan is so taken with you. You are a good person, Kenzie."

"Tell Zan that I will be here after work tomorrow, and every day after that. I hope she can come back to me. There is so much more I want to tell her, and so much more I want to learn about her."

Trey nodded. "I will tell her."

Trey put one foot on the ground and then turned back to Kenzie. "Thank you, Kenzie Caldwell. I hope to see you again soon."

"You're welcome, Trey. Give Zan a hug for me."

Trey stared at her, and then climbed the rest of the way out of the car. She walked to the fence and watched Kenzie pull out of the parking place.

Kenzie stopped and lowered her window. "Are you sure you don't want me to wait for your friend to arrive?"

"I think I see them coming now," Trey said, pointing to a car pulling into the lot. "Have a pleasant evening!"

Trey watched Kenzie pull into traffic and drive away and then headed into the trailhead. Moments later, she reached the transference site and transferred to the ship.

***

Tredoran stopped at her quarters to shed her avatar and change into clothing more suitable for the ship's environment before moving on to Zangendar's quarters. When she reached Zangendar's rooms, she inhaled deeply to compose herself and then pushed the button to announce her presence. The door slid open and she stepped inside. Zangendar was lying on her renewal unit and staring at the ceiling.

Tredoran clasped her hands behind her back and observed her friend. "You are still cloaked in your avatar," she said.

"Yes."

"You were explicitly instructed—"

"I know what I was explicitly instructed to do, Tredoran." Zangendar sat up. "The fact is, I cannot shed the avatar. At least not entirely."

Tredoran walked closer to her friend. "Explain."

"I have been cloaked in the avatar almost exclusively since we generated them. In the beginning, I was able to transfer back to my original form with ease. Per the edict from the council this morning, I attempted to shed the avatar, and was unsuccessful."

"When I first came in you said you were not entirely successful. What did you mean by not entirely?"

Zangendar stood and faced her friend. "Computer, return me to original form," she said.

Tredoran watched as Zangendar's hair returned to its natural green color, and her breasts reduced in size, however, there were no other changes to her facial features or to the smoother curves across her hips and legs afforded by the avatar.

Zangendar raised her arms out to the sides. "This is as far as the transition goes, every time I have tried. It appears my physiology has adapted to the human features, and I assume the longer I am cloaked in the avatar, the less likely my hair and mammary masses will change in the future."

"Is the council aware of this?"

"They are not."

"They will need to be informed, Zangendar."

"I am aware of that. I fear their reaction."

"What can they do? You are the same Zangendar on the inside."

"Am I, Tredoran? Am I the same? I am not as sure as you seem to be. I am different. I feel emotion. I feel affection and attraction for a human female. I have shed tears. I have felt hope and I have felt sorrow. I am not the same. I feel alive, and I am not unhappy about that."

"What is your plan, Zangendar?"

"*This* is my plan. Computer, return me to avatar form."

Tredoran watched as the fullness of Zangendar's breasts returned, and her hair turned dark brown.

"This is who I am on the inside, Tredoran. This is what I want to be on the outside."

"I applaud your courage, my sister. I only hope I am brave enough to make that same choice if my hand is forced."

Zangendar took two steps forward and placed her hand on Tredoran's shoulder. "What are you saying, Tredoran?"

Tredoran lowered her eyes and then raised them again to look directly at Zangendar. "I went to the surface this afternoon and with Kenzie. I understand now how you feel about her. She opened my eyes to so many things, and I have experienced the depth of feeling you speak so lovingly about."

"You have seen Kenzie? Is she well?"

"She is well, but she longs to see you again."

"Wait, you have felt the depth of feeling as well? For whom?"

"Kenzie took me to an establishment for refreshments, and so that we could talk. I believe she called it a bar. While we were there, Charlie came in."

"Charlie? The person she was on the trail with?"

"Yes. He came in and I totally lost all control of my thoughts and my bodily reactions. He called me beautiful, Zangendar. He called me beautiful."

Zangendar held Tredoran by both shoulders and lowered her forehead to hers. "What are we going to do about this, sister? How can we return to a life with no emotion after this?"

"I am not sure that we can."

"Does Kenzie know why I could not come?"

"I explained it to her. She said to tell you that she would be on the trail, waiting for you tomorrow, and every day after that until you come back to her. Oh, and she told me to give you this."

Tredoran closed the remaining distance between herself and Zangendar and wrapped her arms around her friend. Almost instinctively Zangendar's arms rose to hold Tredoran close. "She called this a hug. I believe it is meant to convey intense emotional attachment," Tredoran said.

Tredoran relaxed her hold on Zangendar and rested her head on her friend's shoulder. Before long, all of the tension released from both their bodies as they stood wrapped in their loving embrace. When they parted, there were tears in both their eyes.

Tredoran wiped the tears from her face with the back of her hand. "Thank you for sharing your true self with me, my sister. I am forever changed."

"I am as well. I believe I would not survive this transition without you," Zangendar admitted.

"Here is *my* decision. Computer, return me to avatar form." Within seconds, Tredoran became Trey. "I will go where you go, Zan."

"Thank you, Trey. I need you by my side. You make me stronger than I am alone."

Their attention was suddenly diverted to the door as the call bell erupted.

"Enter," Zangendar called out.

The door slid open and revealed their visitor to be Belander.

"Mother. Please come in," Zangendar said.

"I have come to inform you that the council will allow you to return to the surface upon the new day. I have convinced them that your human avatars are real enough to allow any Vakillian to move about freely. They have also agreed that you may stay on the surface for multiple days at a time."

Zangendar took her mother's hands in hers. "Belander, I cannot thank you enough."

"This reprieve comes with conditions, Zangendar. If Earth is chosen as our new homeland, it is critical that our transition into human society is seamless, so you and Tredoran will be expected to provide continuous and meaningful feedback that can be used to prepare the others for infiltration."

"Of course. That has always been our mission," Zangendar pointed out.

"Belander, if I could be so bold as to ask what swayed the minds of the council members?" Tredoran asked.

"It was the avatars. As you know, the situation on Vakillia is reaching a critical level and as such, the council's goal was to integrate into another alien society, even through force if necessary, but when they realized that you and Zangendar were planning to infiltrate Earth without the humans becoming aware that we are different from them. That was the strategy that convinced them to allow you freer reign."

Chapter 18

Tredoran and Zangendar met the following morning in Tredoran's quarters.

"Trey, given the expectations of the council, we need to find a way to integrate more with the general population of Sedona. I do not believe we can accomplish that by confining ourselves to the hiking trails," Zangendar said.

"I agree. But we cannot depend only on Kenzie to make those connections, especially since she works until later in the day. We need to find a way to get around by ourselves. Our transference site is too far away from the town to walk that distance," Tredoran replied.

"You are correct. We need to be closer. Kenzie has mentioned a hotel several times."

"What is a hotel?"

"I believe it is a place to purchase rooms on a daily basis."

"To purchase rooms, we need currency, Zan. I do not think our fingertip chips will work here."

Zangendar paced the room. "We will also need currency for food if we are to stay on the surface for multiple days. Or a place to store food if we bring it from the ship."

"Can we duplicate currency?" Trey asked.

Zan tilted her head in thought. "Possibly. I will approach Belander to determine if duplication is possible through images available in our research database. Since we do not plan to return to the ship this evening, we will need currency to secure a place to renew tonight."

"How does Kenzie get her currency?"

"Kenzie is a healer, and she works at an urgent care center. Her employer provides currency to her in exchange for her services. Her currency is transmitted to a financial institution and she uses a plastic card to retrieve it."

"That is a very primitive practice," Trey observed.

"I agree, however, it may be one we need to understand and learn if we are to exist among the humans in the near future," Zan replied.

Trey walked to the duplicator and replicated several kinds of snacks for them to take to the surface that afternoon. "Here, put these in your pack. We do not know when we will return to the ship. It will be wise to have provisions. We need to take several bottles of water as well."

***

At four that afternoon, Kenzie entered the locker room at the urgent care center and hung up her white coat. Bree came into the room just as she pulled her pack out of her locker.

"Hey, girl. Have you got plans for this evening?" Bree asked.

"I was actually going to hit the trails. I'm hoping to run into Zan today."

"Didn't you say she was banned from here for now, or something along those lines? Isn't that what Trey said?"

Kenzie was irritated. "I don't know what to think. I mean, Zan is a grown woman. I don't like the idea of someone pulling rank on her. I mean, a girl's got rights, don't you think?"

"I don't know, K. They're not from around here. We have no idea what their customs are like."

"Well, I told Trey I would be on the trails after work, so that's what I'm planning to do."

"The weather report says forty percent chance of rain, so you might want to take your car instead of your bike. It won't be fun biking home in the rain."

"Ugh! In that case, I'll change at home instead of here. I need to go home to get my car anyway. Thanks for the tip, Bree."

"No prob! If you finish early, drop me a text. In fact, drop me a text anyway. I want to know if you hook up with Zan."

***

Kenzie pulled into the parking lot at Little Horse at around four-thirty. She looked at the sky after stepping out of the car and decided that it did indeed look like it might rain. Nevertheless, she'd promised to be on the trailhead that evening, so she was committed to go. She threw her pack onto her back and entered the trailhead. Fifteen minutes later, she reached her usual meditation site. There was no one in sight.

She sat down dejectedly on a nearby boulder. Her day had been especially difficult. For starters, she was nearly late for work when her alarm didn't go off. That was after a restless night that she spent alternating between short naps and marathon pity parties worrying about Zan. Then mid-morning, they had a patient come in with chest pains, who should have gone to the hospital instead. The patient coded and they had been unable to revive him. Finally, the possibility of rain on her hike, and then an empty meditation site when she got there. She closed her eyes and rubbed her temples to ward off a headache that was creeping up on her. She was so ready for this day to be done.

"Kenzie."

Kenzie's head snapped up at the sound of her name. It sounded like it had come from far away. She stood up and looked around and saw Zan and Trey coming up the trail from the chapel. They were still about fifty yards away.

"Kenzie!"

"Zan!" She waved her arms above her head and ran toward them.

They met halfway and fell into one another's arms. Kenzie wrapped her arms around Zan's waist and held on for dear life. "Hold me, Zan. Just hold me. I so need this right now."

***

Zan held Kenzie as close as she could. She didn't know what else to do. She'd had no demonstrations of affection as a child. She knew when Trey hugged her in her quarters that it felt warm and loving, so she strove to convey that same sense of comfort and safety to Kenzie as she held her close.

They were still in an embrace when Trey finally caught up to them on the trail. "It is good to see you, Kenzie," she said.

Kenzie reached one hand out to grasp Trey and pull her into the hug. "It's good to see you too, Trey."

Trey awkwardly wrapped her arms around her two friends for a quick hug.

A crack of thunder broke up their trio.

"I was afraid that might happen. Quick, let's get to my car before the sky breaks loose!"

All three friends ran down the path and almost made it to the car before the sky opened up. They were soaked by the time they got to the car and scurried inside.

"Oh, my God! I am soaked!" Kenzie exclaimed. She looked at Zan, who was in the passenger seat beside her, and broke out laughing. "You look like a drowned rat!" she squealed.

Zan was totally lost, that is, until Kenzie pulled down the visor and opened the mirror. Zan's eyes flew open and before she knew it, she was holding her stomach in laughter.

"What about you, Trey?" Kenzie looked into the back seat and lost it. "Trey, look in the mirror."

It was a good ten minutes before the three of them stopped laughing and composed themselves enough to pull out of the parking lot.

***

"Come in. Make yourselves at home." Kenzie closed the door behind them and turned the lights on in the living room. "I'm going to go change my clothes and towel-dry my hair. There are more towels in the bathroom cupboard. Zan, you know where the bathroom is."

Zan went to the bathroom cupboard and pulled out two towels. She threw one to Trey.

"Do you believe we were actually laughing in the car, Zan? I don't know that I have ever laughed before."

"I can't remember laughing before either," Zan said. "It felt nice."

Kenzie stood on the other side of the door and listened to their conversation. *They've never laughed before? What kind of cult do they live in?* she thought to herself.

Kenzie threw the bedroom door open and walked into the living room. "It feels good to be dry again." She stopped short. "Did you bring a change of clothes with you?"

"Yes, we did. Several changes in fact," Trey replied.

"Several?" questioned Kenzie.

"Yes. We were going to ask you to help us find a hotel close by. We will be here for several more days. The place we are staying in right now is too far from town," Zan said. "In fact, it is beyond the hiking trails."

"Sure. There's a motel just up the street. I'd be happy to take you there," Kenzie said. "For now, you need to get out of those wet clothes. One of you can use the bathroom, and the other can use my bedroom to get changed. I'll just park my butt here on the sofa."

A few minutes later, her guests reemerged fully dressed in dry clothing. "Give me your wet things. I'll throw them in the dryer."

Kenzie took the wet clothes and towels from them and pulled open a closet door in the kitchen, just beside the pantry. Inside, was an apartment sized, stackable washer and dryer. She opened the dryer, threw the clothes in, and set the timer.

"That is a convenient appliance," Zan said.

"Yes, and it's just the right size for one or two people." Kenzie closed the closet door and turned to her guests. "I hope you're hungry because I ordered pizza while you were changing. Vegetarian."

"Pizza?" Zan said.

"Really? You don't know what pizza is? We seriously need to talk. What kind of conditions do you live under that you've never experienced pizza?"

Trey looked nervously at Zan.

Kenzie squinted her eyes at them. "What is going on with you two? I mean, should I be worried that you know where I live?"

Zan stepped forward and sat beside Kenzie. She took her hand between her own. "Kenzie, I would die before I would do anything to hurt you. You have nothing to fear from us."

Once again, Kenzie felt intense energy pass through her at Zan's touch and she had to consciously make an effort to not allow it to distract her.

"So, what's the deal? Honestly, I was surprised to see you on the trail today. The last I knew, you were being confined for some reason."

"All of that has changed. We have convinced the council to give us freer reign. There won't be any more restrictions from this point on," Zan explained.

"Look, I know Trey told me not to question your methods, but you are grown women. No one should be telling you where you can go or who you can see, and you certainly shouldn't have a curfew. This is just a little creepy, you know?"

"Trey is correct. Our community has rules that might seem unusual to you, but we are foreigners in a foreign land, and the rules are designed to keep us safe. Believe it or not, our council has the same concerns about you that you have about us."

"Have you told them about me?" Kenzie asked.

"Yes. I have told them," Zan replied.

"And?"

"They have no opinion of you. Their only interest is if our kind will be able to integrate with your kind," Zan said.

Kenzie got up and walked across the room. She turned to face them. "Your kind? My kind? What exactly do you mean by that?"

Trey traded nervous glances with Zan. She stood and approached Kenzie. "I'm sorry, Kenzie. We have had to learn English through recordings and videos. I am afraid we do not always know the correct words to use. The truth is, we are different from the people who live here, and we are nervous about being accepted."

Kenzie walked back to the sofa and sat beside Zan once more. She took Zan's hands in her own. "Is that what you meant?"

Zan looked directly into Kenzie's eyes. "That is what I meant. I regret my words have upset you. Maybe we should go."

Zan tried to pull her hands from Kenzie's grasp, but Kenzie held fast.

"You are not going anywhere, Zan. If you are going to live here, you need to get used to being challenged, and you need to learn how to stand your ground. You can't run off any time someone questions you." Kenzie cupped Zan's face between her hands. "You are so gentle and sweet, and those are amazingly wonderful traits, but it leaves you vulnerable. Even to me."

A sharp rap drew their attention to the front door.

"The pizza is here!" Kenzie said. She jumped up and ran to the door while Trey made herself comfortable in the chair beside the sofa.

After paying the delivery boy, Kenzie placed the pizza on the coffee table in front of the sofa. "I'll be right back," she said, and she went to the kitchen for paper plates, napkins and three bottles of beer, which she placed on the table beside the pizza before sitting on the sofa cross-legged beside Zan.

She handed out the paper plates and then opened the cover on the pizza box. The tantalizing aroma of fresh baked pizza filled the room. "Dig in! This pizza is to die for!"

Zan looked startled. "Do you mean to say we will die if we eat this?"

Kenzie threw her head back and laughed. "Oh, my God, no! That's just a saying. It implies that it's so good, you'd be willing to fight to the death just to eat it. Go ahead, take a piece."

Trey looked at her plate and then at the pizza. "How?"

"Just grab a slice with your hand. Like this." Kenzie demonstrated the proper retrieval of a slice of pizza, followed by the proper first bite, after folding it, of course.

"So, there is a ritual involved with eating pizza?" Zan said.

Kenzie raised her eyebrows and saw that Zan was struggling to keep a grin off her face.

She put her pizza on the table. "You're making fun of me, aren't you?"

Zan tried to keep a straight face. "I would never do that."

"Why you little shit!" She poked Zan in the ribs and got the expected reaction. She poked her again. "Are you ticklish?" Kenzie asked.

"What is ticklish?"

"This!" Kenzie launched a full-on attack, tickling Zan's midsection.

Zan tried hard to fend her off but was incapacitated by the laughter. "Stop! Please stop!" she pleaded.

Kenzie stood on the sofa and did a victory dance, with her arms in the air. "I'm the man! I'm the man!" she said.

Trey looked at them both in astonishment.

Kenzie sat down again and picked up her pizza. She looked at Trey. "What?"

Trey just shook her head and grabbed a slice of pizza.

***

Kenzie looked out the window at the sky. "It looks like the rain has stopped. I think we can walk to the motel. It's just a couple of blocks up the street."

"You have said motel two times now. How does it differ from a hotel?" Trey asked.

"Hotels generally have multiple floors of rooms, all in one building. Motels, on the other hand, tend to be two or three-story buildings laid out in a campus. The facility down the street is a motel. The *m* in motel stands for motor. There are usually parking places near each of the individual buildings for parking cars or motor vehicles."

"Clever terminology," Trey noted.

Zan drank the last of her beer and held the empty bottle in her hand. "That was good pizza. And what do you call this beverage?"

"Beer," Kenzie said. "It is much less intoxicating than the coladas you drank the other night. I figured just one wouldn't hurt you."

"Beer," Zan said. "I very much enjoyed it, and the pizza as well. Thank you."

"I think beer and pizza is my new favorite meal," Trey said.

"I'm glad you enjoyed it. Oh! Before I forget, I need to get your clothes out of the dryer."

Kenzie retrieved two pairs of shorts and two shirts from the dryer and folded them on the kitchen countertop. She handed a set to each of her guests. "Here, put these in your packs."

While Zan and Trey readied their bags, Kenzie tidied the living area and then collected the paper plates, pizza box and bottles, which she carried to the door with her.

"May I ask where you are bringing those items?" Zan said.

"The recycling bin is on the porch."

"Recycling?"

"Yes. We minimize the amount of trash that's in the landfills by reusing as much paper, cardboard, metal, glass and plastic as we can. It's good for the environment."

Zan nodded her approval.

"Trey, would you mind getting the door? My hands are full," Kenzie said.

Trey opened the door for all to pass through, and then closed it behind them.

After disposing of the recycling, Kenzie led them down the stairs and onto the sidewalk. "Follow me. The motel is about a ten-minute walk away."

Kenzie made a point of walking beside Zan on the way to the motel, and allowed her fingers to *accidentally* brush against her hand as they walked. Each contact was met by a glance and a smile from Zan.

"One more block and the motel will be on your right," Kenzie said.

She subtly slipped her hand inside Zan's during this declaration and clasped her fingers. Zan looked down at their hands but made no attempt to pull hers loose.

Kenzie looked directly at her and smiled. "Is this okay?"

Zan nodded. "It feels pleasant."

"I agree."

***

Kenzie waited outside the motel office while Zan and Trey reserved a room. Before long, they exited the office carrying their backpacks and a small envelope containing two plastic cards. Zan showed them to Kenzie. "The clerk indicated these would unlock the door. I am hoping you can show us how."

Kenzie took the envelope from Zan and looked at the numbers written on the front. "Building three, Room two-eleven. The two indicates the second floor, and the other number means you are in room eleven. The first thing we need to do is find building three."

Moments later, they stood in front of room two-eleven. "All you need to do is wave the card in front of this panel right here, and when the light turns green, you turn the handle and push the door open."

Kenzie stood aside and watched Zan unlock the door. All three walked into the room. There were two queen-sized beds, a television, small kitchenette and a relatively large bathroom.

"This is nice," Kenzie said. "You should be comfortable here." She looked at the kitchenette. "Do either of you know how to cook?"

Trey dropped her bag on the bed closest to the bathroom. "Cook?" she said.

"Yeah, food preparation. Can either of you cook?"

"Our plan was to eat prepared food that we bring from the community," Zan said.

"So, neither of you can cook," she said. "Jesus! It's good that you're close enough to my place for a home-cooked meal once in a while."

She looked at Trey, who was now reclining on the bed, and then at Zan. Both of them had slight grins on their faces.

"Why do I get the impression that this is the first time the two of you have been on your own?"

Chapter 19

Zan closed the motel room door and directed Kenzie to the stairs leading to the parking lot. When they reached the sidewalk, she offered her hand to Kenzie.

Kenzie slipped her hand into Zan's. "Thank you for walking me home."

Zan had to consciously focus on what Kenzie was saying, as the feel of Kenzie's hand in hers was very distracting. "Trey will not miss us. She was sleeping before we left the room, and besides, it will be dark soon and I didn't want you to walk home alone."

They walked along in silence for a bit, and then Zan spoke.

"You were correct about Trey and I never being on our own before. We have lived very sheltered lives within the community."

Kenzie glanced at Zan as they walked. "I'd like to know more about where you come from, Zan."

Zan continued to look straight ahead as they walked. She had a very solemn look on her face. "I am not sure you would understand. And you may not approve."

"Still, I'd like to know."

"It is quite different from here. In some ways, it was less repressive and less controlling that the community you lived in as a child, but in other ways it was more so."

Kenzie stopped, forcing Zan to look at her.

"What do you know about how I grew up?"

Zan felt a surge of anxiety in her chest. She could not tell Kenzie that she had invaded her mind at least twice without her knowledge. "I assumed that since you left home under less than optimum circumstances that your upbringing was difficult. Forgive me if that assumption is incorrect."

They continued walking.

"Well, I'd say you were definitely correct on that one. I lived in a community that valued women only for their ability to bear children and to provide housekeeping services for the men of the community. And I've already mentioned they were not thrilled with the fact that I am attracted to women."

"That is unfortunate."

"That's an understatement! I had to leave. They gave me an ultimatum. It was either denounce my attraction for women, or be excommunicated. I chose my lifestyle."

"You were very brave," Zan said.

"What about you? Does your community frown on same sex relationships?"

Zan looked at Kenzie. "On the contrary. My community is very liberal relative to women being attracted to women, yet I have to admit that there is considerable repression of other kinds required of those who live in my community."

By this time, they had reached Kenzie's apartment. Kenzie led Zan to the step leading to the porch. "Do you have time to sit for a bit? I'd like to learn more."

Zan sat beside Kenzie on the steps.

"What else would you like to know?" Zan asked.

Kenzie reached for Zan's hand once more and held it between both of hers. "I have to say, Zan, that after living in a cult-like community myself, I am very wary of what goes on there. Tell me, what kind of repression do you have to deal with?"

Zan was unsure of how honest she should be with Kenzie. She was afraid of losing her if she revealed too much.

"Emotional suppression is the most significant kind of repression we live under," Zan said.

"Emotional suppression?"

"Yes. We are taught from an early age that emotions cause one to become weak."

"Are you serious?"

"Quite serious. We are not allowed to express emotion outwardly, and as such, most of us have learned to suppress them internally as well."

"My God, that's horrible!" Kenzie exclaimed.

"To be truthful, it is something I was born into, and I never questioned it. Until I met you."

"Until you met me?"

"Yes. You display your emotions quite openly, Kenzie, and you make me feel things that I have never felt before. I have come to realize that I have been missing out on something I did not even know existed."

Kenzie touched the side of Zan's face with her fingertips. "I can't imagine going through life never feeling happiness, and never feeling love. My heart breaks for you, Zan."

Zan wiped away a solitary tear that rolled down Kenzie's cheek. "Never feeling heartbreak is one of the benefits of an emotionless existence."

Kenzie captured Zan's hand, with evidence of her tears still on Zan's fingertip. "No, Zan. Emotions make you feel alive, even the bad ones."

Zan nodded, and was unable to look away from Kenzie's eyes. "Yes. I have learned that since meeting you. I have physical pain in my heart when we are apart, and when we are together. When we are together, my mind is so full of emotion that I cannot think clearly."

Kenzie leaned closer to Zan. "I feel the same way about you."

Zan found it suddenly difficult to breathe. "What is happening, Kenzie? This is a feeling that is totally foreign to me."

"You are, no, *we* are falling in love. Don't ask me how this is happening in such a short amount of time. But we are falling in love."

Zan raised one trembling hand to Kenzie's cheek. "I want to kiss you," Zan whispered hoarsely.

"What are you waiting for?" Kenzie replied.

Slowly, Zan lowered her lips to Kenzie's and lightly made contact. An intense spasm passed through her abdomen and she pulled back. She felt nearly on the edge of an emotional breakdown.

Kenzie took Zan's face between both her palms and looked directly into her eyes. "Don't be afraid. What you are feeling is completely normal."

Zan made the conscious decision to trust Kenzie and she lowered her lips once more. This time with increased urgency. She was trembling and breathing sporadically by the time their lips parted. She touched her forehead to Kenzie's and attempted to regain control.

Kenzie was on fire. The feel of Zan's lips on hers was nearly her undoing. She could feel Zan's body trembling, and she knew that Zan was feeling the same. She was almost thankful when Zan broke the kiss and touched their foreheads together.

"You haven't done this before, have you?" Kenzie asked.

"I have not." Zan pulled her face away and looked directly into Kenzie's eyes. "Teach me."

Kenzie stood and offered her hand to Zan. "Come with me." She led Zan into her apartment and straight to her bedroom. "Are you sure about this, Zan? There will be no turning back."

An expression of fear and anticipation graced Zan's features. "I am sure."

Kenzie grasped the hem of Zan's T-shirt and gently pulled it over her head. She was wearing an athletic sports bra beneath it. Kenzie could see the outline of erect nipples protruding through the material. Seeing the evidence of Zan's arousal was staggering and she struggled to take things slow and easy.

She looked into Zan's face and saw a mixture of excitement and anxiety there. Again, she cupped Zan's face between her hands. "Are you okay? You're trembling. We don't have to do this."

Zan placed her palms on Kenzie's hips. "I want to," she whispered.

"If I do anything that makes you uncomfortable, I want you to stop me. Okay?"

Zan nodded.

Kenzie kissed the hollow at the base of Zan's neck.

Zan closed her eyes and tilted her head back. A soft moan escaped her throat.

Kenzie slipped her hands into the waistband of Zan's shorts and pushed them down past her buttocks. They floated gently to the floor around her ankles. She allowed her hands to explore the rounded muscles of Zan's bottom, and she gently squeezed.

Her own ardor increased exponentially and prompted a sharp intake of breath and a spasm to course through her. She fought hard to control her own desire. The last thing she wanted to do was to move too fast. She wanted Zan's first time to be nothing short of phenomenal.

Kenzie dropped to one knee in front of Zan and removed her sandals and the shorts that were in a pile around her ankles. Zan placed her hand on Kenzie's shoulder and lifted each foot as commanded.

Kenzie stood again and pulled her own shirt off. She watched as Zan's eyes grew large when her lacy bra was exposed.

"Go ahead," Kenzie said.

Zan traced the exposed parts of the Kenzie's breasts with her fingertips. "They are so soft," she whispered.

Kenzie reached behind and unhooked her bra. It immediately slid down to her wrists, exposing her breasts fully to Zan's view. Zan's reaction was visible as her trembling increased.

Kenzie looked into Zan's eyes and the raw desire she saw there, added to her own struggle to maintain control. She kicked off her shoes and pushed her shorts and panties down and was soon standing totally naked in front of Zan.

"You are so beautiful," Zan said in an unsteady voice.

Kenzie stepped forward once more and slipped her hands under Zan's sports bra. A moment later, it joined the growing pile of clothing on the floor. Kenzie ran her hands around Zan's breasts and then placed a gentle kiss on each nipple. Zan nearly doubled as her legs threatened to buckle.

"I fear I will fall," Zan said.

Kenzie continued to place a trail of kisses from Zan's breasts, to her ear where she softly whispered to her, "One more thing, and then we can retreat to the bed." She knelt once more in front of Zan and gently removed her panties, and in the process, placed a gentle kiss just above the dark triangle of hair that covered her pubis.

Zan held herself up with a hand on Kenzie's shoulder, which she quickly removed when Kenzie gently pushed her back onto the mattress until Zan was completely supine on the bed. Kenzie spread Zan's legs and lay down between them, with her upper body supported by her arms.

Kenzie could feel Zan's entire body tremble as she hovered above her. With her nose within an inch of Zan's, Kenzie smiled and then placed a searing kiss on her lips. Zan's mouth easily opened, creating an opportunity for Kenzie's tongue to explore. Zan's hands captured Kenzie's face between then, and she pulled her in closer to devour her very essence.

Kenzie broke the kiss. "My God, Zan. I want you more than I have ever wanted anything in my life."

"I am yours," Zan said.

Kenzie dove into Zan's neck and left bite marks that would surely bruise the next day. She was on fire and she so wanted to just take Zan, take her fast and hard, but she knew she had to be careful. She knew she had to go slow. She knew she could not scare the fragile woman beneath her. She forced herself to slow down and to savor every moment of making love to Zan.

Kenzie moved her body lower so that her abdomen rested on Zan's core and she had access to Zan's breasts. She struggled to maintain control of her own climax as she felt Zan's wetness on her stomach. She placed a line of kisses from Zan's throat to the space between her breasts, and then, without warning, she inhaled one of Zan's nipples into her mouth with an intense sucking motion, causing Zan's upper body to come almost off the bed.

"Kenzie!" Zan cried. Her hands flew up to hold Kenzie's head firmly in place.

Kenzie reached up and took Zan's wrists. She pinned them to the bed and then looked directly into Zan's eyes. "Sweetheart, relax and enjoy this. I promise, I am not going anywhere."

Zan nodded and unclenched her fists. "I'm sorry," she said.

Kenzie smiled. "No reason to be sorry. I remember my first time. It was very much like this, intense and so out of control." Kenzie released her wrists and leaned in to kiss her again. "I desire you more than I can possibly explain."

Once again, Kenzie placed tender kisses along Zan's jaw line and neck and stopped to feast on her breasts that were so begging to be sucked. Zan's moans and gyrations only served to heighten Kenzie's desire as she struggled to keep herself from going over the edge too soon.

Kenzie shifted once more to position herself between Zan's legs. Zan lifted her upper body and looked worriedly at Kenzie.

Kenzie glanced upward. "Don't look so worried, love. I promise you will enjoy this."

Zan nearly lost consciousness when she felt Kenzie's tongue delve into her folds. A barrage of thoughts entered her mind as she strove to absorb everything this amazing woman was doing to her. *This was not how the elders said it would happen. Why did they not tell me about amazing this feels? Does it feel this way for all Vakillians, or is it the human avatar that makes me feel this way? The elders. Did they not say I needed to be in water?*

After new minutes, Kenzie repositioned herself to lie beside Zan. She kissed her tenderly. "Are you all right?" she asked.

Zan nodded vigorously.

"Do you want me to continue?"

Zan was barely able to speak. "You are making me feel things I have never experienced before. Please, I need more."

Kenzie smiled. "My pleasure, love." She kissed her again and then once more set out to explore Zan's body. When she reached her midsection, she laid her head on Zan's abdomen and then ran her fingertips into the dark triangle of hair. She felt Zan stiffen when her fingers made contact with her clit.

"Does that feel good, love?"

Kenzie listened as a moan emitted from Zan's throat. A light feeling filled her chest and a mist formed in her eyes as she realized that she was the first one to bring such pleasure to the woman beneath her.

She slipped two fingers inside her and held on as Zan's pelvis rose from the bed.

"Ah! Kenzie!" Zan slammed her head into the pillow and arched her pelvis even higher.

"Am I hurting you?" Kenzie said, suddenly concerned by the intensity of Zan's reaction.

"No! No, it feels amazing. More. Please, more."

Kenzie added another finger and set up a cadence that Zan met with the trusts of her pelvis.

Zan grasped a handful of sheets in an attempt to anchor herself against the sensual assault she was so willingly submitting herself to. She could feel the pressure build up in her temples, and she feared she would lose consciousness.

She thought she should be concerned about how out of control she felt. This was not something that would be encouraged by the community. Never in her life had she been in such a heightened emotional state. She literally felt that the top of her head might explode. But she curiously did not feel afraid. What she *did* feel was an intense and all encompassing need to have Kenzie in her life. Was this love?

Suddenly, Zan felt a surge of heat, originating from deep within her abdomen, and she felt the need to escalate.

Kenzie felt a sudden tightening around her fingers. She knew Zan was close to climax. She scurried quickly to her knees and positioned herself to be able to increase the intensity and speed of her thrusts to match Zan's growing need.

Zan's climax came in an explosion that even Kenzie didn't anticipate. A prolonged guttural moan escaped Zan's lip.

"Let it go, baby. Let it go. Don't try to resist it," Kenzie encouraged as she rode the wave of Zan's orgasm. "I've got you, love. I've got you."

Zan felt her entire body spasm again and again. The heat that had originated in her abdomen exploded throughout her entire being. She was unaware that her body had the ability to experience such emotional and physical intensity. At that moment, she wanted nothing more than to spend the rest of her life in Kenzie's arms.

Finally, the crescendo peaked and the spasms eased. Awareness resurfaced, and she reached down to touch Kenzie's head.

Kenzie looked up at her.

All Zan could do was nod.

Kenzie crawled up Zan's body and lay down beside her. She gathered her into her arms and held her close. Zan wept.

"Are you okay, Zan?" she whispered.

"That was the most amazing experience of my life. Thank you," Zan said in a shaky voice.

Kenzie felt another tremor pass through Zan.

"Will it stop?" Zan asked.

"Yes, it will stop. For now, just relax and enjoy it."

"Is it always that intense?"

"Not always, but it *is* always wonderful, especially if you are with someone you love."

Zan lifted her head from Kenzie's shoulder. "What about you? Is it customary for both individuals to...to,"

"Come? Climax? Reach orgasm? Yes, it is customary. At least when it's two women."

Zan lifted herself onto one elbow. She looked directly into Kenzie's eyes. "I must reciprocate. I want you to feel what I feel. Tell me what to do."

"Women know what women like, so just do what I did to you. I will tell you, it won't take long. I nearly climaxed myself when you came."

Zan kissed Kenzie tenderly at first, but then again with increased ardor. Interestingly, she felt another surge of desire build deep within her as she made love to Kenzie. She was concerned about whether she could satisfy Kenzie the way Kenzie had satisfied her, but she persisted and used her own experience to guide her.

Kenzie's chest rose from the bed when Zan sucked on her nipples. Zan felt Kenzie's hands grasp the sides of her head to convey her desire for more. Zan was intrigued by the low growl coming from her throat. She glanced at Kenzie and the look on her face caused her own desire to escalate even more.

"Zan, I need to feel you inside me," Kenzie said in a raspy voice.

Zan reached her hand down and slipped her fingers between Kenzie's folds. She was amazed at how wet Kenzie was. The heat and energy she felt surge through her hand at the contact sent yet another spasm running through her body.

Control yourself, Zangendar. This moment is for Kenzie.

"Inside. Please," Kenzie said.

Zan thrust two fingers deep within Kenzie and her hips immediately raised off the bed.

"Ah, more!" Kenzie yelled.

Kenzie met each thrust of Zan's rhythm, each one accompanied by a loud moan. Instinctively, Zan increased the speed of her thrusts and Kenzie became more and more vocal. With each thrust, the intensity of Zan's own desire also rose.

Before long, she felt Kenzie's body tighten around her fingers and then suddenly, Kenzie's pelvis rose and suspended above the bed for a few seconds before they both plummeted into climax.

Zan lowered her forehead to Kenzie's chest and savored the feel of Kenzie's body pulsing around her fingers, and her orgasm climaxing in rhythm with Kenzie's.

Zan removed her fingers from Kenzie when she felt Kenzie's hand on the back of her head. She pulled herself upward and wrapped her arms around Kenzie as aftershocks pulsed through them both.

"Did you come again?" Kenzie asked.

"Yes. I'm sorry."

Kenzie took Zan's face between her hands. "No, don't be sorry."

"Do you feel as fulfilled as I do, Kenzie?" Zan asked.

Kenzie smiled. "I feel wonderful, Zan. That was amazing. Thank you."

Zan kissed her tenderly and then laid her head on Kenzie's shoulder. "I love you, Kenzie," she said softly.

"I love you, too, Zan."

Within minutes they were both fast asleep.

Chapter 20

Zan awoke in the wee hours of the morning. She was disoriented.

She felt a weight on her left shoulder and realized that Kenzie's head was resting there. Zan frowned and tried to remember how she came to be in Kenzie's bed. Her tense features were slowly replaced by a smile as she remembered the amazing lovemaking from a few hours earlier.

She glanced at the digital clock on Kenzie's bedside table. It was three in the morning. She needed to return to the room before Trey realized she was gone.

Zan very carefully moved Kenzie's head and gently placed it on the pillow. Kenzie rolled onto her back, but remained asleep.

She pushed herself into a seated position and swung her legs over the side of the bed. The movement caused an uncomfortable feeling in her abdomen as though she had done multiple crunch exercises. A slight spasm ran through her as she recalled the exact exercises from the night before. She smiled again and inhaled deeply to regain control.

She felt a hand on her back just as she was about to push off and stand.

"Zan? Where are you going?"

Zan lay back down and took Kenzie into her arms. "I need to go back to the room. Trey will be worried if she finds me gone in the morning."

"Stay with me. You can leave after sunrise and then tell her you and I met for an early morning walk."

"You are asking me to deceive Trey?"

"I am asking you to make love to me again."

Zan smiled and looked into Kenzie's eyes. She could see passion smoldering there. "How can I resist you?" she said.

"You can't."

***

Several hours later, Kenzie and Zan walked hand in hand down the street toward the motel. Kenzie was freshly showered and dressed in her work scrubs. Zan, on the other hand, had not brought a change of clothes from the day before, so she would shower when she reached the motel.

"What's on your agenda today?" Kenzie asked.

"We must report back today on the customs and social activities of the natives. Trey and I will be spending time visiting social centers. If you have any suggestions, we would much appreciate it."

"Social centers? Do you mean places where people gather?"

"Yes. Exactly."

"People gather for a lot of different reasons. If we were in a big city, I would recommend musical or sporting events, but in a place like Sedona, well, maybe the shopping centers and churches."

"There were many people gathered at the chapel on the trail when we first met."

"Yes, but they were tourists. Chances are, very few of them actually live in the Sedona area. I assume you want to observe local people."

"That is a good assumption."

"Okay, then I recommend shopping areas and churches to start with. You should be able to find a list of them in the telephone directory or in the local information directories in your motel room."

They continued to walk in silence until they reached the motel.

Zan turned to face Kenzie without releasing her hand. "Will I see you tonight?" she asked.

Kenzie looked at the chronogram on her watch. A smile came to her face. "It's Friday! That means we have two full days together coming up, but I have to admit that I did feel a little guilty about deceiving Trey, so we'll need to do something that includes her."

Zan glanced at their room on the second floor. "I agree, although she might get in the way of our intimacy."

Kenzie stepped closer and placed a tender kiss on Zan's lips. "I promise we will find time to make love." She glanced at her watch again. "I've got to get going or I'll be late. I'll stop on my way home and we'll make plans then."

Zan stole one more kiss before she released Kenzie and watched her walk away. She continued to watch her until she was out of sight and then turned to climb the stairs to the second level. She couldn't wait to tell Trey about how she felt.

Zan waved her entry card in front of the reader and pushed the door open. The first thing she noticed was that Trey was not in her bed.

"Trey?"

The door to the bathroom swung open.

"You coupled with her, didn't you?" Trey said.

"I, I,"

"Don't bother to answer, Zan. I can see it in your demeanor. I can see it on your face. And you smell different."

Zan crossed her arms. "Then take a good look, Tredoran, because *this* is what happiness looks like."

"So, you coupled with her."

"Yes, I did, and it was the most amazing experience of my life."

Trey sat on the bed. "So, what happens now, Zan? What happens to you, to us? What happens to our mission?"

Zan crossed the room and sat beside Trey. "Trey, nothing happens to us. I won't deny that I love Kenzie. And yes, before you say it, what I feel for Kenzie is not defined by anything you and I have ever been allowed to feel. I now know what love is. I now know that love comes in many forms. What I feel for you, and for my birth units, is love, but a type of love that is so different from what I feel for Kenzie. We have spent our entire lives closing our hearts and minds to this emotion. I can no longer live in such a sterile, emotionless environment. I *will* no longer do that."

"And our mission?"

"I am more determined than ever to succeed. I will die if we fail and have to leave this place."

Trey spent several long moments just looking at Zan. Finally, she spoke. "You look different."

"Different, how?"

"The lines on your forehead are gone. You look more relaxed. You are less stiff. You are more human. Tell me, Zan—what was it like?"

Zan stood and walked to the other side of the room. "I have no words to describe it, Trey. The experience was partly physical and partly emotional, and at any one time they overruled one another. It was intense and so fulfilling. I cried several times, and so did Kenzie. I never imagined two beings could connect on such a primal level. We were inside one another's hearts, minds and bodies."

"Do you plan to do it again?"

"I plan to spend the rest of my life making love to Kenzie."

Trey tilted her head to the side. "I wonder if procreation with our own kind will be as fulfilling."

Zan frowned but did not respond.

Trey's eyebrows rose on her forehead. "You *do* remember that it is each of our duties to procreate with our own kind. That is why we are here."

***

Kenzie went directly to the locker room to grab her lab coat when she arrived at work. She ran into Bree on the way to the break area. "Got time for a coffee before our staff meeting this morning?" Kenzie asked.

"Sure. I'll be right there," Bree said.

Kenzie stood with her back to the door while she waited for the second cup of coffee to brew. She glanced over her shoulder when Bree walked into the room. "Here's your coffee, Bree. My cup should be done in just a minute." She picked Bree's coffee up and handed it to her without looking directly at her.

"Thanks!" Bree stood close to Kenzie and rested her backside against the countertop to wait. She took a sip of her coffee and glanced sideways at Kenzie. "So, did Zan show up on the trail last night?"

Kenzie didn't look at her. She focused instead on watching the coffee brew, and fighting the battle to keep a grin off her face.

"Wait. What's that grin for? Kenzie look at me."

Kenzie glanced coyly at Bree from the corner of her eye and failed miserably to hide the grin.

Bree put her coffee on the countertop and took Kenzie by the shoulders. Kenzie tried to look away.

"No, you don't, girlfriend. Eyes here." Bree formed a V with two fingers, and pointed to her own eyes. "Your face is like a beacon in the dark."

"Huh?"

"There is such a glow about you that I think I'll need sunglasses just to work with you today."

"Get out!"

"I'm not kidding, Kenzie. You don't need to answer my question about Zan, it's written all over your face. And your neck."

"What?"

"Come with me."

Bree took Kenzie by the hand and dragged her back to the locker room. She opened her locker and pulled a silk scarf from the hook inside, which she arranged fashionably around Kenzie's neck. "That should hide it. Thank God it's Friday. It should be gone by Monday."

"What are you talking about?" Kenzie asked.

Bree pushed her in front of the mirror and pulled part of the scarf down. "Look."

Kenzie's eyes grew wide. "I've got a hickey! I've got a goddamned hickey!"

"And I'm sure it didn't get there by itself. So, was it good?"

Kenzie looked at her watch. "We've got a few more minutes before our meeting. Let me go get my coffee and we'll talk."

***

"So, she *was* a virgin!" Bree said.

"Oh, yeah. She was terrified, Bree. I almost stopped, but she insisted."

"So, how did it all happen?"

"I met both Zan and Trey on the trail. It turns out the issue with her community was nothing but a misunderstanding. Not only were they on the trail but I helped them to settle into the motel three blocks from my place. Zan walked me back to the apartment, and, well, she didn't leave until morning."

Bree studied Kenzie's face while she talked. Kenzie had always been expressive, but this morning, light literally radiated from her eyes as she spoke, and her face and hands were more animated than usual.

Bree continued to study Kenzie's face, even after the stopped talking.

"You're making me nervous here," Kenzie said. "What are you thinking?"

"You're in love with her, aren't you?"

Kenzie's eyes misted. She placed her hand on her chest. "I struggle to breathe when she touches me, Bree. She is all I can think about, day and night. I don't know what I'll do if her people decide to leave and she goes with them."

"You don't know that she will go with them, Kenzie."

"I don't know that she *won't* go, either. I'm scared, Bree."

Bree put her hand on the table, palm up. Kenzie's hand went willingly into it. "Let's not invite trouble, okay? I was worried that you'd invest your heart too soon. Maybe you should pull back a bit."

Kenzie shook her head and looked at their clasped hands. "It's too late for that, Bree. I am in so much trouble."

Bree grinned. "Well, let's hope it's good trouble."

"Charlie offered to take us on a tour of the vortex sites from the sky. I think I'll give him a call and see if he's free this weekend. That's something Zan and Trey might really enjoy."

"It's a beautiful tour. Jimmy and I have been up with him a few times. But, instead of calling him, why don't you join us for karaoke tonight at The Vortex. I suspect Charlie will be there as well."

"You want me to sing in front of Zan?"

"You have an amazing voice, K. You'll knock her socks off, not that you couldn't get her socks off any another way, along with every other piece of her clothing."

Kenzie retrieved her hand and pushed Bree's shoulder. "Shut up!"

Bree stood up walked away. "Kenzie and Zan, sitting in a tree, K-I-S-S-I-N-G!"

"Don't make me kick your ass, Bree!" Kenzie growled as she followed her out of the room.

***

Zan was waiting for Kenzie on the sidewalk at her motel. Kenzie walked directly into Zan's arms and wrapped her arms around her waist.

"Hmm. This feels so good. I missed you today," Kenzie said.

"And I missed you," Zan replied. "What are you wearing on your neck? I don't remember seeing it this morning."

Kenzie chuckled. "It's camouflage."

"What is camouflage?"

"Camouflage is a way of hiding something. It's a way of covering something up so no one can see what is beneath it."

She is describing my avatar, Zan thought. "So, what are you hiding beneath this camouflage?"

"Bree took one look at me and knew that we had been intimate last night, because of what is beneath this camouflage." Kenzie pulled the scarf away and showed her neck to Zan.

"What are those marks on your neck?"

"They are called hickeys, otherwise known as love bites. Someone I know and love was just a bit rambunctious last night."

"*I* did that to you? I am sorry."

Kenzie grabbed Zan's arm. "Well, I'm not. I loved every minute of it. It's just that next time, remind me to check my neck before I leave for work. Now, come on, I have a suggestion for tonight's activities for you and Trey to consider."

"What is karaoke?" Trey asked.

"It's singing. It's normally done in a bar. The words to the song are displayed on a screen and the music for the song is transmitted through speakers, and the person who chose the songs gets up in front of all the other bar patrons and sings."

"And you *enjoy* this activity?" Zan asked.

"Yes, I do. I have loved to sing since I was a young child. Oh, and this is a good opportunity for you to collect information about social gatherings. Bars are very popular places for people to congregate and socialize."

"If you enjoy this, then I am willing to go," Zan said.

"Trey?" Kenzie said.

"Will your friend Bree be there as well?" Trey asked.

"Yes, and her boyfriend, Jimmy. Oh, and Charlie will most likely be there as well."

"I will go!" Trey said quickly.

Kenzie grinned. "Awesome! So, I need to go home to get out of these work clothes and get a bite to eat before we head to the bar. I'll drive here in my car to pick you up in say, two hours?"

***

"I believe Kenzie is upset with me," Zan said.

Trey pulled two rations from her backpack and handed one to Zan. "Why do you say that?"

"Because she did not ask me to go with her to her home."

"She will only be gone for two hours. If she were upset with you, she would not come back."

Zan fell silent. "I am hoping you are right."

"I am nervous about going to this bar tonight, Zan."

"Because Charlie will be there?"

"Yes. Tell me, Zan, how did you get past your fear of being with Kenzie?"

"I did what we have been taught *not* to do, I listened to my heart instead of my head."

"Could the elders have been wrong, all this time?"

"I have come to believe that the elders are a group of misguided individuals who are afraid of modern progress. They have maintained control all these years by enforcing what I have come to feel are unreasonable rules and restrictions on all of us. However, after experiencing what I have with Kenzie, I can understand why they expect such sacrifice from us."

"Explain."

Zan sighed heavily. "I have been giving this a lot of thought, Trey, but if the elders choose not to settle here, I will not leave with them. I will choose to remain here with Kenzie."

"I thought as much, sister, but how does that justify the teachings of our people."

"Exactly what they fear is what is happening with me. I have questioned their authority. I have broken their rules, and I have learned what they have kept hidden from us our entire lives. I have learned that there is so much more to experience in life. I have learned that it is good to feel emotion, and it is good to feel alive. I have learned that we *can* be independent, and happy."

Trey nodded. "I will choose to stay as well, sister."

Chapter 21

"Are you ready, Trey? Kenzie will be here soon." Zan took one more look at herself in the mirror and smoothed an errant lock of hair.

"Just a few more moments. I am not used to this type of clothing. I believe I had the leg coverings on backward."

Three sharp raps drew Zan's attention to the door. "I believe Kenzie is here." Zan opened the door and stopped short.

Kenzie stepped into the room. She grinned at Zan's reaction. "Close your mouth, you're catching flies," she said.

"You…you are stunning." Zan was quite taken by the form-fitting, and very short, teal-colored dress Kenzie was wearing.

"You're not so bad yourself. You clean up well. This is the first time I've seen you in anything other than workout gear." Kenzie lecherously assessed how the slim fitting black slacks and sleeveless black shirt accented every curve of Zan's body. She stepped into Zan's personal space and whispered into her ear. "What do you say we send Trey to the bar alone and spend the rest of the night making love?"

"A temping thought," Zan said. "But I suspect she will not go without us."

"Hmm. I'm afraid you're right."

Just then, the door to the bathroom opened. "Kenzie, I am happy you are here," Trey said.

"Wow! You look really cute in that outfit," Kenzie said.

"Thank you, but I was hoping you would help me with facial enhancements."

Kenzie looked puzzled. "Do you mean, makeup? Ah, sure."

***

Kenzie looked around the room when they got to the bar and noticed Bree and Jimmy were already there. They had secured a large table in the corner. She looked over her shoulder at Zan and Trey. "Bree and Jimmy are there in the corner."

Zan held Trey back from directly following Kenzie across the room. "Do not forget that we are here to observe social interactions."

"Yes. I remember."

Zan and Trey once again followed Kenzie, who by this time had reached the table in the corner.

"Hey there, beautiful!"

Zan and Trey stopped and turned to see who was standing behind them.

"Charlie!" Trey exclaimed.

Charlie was carrying three bottles of beer. "Bree didn't tell me you'd be here tonight. I'm really glad I came now." Charlie looked her up and down. "You look amazing."

Trey blushed. "Thank you."

"You must be Zan. I remember seeing you on the trail. I'm glad you could join us tonight. I'd shake your hand, but they're kind of full at the moment."

Zan nodded.

"Come on. Let's join Bree and Jimmy and I'll get us a few more drinks."

When they reached the others, Charlie placed the three bottles of beer on the table. "What are you drinking?" she asked the newcomers.

"Beer is good," Kenzie said.

"I would like a beer, as well," Zan added.

"And you, pretty lady? What would you like to drink?" Charlie asked.

"Beer sounds good," Trey said.

"Great. I'll be back in a jiff."

"Where did you go?" Kenzie asked. "I turned around and you weren't behind me."

"We encountered Charlie," Zan said.

Kenzie slipped her arm into Zan's. "I want to introduce you and Trey to Jimmy."

"Jimmy, this is Zan Tafadon."

Zan extended her hand to Jimmy and firmly shook his. "It is nice to meet you, Jimmy," she said.

"You too, Zan. I've heard a lot about you. Bree tells me you're on a scouting mission to find a new home for your community."

"That is correct."

"Well, I hope you find that Sedona meets your needs. It appears our Kenzie here is quite infatuated with you," Jimmy said.

Zan looked at Kenzie and smiled. "The feeling is mutual."

Kenzie turned to Trey. "Trey?"

Trey had her back to the group and didn't hear Kenzie call to her.

Kenzie reached around Zan and touched Trey's arm. "Trey?"

"Oh! I am sorry, Kenzie. I was watching Charlie."

Kenzie chuckled. "Of course you were, but right now I want to introduce you to Jimmy. Don't worry, Charlie will be back with our beers in no time."

Kenzie pulled Trey to the table. "Jimmy, this is Trey Harlax."

"Wow! No wonder Charlie is so taken with you. You are beautiful," Jimmy blurted.

Trey blushed.

Bree elbowed Jimmy in the ribs. "Jimmy, you're embarrassing her!"

"Charlie is taken with me? What does that mean?" Trey asked.

"It means he really, really likes you," Bree explained.

"Speaking of the devil, here he comes," Kenzie said.

Charlie put the three new bottles of beer on the table. "Okay, kids, have a seat and enjoy your beer."

Kenzie, Zan and Trey sat on one side of the table, while Bree and Jimmy sat on the other. Charlie seated himself at the end of the table where he was closer to Trey.

Charlie took a swallow from his beer and placed it back on the table. "So, have you thought about the aerial tour I offered to take you on? I'm available this weekend if you're free."

"You've read my mind, Charlie. I was going to ask you about that tonight," Kenzie said.

"Aerial tour?" Zan asked.

Kenzie put her hand on Zan's. "I'm sorry, love. I forgot to tell you. Trey and I ran into Charlie earlier in the week and he offered to take the three of us on an aerial tour of the vortex sites by helicopter. Is that something you'd like to do?"

Zan looked at the anxious expectation on both Kenzie and Trey's faces. She could not bring herself to disappoint them. "If this is something you are interested in doing, then I am willing to do it as well."

"Awesome!" Charlie said. "Let's plan to do it tomorrow afternoon then. Maybe three o'clock? That will give us time for the tour and to catch the sunset."

"Great! Where should we meet you?" Kenzie asked.

"Meet me near the Airport Mesa Vortex. We'll take off from there."

Their conversation was interrupted by an announcement from the DJ.

"Ladies and gentlemen, it's time for karaoke! Here's how it works. Choose a song and then write it on the white board. They will be played in the order they are written."

"Go on, Kenzie. Put your name on the board," Bree encouraged.

"I don't want to go first, Bree," Kenzie said.

"I guess I can't blame you. If you go first, no one else will want to sing. You're a tough act to follow," Bree added.

"Stop. I'm not *that* good."

"I agree with Bree," Charlie said.

"Look there's two others up there right now adding songs to the board," Bree said. "You are no longer the first one. Now, get your butt up there."

"Okay, okay! Come help me pick out a song," Kenzie said to Bree.

"I'm going to make another beer run," Charlie said.

"I'll go with you. You're gonna need help carrying them back," Jimmy offered.

Zan narrowed her eyes as she watched Charlie and Jimmy walk away.

"There is something on your mind, Zangendar. I can see it in your face," Trey said.

"There is something not right about Charlie," Zan said.

"What do you mean?"

Zan looked at the worry etched on Trey's face. "I know you are attracted to Charlie, but something is not right."

"They are coming back," Trey said.

Jimmy and Charlie returned to the table and handed out the beer. Jimmy looked over his shoulder. "I see that Kenzie and Bree are still picking out songs to sing. I wonder if Kenzie will talk Bree into singing this time."

"Not on your life!" Charlie said.

Kenzie and Bree finally returned to the table.

"It took you long enough to choose a song, Kenzie," Jimmy said.

"I actually picked out a few," Kenzie replied. "There are two singers ahead of me."

"So, what song are you going to sing tonight, Bree?" Charlie asked.

"Shut the fuck up, Chuckles. There is no way in hell I am going to sing in front of people," Bree exclaimed.

"One of these days, you'll consume enough liquid courage to get up there and sing," Charlie said.

"Not happening!" Bree said.

Charlie sat down again beside Trey. "Do you sing, pretty lady?"

"I'm with Bree on this one," Trey replied.

"Do you dance?" he asked.

"I have never danced."

"Then maybe it's time you learn." Charlie stood and offered his hand to Trey. "Come with me."

"I wanna dance too. Jimmy, come dance with me." Bree jumped up and dragged her boyfriend to the dance floor.

Kenzie leaned into Zan and kissed her on the cheek.

Zan looked at her and smiled. "Thank you. That was pleasant."

Kenzie placed the next kiss directly onto Zan's lips. "Thank you for coming out tonight. I hope you enjoy it."

"This is very different from Vakillian gatherings."

"In what ways?"

"It is dark in here, and noisy. The Vakillians also do not dance. What is this ritual?"

Kenzie tilted her head and contemplated the woman before her. In comparison to Trey—who was on the dance floor and who was clearly enjoying the dance lesson Charlie was giving her—Zan sat sullen and quiet.

"Dancing is a way of releasing your spirit to the world. It can be a lot of fun if you let yourself enjoy it."

"Explain."

"The trick is to not just *listen* to the music, but to allow yourself to *feel* it to the very depths of your soul. Once you let the music consume you, your body will know what to do."

"So, you put yourself in a trance-like state?"

Kenzie grinned. "Something like that."

"It sounds dangerous. Does that not leave you vulnerable to others?"

Kenzie sat up straight. "Zan, you really need to relax. Look at Trey. She's out there having a good time. Why do you have to be on guard all the time? Life is about enjoying your time with those you love."

"Relax?"

"Yes. Chill out. Let yourself have fun. Does it make you more vulnerable? Yes, but you need to trust the ones around you."

Zan looked around the room. "But I do not know these people."

Kenzie turned Zan's face toward hers. "No, you don't. But you know us, me, Bree, Jimmy and Charlie. Do you really think we'd let anyone harm you if we could stop it? You need to trust, Zan, or life here will never be enjoyable for you."

Just then, the song ended, and the others returned to the table. Trey sat down next to Zan and picked up her beer. She took a long drink and then smiled at Zan. "Dancing is fun," she said. "I am not very good at it, but it was fun."

"You did awesome," Charlie said. "There were others on the dance floor with less rhythm than you. Let me know if you want to go again. I love to dance."

"Trey, Kenzie tells me you need to *feel* the music. Did you experience this feeling?" Zan asked.

"I did. It felt like lightness in my chest and my body just moved on its own. It was pleasant and it made me less afraid to try."

"Maybe I will try this dancing." Zan said.

"Let's give a hand to Melissa for having the courage to sing our first song tonight," the DJ announced.

The bar filled with the sound of clapping, as well as a few whoops and hollers.

"Why are they doing that?" Zan asked.

"It's a way to show appreciation."

"Interesting."

"Next up is Kevin, singing *Lady*, in the style of Kenny Rogers," the DJ announced.

"No time like the present," Kenzie said. She offered her hand to Zan, who nervously took it. "Don't be afraid, this is a slow song, and it's perfect for your first dance. When the music starts, I want you to open yourself to how it makes you feel."

The dance floor filled almost immediately with couples, including Charlie and Trey, as well as Bree and Jimmy.

"This appears to be a popular song," Zan said.

"It is a romantic song. When the music starts, I want you to really listen to the words, and allow your mind to feel what they mean to you."

"I will try."

Kenzie led Zan to the middle of the dance floor and stepped in close. "Put your hands on my hips and I will put my arms around your neck. When the music starts, we will sway back and forth. Let me lead and I think you'll get it after a few seconds."

Zan nodded as the music began. Her eyes widened as she listened to the words. Her hands instinctively moved from Kenzie's waist to her back as she pulled her in closer and fell into the swaying rhythm Kenzie had established.

"This song speaks of love," Zan whispered.

"Yes, it does. The words in this song express exactly how I feel about you, Zan. You are my knight in shiny armor. You have rescued me from a life of loneliness," Kenzie replied.

Zan felt a swelling in her chest that moved slowly upward into her mind. When Kenzie laid her head on her chest, just above her breasts, Zan felt her heart would burst. She laid her cheek on the top of Kenzie's head and closed her eyes.

"I did not realize how empty my life was before I met you, Kenzie. Like the song says, you have made me whole."

"You are the only thing I need in my life, Zan. You *are* the love of my life."

By the time the song finished, there were tears in both their eyes.

Kenzie pulled out of Zan's grasp and looked into her eyes. "That was beautiful, Zan. Did you feel it?"

"I did. Thank you for sharing this experience. I believe I like this dancing thing."

"A round of applause for Kevin! Next up—Kenzie!" the DJ announced.

"My turn!" Kenzie said. "I hope I don't make a fool of myself."

Zan turned to head back to the table but felt an arm slip through hers. It was Bree.

"You are in for a treat," Bree said. "Your girl has an amazing voice."

The group of friends settled back into their seats as the DJ queued up Kenzie's song.

Zan leaned toward Bree. "She appears nervous."

"She always looks nervous, at least until the song starts. Then she knocks it out of the park."

Zan read the title of the song on the monitor. "*At Last*, in the style of Etta James. Is this a popular song?"

"Wait until you see the audience's reaction. That will tell you how popular it is," Bree replied.

Zan felt like she had been punched in the gut as soon as the song began. Kenzie's voice was pure and pitch perfect and Zan felt like she was singing this song only for her.

Zan couldn't look away from the stage. Kenzie's voice was powerful. Powerful enough to cause Zan's heart to flip in her chest several times throughout the song. She looked around the room and noticed a sense of appreciation on the faces of the patrons and she felt a sense of pride that this beautiful human was hers.

Kenzie finished the song while looking directly into Zan's eyes.

Bree glanced at Zan as Kenzie finished her song and noted there were tears freely running down her face. She reached out and placed her hand on Zan's. She was pleased when Zan's fingers enclosed around hers.

"That was for you, Zan. She truly loves you with all her heart," Bree said.

Zan met her gaze. "And I love her with all my heart in return."

The entire bar erupted in applause, louder than any so far that evening. Zan's heart swelled with almost overwhelming emotion as Kenzie graciously left the stage and walked toward their table. Zan quickly rose to her feet and met Kenzie halfway. She took her into her arms and kissed her soundly, right on the dance floor. "That was beautiful," Zan whispered.

"Well, I guess we all know who Kenzie sang *that* song for!" The DJ said. "Let's get another round of applause for Kenzie!"

Once again, the room erupted in applause, and several patrons personally complimented her as they made their way back to the table.

No sooner had they sat down when the next song began, *Let's Get It On*, by Marvin Gaye.

Kenzie sprang back to her feet. "Oh, my God! I love this song! Come dance with me, Zan."

"Me too!" Charlie said. "Are you up for it, Trey?"

Kenzie looked at her friends. "Bree? Jimmy?"

"No, I think we'll sit this one out. But go on. Boogie away," Bree said.

***

Bree and Jimmy sat close together at their table and watched the others dance to the slow and sensual song.

"Wow! You can almost see the sparks coming off them," Bree said. "I've never seen Kenzie glow like she does when she's around Zan, and the look in her eyes when she talks to me about her at work. Well, let's just say she is totally smitten. I'm just little concerned that she's jumping in too quickly."

"Kinda like when we first met. Wouldn't you say?" Jimmy asked. "I know I was all in after our first date."

Bree looked at Jimmy and kissed him tenderly. "Me too." She looked back to their friends on the dance floor. "I only hope it works out for them as well as it's worked out for us."

***

Kenzie looked at Zan as they swayed. "Are you listening to the words?"

"Yes, but what does let's get it on mean?"

Kenzie chuckled. "It means, let's make love."

Zan's eyebrows shot high onto her forehead. "Do all of your songs speak of love?"

"Not all of them. Some of them are just fun and perky, but my favorites by far are the love songs. If you'd like, I'll create a playlist in my phone with just that type of song that we can listen to while we make love."

Zan lowered her forehead to Kenzie's. "You are making me want you, right here on the dance floor."

Kenzie smiled. "Those very thoughts have been going through my mind since you answered the door in your motel room. Maybe you can stay with me tonight?"

Zan lowered her lips to Kenzie's and kissed her long and passionately.

***

"Damn! I can feel their passion even from here," Bree said.

Jimmy turned Bree's face to look into her eyes. "It reminds me of how much I love you, even if I don't say it often enough."

"I love you too, sweetheart."

Bree and Jimmy continued to watch their friends as they danced.

"It looks like Charlie has fallen for Trey," Jimmy said. "They're practically having sex on the dance floor. I just hope she doesn't break his heart when she finds out."

"I know. I've been worried about that too. In the beginning, I was hoping Kenzie would hook up with him, but she was adamant that she didn't feel sexually attracted to guys. But I have to say that Trey seems sweet, and she certainly is beautiful. Like you, I hope she doesn't break Charlie's heart."

They watched as Zan kissed Kenzie passionately on the dance floor.

"What do you think of Zan?" Bree asked.

"She's attractive, in a butch, bad-boy kind of way. But then, Kenzie is very feminine, so I guess they complement one another."

"If she breaks Kenzie's heart, she will have to deal with me."

"There you go again, Bree. You're such a mother hen when it comes to Kenzie," Jimmy said.

"I can't help it, Jimmy. She grew up not knowing her own worth. She's beautiful, smart, and so loving, despite the repression she lived under. She deserves so much more than what Jessie gave her. I just hope Zan doesn't end up hurting her too."

***

Two hours into the evening, the DJ took a break and the group retreated to their table.

"Who's ready for another beer?" Kenzie asked. "I, for one, am parched from all that dancing and singing."

"Let me get it this time," Zan said.

Trey stood. "I will go with you."

Zan grabbed an empty bottle from the table and took it with her to the bar, where she used it to order six more of the same brand. They stood aside while they waited to allow other patrons to have access to the bar.

"It is clear to me from watching you on the dance floor that you have feelings for Charlie," Zan said.

Trey couldn't keep the smile from her face. "I admit that I do. He makes me feel lightheaded and hot in my abdomen."

"I know the feeling. Could it be that you are falling in love with Charlie?"

"I don't know what love feels like, Zan. But if this is it, then it is something I always want to feel for him."

Zan looked at their friends at the table and frowned. "I still feel that something is not quite right with Charlie." She pulled her omni-spectrometer from her pocket and pointed it at him.

"What are you doing, Zan?" Trey demanded. Alarm tinged the edges of her voice.

"I am collecting biometric data on Charlie."

"Is that necessary?"

"We need to know that you are safe, Tredoran." Zan looked at the biometric data displayed on the screen and had to struggle to keep a shocked expression from her face.

"What is it?" Trey demanded.

Zan simply handed the device to Trey.

Trey scanned the data displayed on the screen. Her head snapped up and she turned sharply to Zan. "Are you sure?"

"The data is all there. I am sure," Zan replied.

Trey looked at Charlie and then back at the device. *Did* it matter? She looked again at Charlie and examined how she felt. Her heart still pounded in her chest. She still found it difficult to think. The thought of coupling with Charlie still caused spasms to rip through her abdomen.

Trey handed the omni-spectrometer back to Zan. "It does not matter."

"But he is pretending to be something he is not."

Trey looked directly into Zan's eyes. "And so are we."

Chapter 22

At the end of the evening, the friends lingered outside the bar to say their goodbyes. Zan observed that Trey and Charlie walked several feet away from the rest of the group. She watched as Charlie kissed Trey several times before they separated and rejoined the rest of them.

After wishing the others a good evening, Zan and Trey waited by Kenzie's car as she said her goodbyes to Bree and Jimmy.

"Are you planning to stay with Kenzie tonight?" Trey asked.

"We need to talk about that, Trey. I would like to spend *every* night with Kenzie, but I do not want to leave you alone."

"As Kenzie is fond of saying, you are a grown woman. If you wish to spend the nights with Kenzie, you should not allow me to stop you."

"Are you sure about that, Trey?"

Trey looked toward their group of friends, and then back at Zan. "I asked Charlie to come to the motel tonight."

Zan raised her eyebrows. "I am not sure that is a good idea. I am concerned for your safety, Trey."

"I will be safe. Do you not remember that we brought weapons with us? I will not allow Charlie to do anything that I don't want him to do. I promise."

"Trey,"

"No, Zan. Why should you be the only one to experience what making love feels like?"

Zan took a deep breath and then exhaled. She put her hand on Trey's shoulder and touched her forehead to hers. "I understand. Promise me you will protect yourself if you need to."

"I promise."

"Hey, are you two all right?"

Zan broke contact with her friend. "We are fine."

Kenzie opened the door to her car. "Okay, then. Let's head back to the motel."

"I will get a change of clothes and go to your house tonight," Zan said.

"Really?"

"Yes. Trey and I have discussed it."

Kenzie looked at Trey. "Will you be all right alone at the motel?"

Trey blushed.

Kenzie's eyes opened wide. "Oh! I see! Well then, let's get you home and get us out of your hair as quickly as possible!"

***

"Ugh! I stink!" Kenzie exclaimed

"What did you say?" Zan asked.

"I said I stink. As much as I love to dance, I always work up a lather and then stink to high heavens afterwards! I need a bath."

"Would a shower not be quicker?"

"Yes, but then I wouldn't be able to make love to you in a nice warm bubble bath."

Zan walked up to Kenzie and grasped her face between her palms. "I see now that you have ulterior motives." She lowered her lips to Kenzie's and kissed her soundly. That simple kiss led to intensive groping.

Kenzie stepped out of Zan's grasp. "Wait. Let me get the tub running first."

Zan followed Kenzie into the bathroom and while the tub was filling, they resumed their previous groping, and unclothing session. By the time the tub was filled with billowy clouds of bubbles, they were both naked and worked up into their second lather of the night.

Zan stepped into the tub first and gingerly lowered herself into the hot water. Once she was settled at the far end of the tub, Kenzie joined her and sat between Zan's legs, with her back resting against Zan's chest and her head on her shoulder.

"Ah, this feels so good," Kenzie said. "There's nothing like a nice warm soak."

Zan kissed the side of Kenzie's head. "This really does feel amazing."

"Did you have fun tonight, Zan?"

"It was very enjoyable. Your voice is mathematically pleasing, Kenzie. I felt pride when the other patrons showed their appreciation."

"First time ever that I've been good at math!" Kenzie laughed.

"I am being sincere. It was very pleasing."

"You did pretty well with the dancing, too. It isn't as hard as it looks."

"Your advice to let myself feel the music was helpful. I enjoyed the dancing—especially the slow and close dancing."

Kenzie shifted so that she was on her knees between Zan's legs, facing her. "The slow dancing made me so hot. I wanted to rip your clothes off and take you right there on the dance floor."

"My feelings exactly."

"Wait a minute!" Kenzie rose higher on her knees and wiped her hands on the towel beside the tub, and then she reached as far as she could for her cellphone that was on the sink vanity, just opposite the bathtub. She sat back on her heels and searched through her phone until she found what she was looking for. Then she slipped her phone back onto the vanity. Within seconds, slow, romantic music sounded. She sat back on her heels once more and then leaned forward to place a searing kiss on Zan's lips.

Zan's hands darted out of the water and she grasped Kenzie's head to deepen the kiss. Kenzie moaned and opened her mouth to allow Zan's tongue access. She heard a low growl come from deep within Zan's chest and her own passion increased exponentially.

Kenzie found herself suddenly flipped as Zan assumed the position above her. She vaguely acknowledged a considerable amount of water splashing out of the tub and onto the floor, but she was in such a state of arousal, that she paid it little heed.

Zan moved from Kenzie's mouth, to her neck, and then to her breast where she vigorously inhaled Kenzie's erect nipples into her mouth, one at a time. Zan sucked so hard that it was almost uncomfortable, but the overall effect nearly pushed Kenzie to climax. She knew that if she didn't take control, it would be finished for her long before she could bring Zan to climax.

Kenzie pushed at Zan's shoulders until she finally got the message to stop. She pushed herself up into a seated position with her back against the far side of the tub. "My turn," she said. "Come here."

Zan scurried to her knees and straddled Kenzie's legs, putting her breasts exactly within reach of Kenzie's mouth.

Zan held onto the sides of the tub for support while Kenzie drove her mad sucking and nibbling her nipples. She felt a heat so strong in her abdomen that she thought she might explode, and she had no control over the loud moans emitting from her throat.

"Kenzie. I can't hold it back. Help me, please!"

Kenzie reached her right hand under Zan and her left hand between her own legs. She pumped into Zan as hard and fast as she could with Zan sitting above her. Zan finally matched her upward thrusts with her own downward ones. Moans and cries of *more* rang out loudly in the small bathroom.

Kenzie felt Zan pause in mid-air. Zan's body had tightened so much around Kenzie's hand that she could barely move it, and Kenzie knew it would be only a matter of seconds before Zan came crashing over the cliff.

"Kenzie!" Zan cried.

Kenzie no longer fought to hold her climax back as she delved into her own core and released them both to plummet into the warm depths of one another's love.

For several long moments, waves of passion passed through both of them, until, finally exhausted and spent, Zan collapsed limply against Kenzie's shoulder.

"I've got you, love. I've got you, Kenzie whispered.

They remained in this position for at least another ten minutes while their breathing and respiration returned to normal.

And then it happened. One last, intense spasm wracked Zan's body and she suddenly sat back and grasped the sides of the tub. She looked down at Kenzie. Her eyes were wide with surprise. The spasm continued for several moments.

Kenzie became concerned that Zan was having a seizure. "Are you all right, love?"

The spasm slowly subsided and Zan collapsed again against Kenzie's shoulder.

Kenzie wrapped her arms around Zan and held her while the final tremors left her body. "Are you okay?"

Zan slowly sat back on her heels. "Yes. That last wave was unexpected. And it was different than the rest."

"Are you sure you're okay?"

"I am fine." Zan leaned down again and placed a tender kiss on Kenzie's lips. "The water is becoming cool. I recommend we shower and then retire to the bed."

***

Charlie and Trey lay entwined on Trey's bed, both fully clothed.

"You are so beautiful, Trey. I can't tell you that enough."

"Hmm." Trey moaned and turned her head to the side to allow Charlie easier access to her neck. "This feels so good."

"If you let me, I can make you feel even better," Charlie said.

Trey opened her eyes and looked at him. "Better than this?"

Charlie scurried off the bed. "Wait! You've never done this before, have you?"

Tray shook her head.

"Jesus!" Charlie ran a hand through his hair. "I...I'm maybe not the one you want to do this with for the first time."

Trey pushed herself into a seated position with her legs over the side of the bed. Charlie was within her reach. She grabbed his waistband and pulled him toward her, and then looked up into his face. "But I do want to do this with you. You make me feel things I have never felt before."

Charlie put his palms on Trey's shoulders. "Look, Trey. If I didn't care about you, we'd both be naked and writhing on the bed right now, but the fact is, you also make me feel things I've never felt before, and I don't want to ruin the possibility of a real relationship between us by starting things out this way."

"In what way?"

"There are things you don't know about me, Trey. One thing in particular that may be a deal breaker for you."

"Stop. I already know, and I do not care," Trey said.

"What do you mean, you already know? Did Bree or Jimmy tell you?"

Trey shook her head. "They did not tell me. I just know." Trey unhooked Charlie's belt and the top button on his jeans and then pulled down the zipper. She slipped her hands inside his briefs and pushed both the jeans and the briefs off his hips and down his legs. She looked down and saw the prosthetic lying inside his briefs on the floor. Slowly, her eyes drifted upward, taking in every detail of his body until their eyes met.

"You are perfect. Now, make love to me."

***

Kenzie pulled her car into the parking lot at the motel at noon the next day. She and Zan had awakened around eight o'clock that morning and for the second time within twenty-four hours, they made love, and then promptly fell back to sleep, wrapped in one another's arms. It was nearly noon before they were up and about, showered, and ready to start their day.

They climbed the stairs to the second level and stopped in front of room two-eleven. Zan pushed the door open and they stepped inside.

The room was a mess. Clothing was strewn from one end of the room to the other as well as random shoes and boots.

Kenzie looked at Zan. "Ah, maybe we should leave."

Just then, the bathroom door opened, and Trey came out, naked as a jaybird, with Charlie right behind her. Charlie immediately covered his privates with his hands.

"Zan!" Trey exclaimed. "I...I didn't expect you back so soon."

"It would appear so," Zan said.

Kenzie covered her mouth to hide her grin as Trey and Charlie went back into the bathroom and re-emerged with towels covering themselves.

"Sorry about that, guys," Kenzie said. "We just thought you'd want to get some lunch. We didn't expect Charlie to still be here."

Charlie put his arm around Trey's shoulder. "To be honest, I didn't expect to still be here either, but Trey's put a spell on me and now I have agreed to be her sex slave for the rest of my life."

Kenzie examined Charlie with a nurse's eye, the six-pack abs, muscular arms and shoulders, slim waist, and two other things that looked out of place.

Charlie squirmed under the scrutiny and crossed his arms to protectively cover his chest.

"When did you transition, Charlie?" Kenzie asked.

"What?" Charlie exclaimed.

"Please lower your arms. Now, I'll ask it again. "When did you transition?"

Charlie lowered his arms, revealing four-inch scars about three inches below each nipple. "You mean these? These are from an injury when I was in the sandbox."

"Are you forgetting that I'm a nurse, Charlie?"

Charlie put his hands on his hips. "Shit. I was hoping you'd never find out."

Kenzie chuckled. "Well, if Bree had had her way, I would have found out sooner or later. She tried to hook us up."

"What?" Charlie said.

"Yes. When I told her that I thought you were a really great guy, but that I wasn't attracted to men, she told me that you were not a typical guy. I didn't get it at the time, but now I see what she meant."

"So, what now?" he asked.

Kenzie picked up his pants from the floor and threw them at him. "Now you both need to get your asses dressed so we can get some lunch. I'm starving! Zan and I will wait outside."

***

Charlie pulled his Jeep Gladiator into the employee parking lot of the Airport Mesa Vortex facility. He and his three guests climbed out.

"Follow me." Charlie opened a door to a large building and invited them into a room that held communication gear. He selected several sets of headphones and passed them out to each of them.

"What are these for?" Zan asked.

"They are Bluetooth headphones. They will allow us to communicate with one another while we're in the helicopter. It's a bit noisy and this will help to cancel some of it out," Charlie replied.

Charlie then led them into a large hangar where several small airplanes were in storage.

"Wow! This is awesome!" Kenzie said.

"What are these called?" Trey asked.

"They're airplanes, of course. What are they called where you come from?" Charlie asked.

"I don't recall seeing machines like this," Trey replied.

"You've never seen an airplane?" Charlie was shocked.

"No."

"Okay. This promises to be quite an experience for you then. The helicopter we're taking today is right outside this building. Follow me."

The group exited the hangar and walked into a large fenced-in area.

"Here we are. This is the one I fly most often." Charlie opened a large sliding door on the side of the helicopter. "Climb in."

Kenzie was the first one in. She turned to lend a hand to Zan and Trey and was surprised to see them both still on the tarmac. "Are you coming?" she asked.

"What is this machine? It does not look safe," Zan said.

Charlie put his hand on Zan's shoulder. "This machine is safer than the airplanes we saw in the hangar, and it's much more maneuverable. I've used it every day for the past three years to take people on aerial tours of the vortex sites. I haven't lost anyone yet."

Kenzie reached her hand out again. "Come on, Zan. It'll be fun. Do you think I would go if it wasn't safe?"

Zan looked at Trey and then at Kenzie. "I suppose not."

"Come on, then. I want to have enough time for the tour and the sunset."

Zan grabbed Kenzie's hand and allowed her to help her into the chopper, followed by Trey.

Charlie was already in the pilot's seat. "Just slide that door closed and latch it, and we'll be ready to go. Trey, why don't you come sit up front with me?"

As soon as the door was closed, Charlie initiated the rotors and waited for them to be at full rotational speed. The faster they spun, the louder the hum became. Charlie put his headphones on and motioned for everyone else to do the same. "Can everyone hear me?"

After their affirmative responses, he increased the lift on the rotors and the helicopter gently lifted off the ground. Soon, the helicopter was moving forward and soaring above the treetops.

"How are you two doing back there?" Charlie asked.

"This is amazing," Kenzie said.

"Zan? How about you?"

"I can think of better places to be right now," Zan replied.

Kenzie reached for Zan's hand. "Relax and enjoy this, sweetheart. Have I steered you wrong yet?"

Zan squeezed Kenzie's hand. "No, you have not."

"Okay then, look out your window. It's an awesome view."

"How about you, Trey? Are you doing okay?" Charlie asked.

Trey was studying the gauges and controls on the dashboard. "I am fascinated by how this technology applies the principles of torque and lift to allow bidirectional flight."

"Are you telling me that you understand the fundamentals of aerodynamics?" Charlie asked.

"Yes, indeed. I have created many algorithms that optimize the torque/lift sequence."

"But how can that be if you didn't even know what an airplane was?"

"The work I did was for much larger, space vehicles."

"You worked on the space program? Wow! Charlie looked at Kenzie in his mirror. "Did you know about this, Kenzie?"

"I knew they were smart. Zan here is an environmental engineer."

He looked at Trey again. "Wow! If you need a job, let me know and I'll hook you up with the company that makes these birds."

***

Charlie spent the next two hours traversing all the popular helicopter tour sites. The maneuverability of the helicopter allowed them to fly close to several of the famous landmarks, as well as learn about some of the history of Sedona, including a flyover of the Anasazi cliff dwellings.

Near the end of the flight, Charlie flew the helicopter in the direction of the Chapel of the Holy Cross. When they arrived, he hovered the machine above the church, close enough to afford his guests a front row view, but high enough not to endanger the tourists they could see outside the structure.

"I wanted to end the tour here because of the amazing sunset. And here it comes, above the horizon," Charlie said.

"I've been inside the church when the sun sets," Kenzie said. "Beams of orange light shine straight through those windows in the front, all the way to the back of the chapel. It's a very spiritual experience."

"I remember," Zan added.

Kenzie looked at her. "You've been there at sunset?"

"Yes, with you."

"I have never been there with you at sunset, Zan. In fact, I've never been *inside* the chapel with you."

A momentary look of panic crossed Zan's face. "I...I must be mistaken."

Chapter 23

They landed at the Airport Mesa Vortex just before dark. Charlie invited them to dinner, but Zan and Kenzie declined in favor of a quiet dinner at home. Trey, on the other hand, accepted.

Charlie pulled up in front of Kenzie's apartment and all four of them climbed out of the car. Trey took Zan aside.

"Will you be home tonight, Zan?" Trey asked.

"I do not know at this time. I will ask Kenzie to call the room and leave a message if I will not be home. Will *you* be home tonight?" Zan asked.

Trey laughed. "Same answer."

"We will need to report to the community tomorrow. So, we both need to plan to be at the motel in the morning," Zan said.

"I agree. In the morning then," Trey replied.

While Kenzie hugged Charlie, she saw Trey climb back into the passenger seat of the Jeep. "Do me a favor and treat her with kid gloves. She's kind of an innocent."

"I would never do anything to hurt her, Kenzie. I promise."

"Good. Thank you for the tour, my friend. It was amazing. I really enjoyed it." She started to walk away, but then returned and lightly punched him in the shoulder.

"Hey! What was that for?" he complained.

"That was for not trusting me."

"Okay, okay. I guess I deserved that. I owe you an apology," Charlie said.

"Apology accepted." Kenzie kissed him on the cheek. "I'll see you later."

While Kenzie said her goodbyes, Zan waited for her at the bottom of the stairs, and together they went into the apartment. Zan dropped the backpack she had brought with them, on the floor beside the door. Kenzie went into the kitchen and opened the refrigerator.

"Are you hungry?" Kenzie said over her shoulder.

"Not especially," Zan replied.

Kenzie continued to stand in front of the open refrigerator.

"Are you all right, Kenzie?" Zan asked. "You were very quiet on the way home from the airport."

Kenzie closed the door and turned around to face Zan. She crossed her arms. "I'm concerned about something you said in the helicopter."

Zan clasped her hands behind her. "You are referring to my comments about the sunbeams inside the chapel."

"Yes. Do you care to explain?"

"I deceived you."

Kenzie walked up to Zan. "Why?"

"I did not want to alarm you with my presence in the chapel."

"So, you were there?"

"Yes."

"When?"

"On the day the caretaker asked you to leave so she could close the church."

"Where were you? I don't remember seeing you."

"I was sitting on the bench behind you."

"There was no one on the bench behind me, Zan. I was alone in the chapel."

"I was there. You were consumed with your meditation. You were not aware of me."

Kenzie walked a few feet away. She turned to face Zan once more. "When Bree and I met you and Trey outside the chapel, I felt like I had known you from somewhere. You felt familiar to me. Had you seen me on the trails before that day?"

"Yes. I had seen you several times."

"Then why didn't I see you?"

"I kept myself hidden."

"Why?"

"I cannot say."

Kenzie charged Zan and pushed her backward with both hands. "How dare you? Why are you here, Zan? Is it really to seek out a new settlement, or am I being played for a fool?"

Zan walked to the door and picked up her bag. "You are not a fool, Kenzie. That would be me. I had convinced myself that I might be able to fit in here. I was wrong." She reached for the door handle and paused with her back to Kenzie. "I never meant to hurt you, Kenzie. I would rather die first. I am sorry."

Kenzie charged across the room, grabbed Zan's arm and swung her around. "Don't think for one minute that I will allow you to walk away from me. I trusted you, Zan. I trusted that you would not be like Jessie. I trusted you."

Zan looked at the floor. "I am not Jessie."

"Jessie deceived me, too."

Zan looked directly at Kenzie. "I am not Jessie!" she said angrily.

"Why did you lie to me?"

"It was necessary."

"Why?"

"I couldn't risk you seeing me."

Kenzie pushed on her shoulder again. "Why?" she shouted.

"Because I would have repulsed you!" Zan yelled.

"What? Why on earth would you repulse me? Zan, I have never met anyone in my entire life that makes me feel the way you do. I love the way you look. I love the way you make me feel."

Zan dropped her bag on the floor and leaned her back against the door. She rubbed her face with her hands. "I haven't always looked like this," she said.

"And *I* haven't always looked like *this*!" Kenzie replied. "You wouldn't have recognized me three years ago."

"Kenzie, it is not the same."

"The point I'm trying to make, Zan, is that we can't base our relationship on lies. I won't tolerate it. I put up with too many lies from Jessie. I won't do that again."

"I am sorry, Kenzie."

Kenzie stepped forward and touched the side of Zan's face. "I love you, Zan. I love you more than I have ever loved anyone. You need to be honest with me. We need to be honest with one another."

Zan lowered her forehead to Kenzie's. "There is so much I need to tell you, and I promise I will tell you everything I can as soon as I can."

"Tell me now."

"I cannot. Please understand. I will tell you soon."

"I want to trust you, Zan. I *need* to trust you. Please give me some assurance you won't lie to me again."

"On my life, I vow."

***

Kenzie sat in the corner of her bedroom, in a chair by the reading lamp. The room was illuminated only by the moonlight shining through the window. She glanced at the clock on her bedside table across the room. It was nearly one in the morning and she was wide awake, while Zan slept peacefully in her bed.

They did not make love that night. The anger and hurt she felt at Zan's deception rested like a barrier between the two of them. Her anger had dissipated several hours ago, but still, the hurt lingered.

What did she really know about Zan? For all she knew, Zan was an axe murderer just waiting for the opportune moment to strike. But then, wasn't Zan taking that same chance with her?

What was up with this community she spoke of so often? Why did they seem to have so much power over her? What would happen if they chose not to settle in Sedona?

For the hundredth time, Kenzie thought again about what Zan had said during their argument, *I would have repulsed you!* Why on earth would Zan think she could ever be repulsed by her? She was gorgeous and amazingly sexy. Her slim build, butch attitude, boy-cut dark hair, amazing green eyes, full lips, and that cleft in her chin. Hell, Kenzie got all hot and bothered simply by thinking about her!

What she *did* know is that the attraction between them was more intense than anything she had ever known. What *she* did know is that Zan filled that empty space in her heart that had felt like a gaping chasm for most of her adult life. What she *did* know is that she didn't want to live without her, even if she did turn out to be an axe murderer.

Kenzie made the conscious decision to push her hurt into the far recesses of her heart. Zan was right—she wasn't Jessie, and it wasn't fair for her to hold Zan accountable for Jessie's transgressions.

Zan was unable to sleep. She knew instinctively that Kenzie was not in bed beside her. She had felt her leave their warm nest more than an hour ago. She thought back to their argument earlier in the evening. Kenzie was right. She had no right to deceive her. She knew when she probed Kenzie's mind that she was violating her, but she couldn't help herself. She was unable to resist the power Kenzie had, even from very first time she found her meditating on the trail.

Zan was terrified that Kenzie would never really forgive her. That she would store the memory of her deception in the back of her mind, where it would always be ready and willing to come forth again to remind Kenzie of her untrustworthiness. She knew Kenzie was still angry with her. She chose not to be intimate with her that night. Zan was full of self-loathing for betraying Kenzie's trust. She had to find a way to fix it. She knew she would die should Kenzie choose to end their relationship.

Kenzie felt a stirring deep with the pit of her being as she watched Zan sleep. In so many ways, she was an innocent. Kenzie suddenly regretted being so hard on her earlier. Maybe she didn't know any better. Maybe she really *was* afraid of how Kenzie would perceive her. She felt a sudden need to be near her.

Slowly, Kenzie rose from the chair and tiptoed to the bed. She removed her nightshirt and panties and crawled in between the covers. Zan's back was to her, so she carefully spooned her naked form against her and slipped her arm around Zan's waist.

She kissed the back of Zan's neck. "I love you, Zan," she whispered. "Sweet dreams."

Kenzie forced herself to relax and soon, fell asleep.

Zan tensed when she felt Kenzie come back to bed. She feared that Kenzie would seek another confrontation, but when she felt Kenzie mold her body around hers, and then whisper her love to her, Zan had all she could do not to cry. Instead, she forced herself to relax and to enjoy the feel of Kenzie's love.

"Sweet dreams to you as well, Kenzie. I love you, too," she whispered into the dark.

***

Kenzie handed a cup of coffee to Zan. "Where are you meeting with the council, this morning?" she asked.

"Thank you." Zan sipped the coffee. "This is very good. We are meeting on the trail."

"Little Horse Trail?"

"Yes."

"That's an odd place to meet."

"It is what they are familiar with. The area feels safe to us. And besides, I wanted to show them the chapel."

"When will you be finished with your meeting?"

"I believe the meeting will require no more than three hours."

"How did you and Trey plan to get to the trail? I could drop you off at the trailhead if you'd like."

Zan tilted her head and smiled at Kenzie. "You are kind. That is one of the things I love about you."

Kenzie stood on tiptoe and kissed her. "Thank you, love." Kenzie went back to stirring the scrambled eggs. "So, what do you plan to tell them?"

The toast popped up before Zan could answer. "I will apply butter to them for you," she said. Zan glanced at her while she carried out her task. "Trey and I agree that Sedona has a lot to offer our people. The resources are plentiful and from our experience, the local natives are very accepting and kind. We learned on our tour yesterday that the area is rich in history as well. I think we could fit in here."

Zan handed the slices of buttered toast to Kenzie who put them on two plates filled with sausage and scrambled eggs and carried them to the breakfast bar where they sat on stools, side by side.

"Do you think they'll take your advice?" Kenzie asked.

"We were sent here to form an opinion about our culture merging with yours. It is our belief that it is not only possible for that to happen, but that it can happen quite successfully. The council is duty-bound to consider our recommendations."

"But what if they don't accept your recommendations?"

Zan sighed heavily and remained silent before she looked at Kenzie. "We feel confident that they will."

"I'll be crossing my fingers for you this morning."

Zan took a bite of sausage and stopped mid-chew. "What is this that I am eating?" she asked.

Kenzie's eyes opened wide. "Oh, shit! I'm sorry, Zan. I put sausage on your plate."

"It is very pleasant tasting," she said.

"But, but it's meat," Kenzie said.

Zan chewed a little more. "Very pleasant. I did say I wanted to try your meat."

Kenzie laughed. "That horse left the barn several days ago, sweetheart!"

Chapter 24

Kenzie dropped Zan and Trey off in the parking lot of Little Horse Trail around ten. She kissed Zan tenderly before she got out of the car. "I'll get hold of Charlie and see if he feels like hiking this afternoon. If he does, we'll both be back around one o'clock. Otherwise, it will be just me. Okay?"

"Yes. We should be finished by then. We will meet you right here in the parking lot," Zan said.

"Okay. Good luck, and knock 'em dead with your proposal," Kenzie said.

Trey, who had already exited the car and was standing outside Zan's window, leaned forward. "You want us to kill them?"

Kenzie laughed. "Oh, my goodness. I really need to teach you two our figures of speech! It means good luck and awe them to the point they cannot refuse."

"Oh! Your people have odd ways of expressing themselves," Trey said.

Zan kissed her again. "We will do our best to knock 'em dead. Thank you for the ride."

***

"Zangendar, why do you appear before the council while cloaked in your avatar when you were specifically instructed not to do so while on the ship?"

Zangendar stood with her hands clasped behind her. "I appear to have lost my ability to return to Vakillian form. I do not understand why."

"What do you mean, you cannot return to Vakillian form?"

"Allow me to demonstrate. Computer, return me to Vakillian form," Zangendar said.

Nothing happened.

Zangendar's birth unit, Belander, leaned forward with apparent interest in her daughter's predicament.

"How did this happen?" the councilwoman asked.

"I do not know the exact reason, however, I believe the longer I am on the surface, the more my physiology adapts to the planet," Zangendar looked at Tredoran who was not cloaked. "I cannot explain why Tredoran is unaffected."

"Would you assume then, that should the population of Vakillia relocate to the surface, that time passed, some would become more human rather than Vakillian?"

"I cannot say unless it is determined why it has affected me and not Tredoran," Zangendar said.

Zangendar and Tredoran exchanged glances as the members of the council whispered among themselves. When the whispering stopped, the chairwoman stood and walked toward them.

"Tell me about the humans," she said.

Tredoran stepped forward. "We have collected biometrics on thousands of humans, and we have had opportunities to interact with hundreds of them. We have found them to be diverse, tolerant, accepting, peaceful, and interactive. The data for these humans and encounters have been downloaded into the primary database."

"Tell me about their relationships," the chairwoman said.

Zangendar looked at Tredoran, who nodded to yield the floor to her. "The humans are very interactive with one another. They show no fear when approached by others unknown to them. Similar to the Vakillians, the humans we have encountered are not a violent race unless provoked or are protecting themselves. They tend to form romantic relationships with one other human at a time. Some of these relationships last for many decades, while others are short-lived. The humans rely on trust to maintain these relationships."

"And do these relationships produce offspring?"

In the human race, it requires the blending of genetics from a male and a female to produce offspring. This coupling can happen physically between two humans, or it can be duplicated under scientific conditions and implanted in a human female.

Human males are incapable of carrying offspring. We have had the opportunity to observe human offspring at various ages. The biometrics for these encounters have been downloaded into the database. I must admit that it was somewhat odd to observe these various ages of off-spring."

"Odd? In what way?"

"On Vakillia, the generations are only in increments of fifteen earth-years. On Earth, there are children and adults of all ages, shapes, sizes and colors. Each one appears to be very individualistic."

"Interesting, but easily explained by the Vakillian manifestation cycles. And the environment—is it safe?"

"Madame Chairwoman, we have already proven that the atmosphere is compatible with our kind. The air is relatively clean, and the humans have taken additional measures to assure the environment is clean as well. They are required to recycle certain materials to minimize waste."

"Are there large bodies of water in the vicinity? As you know, water is essential for the reproduction of our species."

"There are relatively few large bodies of water in the immediate Sedona area, however, there are some of moderate size a short distance away, and there are massive bodies of water the humans call oceans at the borders of the continent we are on. Water is plentiful. So plentiful, in fact, that the humans bathe in it."

"They bathe in it?" the councilwoman asked incredulously.

"Indeed they do. I have tried it. It is quite pleasurable." Zan did not tell the council that she shared said bath with Kenzie. She could feel the heat rise into her face as she recalled how extremely pleasurable it was to make love to Kenzie in a tub of warm water.

The chairwoman stopped pacing and stood in front of Zangendar. "Tell me, Zangendar, if we adopt your recommendation of cloaking in avatars to integrate into human society, what is the one thing we will need focus on to adapt and to survive?"

"Our people will need to understand and experience emotion, Madame Chairwoman."

"Emotion. That is the one thing that weakens us the most."

"The humans do not feel that way. The humans believe that emotion makes them stronger rather than weaker."

"And how is that so, Zangendar?"

"It makes them feel alive. Even the negative emotions. It teaches the humans how to deal with adversity and how to compromise. It allows them to celebrate good times and mourn bad times. It allows them to feel empathy for others." Zangendar replied.

"And what about you, Zangendar? You have spent a significant amount of time on the surface. Have you experienced these emotions?"

"I have, Madame Chairwoman," Zangendar admitted.

"And do you feel more alive?"

"If I had to choose between how I feel on the surface, and dying because of the nonproliferation of our race, I would choose human emotion."

"I see," the chairwoman said. She walked to Tredoran. "And you, Tredoran. Would you make the same choice?"

"With all due respect, Madame Chairwoman, yes, I would," Tredoran replied.

***

"Enter," Zan said when the door alarm sounded.

The door slid open and Tredoran entered.

"You are not in your avatar," Zan observed. "In fact, you were not in your avatar at the council meeting."

"I am not as brave as you, sister. I chose not to disobey the council's orders regarding the avatars," Trey said.

"I have tried to transition back. As I demonstrated to the council, I cannot."

"I am concerned that you may never be able to return to Vakillian form again."

"Scan my biometrics," Zan said. "I am curious as to whether it will detect Vakillian signatures."

Trey pulled the omni-spectrometer out of her pocket, scanned Zan, and then showed her the results.

Zan frowned. "There are still Vakillian signatures in these readings, however, my appearance is human. It seems from this point on, I may always present as human. Let me scan you, sister."

Zan scanned Trey. "Your readings are Vakillian as well, yet you retain the ability to transition back and forth."

"What if you are never able to transition back to Vakillian form, Zan?"

"I don't see where that is a problem, Tredoran, considering I plan to live on the surface, whether the council agrees to stay or not."

"What if the council refuses to let you stay, Zangendar?"

"I am hoping it will not come to that, but if it does, I will find a way."

Trey smiled. "As will I."

"We should formulate such a plan in the event that we need it, however, right now we have orders to collect additional environmental data."

"When will you be ready to return to the surface, sister?" Trey asked.

"It is not yet one o'clock, so we have time if there is anything else you need to do while we are on the ship."

"I would like to duplicate additional clothing, rations and currency," Trey said.

"I had the same thoughts. I will meet you in the transference room at twelve-thirty."

"I will be there."

Zan watched Trey leave and then got to work duplicating and packing her new clothing and rations. She also took the time to download the literature on the environmental conditions required for successful Vakillian reproductions. She suspected there were specifications regarding water purity levels, and it would be useful to have that information on hand when she collected and tested water samples.

Zan felt lightness in her chest as she walked to the transference room. She attributed it to the fact that she would be seeing Kenzie again soon. As promised, Trey was there waiting for her, cloaked in her avatar. Moments later, they appeared at their usual transfer site on the trail.

Zan felt lightheaded once the transfer was complete. She grabbed Trey's arm to steady herself.

"Are you not well, sister?" Trey asked.

"My head feels cloudy. I will be fine in a moment or two."

"Come sit on that rock."

Trey led her to a nearby rock and waited while Zan recovered. She pulled her omni-spectrometer from her pocket and collected biometrics on her. "The readings indicate your heart is beating rapidly and your respiration is irregular. Maybe we should return to the ship."

Zan put out her hand. "No. I will be fine. I just need a few moments."

"Are you having other symptoms?" Trey asked.

"My stomach is not right," Zan replied.

Trey scanned her again. "The readings also indicate dehydration."

"Of course," Zan said. "I have not had enough water intake today. That makes perfect sense." She pulled a bottle of water from her backpack, thirstily drank the entire thing and then shoved the empty container back into her pack. "I am beginning to feel better. I believe we can go now."

Fifteen minutes later, they returned to the parking lot where Kenzie was waiting for them.

"I do not see Charlie with her," Trey said as they approached.

Kenzie hugged both women and then slipped her hand into Zan's arm to walk toward the car. "I missed you," she said.

"Where is Charlie?" Trey asked.

"He sends his apologies. He had a tour scheduled. That's the problem with working in the tourist industry. It's rarely a Monday through Friday, nine to five job. He *did* ask me to tell you that he would pick you up for dinner around six tonight."

Trey grinned. "Thank you for telling me, Kenzie."

"So, how did it go with the council?" Kenzie asked. "Did they enjoy the chapel?"

Zan and Trey shared a nervous glance.

"We did not have time for the chapel on this trip. We will have to do that another time," Trey said.

"If you didn't have time, that must mean you had a pretty involved meeting with the council. Are they considering your recommendations?"

"Unfortunately, they have given us more tasks to do before they make their decision," Zan said.

"What kind of tasks?"

"Mostly environmental in nature. We need to collect and test water and soil samples, and they asked for a mapping of all the bodies of water in the nearby vicinity," Zan added.

"Bodies of water? You've already seen that water is plentiful here, even in the middle of the desert. I'm becoming just a little suspicious of the council's intentions, Zan. I can understand their desire to live in a clean environment, but you've already said it would meet your needs."

"I'm sure the council is just being cautious. They want to be sure both the environment and the people will welcome us here," Trey said.

"Of course, the people will welcome you. You've seen that for yourself. Look, I know the immigration laws in Arizona are tough, but if you and your people go through the proper channels, and your documentation is in order, there's no reason why you won't be approved. The government is generally willing to approve immigrants with exceptional skills like yours."

"I hope you are right. Maybe you can help us to determine what needs to be done to start the immigration process," Zan said.

"Sure! We can find the information online, and even download the application forms."

***

Kenzie pulled into the parking lot of the motel and Trey climbed out of the back seat. "Are you sure you don't want us to wait with you until Charlie gets here?" Kenzie said.

"No. I plan to shower and rest before dinner. Go home and enjoy your evening."

"I will see you in the morning, then," Zan said.

"In the morning," Trey repeated.

Kenzie drove the rest of the way home in silence. She pulled into the driveway and turned off the car. "Are you okay, Zan? You've been awfully quiet."

"I am not feeling well. It began after the council meeting today," Zan admitted.

Kenzie felt her forehead. "No fever. What doesn't feel well?"

"I was lightheaded earlier, and my stomach is not right."

"Have you eaten since breakfast this morning?"

"No, I have not."

"Well, then, maybe you're hungry. Come inside and I'll heat some soup for you."

"I really do not feel like eating."

"Hmm. Come on. Let's get you inside."

Kenzie led Zan to one of the stools in front of the breakfast bar. "Sit. I'll be right back."

She returned a few moments later with her blood pressure cuff, stethoscope and digital thermometer. "Open," she said, and placed the thermometer under Zan's tongue.

"What are you doing?" Zan asked around the thermometer.

"I'm checking your vitals. I'm guessing you're just overtired, and maybe you need something light to eat, but I want to be sure."

The thermometer beeped and Kenzie removed it from Zan's mouth. "Ninety-six point three degrees. Do you normally run on the cool side?"

"I do not know."

"It's a little lower than it should be, but not dangerously so. If it drops much lower than that, I will recommend tests."

"What happens if it is too low?" Zan asked.

"If your temperature drops too low, it can cause your body and brain not to function properly. The medical term for it is hypothermia."

"What is normal?"

"Ninety-eight point six degrees Fahrenheit. Like I said, ninety-six point three is a little on the low side, but the point at which you might need medical attention is in the ninety-five degree range, so you're still okay. Some people naturally run low. You might be one of them."

Kenzie next wrapped the blood pressure cuff around Zan's left arm.

"And what is this for?"

"I'm checking your blood pressure." She stopped and looked at Zan. "Have you never had a checkup before?"

"We have different medical methods in our community."

Kenzie placed the ear tips of her stethoscope in her ears and the diaphragm inside the crook of Zan's arm. She pumped the pressure ball, but stopped when Zan squirmed.

"Hold still or I won't get an accurate reading," she scolded.

Zan's eyes grew wide as the cuff tightened around her arm.

Kenzie slowly released the air pressure while she carefully watched the regulator gauge. She frowned when the air was almost released and then tightened the value and pumped the cuff up again.

"What are you doing?" Zan asked.

"Shhh." Kenzie once again released the pressure while she watched the gauge and listened for Zan's heartbeat in her ears. "One forty-three over eighty-six. That is not good, Zan."

"What is good?"

"For someone your age and in your condition, it should be around one ten over seventy. I think you should come to work with me tomorrow for blood work."

"What causes blood pressure to rise?"

"Stress, diet, lack of exercise. Too much exercise, and sometimes it's just genetic. But when it's too high, it really needs to be treated or it could cause damage elsewhere in your body, like your kidneys. I'm not surprised you were lightheaded."

"So, if I relax it should be better in the morning?"

"Yes, if stress is what's causing it," Kenzie agreed. Kenzie noted the worry on Zan's face. She lifted her chin up with the tips of two fingers. "Look, I'll take it again in the morning, and if it's down, we'll just keep an eye on it for a few days. If it stays down, we'll attribute it to the stress of meeting with the council, but if it's still elevated, I want to do some blood work. Okay?"

Zan nodded.

"I really do think you should eat something. Maybe some chicken noodle soup?"

"Chicken is meat. Yes, I would like to try that."

***

After dinner, Zan and Kenzie sat on the bed with her laptop and searched for immigration paperwork. Kenzie stored the portable document format versions of the application forms on her hard drive to print out later. Afterward, they snuggled down together and watched several episodes of the old television series, *I Love Lucy*.

Part way through, Kenzie went into the kitchen and made a bowl of popcorn, which they devoured in the span of one episode.

"This is very enjoyable," Zan said. "What is it called?"

"Popcorn. With butter on it. Lots of butter."

"We should have this often."

"If I ate this as often as I would like to, I'd need to go to the gym every day, in addition to hiking. As good as it tastes, too much butter is not good for us."

Kenzie put the empty popcorn bowl on the bedside table and glanced at the clock. "Wow. It's ten o'clock already. Where has the evening gone?" She rolled back over and snuggled into Zan's shoulder.

"I enjoyed this evening, Kenzie. It was very relaxing, and Lucy made me laugh. Thank you for sharing that with me."

Kenzie kissed her gently. "Thank you, love. I enjoyed it too."

"Why do you call me love?"

"It's a term of endearment. I sometimes call you sweetie too. It's my way of letting you know that I love you."

"Sweetie. I like that."

"I'm glad." Kenzie yawned. "I really need to get some sleep. I gotta work tomorrow."

Zan kissed her on the nose. "Yes. I am tired too. It was a busy day for me. Sleep well."

Kenzie rolled with her back to Zan and spooned into her. "Sweet dreams, Zan."

"I love you, sweetie," Zan said.

Kenzie grinned into the dark.

"I love you, too, Zan."

Chapter 25

Kenzie awoke the next morning just before the alarm. She disabled it before it awakened Zan, who was sleeping on her side, facing Kenzie. A warm feeling filled her heart. For several long moments, she just looked at Zan's face and resisted the urge to kiss her eyelids. She looked so sexy and vulnerable with her defenses down and her hair all tussled.

Kenzie realized they had met less than a month ago, but it felt like so much longer. Zan had an innocence and vulnerability about her that made Kenzie want to protect her. She could only imagine how Zan felt, being a foreigner in a strange land and not knowing the customs. She knew so little about this woman, yet she felt safe in her presence.

Who are you, Zan? Where do you come from? How have you invaded my mind and my heart so easily? she wondered.

Kenzie thought about the possibility that Zan's people would decide Sedona was unsuitable and would ultimately move on. That thought caused a deep sense of fear to fill her soul. She wondered if Zan would have the choice to stay, or if she would be forced to go with them. The more Zan told her about the community, the more she felt that it could be a cult that controlled the actions and very thoughts of its members. In a lot of ways, the religious community she'd escaped from a few years earlier had had similar control when it came to her. It had taken an exceptional level of bravery, determination and sacrifice to break away. She only hoped Zan would want to do the same if faced with a choice of leaving with them, or staying with her.

Kenzie softly kissed Zan on the forehead and climbed out of bed. She quietly collected a clean set of scrubs and underclothes and left the bedroom to shower and dress for work. She stopped in the doorway of the bedroom and looked back at the sleeping woman.

"Have an amazing day, my love," she said under her breath.

***

"Hey, Kenzie. How was your weekend?" Bree asked when Kenzie entered the break area for her first coffee of the day.

"It was good. How was yours?" Kenzie replied.

"It was fun, actually. Jimmy and I spent it backpacking and primitive tenting. It felt good to get away from everything for a couple of days. What did you do?"

"Well, on Saturday, Charlie took us on the aerial tour of the vortexes. That was awesome, and then on Sunday, Zan and Trey had a meeting with their council, and when they got back, Zan and I just chilled out for the evening. It was nice to do nothing but relax for a change. We watched old reruns of *I Love Lucy* while snuggling in bed with a bowl of popcorn."

"I love snuggle-bug days like that. We all need that now and then. What did Trey do while you were all snuggled down in your bed?"

"I suspect she was with Charlie. They had a dinner date for last night. I think they've pretty much been together since after karaoke on Friday. Except for their meeting with the council, that is."

"What is up with that council?" Bree asked. "If you ask me, they seem to have an inordinate amount of control over Zan and Trey."

"I've been thinking about that, myself," Kenzie admitted. "I know how much power cults can have."

"Well, I hope Zan's love for you overpowers her loyalty to the council if it comes down to that."

"My thoughts, exactly!"

"So, what's on Miss Sexy-pants' agenda for today?" Bree asked.

Kenzie chuckled. "She *is* sexy, isn't she? I believe she and Trey will be collecting environmental samples today. Orders from the council. She was still sleeping when I left this morning."

"She's one of those late sleepers, huh? I think Jimmy would sleep until noon every day if I let him."

"I don't think she's necessarily a late sleeper, but she didn't feel well yesterday, so I think the extra sleep will do her good."

"She was ill?"

"Yes. Light-headed, and stomachache. I took her vitals. Her temp was a little low, but her BP was really high. It could have been caused by stress about meeting with the council, but I've told her if it doesn't come down and stay down that I would bring her in for blood work."

"High blood pressure is nothing to mess with. I hope she listens to you."

"I'll take it again when I get home. Hopefully, it will be lower. She's in great shape, so I don't think it's anything serious."

"Hopefully, whatever ails her works its way out of her system in the next few days. Don't forget, we need to be in Phoenix for the next two weeks for the genetics genome training. That should be right up your alley."

"Shit! I forgot all about that!" Kenzie exclaimed. "Wow! Two weeks is going to feel like a lifetime."

Bree sighed. "Ah, young love. I remember when Jimmy and I were at this stage, when every moment apart seemed like an eternity. Just think about how hot the sex will be when you get back home!"

***

Zan slept until nearly nine that morning. The moment she opened her eyes, she realized she was alone. She swung her legs over the side of the bed and sat up. She had to grasp the bed on either side of her to remain upright.

What was this feeling in her head? Why was she so unsteady?

After a few moments, Zan regained her equilibrium and she was able to navigate her way into the bathroom and then to the kitchen to make herself a cup of coffee. She saw the note from Kenzie next to the coffee maker.

Good morning, love. I hope you feel better today. Make yourself at home. There are bagels and cream cheese in the fridge if you're hungry. And of course, you know how to use the coffee maker. I recommend you eat something before you head out. Maybe if you're up to it, we can hike Bell Rock after work today? Good luck gathering samples! I will see you when I get home. Much love, Kenzie.

Zan heard a knock on the door just as the coffee pot finished brewing. It was Trey.

"Have you just finished renewing?" Trey asked when Zan opened the door. She looked at Zan closely. "And do you always greet visitors when you are unclothed?"

Zan looked down at the T-shirt and panties she had on. "To answer your questions, yes, I finished renewing not too long ago. As you know, I did not feel well yesterday. I assume I needed the extra rest. Secondly, this is the clothing I renewed in last night, and had it been someone other than family, I would have put additional clothing on before I admitted a visitor."

"I am glad I am considered your family, my sister. How are you feeling today?"

"Still not well, but I am better than yesterday. I am hoping some nourishment will help. Would you care to join me?"

"I have already taken nourishment."

"I will not be long."

"We are in no hurry, sister. Enjoy your nourishment. I hope you are improved after you have consumed it."

Zan cut a bagel in half and slipped it into the toaster, and then retrieved both the cream cheese and creamer from the refrigerator.

Trey watched her every move.

"I find the way humans take nourishment to be primitive. It is much simpler to give the duplicator a command and have it provide you with ready-to-eat rations," Trey said.

Zan pulled the bagel halves out of the toaster and spread cream cheese on them. "I agree that duplicators are much more efficient, but I find I gain a certain satisfaction from preparing rations for myself. It is also a way to show another human that you care for them."

"Explain."

"It pleases Kenzie when I prepare coffee for her. She readily expresses appreciation when I do so."

"Interesting."

Zan looked up from her task. "I assume you were with Charlie last night?" she asked.

Trey smiled and her face turned pink. "Yes. I am enjoying my time with him."

"If he makes you feel the intensity of emotion that I feel with Kenzie, then I believe you are falling in love with him."

"Falling in love?"

"Yes. That is what the humans call it when the relationship between two people is so intense that they want to spend the rest of their lives together."

"I see. In that case, yes, I am falling in love with Charlie."

"And is he returning the same level of feeling for you?" Zan asked.

"I believe so, but I will ask him."

Zan carried her coffee and bagel to the breakfast bar. "Are you sure you do not wish to partake in nourishment, Trey?" she asked.

"That does look enticing," Trey responded.

Zan slid her breakfast to Trey and returned to the kitchen to toast a second bagel. A few moments later, they were enjoying their breakfast together.

"What are your thoughts on the council meeting yesterday, Zan?" Trey asked.

"We have been here for nearly three weeks, and we have provided a significant amount of data on the environment and the people. It concerns me that the council feels they need additional information."

"They have asked for information on the governments across the planet as well as more environmental data. Some of that data will be difficult to obtain."

"I have seen information on the governments and political issues on something the humans call, television. I believe there is a television in the motel. We will both need to consume more information from that source to fulfill the council's request," Zan said.

"I agree. I find myself wondering what data the other research missions are collecting from the planets they have been assigned to and how it compares to the data from Earth," Trey said.

"Some of the other planets are uninhabited. The council will need to weigh the benefits of settling in a place that is already established, like Earth, against the possibility of starting with a blank canvas, so to speak, and molding it into a specialized Vakillian society. There are valid arguments for both cases."

"Settling on Earth, or on another inhabited planet, would certainly allow the procreation process to begin sooner. There would be no need to build an infrastructure to support it first," Trey reasoned.

"That is a good point, sister. I will use that argument at the next council meeting."

Trey fell silent for a few moments, and then looked at Zan. "Zan, how are you feeling about the procreation process?"

Zan inhaled deeply. "Before I met Kenzie, I never questioned it. It is our duty to participate in the process to further the reproduction of our species, however, my thoughts about procreating with another Vakillian when I feel the way I do about Kenzie are not agreeable to me."

"I have been having the same thoughts, Zan. I can only hope that Charlie will understand."

"I hope that Kenzie will understand as well. I hope we will not be forced to choose between duty and love."

"All of that will be futile if the council does not choose Earth as our new homeland."

Zan studied her friend's face for several long moments. "We need to be prepared for that, Trey. We may be forced to choose, but for now, we need to do everything in our power to sway the council toward choosing Earth. To do that, we have work to do during the next couple of weeks. Let us finish our nourishment and get started."

Chapter 26

The council chairwoman rose and addressed the assembly. "It has been seven cycles since Zangendar and Tredoran last appeared before this body with their recommendations. Within seven additional cycles, they have committed to provide their final analysis on purity levels for the water and other natural resources to assist us in our final decision. I have gathered us here today for a preliminary assessment of what we know based on the data already collected, and the feedback provided by Zangendar and Tredoran in our last council meeting with them. Lorhonder, as forewoman of the council, please summarize the findings."

Lorhonder stood and cleared her throat. "Madame Councilwoman and members of the council, I will read to you a list of findings on the suitability of Earth as a future homeland for Vakillians, as presented to us by Zangendar Tafadon and the engineers in residence on this ship. We will have the opportunity to debate and discuss each one after the list is fully presented to you.

"Environmental factors analyzed to date. It has been determined that the Earth's atmosphere is compatible with sustaining Vakillian life. The ratio of oxygen to hydrogen is not in exact concurrence with Vakillia, but it is within adaptable ranges. We believe this to be true regardless of where on the planet Vakillians may wish to migrate to.

"Relative to natural resources, the soil quality in the immediate vicinity of Sedona is dry but is adaptable to irrigation and is believed to be able to support plant-based food growth. The data also suggests that areas outside the immediate vicinity have more than enough water supplies to support ample food growth for thousands of years to come.

"Relative to climate, the area we have chosen to collect data from is relatively warm and dry, however, indications are that other parts of the planet vary in temperature significantly, depending on location. Data we have collected confirms that the closer the location is to the poles, the colder that location becomes and the less able it is to sustain life. We know from our research that this planet rotates on its own axis and circles the light source every three hundred sixty-five days. The combination of Earth's rotation and orbital path indicates that temperatures and weather occur seasonally in all non-polar locations on the planet.

"There is also data to support the occurrence of natural disasters in many locations across this planet. These disasters include those relating to water, wind and fire, as well as shifts in the tectonic plates beneath the surface. In short, if we choose Earth as our new homeland, we will need to learn to adapt to various climate conditions. The question we need to ask ourselves is whether these conditions are better or worse than those we currently face on Vakillia."

Belander stared at her hands, clasped together and resting on the table before her, as she listened to the forewoman read from her report. The enormity of the task before Zangendar and Tredoran seemed unachievable in the amount of time they had been given to complete it, and she feared that even if they were able to fulfill the council's requests, that the council was predisposed to reject their findings. Earth was, by far, not the best planet in the universe, however, their time was running short on Vakillia, and the council needed to prevent their criteria from eliminating viable worlds, regardless of their imperfections.

The forewoman continued.

"Relative to government and politics, we have few details at this point, however, we understand there several types of governments across the planet that practice varying degrees of personal and political freedoms. Some have pursued equal rights among all residents, where others have class-based systems in which the higher classes have greater rights, wealth and freedoms than the lower classes. There are also some areas of the planet that govern based on tribal rules and regulations. Without more information, it is unclear where on the spectrum the Vakillian community will fit in. One disturbing aspect of life on Earth is that nearly everywhere on the planet, the female portions of the populations are not on equal par with the males. They are often disadvantaged politically, socially and economically. It is our hope that the additional data we have asked Zangendar and Tredoran to collect will help to refute these preliminary findings.

"Finally, with regards to the humans, Zangendar and Tredoran have collected biometrics on thousands of them and we have determined that some of their physical characteristics are similar to our own, and as such, the data indicates the Vakillian race could easily adapt to the environment. The data also indicates that humans suffer from a range of health issues, some of which are life threatening and for which adequate cures have not yet been developed. If the council decides to settle on Earth, this is an area where our advanced technology may be able to help. It should be noted here that there are health issues on Vakillia as well, but should Earth become our new homeland, the types of health issues will be different.

"That is the end of my report. More data will be forthcoming when Zangendar and Tredoran complete their analysis during the next seven cycles."

The council chair stood. "Thank you, Lorhonder." She looked around the room. "As you can see, there is much to think about. I have not reached a final decision for myself; however, I am concerned about the information Zangendar shared with us previously, about emotion. We have spent generations training Vakillians to be strong in the face of emotional situations, and it has served us well. We will need to consider this, as well as the positive and negative points we have learned through our research before we make a final decision.

"We will meet again when Zangendar and Tredoran have completed their mission. Dismissed."

***

Belander returned to her quarters and greeted Molinder, who was waiting for her there.

"How was the council meeting?" Molinder asked.

"It went as well as could be expected. Zangendar and Tredoran have collected a significant amount of data that indicates Earth is indeed a suitable habitat for our species. I believe the council was impressed," Belander replied.

"I sense there is more you want to say."

Belander nodded. "Yes. The environmental data is conclusive. Earth is compatible, but I am not sure the council was impressed with their data on the humans."

"How so?"

"Zangendar pointed out that the humans are emotional. That did not impress the council. I wish she had not been so forthcoming with that information."

"Our daughter was taught to always be truthful, Belander. I would expect no less of her." Molinder approached Belander and traced the side of her face with her fingertips. "Throughout my lifetime with you, I have learned that emotion is sometimes a positive thing. You are not a typical Vakillian, Belander, and I am grateful for that."

Belander nodded. "And our daughter is not typical as well. Others could benefit from her example."

"I agree. So, I assume the council did not reach a decision."

"You are correct. They have decided to wait for the remaining data they have asked Zangendar and Tredoran to collect. We should have a decision from the council in the next ten to fourteen cycles."

***

Zan and Trey sat side by side on Kenzie's bed with a bowl of popcorn between them.

"This is very pleasing," Trey said. "You said it was called popcorn?"

"It is called Popcorn with butter on it. Lots of butter. Kenzie and I often enjoy it while watching the television."

"I see." Trey looked at the television. "There appears to be a lot of unrest on this planet."

"Unfortunately, the unrest is often caused by humans seeking power," Zan said. "It seems the humans do not always make wise decisions about who they choose for leaders. From what I have been able to determine from this television, there is a lot of division among these humans and the current leaders are making it worse rather than working to bring the humans together. I fear there is too much power given to too few leaders. The Vakillian rule by council appears to be a more balanced approach."

"If the council chooses Earth for our new homeland, will the rules of our council override the rules of the human leaders?" Trey asked.

"I suspect it will not," Zan replied. "Not unless the Vakillians live separate from the other humans, and even then, I believe the laws and regulations of the land will override the council."

"I believe the council will not approve of that arrangement."

"I believe you are correct. We need to hope that the other benefits of choosing Earth will outweigh the politics," Zan said. "The council will decide when they have all the data."

"Speaking of all the data, we have provided the environmental samples they requested seven cycles ago. When do we need to provide this government analysis?" Trey asked.

"We need to provide it within the next seven cycles," Zan replied. "I am looking forward to having this data collection completed and the decision to choose Earth concluded. I feel like we need to move forward with our lives. I would like to plan a future with Kenzie."

"Do you miss her?" Trey asked.

"I do. But she will return in another seven cycles. The conference on genetics genomes is important for her work as a healer."

"Do you miss the intimacy?"

Zan smiled and felt her face grow warm. "I do. Making love to Kenzie is the most amazing experience. Even though she has only been gone for seven cycles, we have not made love for about three cycles before she left, because of my illness."

Trey frowned. "Are you still ill?"

"To some degree, yes, but it is improved."

"Does Kenzie know you are still ill?"

"I have not told her."

"But she calls you every day on that communication device." Trey pointed to the phone on the bedside table.

"Yes, but I have not told her. I do not want it to distract her from her training."

"What do you believe is causing the illness, Zan?"

"I do not know. I have discontinued talking the medication Molinder formulates for me. That is a potential, however unlikely cause."

"You stopped taking your medication? Why? Do you think that is wise, Zan?" Trey demanded.

"I stopped taking the medication when I first transported to Earth on my research missions nearly a full moon cycle ago. I did not want it to interfere with my ability to adapt to Earth's environment. I reasoned that if we relocated to Earth, then Molinder may not have access to resources to formulate it. I wanted to determine if I could survive without it."

"It appears to me that this illness you are experiencing is proof that you cannot survive without it," Trey pointed out.

"I do not agree. This illness only began two days before Kenzie left for her training. It has only been nine cycles that I have been feeling this way, whereas, we have been on Earth for nearly thirty cycles. If a lack of medication were causing my illness, I surmise I would have fallen ill much sooner than twenty days after I stopped taking it."

"Then what could be the cause?" Trey asked.

"I do not know. I have added meat to my diet at about the same time I fell ill. It could be that ingesting different types of food than I am used to may be causing it. In any event, the frequency and severity of the illness appears to be lessening."

"I do not like that you have not told Kenzie," Trey said.

"It was my choice not to tell her."

"If you are still ill when she returns, will you tell her then?"

"I will take it under advisement," Zan said.

"If you do not tell her, then I will."

Chapter 27

Kenzie pulled into Bree's driveway and slipped the car into park. She opened her arms to hug her friend.

"Thanks for the ride, K. The next time we have training out of town, I'll drive," Bree said.

"No problem. Give Jimmy a big hug for me, okay?" Kenzie replied.

"Only if you give Zan one for me."

"It's a deal."

Kenzie waited until Bree was inside her house before she pulled out of the driveway and headed home. Twenty minutes later, she pulled into her own driveway and turned off the ignition. She sat back and sighed heavily. It had been a hectic two weeks of intensive genome training and she was exhausted and starved.

Kenzie opened the back door and grabbed her suitcase and then went into the house. She walked into a relatively dark living room and it took a moment for her to realize that Zan had prepared an elaborate dinner of Chinese takeout, complete with a lit candle in the middle of the dinette table. Zan stood behind the table with an expectant look on her face.

Kenzie dropped her bag by the door and covered her mouth with her hands. "Oh, my God. This is so sweet!" she exclaimed. She wiped a tear from her eye and crossed the room, directly into Zan's arms. Kenzie closed her eyes and melted into Zan's embrace.

"Welcome home, love," Zan said softly. "I missed you."

"I missed you, too, Zan," Kenzie replied. She wrapped her arms around Zan again and placed her cheek on Zan's chest, just above her breasts. "I want to stay like this forever," she whispered.

"I would be happy to accommodate, however, your dinner may get cold," Zan said.

Kenzie looked at the table and chuckled. "I guess you're right."

"There will be time to make love after dinner," Zan said. "Are you hungry?"

"I am famished. Thank you so much for doing this."

Zan held Kenzie's chair for her as she sat down and hungrily dug into the appetizers. "I love Chinese takeout. How did you know?"

"I found several takeout menus in the kitchen when I was putting rations away," Zan explained.

"Rations?"

"Trey and I purchased food items. I thought it was only right to replace what I had consumed."

"You walked all the way to the store and back?"

"No. Charlie provided us with transportation."

"I see. Thank you for doing that. To be honest, I am too exhausted to have done it myself."

"How was your training?" Zan asked.

"It was amazing. I learned so much. It makes me wish I was still working in the genetics field."

"Do you not work with genetics at your Urgent Care Center?"

"Not much. The urgent care center is specifically for that, urgent care. We are like a mini emergency room for less critical illnesses. Bree and I signed up for the genetics class last year because we thought it would be fun. I didn't realize how much I missed it."

"Maybe you should consider returning to that type of work."

"Bree and I chatted about that about a month or so ago. I am definitely giving it some thought. It means I would have to leave the urgent care center and work in Flagstaff, but it's close enough from here to commute. I am definitely giving it some thought."

"I am glad you enjoyed your training."

"I did. Thank you for asking. So, what did you and Trey do while I was gone?"

"We collected more data for the council."

Kenzie took a bite of her egg roll. "What type of data?"

"Water and soil samples and information about the government and politics."

"Oh, my God! You couldn't have picked a worse time to collect data on our politics. For the past few years, this country has been under the rule of the most narcissistic, xenophobic, sexist, racist, corrupt piece of shit we've ever had for a president. He is clearly an anomaly, and not what our founding fathers envisioned in a president when our country was formed. We have become so polarized as a nation, it's truly scary. We have a lot of healing to do, and hopefully, that will happen soon. Please be careful when you provide that data to the council. It is truly not who we are as a nation."

Zan's eyebrows were high on her forehead. "I have already provided information on the current president to the council, but I have also provided a history of this nations' politics from the time the country was founded. I am sure the council will see that the current state of affairs is not typical."

"I sure hope so. I would hope they would not allow that asshole's less than stellar performance to cloud any decision they may make on settling here."

"I will reiterate that point to them again before they make their decision," Zan said.

"Good. So, do you have any idea when they may decide?"

"We are nearly finished collecting data. We are required to present our final report within the next three days. I suspect their decision will be soon after that."

"Good. I am looking forward to making more long-term plans with you," Kenzie said.

Zan smiled. "I was discussing that very thing with Trey just yesterday."

"I have to admit, Zan, that I am worried they will expect you to go with them if they decide not to stay."

"I have given that a lot of thought as well. I want to stay, Kenzie, if you will have me."

"That is not even a question, Zan. I'll hold you hostage if I have to. I want you here with me. I will not let you go easily."

"I will not go easily."

Kenzie looked around the table. "Soy sauce and chopsticks. I'll be right back."

Kenzie jumped up from the table and went into the kitchen to grab the soy sauce from the refrigerator. The first thing she noticed was that the lower shelves of the refrigerator were filled with beer. She then grabbed two pair of chopsticks from the silverware drawer and while doing so, noticed that one of the cupboard doors was not closed all the way. She pushed on it, but something was blocking it from closing completely. She pulled the door open and saw that it was packed full of boxes of microwave popcorn. "Geez Louise!" she exclaimed.

Zan looked up. "I wanted to be sure we had sufficient popcorn with butter on it, lots of butter. I enjoy that very much."

"And beer?"

"Yes. I enjoy that, too. Oh, and there are several frozen pizzas in the freezer as well."

Kenzie returned to the table and kissed Zan on top of her head. "I like the way you grocery shop. Remind me to send you again." She handed Zan a set of chopsticks.

"What are these for?" Zan asked.

"You've never used chopsticks before? Well, you're in for a treat!" Kenzie said.

By the end of the meal, Zan had more food on herself and on the floor around her chair than had made it into her mouth. She had also had more fun and laughter than she ever had in her life.

***

Zan and Kenzie worked together to package up the leftovers and to clean up the mess around Zan's chair. Kenzie rinsed their dishes and handed them to Zan to put into the dishwasher. Zan then washed the table and the countertops while Kenzie rearranged room in the refrigerator for the leftovers.

Kenzie closed the refrigerator door and turned around to face Zan who was standing close behind her. Zan took a step forward and backed Kenzie up against the refrigerator. She placed her hands on the refrigerator on either side of Kenzie's head. Her nose was within an inch of Kenzie's.

"I have missed you so much. Let me make love to you," Zan said in barely more than a whisper.

"I was hoping you'd say that. Take me to bed," Kenzie replied, huskily.

Zan placed her left hand behind Kenzie and scooped her up with her right arm under her knees.

"Wow, you're stronger than you look," Kenzie said breathlessly.

Zan pushed the bedroom door open with her foot and carried Kenzie to the bed where she laid her down gently and covered her body with her own. Zan's tongue invaded Kenzie's mouth with an urgency that nearly overwhelmed her.

"I have been waiting for this moment since you left," Zan growled. "I have dreamt about making love to you every night."

Kenzie spread her legs farther apart to allow Zan to settle more comfortably between then. She bent her knees and lifted her pelvis into Zan's abdomen to demonstrate her own need. "I need you, Zan. I need you now. Please."

Kenzie reached for the hem of Zan's shirt and pulled it over her head. With a sense of urgency that threatened to overpower them both, Zan rose to her knees and forced Kenzie's legs up and around her waist while she pulled her sports bra off and allowed Kenzie access to her breasts.

With abdominal strength Kenzie didn't know she possessed, she rose from the bed and inhaled Zan's nipples, one at a time, into her mouth. Zan leaned backward and supported herself with her hands behind her on the bed, taking Kenzie with her. Her head was thrown back and the cords on her neck stood out prominently while she moaned out her pleasure at what Kenzie was doing to her.

The surge of passion that filled every part of Zan's being overwhelmed her and she rose once more to push Kenzie into the bed beneath her. With an urgency that surprised them both, she tore off Kenzie's clothes and ravished her neck and breasts while Kenzie squirmed beneath her.

"Off!" Kenzie growled as she pushed down on the waistband of Zan's shorts. The moment the offending garment was out of the way, Kenzie thrust her fingers into Zan. Zan curled her body and struggled to control her climax against the assault Kenzie was making on her.

"My God, Zan. You are so wet," Kenzie exclaimed, and she struggled to hold back her own climax. "I need you inside me. Please. I can't hold it back."

Without waiting for Zan to comply, Kenzie pushed her off and onto the bed beside her. She quickly reversed her position and climbed on top of Zan so that they each had oral access to one another.

Zan momentarily panicked with this new position until she felt Kenzie suck her clit into her mouth and plunge two fingers deep within her. She quickly followed suit.

She was sure she temporarily lost consciousness as they climaxed together, and she floated above them and watched as their minds, hearts and bodies melded into one.

I love you, Kenzie. I will never leave you, she thought as the spasms subsided and Kenzie moved to lie beside her.

Within moments, fully sated, they both fell into a deep sleep.

In the wee hours of the morning, they awoke and made love once more, slower, and with more tenderness. Later, Zan lay with her head on Kenzie's stomach, and Kenzie's hand ran through Zan's hair.

"I am sorry I was so urgent and rough, earlier," Zan whispered into the dark.

"Don't be sorry. It was exactly what I wanted, and needed," Kenzie whispered back.

"Welcome home, Kenzie."

"I love you, Zan.

Chapter 28

Kenzie awoke the next morning to an odd sound.

"What the hell is that?"

She noticed that Zan was not in bed. She propped herself up on one elbow and listened. Her eyes grew wide.

"Shit!"

Kenzie scurried out of bed and went directly to the bathroom. Zan was there, kneeling in front of the toilet and vomiting.

She dropped to her knees beside Zan. "My God, Zan. Are you all right?"

Zan pushed Kenzie away and retched once more. "Please. I'll be okay." Zan retched again. "Please go."

Kenzie realized she was making Zan uncomfortable and quickly left the bathroom.

"She hovered outside the bathroom door until the retching sounds ceased and the toilet flushed. "Zan? Are you all right? Can I come in?"

She heard the toilet seat cover come down, and then the door cracked open. She pushed the door open farther and found Zan sitting on the seat. She was unnaturally pale. Kenzie dropped to her knees again and lifted Zan's chin. "Sweetie, tell me what's wrong."

"I do not know," Zan said weakly.

Kenzie frowned. "Zan, you told me you were feeling better before I left for Phoenix. Has this been happening for the past two weeks?"

Zan didn't answer her.

Kenzie climbed to her feet. "Damn it! I would never have left if I knew you were still sick."

"My point, exactly," Zan said.

"Ahh! You infuriate me sometimes! Come on, we need to put some clothes on. I'm taking you to the clinic."

Kenzie grabbed Zan by the arm and pulled her into a standing position. She led her toward the bedroom.

"I don't want to go. Please, no hospital," Zan said.

"Well, I'm not giving you a choice," Kenzie replied. "Have you been sick the whole time I've been gone?"

"It was getting better."

"Damn it!"

Kenzie sat Zan on the bed and pulled a set of clean clothes out of the dresser. She handed them to Zan. "Here, put these on."

Kenzie dressed herself quickly and then called Bree.

"This better be good, Kenzie. Do you know what time it is? And on a Saturday to boot?" Bree said.

"Bree, I need help."

Bree was immediately awake. She sat up quickly and climbed out of bed. "Kenzie, are you okay?" She quickly made her way into the living room to avoid waking Jimmy up.

"I'm okay. It's Zan."

"What's wrong?"

"Do you remember me telling you before we went to Phoenix that she had been sick?"

"Yes."

"Well, she's still sick. Apparently, she's been sick the whole time. I found her in the bathroom his morning puking her guts up."

"Jesus, Kenzie."

"Can you meet me at the clinic?"

"It's Saturday. The clinic is closed today."

"Yes, but you and I both have keys. I just want to do the standard blood and urine workup. I don't really want to wait until Monday, and she is adamant that she will not go to the hospital."

"Okay. Sure. I'll meet you there in about twenty minutes."

"Thank you, Bree. You're a good friend."

"Ditto, sister. I'll see you soon."

***

"Don't bother with the blood work, Kenzie. We have our answer."

Kenzie looked at the test result that Bree had taken. Her eyes grew wide and she shook her head side to side. "No way. This can't be!" Kenzie said.

"We can wait a while and do another test, but I suspect we'll get the same result. The test results match the symptoms. Zan is pregnant."

"How can that be?"

"You're a nurse, Kenzie. You know exactly how that can be."

"But she's been with me for more than a month."

"We don't know how far along she is. She could have become pregnant before you ever met her. Oh, and she's been on her own for the last two weeks. You have no idea what she's been doing while you've been gone."

"No, I don't believe it. She wouldn't do that to me."

"Are you sure about that? What do you *really* know about her, Kenzie?"

Kenzie walked toward the door of the lab. "I need to take her home. Thank you for helping me, Bree."

"Kenzie, wait." Bree crossed the room and took her friend by the shoulders. "I'm sorry I was so negative. Don't jump to conclusions before you give her a chance to explain, okay? I won't lie to you, K. This has shaken my confidence in her, but I can see the difference she has made in your life, and I would hate like hell for you to lose that."

Kenzie hugged her friend. "Thank you, Bree. I really need to take her home."

***

Zan sat on the sofa while Kenzie paced the room in front of her. An intense fear had begun to grow in her chest the moment Kenzie came to retrieve her from the clinic waiting room to take her home. Kenzie was silent the entire way.

"Kenzie, please tell me what is wrong," Zan said.

Kenzie stopped pacing and faced Zan. "What exactly did you do for the two weeks I was gone?" she asked.

"Trey and I completed our research, and when Trey returned to the motel, I was here."

"You were here, in this apartment?"

"Yes."

"And you didn't go anywhere, or see anyone else during those two weeks?"

"Only Trey. Oh, and Charlie."

Kenzie paced again. Zan stood and stopped her in her tracks by grabbing her arm.

"Kenzie, tell me what you and Bree found at the clinic."

"You're pregnant, Zan."

"Pregnant?" Zan said.

Kenzie shook off Zan's hand on her arm. "Yes, pregnant. You know, knocked up, bun in the oven, expecting, with child! What you've got is morning sickness. It's pretty common with pregnancy. It also explains why you feel better later in the day."

Zan's legs suddenly felt weak. She reached back for the sofa and sat down again. "I…I am with child?"

Kenzie folded her arms across her chest. "Yes. Care to tell me who the father is?"

Zan was confused. "I…"

"I trusted you, Zan. I trusted you! I go away for two weeks and I come back to this!"

Zan stood again and looked around the room like she had to escape. "I need time to process this."

"Take all the time you need, Zan. This is finished. I can't be with someone I can't trust."

Zan felt like she had been punched in the stomach. She grabbed her backpack that sat in its usual place by the door and she left.

She had all she could do to stumble down the front steps and make her way the three blocks to the motel. Once in the room, she threw herself on her bed and sobbed heart-wrenching tears. She had never experienced such an intense sense of loss in her entire life and the feeling consumed her. The emotional release drained her to the point that she succumbed to sleep, only to awake in the middle of the night to more intense tears. Come morning, she was resigned to return to the ship and never step foot on Earth again.

***

Trey found Zan curled into a fetal position when she returned to the motel room later that morning. She knew immediately that there was something seriously wrong. She rolled Zan onto her back and was met with a blank stare on her friend's face.

"Zan. Zan, what happened? Are you ill?" Trey asked urgently. "Is Kenzie okay?"

Trey watched the focus return to Zan's eyes at the mention of Kenzie's name.

"Kenzie?" Zan whispered.

Trey pulled Zan into a seated position. "Zan, you are beginning to worry me. What is wrong?"

Zan met Trey's gaze.

"I am with child."

Trey abruptly stood. "What?"

"I am with child. That is why I have been sick."

"How could this happen?" Trey asked.

"It should not have been possible. I have not yet seen my three hundredth year. It was not my time."

"Have you engaged in the manifestation ceremony?"

"Yes."

"With Kenzie?"

"Yes."

"And were you both immersed in water, sister?"

"We were bathing together, and we made love."

"And did you reach simultaneous fulfillment?"

Zan's head snapped around to face Trey. "Yes, and several minutes after, a final wave of spasms ripped through me that was so intense, I thought I might lose consciousness. I have been ill every morning since, although the intensity of the illness was greater yesterday that it had been previously."

Trey returned to Zan's side and sat down beside her. "How did you find out?"

"I was sick yesterday morning and Kenzie took me to the clinic. Bree did a test."

"So, Kenzie knows."

"Yes." The tears flowed freely from Zan's eyes. "It is over, Trey."

"What do you mean?"

"Kenzie believes I was unfaithful while she was gone. We are done."

"But you were ill before she left."

***

Kenzie lay curled up on her bed. She hadn't slept well the night before and her face was tear-stained and puffy. The combination of tears and little sleep had caused a raging headache to settle in behind her eyes.

She pondered again and again in her head, the sequence of events that had led to the disastrous confrontation with Zan the day before. How could she be so stupid as to fall a second time for someone who would break her heart?

For the hundredth time, she asked herself what she actually knew about Zan. There were warning flags. Like why she was only able to meet her on the trail. The odd arrangement she seemed to have with Trey. The whole council business. And why she seemed so ignorant about their language and cultures. Why did she allow herself to ignore these warning signs?

Kenzie's thoughts were interrupted by a banging on her front door. She tried to ignore it, but it persisted. Finally, she couldn't deal with the irritation any longer and she went to see who was disturbing her misery on this Sunday morning.

It was Zan.

"Kenzie, open the door. We need to talk," Zan said.

Kenzie stood in front of the locked door and looked at Zan through the window. "Go away. We have nothing to say to one another," she said angrily.

"I have plenty to say. Please open the door."

"No!" Kenzie started to walk away.

"Kenzie!" Zan shouted. "You are the father!"

Chapter 29

Kenzie flung the door open. "How stupid do you think I am, Zan?"

Zan stepped into the room. "Kenzie, you need to listen to me." She reached out to take Kenzie's hand.

Kenzie snatched her hand away. "Don't you touch me."

"Kenzie, please. Just listen to what I have to say."

"No, Zan! You need to listen to *me*! I loved you. I loved you more than any human being I have ever known. And you betrayed me."

"Kenzie, I am not a human being."

Kenzie stepped into Zan's personal space. "Not a human being, huh? Then what the fuck are you?"

"I am Vakillian. I am an alien."

"I *know* you're an alien! Why do you think we spent so much time finding immigration applications for you?"

Zan ran a hand through her hair. "No. You don't understand."

"It's *you* who doesn't understand, Zan. You've played me for a fool for too long already. I trusted you, Zan. I invited you into my home, and into my bed, and then the minute I'm out of town, you get yourself knocked up. I refuse to be your immigration meal ticket, Zan."

"Kenzie, I became ill *before* you went out of town. I have not been unfaithful to you."

Kenzie put her hands on her hips. "If that's true, then that means you were pregnant before I went out of town."

"Yes."

Kenzie began to pace. "You know what, Zan? I really shouldn't blame you for this. I should blame myself. Gullible Kenzie. So, were you planning to make me fall in love with you, so I'd marry you and give you legal reason to stay in this country, or to maybe provide you the opportunity to have your anchor baby born here? Don't get me wrong, Zan, I believe in immigration. I believe everyone deserves a fair chance at a better life, but what I object to is achieving that better life by lying and cheating and taking advantage of innocent people. And then to top it all off, you are trying to convince me that I fathered this child? News flash, Zan, we are both women. Conception is impossible between two women!"

"It is not impossible on Vakillia."

"There you go with the Vakillia thing again! That must be some awesome country if women can make other women pregnant there!"

"Vakillia is not a country. It is a planet. Like I said, I am an alien."

"And how did you get here, Zan, in a spaceship?"

"Yes."

Kenzie pulled her cellphone out of her pocket.

"What are you doing?" Zan asked.

"I am calling the police. You are out of your freaking mind."

Zan grabbed her phone. "Please do not do that. Let me prove it to you."

"You're going to prove to me that you're an alien from another planet?"

"Yes."

"How?"

"Come with me to the trail."

"Do you think I'm stupid enough to get into a car with you?"

"I would die before I would hurt you, Kenzie."

Kenzie turned her back on Zan and walked to the window where she stood for several minutes in silence.

"Kenzie, I promised that I would tell you everything when I could. The time has come for me to be completely honest with you, but I cannot do that if you don't trust me."

"Considering the circumstances, you are asking a lot of me, Zan."

"Yes. But if you feel you have already lost everything, you have everything to regain if I am telling the truth."

***

Kenzie and Zan stopped at Kenzie's meditation site on the Little Horse Trail.

"The very first time I saw you was in this location. You walked to the edge of that cliff and you took a photograph of the structure in the distance."

"Yes, I did."

"Please hand your mat to me," Zan said.

Kenzie handed her the mat, and Zan rolled it out in the exact location it had been on their first encounter.

"After you took the picture, you sat in the middle of your mat and meditated. Beside you, were two bottles of water and your sunglasses."

"That's right. How did you know that?" Kenzie asked. "Were you watching me?"

"Let me continue," Zan said. "When I was sure you were in a meditative state, I mind probed with you."

"You what?"

"I mind probed with you. I placed my hands on the sides of your head and read your thoughts. I saw your memories. I saw the repression from your childhood. I saw Jessie, and I felt your emotions. That was the first time I had ever felt emotion in my entire life.

"After I broke the probe, I drank the water from your bottles. I had not brought water with me because I had not anticipated the arid nature of your planet when I first arrived."

Kenzie threw her hands into the air. "This is bullshit, Zan."

"Please let me finish." Zan waited until she had Kenzie's attention again. "I drank your water and then went through your pack. When I pulled your cellphone out and turned it on, the battery drained almost immediately, so I returned it to your pack. I then took your sunglasses because your sun was too bright, and I had not yet created lenses to reduce the amount of light allowed into my eyes."

"You took my sunglasses?"

"Yes. I took them back to the ship with me and showed them to Trey. Later that night, I lay on my unit and I put them on, and when I opened my eyes, I saw images that I assumed were things you had seen when you were wearing them. I saw images of a woman with long yellow hair, running into a massive body of water."

"Jessie," Kenzie said under her breath.

"I returned them the next day when you and Bree came to search for them."

Kenzie stepped a few feet away. "You are freaking me out here, Zan."

"Do you recall seeing a flash of something on the trail that day, just before Bree spotted your sunglasses beside the shrub?"

"As a matter of fact, I do."

"That was me. I had to uncloak to return your glasses, and I was not fast enough to re-cloak before you saw a glimpse of me."

"The next thing you're going to tell me is that you were the shadow I chased shortly after that," Kenzie said in jest.

"That was me as well. It was because of that encounter that we realized we had a bug in our cloaking mechanism that neglected to cloak our shadows."

"This is just too far-fetched to believe, Zan. You could have made this up just by watching me that day on the trail."

"I have one more thing to show you." Zan offered her hand to Kenzie. She looked at it suspiciously. "I will not harm you, Kenzie."

Kenzie finally relented and put her hand in Zan's. Zan led her to the edge of the cliff facing Cathedral Rock.

Zan stood on Kenzie's right side. "Look at the shrubs below."

Kenzie gasped and dug her cellphone from her pocket. She opened the photo folder and quickly located the mystery picture she had taken in this very spot several weeks earlier. The two shadows in the picture perfectly matched the two shadows being projected on the shrubs at that exact moment.

"It was you," Kenzie whispered.

"Yes, it was me. Do you recall feeling like you had made contact with something when you threw your pack over your shoulder?" Zan watched Kenzie nod. "That was your arm coming in contact with me. I was standing very close, as you can see in the picture. Even then, I wanted to be as close to you as I could get."

"And in the chapel?" Kenzie said.

"Yes. I was there, sitting cloaked on the bench behind you. That is how I knew the sunbeams extended throughout the chapel. I mind probed with you on that day as well. Your memories and emotions touched me deeply. I believe I had already fallen in love with you by that time. I believe I had fallen in love with you the very first day I laid eyes on you on the trail, but I had no name for that emotion. At that time, I had no name for any emotion."

Kenzie walked a few feet away and turned to face Zan. She ran a hand through her hair. "This is all so overwhelming. Why here? Why Sedona?"

"The vortexes afforded us the easiest point of entry."

"The vortexes?"

"Yes. They are more than just spiritual sites. They also serve as tears in the time-space continuum that are easily penetrated."

"Like portals," Kenzie said.

"In a manner of speaking, yes."

Kenzie and Zan walked slowly down the trail to the Little Horse parking lot.

"I don't know what to think about all of this, Zan. It seems impossible to believe."

"I have not lied to you, Kenzie. I have not always given adequate explanations for things I have said, but I have not lied to you. I am from Vakillia, and Vakillia is dying. Our water sources are depleting and as such, we are unable to reproduce.

"My people are in search of a new homeland, and I am hoping that Earth will be chosen, but there many other missions like this one, to seek out and explore other destinations as well. We are a peaceful species, and we do not intend to dominate, but rather to co-exist and to use the resources of other worlds to procreate."

Kenzie stopped walking. "Wait! You use the resources of other worlds to procreate? Is that secret code for finding natives of these worlds to become baby-daddies for your offspring?" Kenzie asked. "Is that what I am to you?"

"I promised not to lie to you again, Kenzie, so I will tell you the truth. Procreation is impossible on Vakillia, so every fifteen Earth-years, those of my people who are between the ages of thirty and forty-five Earth-years, seek out host planets with plentiful enough resources to allow us to procreate among *ourselves*, and then return to our home world. It has never been our intention, nor our practice to procreate with the natives of these worlds. Until you, I wasn't even aware it was possible to do so."

"Until me. That assumes I believe you."

Kenzie turned and continued down the trail to the parking lot. When they reached the car, both climbed in and they headed back toward town without another word exchanged between them.

Kenzie pulled into the parking lot of the motel and put the car into park. She looked at Zan, who sat in the passenger seat, dejectedly studying the hands clasped in her lap. "I think it's best if you stay here tonight. I have a lot to think about."

***

"I told her everything, Tredoran."

"Everything?"

"Yes. I told her we are from another planet. We went to the trail and I told her everything I had seen and done to her on the earlier visits. I told her about Vakillia and about our treks to other worlds to procreate. I will not lie to her again."

"And the child?"

"I believe the child is hers, Trey. I believe it with every part of my being, but I do not know if Kenzie believes it. Her race cannot produce viable offspring without the genetic union of male and female components. It may be beyond her comprehension."

"You may not be giving her the credit she deserves, Zan."

"What do you mean?"

"She is a healer. She is a genetic scientist. You said you downloaded the process documentation and specifications for Vakillian procreation before you left the ship. Share that with her and let her decide for herself."

***

Kenzie sat on the sofa with her legs curled under her and a box of tissues on the cushion beside her. She couldn't stop crying at the sense of loss and confusion that filled her heart and mind.

Everything that Zan had shown her and told her on the trail could only be known if she was there. She *knew* things that Kenzie had never told her. Things she had never told anyone.

All those times it felt like I was being watched. Was that Zan? she wondered.

Kenzie reached for another tissue just as a knock sounded on her door. She pulled the shade back from the window and saw Trey standing on the porch. She opened the door.

"Trey, I really don't think…"

"I am only here to bring this to you." Trey handed her a tablet. "It contains the scientific process for Vakillian procreation. I urge you to read it. It may give you a better understanding of what is happening."

"Thank you."

Trey stood there for a few moments just looking at Kenzie. "I understand how overwhelming this is, Kenzie. It is overwhelming for us, as well. Goodnight."

Kenzie closed and locked the door. She dropped the tablet onto the coffee table before settling back onto the sofa, staring at it for several minutes. Then, she picked it up and began to read.

Chapter 30

Kenzie arrived at work the next morning with dark circles under her eyes.

"You look like hell," Bree said. "I'm taking you to lunch today. I sense you need to talk."

"You don't know the half of it, Bree."

"Rough night?"

"Rough weekend."

"I assume this has something to do with our discovery yesterday?"

"Grrrr," Kenzie said.

"That bad, huh?"

"Worse." Kenzie wiped tears from the corners of her eyes.

"Ooh, that's not a good sign. Maybe you should take the day off. I'll cover your patients."

"Thanks, but I really need to keep my mind occupied."

"Okay, but if you feel you need to get out of here today, just let me know."

Kenzie threw her arms around Bree and hugged her. Bree held her close, longer than a normal hug. "You're trembling. Go home, K. Take care of yourself."

Kenzie released Bree and stepped back. She was openly crying. "Okay. Thanks, Bree." She took off her white coat and went into the locker room to hang it up. Bree followed her.

"Call me later. I want to know that you're all right."

Kenzie nodded and left through the back door.

By the time Kenzie reached home, she could barely see to pull her car into the driveway. She put the car in park and then climbed out. As she walked to the front of the building, she saw Zan sitting on her front steps.

She hesitated for a split second, during which time, Zan stood and moved toward her. "I was worried about you. Trey said you were crying," Zan said.

Kenzie sobbed. She grabbed Zan's hand and pulled her up the stairs and into the apartment with her. Once inside, she threw herself into Zan's arms.

"Hold me. Please, just hold me."

Zan wrapped her arms around Kenzie and held her close. She had no clue what to say, so she said nothing.

After a time, the sobs subsided, and Kenzie regained control. She took a step back and reached for a tissue on the coffee table. "I'm sorry. I'm such a mess," she said.

Zan took her by the shoulders. "Do not apologize. You were thrust into this against your will. You have nothing to be sorry for."

"You don't understand," Kenzie said. "I read the material Trey brought to me last night. If I had been aware of all of this before anything happened, I might have been a willing participant."

"What do you mean, Kenzie?"

Kenzie placed her hand above her heart. "The thought of having a baby with you brings such joy to my heart, Zan, but the way this is all going down is so confusing and there are so many questions. And I have so many fears."

"Come, sit. Talk to me about this, Kenzie."

"I read the material several times, and if I understand it correctly, the process uses the principles of diffusion and thermal molecular motion. The water as a medium provides the transference mechanism that moves the enzymes from one place to another."

Zan frowned. "I have not heard the process described that way before."

"It's a lot more complicated than what I've described, but from what I read, the enzymes themselves would take the place of male sperm and through a symbiotic relationship between the water and the diffusion process, the enzymes are moved from the donor to the host where fertilization occurs between the donor enzymes and the host egg. I guess that might be possible since enzymes are essential for DNA replication. Thermal molecular motion comes into play with the temperature of the water. Since heat excites molecules, they move faster in warmer environments, so I would assume that warmer water is preferable for this process than colder water."

Zan tilted her head. "I admit that this is the first time that process has been explained to me in terms I can understand. Thank you."

"If this is truly how it works, it most likely happened the night we made love in the bathtub," Kenzie said.

"I assume that to be true. For it to happen, both parties must reach fulfillment at the same time, and as you pointed out, water is required to move all the components. All of those events happened that night, and my illness appeared to begin at the same time."

"I still have doubts, Zan. We are talking about a form of parthenogenesis here. In the human race, spontaneous parthenogenesis is common, but it never develops into a viable fetus that can be carried to term. Instead, it usually becomes a benign ovarian tumor, and could even have disorganized structures in it such as hair or teeth, but it never develops into a child."

"This process is carried out every fifteen Earth-years by the Vakillian people, Kenzie. It has been proven to be viable."

"Yes, but if this child really *is* mine, it is not strictly Vakillian. We don't know what complications might arise from introducing a different species. That part scares me, Zan. It's all I could think about all night. I didn't sleep at all. Bree sent me home this morning almost as soon as I got there because I was such an emotional wreck about this."

"Kenzie, you have said *if* the child is yours. You still do not believe me."

Kenzie stood and walked a few feet away. "Zan, think about what you are asking me to blindly accept here. Yesterday, I discovered the one person I have been waiting for all my life is an alien, and then I discover she's pregnant—supposedly by me—and we're both women. That is a lot to handle without proof, especially since in *my* world, it's impossible."

Kenzie saw the dejected look on Zan's face. "Like I said, Zan, under normal circumstances, I would love to have a child with you, but the scientist in me needs proof."

Zan stood. "If it is proof you need, then I will find a way to get it for you."

"How? We can't do it through medical means here. I can only imagine what the medical community would do with this information. If you are truly an alien, your DNA would be unlike anything the scientists have ever seen. I don't want to risk exposing you like that. And if this is truly my child, I will not do anything that will put him or her at risk, and I will not allow it to become a science experiment for the medical community."

"The child will be a girl," Zan said. "It cannot be anything else."

"How do you know that?"

"Because as you pointed out, there is no sperm in this process, therefore, there is no Y chromosome."

Kenzie nodded. "You are right, of course."

Zan walked toward the door.

"Where are you going?"

"To get your proof. Then, maybe you will believe me."

"I'm going with you."

***

Trey walked back and forth across the motel room. "I believe it may be possible to modify the omni-spectrometer to provide that information," she said. "But I will need to be on the ship to accomplish that."

"When can you go?" Zan asked.

"I prefer to go as soon as possible. I would like to return before nightfall." Trey looked at Kenzie. "If you could transport me to the trailhead, it will allow me to leave sooner."

"Of course. Let's go."

A short time later, Kenzie pulled her car into the parking lot of the Little Horse trailhead. She threw open her car door and stepped out.

"Kenzie, I need you to wait here," Zan said.

"Not on your life, Zan! If you want me to believe you, then you need to trust me. If we have no trust, then we have no relationship. It's just that simple." Kenzie crossed her arms and waited for Zan's response.

Zan looked at Trey, who nodded slightly. She then extended her hand to Kenzie and the three of them entered the trailhead.

Ten minutes later, they reached the transfer site.

"How do they know you're here?" Kenzie asked.

"They continually monitor the transfer site. When they receive a signal from our transmitter, they will retrieve whoever is waiting," Zan explained.

"Are you going back with her?" Kenzie asked.

"I believe I should. I need to discuss the child with my birth units."

"Your birth units?"

"Belander and Molinder. Belander gave birth to me. To use Earth terms, they are my parents."

"Your parents are on the ship?" Kenzie asked incredulously.

"Yes. Belander is a member of the council. Molinder is a medical scientist. It is a pity that you may not meet them. I think they would like you."

"Well, if you settle on Earth, maybe I *will* get a chance to meet them."

"Perhaps."

"Are your parents on the ship too, Trey?" Kenzie asked.

"My birth units are no longer with us. They perished when I was a child. I have been more or less, reared by Zan's birth units."

"No wonder you two consider yourselves sisters. I'm sorry for your loss, Trey."

"It was a long time ago. Are you ready, Zan?"

"Yes." Zan turned to Kenzie. "We will return before nightfall."

"I will be here to pick you up."

Zan nodded and stepped into the transport site with Trey.

"Zan!" Kenzie called out. "I love you."

And then they were gone.

***

Kenzie sat in her car in the parking lot of the Little Horse Trail for the next half-hour, struggling to make sense of what she had witnessed at the transfer site. One minute they were there, and suddenly, they were gone. They vanished into thin air!

The realization hit her that Zan was being truthful with her.

Zan was an alien! The woman she was in love with was a goddamned alien!

Kenzie felt a combination of panic and exhilaration. Exhilaration because of her renewed sense of trust in Zan, and panic because, well, because the women she was in love with was a goddamned alien.

And what about the child? Kenzie struggled more with the concept of female-female conception than she did with Zan being an alien. As a geneticist, it was simply inconceivable to her.

She truly hoped Trey could come up with a way to resolve that question. She didn't know how she would feel if she couldn't.

Chapter 31

Trey and Zan parted ways as soon as they materialized on the transfer pads, Trey to the lab and Zan to her parents' quarters. Trey transformed immediately to Vakillian form before she left the transference room. Without having that same option, Zan remained cloaked in her avatar as she made her way through the ship toward her mothers' quarters.

The closer Zan came to her parents' quarters, the more nervous she became. By the time she reached their door, she was a wreck and visibly shaking. She inhaled deeply to calm herself and requested entry.

The door slid open and she stepped inside. Her mothers were relaxing on the sofa. Molinder was reading, and Belander was working on what appeared to be a work of needlepoint.

Molinder looked up. "Zangendar. We did not expect you to return from the surface today."

Belander put her needlepoint on the sofa beside her, and approached her daughter. She stopped in front of her and examined her closely. "Have you really lost the ability to transition to Vakillian form?" she asked.

"I have. Does that displease you?" Zan asked.

"It does not." Belander walked away. "Is there a reason you are here unexpectedly, daughter?"

"There is. I wanted to speak with you both about the human named Kenzie."

"She is the one you have been studying. Is that correct?" Molinder asked.

"Yes. I have come to know her very well. That is why I am here today."

"You have allowed yourself to feel emotion for her, haven't you, daughter?" Molinder challenged.

Zan clenched her jaw and tried desperately to hold back tears. "Yes, Mother. I have."

"You are on a mission, Zangendar. You should not allow human emotions to cloud your judgment," Molinder added.

"I am afraid it is too late for that. I am in love with her."

"In love with her? And does she return that love?"

"Yes. She has told me many times."

Molinder sat on the edge of her seat. "And how will she feel when she knows what you are, Zangendar? Will she still love you then? Not all species are open to loving someone not of their kind."

"Molinder! That is enough," Belander snapped.

"Our daughter is becoming weak, Belander."

"She is no weaker than you, Molinder, or me for that matter. As you well know, this path she is on is a difficult one. She needs our support right now, not your criticism."

"It is difficult indeed, and that is why I urge her to think long and hard before she chooses it."

"My path has already been chosen, Molinder," Zan said. "What I feel for Kenzie consumes me. I cannot turn away now."

"Have you coupled with her, Zangendar?" Belander asked softly.

Zan looked at her mother and saw a spark of something unexpected in her eyes. She saw sympathy, and that was all she needed to allow the tears to flow down her cheeks. "I am with child."

Belander opened her arms and gathered Zan to her. The floodgates opened and Zan wept into her mother's shoulder.

Then the unexpected happened. The duo grew by one and Zan found herself wrapped in the love of both her parents. That made her sob even more.

Belander looked directly at Molinder and smiled. "We are going to be grandparents, Molly."

***

Belander held Zan by the shoulders. "You have always been different from others of our kind, Zangendar. Even as a child, you challenged authority and questioned our ways. That is one of the reasons I recommended you for this mission. You bring a different perspective to our search for a new homeland. I specifically chose Earth for you and Tredoran to explore. One day soon, you will see the significance of that choice."

"Do you know how the council will rule, Belander?" Zan asked.

"You have given us much to consider. Once you deliver the remaining information, the council will meet and the decision with be forthcoming. I am but one vote, my daughter. I cannot say what the rest of the council will decide."

Zan broke out of her mother's grasp and walked toward the door. She looked at both of them. "Belander, Molinder, you must know that I will choose to stay if Earth is not chosen as our new homeland. I will not leave Kenzie. I love her, and she has the right to be part of this child's life."

Molinder approached her daughter. She touched her forehead to Zan's. "You are truly honorable, Zangendar. It is one of the reasons we care for you deeply. You are also an adult and you must make your own decisions, and live with the consequences, good and bad."

"Thank you for realizing that, Mother," Zan said and she turned to go.

"Zangendar," Belander said, causing her to pause in the doorway. "If the council learns of the child, it will complicate things."

Zan nodded, and then left their quarters.

Belander watched the door slide closed behind her daughter and then turned to her wife. "It appears your concerns are for naught, Molly."

"It appears so, Belinda. It appears so."

***

Kenzie paced back and forth across the transport site on the Little Horse Trail. She had been a nervous wreck all day and unable to concentrate on anything but Zan and the baby.

Where were they? It would be dark soon!

She sat on a nearby rock and rested her forearms on her thighs. She tilted her head back and closed her eyes.

How was this even possible? Conception between two women is impossible, at least on Earth it is. Check that, at least between two human women, it's impossible. But Zan isn't human.

Kenzie jumped to her feet again and resumed pacing.

Did you hear what you just said, Kenzie? she told herself. *Zan is not human! Zan, is, not, human! Are you out of your freaking mind for even thinking about getting involved in this? But wait – I'm already involved. Jesus! What have I gotten myself into?*

Kenzie stopped pacing and stepped out of the way to allow a young family to pass through from the Chapel Trail. The man and woman were holding hands and the father had a young toddler strapped into a pack on his back. The little one was fast asleep with its head on the father's shoulder. Kenzie's eyes were drawn to the baby and a rush of maternal tenderness filled her mind.

I wonder what our baby will look like. I hope she looks like Zan.

Kenzie felt an intense anxiety fill her chest.

Get a grip, Kenzie! You don't even know if it's yours yet! Ahh! Do you realize how crazy this sounds? Two women? Seriously?

Kenzie was about to crawl out of her skin with worry when a faint static sound reached her ears. She recalled having heard that same sound the day she chased Zan's shadow. A second later, Zan and Trey appeared at the transport site.

"Zan!" Kenzie called out.

Zan pulled Kenzie into her arms.

"I was beginning to think you weren't coming back."

"Of course, I would come back," Zan said.

"The delay is my fault, Kenzie," Trey interjected. "It took longer to adapt the omni-spectrometer than I thought it would."

"Look, it's starting to get dark. Let's head to the car while we talk. So, were you able to make the modifications you needed?" Kenzie asked.

"I was successful," Trey replied.

"How will we test it? How can we verify its accuracy and repeatability?"

Zan frowned.

"Why are you looking at me like that?" Kenzie asked.

"You still do not believe me, do you?" Zan said.

"Zan, I'm a nurse. It's routine procedure to do repeat tests or to get second opinions if life-altering situations are at hand. I think this qualifies as a life-altering situation, don't you think?"

Zan stopped on the trail and ran a hand through her hair. "Forgive me, Kenzie. It has been a tiring day. I had an emotional encounter with my parents, and I am afraid it impacted me more than I anticipated."

"Can I assume the meeting with your birth units did not go well, sister?" Trey asked.

Zan sighed. "We are losing our light source. We can talk about this at home."

Kenzie pulled her cellphone out of her pocket as they continued down the trail.

"Who are you communicating with?" Zan asked.

"I'm ordering pizza for the three of us. We can pick it up on the way home."

"It is a good thing we purchased beer," Trey said.

***

"How are we going to test this?" Kenzie asked.

"What will it take to convince you I am not lying?" Zan replied in a combative tone.

"Sister! Are you forgetting that Kenzie has as much to be concerned about as you do in this matter?" Trey said. "I think you owe her an apology."

"Trey, it's all right. I guess I'd be angry too if I were challenged on something this personal," Kenzie said.

"No. Trey is correct," Zan interrupted. "You are right to be concerned. I am sorry."

Kenzie took Zan's hand and held it while she asked her next question. "So, I'm getting the impression that you two are making this up as you go. Is that right?" She looked back and forth between them. "Hmm, I thought so. You have no clue how to proceed," she said when neither responded. "So, what exactly does this device do that you modified on the ship?"

"It will be able to compare blood samples from two or more individuals to determine if common genomes exist between them," Trey said.

Kenzie sat back in her chair. "So, this is really nothing more than a paternity test?"

"Paternity test? I do not understand," Zan said.

"A paternity test does exactly what you just described. It has the ability to determine which man fathered your child as long as you have DNA samples from both," Kenzie explained.

"Yes," Trey said excitedly.

"I sense a *but*, in there," Kenzie said.

"But we have not yet determined how to get a sample from the child without harming it."

"That's easy. The baby's DNA can be found naturally in the mother's bloodstream, at least in humans, it can. I assume in a Vakillian pregnancy, the mother and child share a bloodstream?"

"Yes! Yes, they do," Trey responded.

"Then, problem solved. All we need is a sample of blood from me, and another from Zan."

"I believe you should take samples from me as well. That will allow us to compare my blood to both yours and Zan's in a double-blind study," Trey suggested.

"That's an excellent suggestion, Trey," Kenzie said.

"But will you believe the results?" Zan asked.

"If your device shows a match between you and me, Zan, I will process a paternity test of my own on the same samples of blood."

"But you were concerned about other medical professionals seeing my blood," Zan pointed out.

"Yes, I am still concerned about that, but I have the ability to do that test myself. Right at the clinic."

"And if the device does not show a match?" Zan asked.

Kenzie didn't respond for several moments, instead, she contemplated her hand still joined with Zan's.

"Kenzie?" Zan prompted.

She looked directly at Zan. "I don't know, Zan. I honestly don't know."

***

It was after dark when Kenzie and Zan walked Trey back to the motel and then returned to the apartment. Kenzie unlocked the front door and motioned for Zan to enter before her. Once inside, she closed the door and leaned her back against it.

Zan walked a few feet into the room and turned around to face Kenzie. "I am sorry, Kenzie," she said.

"I wish you could understand how I feel, Zan. Never in a million years did I expect to be in this situation. It is so hard for me to comprehend how this could have happened. It is making me question everything I know, and everything I have been taught my entire life."

"I was not with child when I first came to Earth, Kenzie, and I have not coupled with anyone but you since I have been here. In fact, I have never coupled with anyone in my entire life, except you. I wish you could trust that I am being truthful with you."

Kenzie pushed off the door and walked up to Zan. She placed her palm on the side of Zan's face. "Please know that I am not challenging you, Zan. I am challenging the whole concept of same-sex conception."

A solitary tear rolled down Zan's cheek.

"Sweetheart, please don't cry," Kenzie said.

Zan put her hand on her own chest. "It hurts me here that you doubt my faithfulness. I love you, Kenzie. I love you with everything that I am."

Kenzie sighed and took Zan's hand. "Come lie with me. Come talk to me about Vakillia."

***

Kenzie and Zan lay facing one another in the darkened bedroom. For a long time, they simply looked at one another, each struggling with her own inner thoughts.

"Zan, I know you believe it's your duty to procreate with another Vakillian, but in a loveless society, how does that work? I mean, do you mate only to procreate?"

"That is a difficult question to answer. Technically, we do not have to identify with another female as a couple to procreate, in fact, most Vakillians do not couple with one another for long periods of time. My parental units are not typical in that respect, although there are others besides them that have done so."

"How do you choose your mate?"

"Our mates are chosen for us."

"What? That's pretty barbaric!"

"Our mates are chosen for us based on scientific genome matching for optimized species control."

"Are you seriously telling me you have designer children, that you genetically determine what they will look like and what their abilities will be?"

"Yes. It has been an effective means of preventing defects."

"Holy shit! How cold is that? What would happen if a defect or disability comes through anyway?"

"That rarely happens."

"But if it did?"

Zan rolled onto her back and looked at the ceiling. "Then it would be eliminated."

"Jesus Christ! No wonder your species avoids emotions! That is wrong on so many levels! That is just wrong!"

"It is how things are done on Vakillia. Like I said, it rarely happens."

"Do you realize that if this truly is my child, that she could have some defect or disability simply because she is a combination of Vakillian and human genes?"

"That is a possibility I have been contemplating. I am hoping that is not the case."

"So, how do you decide who gets pregnant? I mean, let's say you and Trey were chosen to couple. Who gets to carry the baby, you or her?"

"It could be either, and in the best of situations, it is both. During the manifestation process, there is transference of enzymes through the water by both participants, and if the host is receptive, conception occurs. Sometimes the process also results in no pregnancy at all."

"Would you raise the child or children together?"

"Again, that depends on the individuals involved. Belander and Molinder chose to raise me together, however, several Vakillian mothers choose to raise their children by themselves."

"It all seems so clinical."

Kenzie traced the side of Zan's face with her index finger and struggled unsuccessfully to hold back tears.

Zan captured her hand and pulled it close to her heart. "There are tears in your eyes, Kenzie," she whispered softly.

"I was thinking about little Zan being raised in an emotionless environment. Did your parents show any affection toward you at all?"

"While I was growing up, Molinder was strict and unyielding. I believe she cared for me deeply, however, she more readily displayed affection for Belander than she did for me. Belander was less strict and more willing to look beyond my rebellious behavior when it occurred. I have always had a special relationship with Belander. I would not describe my relationship with either of my birth units as loving or affectionate. At least not in the ways I have seen Earth parents treat their children."

"It breaks my heart to know that you were never shown love and affection as a child."

"It was part of my culture, Kenzie. I was not aware that feelings as complex as love even existed before you came into my life."

Kenzie wiped a tear from her cheek. "Children need touch. They need love. I,I just can't imagine it."

"I promise you that our child will be raised in a loving environment, even if you choose not to be part of that," Zan said.

Kenzie didn't know how to respond to that. There was such conflict raging inside of her at that moment that she didn't trust herself not to make the situation worse by directly responding to Zan's comment. Instead, she chose a different tack.

"Zan, I'm confused about something. You say your people travel to other worlds every fifteen years looking for suitable places to mate, yet you are not quite twenty-eight years old. Why are you here now? Aren't you a couple of years early?"

"What you describe is true, however, during the past decade, the degradation in both the quantity and quality of the water supply on Vakillia has accelerated at an alarming rate. I have pointed out on several occasions that this mission is primarily to find a new homeland. We endeavored to start this mission two earth years sooner than normal so that we could have time to settle and to build a suitable infrastructure for our people before the time of the manifestation was upon us."

"The manifestation?"

"Yes. That is what we call the time for mating."

"So, this child..." Kenzie began.

"*Our* child," Zan corrected.

"What I'm trying to say, Zan, is that this child was not intentional."

"It was not. What you and I did to create this child was quite different from the manifestation ceremony. And you are not Vakillian. Combined with the fact that I have not yet reached my thirtieth Earth year, all of these factors made conception unlikely. To be truthful, conception was not at all on my mind when we made love."

"Needless to say, it was the last thing on my mind as well," Kenzie said.

Kenzie continued to look directly into Zan's face. She so wanted to kiss her and to tell her everything would be all right, but she honestly didn't know if that was true. There were so many unanswered questions.

"What do you think the council will decide, Zan?"

"I do not know, but it does not matter."

"What do you mean?"

"What the council chooses to do has no influence on what *I* will plan to do. The only one who will influence my plans is you."

Kenzie's head snapped up. "What do you mean by that?"

"If you choose to be part of this child's life, I will fight to remain on Earth with you, even if the council decides to move on."

Kenzie abruptly climbed out of the bed and faced Zan, with her arms stretched out to the sides. "When did I *ever* say I didn't want to be part of this child's life, Zan?"

Zan pulled herself into a seated position with her back against the headboard. "You doubt that the child is yours."

"I won't deny that. It's just impossible in my world." Kenzie climbed onto the bed and sat back on her knees beside Zan. "Look, we'll see what happens after we get the test results, but even if this is *not* my child, it is part of *you*. I love you, and I know I will love this child, *even* if she is defective, and *even* if she's not mine. Either way, I will raise her with you as though she was my own."

Zan's eyes filled with tears. "She is yours. You will see."

Chapter 32

Kenzie left the house the next morning before Zan woke. She wanted to get to the clinic before anyone else so that she could collect three test tubes and syringes for the blood draws she planned to do on her lunch hour. She secured the supplies in her backpack which hung inside her locker and then retreated to the break area for a cup of coffee.

"Good morning, girlfriend!" Bree said as she passed the break area on her way to the locker room.

"'Morning, Bree!"

"I'll take mine with cream and two sugars!" Bree shouted as she walked by.

Kenzie carried both cups of coffee to the table just as Bree entered the room.

"Thank you!"

"You're welcome. I thought you were cutting back on the sugar," Kenzie said.

"I'm having a moment of weakness. Don't judge me. How are you feeling today, by the way?" Bree asked.

"I'm much better. Thanks for covering for me yesterday."

"No problem. How are things with Zan?"

Kenzie studied the contents of her cup. "Better. We have a lot to work out, but things are definitely better."

"Did she give you any explanation?"

"She confirmed that she was pregnant before you and I went to Phoenix."

"I see. And how do you feel about that?"

"Like I said, we have a lot to work out."

"Well, I have some pretty big shoulders if you need to talk."

Kenzie reached for Bree's hand and squeezed. "Have I told you lately that I love you?" she asked.

"Ditto, girlfriend. Ditto."

***

Just before lunch, Kenzie stepped into the charge nurse's office.

"Hey, Bree. I'm heading home for a few minutes to check on Zan. She's still doing the morning sickness thing."

"Okay. Tell her I said to hydrate."

"I'm going to swing into the deli on the way back. Can I pick you up a sandwich or something?"

"Ooh! That sounds good. How about a ham and cheese sandwich with pickles, tomatoes, lettuce and mayo. Thanks!"

"Whoa, let me write this down." Kenzie picked up a notepad and pen from Bree's desk. "Salt and pepper?" she asked.

"Yes, please. Oh, and provolone cheese."

Kenzie finished writing the list. "Okay. I'll be back soon."

Ten minutes later, Kenzie pulled into her driveway and grabbed her pack. She went into the apartment and found Zan and Trey sitting at the dinette table, waiting for her.

She put her pack on the table and pulled out the supplies. Before she began, she felt Zan's forehead and kissed her on the head. "How are you feeling?" she asked. "Were you sick again this morning?"

"Yes, but I'm beginning to feel better."

"That's good. I've only got a few minutes, so let's get this blood drawn. Trey, could you grab a plate from the cupboard? We can put the samples on it for your device to test. The rest of it will go into the test tubes for me to bring back to work."

Trey pulled a plate from the cupboard and showed it to Kenzie. "Is this one okay?"

"Perfect. Who wants to go first?"

Zan and Trey pointed at one another.

"That wasn't so bad, now was it?" Kenzie said. "I even managed to draw my own blood." Kenzie pointed to the plate with three circles of blood. Above each circle were the letters, T, Z and K to identify which sample belonged to each of them.

"Go ahead and take your readings, Trey, while I grab an ice pack from the freezer. These test tubes need to be kept cool until they can be tested. Zan, watch what Trey is doing carefully as a second check that the correct sample is assigned the appropriate name."

Trey pulled her omni-spectrometer from her pocket and pointed it at the circle of blood with the Z above it. She collected the appropriate data and assigned it the file name Z. She did the same for the other two samples, assigning them the appropriate T and K file names. She then programmed the device to test all permutations of the three samples. While they waited, Trey set up a tablet to be able to display the results on a larger screen.

Kenzie wrapped the test tubes and ice packs in a towel and put them into her pack. She then joined Zan and Trey who were watching the omni-spectrometer with rapt attention. Finally, the device beeped. They all looked at one another expectantly.

Trey picked up the device and wirelessly connected it to the tablet.

Kenzie put her hand on Zan's shoulder and squeezed as the data was displayed on the screen.

T to K...No match

T to Z...No match

Z to K...Partial match

Zan looked up at Kenzie and smiled.

"Partial match?" Kenzie said.

"The program would detect a match between you and the child's genomes, but not between yours and Zan's," Trey explained.

***

Kenzie met Bree in the break room and delivered her ham sandwich.

"Thanks, K. What do I owe you?" Bree asked.

"My treat. Here's a bag of chips as well." Kenzie handed her the chips. The bag shook so badly, it rattled.

"Whoa! You are shaking like a leaf, girl! Are you okay?"

Kenzie looked directly into Bree's face.

"Okay. You look terrified. Come with me." Bree scooped up their sandwiches and pulled Kenzie into her office and closed the door. She dropped the sandwiches on her desk and then took Kenzie into her arms. "C'mere, you."

Kenzie wrapped her arms around Bree's waist and allowed her friend to envelope her in a loving embrace. After a few minutes, the trembling subsided.

Bree held her at arms' length. "So, tell me what's going on."

"I need your help, Bree."

"You got it. Anything you need."

Bree locked the front door of the clinic as soon as the final patient left around five. She joined Kenzie in the lab. "All right, so tell me what's wrong," Bree said.

"I'm not sure I'd classify it as right or wrong, Bree."

"So, what's the issue then?"

Kenzie began pacing.

"Pacing is not a good sign. Stop, Kenz. Spill it!"

"I have some tests I need your help with."

"What kind of tests?"

"Paternity tests."

"For Zan?"

"Yes."

"Okay. We need blood for that."

Kenzie picked her pack up from the table and carried it to the lab bench. She unzipped it and retrieved the plastic bag containing the blood samples and ice packs. They were still cool.

"Wow! How long have you been preparing to do this?"

"Just since yesterday. I took the blood samples today."

"So, you know who the potential fathers are, then?" Bree asked.

"I think so. At least I hope so." Kenzie handed the test tubes to Bree. "Zan's sample is labeled with the Z."

Bree looked at all three samples. They were labeled Z, T and M. "Okay. Let's do this."

Bree first did the test on sample Z. She and Kenzie looked at the test results together.

"So, this is the baseline. I definitely see two DNA signatures here. I assume one is Zan and the other is the baby."

"Yes. Let's test sample T next," Kenzie suggested.

Bree processed the test and compared it to Zan's sample. "Hmm. I have an opinion, but I'd like to hear what you think before I say anything," Bree said.

Kenzie examined the comparison carefully. "I don't see anything that matches, Bree."

"I agree. Okay, then. On to sample M."

Bree and Kenzie watched as the test result were calculated.

"Bingo!" Bree said. "We have a match with one of the two DNA streams in Zan's sample. Do you agree?" Bree stepped aside so Kenzie could see the final analysis.

"Zan was right," Kenzie said. A grin spread across her face.

"Right about what?" Bree asked."

Kenzie looked at Bree. Tears filled her eyes. "About this." Kenzie pointed to the results.

Bree frowned. "Kenzie, whose blood is this?"

Kenzie lost the battle to keep the smile from her face. "Mine."

***

"She's a what?" Bree shouted.

"An alien. She's an alien."

"An alien like in an immigrant? Or an alien like in E.T.?"

"E.T."

"Get the fuck out!"

"Bree, I'm not kidding."

"Listen to yourself. An alien? Does she have antennae squirreled away somewhere under her hair? Jesus, Kenzie!"

Kenzie grabbed Bree's arm. "Bree, she proved it to me. I saw her and Trey transport to their ship. They disappeared into thin air."

"They disappeared?"

"Yes. I saw it. Oh, and you know that mystery shadow picture I took? The other person was Zan."

"So, Zan was invisible when you took the picture?"

"Yes."

"And you knocked her up?"

"Yes. Look, Bree. If you don't believe me, take another sample of my blood and test it again against Zan's. Maybe that will convince you."

"I'm going to take you up on that."

Bree drew another sample of Kenzie's blood and ran the paternity test on it. The results were the same.

"Well, I'll be damned."

"Now do you believe me?"

"This is impossible, K. Two women?"

"I know. I've been struggling with it as well, but you've done the test twice now and both indicate my DNA is running through Zan's bloodstream. The only way that could happen is if the child is mine."

"Let's say I'm willing to suspend disbelief for a few minutes. How the hell could this happen?"

"The way Zan explained it, they have this ritual called the manifestation where Vakillian women mate and during the mating process, they are both submerged in water, and when they reach orgasm, enzymes are secreted from their bodies and the water acts as a medium through which the enzymes enter their partners' bodies. The enzymes are the equivalent of male sperm."

"So, it depends on a system of diffusion then?" Bree asked.

"Exactly. Enzymes are the building blocks for DNA, so if you think outside the box a bit, it just might be possible for the enzymes to provide the DNA material normally supplied by sperm."

"So, the water just knows which direction to push the enzymes into? That's pretty far-fetched, Kenzie."

"Oh, I forgot to say that both parties have to climax at the same time for the process to work. During the dual orgasm, both women secrete the enzymes and that supposedly creates a symbiotic relationship between the enzymes and the water."

"So, you're telling me that you and Zan…"

Kenzie nodded.

"Clit banging in the tub?"

Kenzie nodded again.

"Squirting?"

"In stereo," Kenzie said.

"And when did this happen?" Bree asked.

"The night we all went to karaoke. Zan's headaches and upset stomach began the next morning."

"Holy shit! I can't wait to tell Jimmy about this!"

"Ah, Bree?"

"Yes?"

"This needs to be kept secret. Okay? The more people that know, the more danger Zan and my daughter will be in."

"Jimmy can be trusted."

"How do you know?"

"If he ever wants sex again, he'll keep his mouth shut. Trust me on this one."

***

Bree walked Kenzie to her car. She opened her arms and held her friend close. "I guess I should be saying congratulations," she said. "How do you feel about this, Kenzie?"

"I'm over the moon, Bree. I had already decided to stand by Zan, even if the baby wasn't mine, but now that I know it is…well, my heart is so full, I think it will burst."

"Give our girl a hug for me, okay?"

"I will. Thank you for your help today, Bree. I am so fortunate to have you in my life."

"We are both fortunate, my friend. Now go home to your family. I'll see you tomorrow."

***

When Kenzie pulled into the driveway of her home, she saw Zan peering out the window, apparently keeping watch for her. She got out of the car and opened the back door to retrieve her pack as well as an item she had stopped at the supermarket to pick up on her way home. She walked around to the front of the house and climbed the steps to the porch. Before she could reach for the handle, the door swung open and Zan was standing there with anxiety on her face. Kenzie could see Trey in the background, sporting an identical expression.

Kenzie stepped into the house and thrust what she had purchased toward Zan. It was a pink helium balloon with the words *It's a Girl!* printed on it.

"I guess I'm going to be a father!" Kenzie said.

Zan grinned ear to ear and opened her arms to Kenzie. "I knew it would be so," Zan said. "I knew it."

Kenzie held onto her for dear life. "I'm sorry I doubted you," she whispered.

Kenzie felt a tap on her shoulder. It was Trey.

"May I join you?" she asked.

Kenzie grabbed Trey's arm and pulled her into the hug. "Of course, you can, Auntie Trey."

For several long minutes, the trio stood in the middle of the living room wrapped in a tableau of mutual love for one another.

Trey stepped out of the trio first. "Wait! Auntie Trey? What is auntie?" she asked.

Kenzie turned around in Zan's arms so that Zan was wrapped around her from behind. "On Earth, when someone has a child, their sisters are called auntie and their brothers are called uncle. It identifies their relationship with the child as extended family."

"So, does that make Charlie, Uncle Charlie?"

"If you and Charlie were married, or in a long-term relationship, then yes. Also, the custom is sometimes extended to close friends, so Bree and Jimmy will be called auntie and uncle as well." Kenzie turned back around into Zan's arms. "Your moms may be the only grandparents our daughter will ever know."

Zan grew somber. "Only if the council chooses Earth."

Kenzie kissed her on the cheek. "Don't give up hope, love."

Trey wrapped herself around her friends one more time. She was clearly excited for them. "This journey is a turning point in our lives. To experience love and happiness for the first time is truly an amazing experience. I am so happy we found you, Kenzie."

"I am happy you found me too, Auntie Trey."

Trey kissed them both on the cheek and then stepped back again. "I will take my leave and go back to the motel before the darkness falls. I am excited to share the news with Charlie when he comes to collect me after work."

"Don't forget we need to work on our formal recommendations to the council tomorrow. We need to return to the ship the following day to present our proposal," Zan said.

"I will return in the morning." Trey walked to the door and then turned before opening it. "I love you, my friends."

"I love you, too," Zan and Kenzie said in unison.

***

After Trey left, Kenzie took Zan by the hand and led her into the bedroom. She reached for her phone and searched her music library for the playlist she had assembled of romantic music. With the soft melodies playing in the background, Kenzie entered the circle of Zan's arms and placed her arms around her neck. Her right hand slid into Zan's hair on the back of her head. Zan's hands went directly to Kenzie's waist. As the music played, they swayed back and forth and stared into one another's eyes.

Kenzie placed one tender kiss on Zan's lips. "Thank you, Zan."

"For what?" Zan asked.

"For your love. For this child. For making my life complete."

"I should be saying all of this to you, Kenzie. I never knew I could feel such depth of emotion. You were right. Even the bad ones make you feel alive."

"I'm sorry I didn't trust you, Zan."

Zan lowered her forehead to Kenzie's. "I understand why you did not. I will not deny that it hurt, but I do understand. I am just happy that you accept this child as your own. I will do my best to be a good mother to our child."

Kenzie kissed her again. "And I will as well."

They continued to sway in time to the music.

"I hope she looks like you," Kenzie said.

Kenzie felt Zan stiffen in her arms.

"What is it, Zan?"

"I have not been totally honest with you about my appearance, Kenzie."

They stopped swaying.

"What do you mean?"

"Trey and I have been cloaked with human avatars in order to blend in unnoticed."

Kenzie stepped out of the circle of Zan's arms. "What are you saying, Zan?"

"I am saying that our child may have Vakillian features."

"And what exactly does that mean?"

"The most notable differences between humans and Vakillians are the hair color, and the absence of what humans call a nose in the center of our faces. Our breathing devices are right here on our necks." Zan pointed to the sides of her neck, just behind her ears.

"You have gills? Like fish?" Kenzie exclaimed.

"Similar to fish, yes. That is one of the reasons water is so essential to our species."

Kenzie walked a few feet away and then turned to face Zan. "Show me," she said.

"I cannot do that. We need the ship's computers to transition back and forth between human and Vakillian forms, and even if we were on the ship, I seem to have lost the ability to transform back to Vakillian. My body appears to have adapted to this human avatar permanently."

Kenzie lowered herself slowly into the chair by the reading lamp. "What else are you hiding, Zan?"

"There is nothing else. I promise."

Kenzie sat back and closed her eyes in an attempt to wrap her mind around everything she was feeling.

"Kenzie, does it matter?" Zan asked.

Kenzie opened her eyes and saw that Zan had moved to sit on the corner of the bed closest to her chair. A worried look weighed heavily on her face. Kenzie inhaled deeply and rose to her feet. She walked to Zan and stood close to her, forcing Zan to look up at her. She traced her fingertips across Zan's brow and down the side of her face.

"A parent's love should be unconditional, Zan. I will love our daughter, regardless of what she looks like."

Zan wrapped her arms around Kenzie and drew her closer. She placed her cheek against Kenzie's stomach. "Thank you," she said.

Kenzie kissed Zan on the head, a move that prompted Zan to look up at her again. She lowered her face and kissed Zan tenderly. "Make love to me," she whispered.

Chapter 33

Kenzie and Zan lay side by side on their bed, Kenzie with her head on Zan's shoulder. She gently rubbed Zan's abdomen with the palm of her hand.

"Hey, little one. I can't wait to meet you," Kenzie said.

Zan grinned. "Do you think she can hear you?"

"I hope she can. I want her to know she's loved, even before she gets here."

"You are going to be a wonderful mother, Kenzie."

Kenzie propped herself up on one elbow and kissed Zan. "And so will you. I'll be right back. I've gotta pee."

Kenzie climbed out of bed and trod naked through the kitchen and into the bathroom. While she was washing her hands, she heard a banging on the front door.

"What the hell?" she said out loud.

She grabbed her robe from the back of the bathroom door and pulled the door open. Before she could get Zan's name out of her mouth, she came out of the bedroom, pulling a T-shirt over her head.

Zan pulled back the curtain to see who was on the porch. She looked over her shoulder at Kenzie. "It's Trey." She opened the door. Trey came into the room and went directly into Kenzie's arms. She was sobbing hysterically.

Kenzie looked helplessly over Trey's shoulder at Zan before she turned her full attention to the sobbing woman in her arms.

"Sweetie, what happened? Why are you crying?"

"It's Charlie," Trey sobbed.

"Charlie? Is he all right?" Kenzie asked.

"He left me."

"What? Why?"

"I told him about the baby, and I told him about me and Zan."

"I see. Come sit down." Kenzie led her to the sofa. Zan paced helplessly in front of the coffee table. Kenzie grabbed a tissue and handed it to Trey. "So, tell me what happened."

"Charlie picked me after work, and we went to his place. We fixed a nice dinner together and while we were eating, he asked me how my day went, and I told him about the blood tests and the DNA results. I was so happy to share that with him."

"How did he take *that* news?"

"He started to behave differently. He seemed nervous and he insisted it was impossible for you to father Zan's baby. He asked me if I was crazy." Trey wiped her eyes. "Kenzie, that hurt me here." She pointed to her chest.

Kenzie rubbed her back. "Try not to be too hard on him. I had a similar reaction, didn't I, Zan?"

"Actually, Charlie's reaction sounds pretty calm compared to yours," Zan replied.

"You said you told him about you and Zan. How did that go?" Kenzie asked.

"I could not think of what else to say to him to convince him that Zan is carrying your child, so I told him it was totally possible on Vakillia, where Zan and I were from. He asked me where Vakillia was and I told him it was in another galaxy. That is when he really became agitated. He told me to get my things together and that he was taking me home. When he drove away from the motel, his car made a loud screeching noise and there were black marks on the road."

"Juvenile male behavior," Kenzie said under her breath.

"Kenzie, I do not know what to do. I love him so much. I will die without him."

"Zan, would you mind getting my cellphone? It's on the bedside table," Kenzie said.

Zan returned a moment later and handed her the cellphone. "Thanks, love."

Kenzie dialed Charlie's number. "Hello, Charlie? This is Kenzie. Yes, she is here. Yes, I know what she told you. Look, Charlie, you and I need to talk. Yes, right now. No, tomorrow is too late. Charlie, Charlie, listen to me." Kenzie held the phone away from her ear while a loud voice came from the receiver.

Kenzie lost her temper. "Charlie, will you shut the fuck up and listen to me? You need to get your ass into that tire-burning truck and get here. Now! Do you understand? Yes, I said, now! And if you're not here in fifteen minutes, I swear I will get your address from Bree and I will show up on your doorstep. You got that? Okay. Goodbye."

Zan and Trey just looked at her with shocked expressions on their faces.

"Zan, please take Trey back to the motel. I'll come to pick you up after Charlie leaves."

Zan grabbed Kenzie's arm. "Do you think it is wise to be here alone with him?"

"Charlie is in more danger from me than I am from him. Please don't worry. You need to go before he gets here."

***

Charlie came to a screeching halt in front of Kenzie's apartment. He jumped out of the truck and slammed the door. Kenzie was on the porch waiting for him.

Charlie charged the steps. "Did you know about her?" he shouted.

Kenzie pushed the front door open. "If you're going to yell at me, I'd rather it wasn't in public."

Kenzie followed Charlie into the house and shut the door.

"Answer my question, Kenzie."

"I would if I understood what you were asking."

"Did you know she was a whack-job before you let me get all gaga about her?"

"Why do you think she's a whack-job?"

"You should have heard what she was telling me about you and Zan. Are you aware that you knocked Zan up?"

"As a matter of fact, I *am* aware of that, and yes, I did knock Zan up."

Charlie grabbed her by the arms. "What the hell is wrong with you, Kenzie?"

Kenzie raised her eyebrows. "I suggest you take your hands off me, right now."

Charlie moved his hands to his hips. "So, Zan is pregnant and you think you're the father. Listen to yourself, Kenzie."

Kenzie walked to her refrigerator and grabbed two beers. She twisted off the caps and handed one to Charlie.

"Believe me, I didn't handle it well myself when I first found out, but it's been verified by three separate DNA tests. I know it's hard to believe, Charlie, but it's true."

Charlie took a swig of his beer. "Is it also true that Trey and Zan are aliens, like E.T.?"

"Well, I happen to think they are both much more attractive than E.T., but yes, it is true. How else would it be possible for me to knock Zan up? Anyone with half a brain knows a woman can't impregnate another woman, at least human women can't."

"I refuse to believe it."

"People are not always what they appear to be, Charlie. You know that better than most."

Kenzie watched a play of emotions cross Charlie's face as he visibly struggled with what she was saying.

"Do you love her, Charlie?" Kenzie asked.

"I did."

"But you don't now?"

"I don't know."

"Let me ask you something. Did Trey reject you when she discovered you were something other than what you present externally?"

Charlie finished his beer and placed the empty bottle on the dinette table. "That's not fair, Kenzie. It's not the same."

"Isn't it?"

Charlie pulled the dinette chair out and sat with his elbows on the table and his head in his hands. "I don't know what to do, Kenz."

"Tell me what happened, Charlie."

"I went to the motel to pick her up after my last tour. We stopped at the grocery store for salad stuff and then we went back to my place and made dinner together. All the while, she seemed different."

"What do you mean?"

"Well, since I met her, there was always this lingering feeling that she was nervous or anxious about something. Today, she was much more relaxed, almost happy. It's like she couldn't stop smiling. When I asked her how her day went, she told me about the paternity testing. I mean, I wasn't an A-student in school, but I remember my physiology class well enough to know that girl-on-girl conception is impossible."

"Did you tell her she was crazy, Charlie?"

Charlie sighed. "I'm not proud of it, but yes I did, especially when she got into the alien shit."

Kenzie chuckled. "When Zan told me about the alien shit, as you put it, I misunderstood and accused her of wanting to use me as an immigration ticket into the U.S. I didn't get that she meant E.T. alien. Like you, I'm not proud of how I treated her, but then I had to open my mind to the possibility that she was telling me the truth."

"So, you believe they really are aliens?" Charlie asked.

"I know they are."

"And that doesn't bother you?"

"Charlie, I have always believed that love is love, regardless of how it's packaged, and I love Zan's package—alien or not. I can't imagine my life without her, and now that we have a baby on the way, I will do everything in my power to keep her in my life."

Charlie sat back in the chair and stretched his legs out under the table. He toyed with the empty bottle in front of him.

"I'll ask you again, Charlie. Do you still love her?"

"Yes, but this is just so difficult to believe."

"Would it help if you had proof?"

"Proof?"

"Trey and Zan are transporting back to the ship the day after tomorrow. I think you should be there to witness it. In fact, Bree and Jimmy might want to be there as well."

"Bree knows?"

"Yes. She was a little wierded out when she helped me with the DNA tests, but when it comes down to it, she just wants to see me happy. I'm not sure she's totally convinced either, so I'll give her a call tonight and ask her to meet us on the trail."

"They transport from the trail?"

"Yes. The vortexes serve as portals. In any case, back to what I was saying about Trey. Give her a chance, Charlie. She's a wonderful woman. She's sweet, amazingly intelligent and very loving, despite being raised in an emotionless society. Based on Earth standards, both she and Zan have had a rough life up until now. I don't think it's fair of us to make it any rougher. In a lot of ways, she is an innocent. She has been exposed to a whole new way of living that gives her more freedom to be herself, and that has made her vulnerable to prejudice. You know what that's like, Charlie."

Charlie picked up the empty bottle on the table and showed it to Kenzie. "Got any more of these?"

"Yes, but you need to drive home."

"Just one more. I want to know how you knocked Zan up and I think I might need the reinforcement before you tell me." Charlie raised his eyebrows up and down lecherously.

Kenzie took the empty bottle from him and then hip-checked him nearly off the chair. "You are *such* a guy!"

***

Kenzie knocked on the motel room door and waited. Zan opened the door.

"Kenzie. Are you okay?" Zan studied her.

"Sweetheart, I'm fine. I told you not to worry. Are you ready to go home?"

Kenzie could see Trey curled up in a ball on her bed. Her face was tear-stained and puffy.

"It does not seem right to leave her like this," Zan said.

"She won't be alone," a baritone voice to Kenzie's right said.

Zan stepped outside and saw Charlie standing out of direct view of the door.

Zan blocked the doorway. "I think you should leave," she said.

Kenzie touched Zan's arm. "No, it's all right, love. Let him in."

Zan narrowed her eyes at Kenzie.

302

"Trust me," Kenzie whispered.

Zan stepped aside and allowed Charlie to enter the room.

The moment Trey saw him, she sat up on the edge of the bed and opened her arms.

Charlie went directly to the bed and fell to his knees in front of her. He wrapped his arms around her and held her close. "I was wrong, Trey. Please forgive me. I'm so sorry."

Trey rested her cheek on top of Charlie's head. "I am sorry too. I should not have kept that from you for so long."

Charlie looked up at her. "No more secrets, okay?"

"No more secrets," Trey returned.

Kenzie pulled the door closed behind them and then took Zan's arm. "Let's go home, love."

Chapter 34

Zan stood in front of the full-length mirror in the bathroom and adjusted her collar. "How do I look?" she asked.

"Good enough to eat, and if you didn't have this meeting with the council, that is exactly what I would be doing right now," Kenzie said.

Zan grinned. "I think making love to you is one of my favorite Earth things to do."

"Are you nervous?"

"My stomach is a bit unsettled, and I do not think it is the morning sickness making me feel that way."

"Hopefully, the morning sickness will stop soon, although some women have it through their entire pregnancy."

"Okay. I think I am ready," Zan said.

"Come have a cup of coffee with me while we wait for Trey."

Zan sat at the breakfast bar and waited while Kenzie made the coffee.

"What do you think the council will decide, Zan?"

"I honestly do not know. The data Trey and I have collected clearly indicates that Earth's environment is physically suitable for Vakillians, but that is only one of the factors they will use to make their decision."

"Do you remember the list of documents I asked you to get while you're on the ship?"

"Yes, birth certificate, educational records and transcripts, work histories."

"You are going to need these records to get a green card, and eventually citizenship. Of course, we could always apply for a fiancée visa for you."

"Fiancée? What is that?"

Kenzie walked around the breakfast bar and put Zan's coffee in front of her. She then swung Zan's stool around to face her and she walked into Zan's space between her legs. She put her arms around Zan's neck. "A fiancée is what we call our partner when we are engaged to be married. You know, committed to one another for life."

Zan raised her eyebrows. "Are you asking me to be married to you?"

"I guess I am. I can't think of anyone else I would want to spend the rest of my life with."

Zan kissed her tenderly and then reached up to wipe a tear from the corner of her eye. "I accept," she said.

"Thank you, Zan."

"For what?"

"For loving me, for our daughter, for giving me the opportunity to experience the depth of love I didn't think was possible."

"You are welcome, but I should be thanking you, for all the same reasons."

"Then, you're welcome as well." Kenzie kissed her. "Drink your coffee before it gets cold."

"Yes, boss," Zan joked.

A knock came at the door.

"Come in, Trey," Kenzie called out.

Trey pushed the door open and entered, followed by Charlie. "Good morning," she said.

"'Morning, sweetie. Oh, Charlie's with you!" Kenzie said.

"Is that okay?" Charlie asked. "You told me I should be there for the send off."

"No, it's fine. I just thought you'd meet us there. No worries!"

"That's good. I don't get up this early for just anyone. It's barely daylight out there," Charlie said.

"Bree and I need to be at the clinic by eight, so Zan and Trey graciously accommodated an early departure just for us."

"The early start will give us time to do some paperwork before our meeting with the council," Zan said.

"We have time for coffee if you're interested," Kenzie offered.

***

At seven that morning, they set out for Little Horse Trail. Bree and Jimmy were waiting for them in the parking lot.

Bree hugged everyone. "This better be worth getting up at five." she complained.

"If it makes a believer out of you, then it will definitely be worth it," Kenzie said.

"I'm already a believer," Bree replied. "I was convinced by the paternity tests."

"I have to admit that I'm a bit skeptical," Jimmy said.

Kenzie hugged him. "Thank you for having an open mind, Jimmy."

"Okay then. Let's get this show on the road," Charlie said. "I for one need to see this for myself."

The group of friends entered the trailhead and arrived at the transfer site ten minutes later.

Kenzie hugged Zan and then looked up into her face. "I just had a thought. This won't hurt the baby, will it?"

"The transfer process?" Zan asked.

"Yes."

"No, it is safe. Please don't worry."

"All right then. Gimme a kiss and be on your way. The sooner you get up there, the sooner you can finish this meeting with the council. I'll pick you up before dark, okay?"

Zan kissed her tenderly and then released her.

"Knock 'em dead, love," Kenzie called out.

"I will try," Zan replied.

Charlie took Trey's face between his hands. "Come back to me. We have a lot to talk about."

"I will," Trey whispered. "I love you."

"Love you back," Charlie said. "You'd better get going."

Trey joined Zan in the transfer area.

"Please verify there are no other hikers in the vicinity," Zan called out.

Jimmy, Bree and Kenzie all looked around. "You're good to go," Jimmy said while giving them a thumbs-up.

A few second later, they all watched as Zan and Trey dissolved into thin air.

"How cool is that!" Jimmy exclaimed. "It's just like Star Trek!"

"You know, that's a thought," Kenzie said. "I wonder if Zan would enjoy those campy old Captain Kirk episodes. Something to keep in mind."

"Yeah, but I'd rather watch Seven of Nine," Jimmy said.

Bree punched him in the arm. "You're such a pig!"

"Oink, oink!" Jimmy replied.

Jimmy and Bree led the pack back down the trail to the car. Kenzie lagged behind to walk with Charlie.

"You okay?" Kenzie asked. "You're awfully quiet."

He looked at her out of the corner of his eye. "I'm feeling like a real heel for not believing her, worse yet for mistreating her like I did."

"Not all lessons are easy, Charlie. I made the same mistake with Zan."

"She *will* come back, won't she?"

"She'll come back. My only concern is what the council will decide."

"What does it matter what the council decides? They're grown women with the right to do what they want, aren't they?"

"One can only hope that the council can't stop them from remaining on Earth if they decide to move on, but I am not so sure that will be the case, especially if they find out Zan is pregnant."

"How so?"

"This entire mission is to find a new homeland to proliferate their species. There isn't an ice cube's chance in hell that they are going to let Zan and the baby leave, never mind Trey. It's all about the numbers to them. Zan and Trey have spent their entire lives being taught to comply with the will of the council. I suspect the council will not tolerate defectors easily."

***

Zan and Trey went directly to Zan's quarters as soon as they arrived on board and began creating the documentation

Kenzie had specified. Part way through this process, the call button went off on Zan's door. She glanced at the panel on the wall by the door and identified her visitor as Belander.

"Enter," Zan said.

Belander entered the room. "The transference room technician alerted me of your arrival. You are here early."

"Yes, Trey and I have some documentation to take care of before we meet with the council."

"Documentation? What kind of documentation?" Belander asked.

"Documentation that will identify us on Earth. As I have told you and Molinder, I will be remaining on Earth even if the council chooses not to."

"I will as well," Trey added.

"They will not let you go easily," Belander said.

"I know," Zan replied.

"May I see your documentation?"

Zan handed the paperwork to her mother. "Interesting. It says here you were born in Switzerland."

"Mother,"

"Do not worry, Zangendar. I will not give away your secret. The council *may* vote to stay on Earth and then all of this will not matter."

"*Will* they vote to stay, Mother?"

"I do not know, Daughter."

Belander walked toward the door and then stopped. "Good luck at the council meeting this afternoon."

"Thank you, Mother."

Trey paced back and forth across Zan's quarters. "Why does this environment no longer feel comfortable?" she said.

"Because this is no longer our home," Zan replied. "Kenzie is my home now, and Charlie is yours."

"I look forward to this council meeting so we can return to Earth."

"I agree, sister, but right now, we need to focus on our message and convince the council that Earth meets our needs."

"I hope they agree with us, Zan. Belander is correct, they will not let us go easily."

Zan looked at the timekeeper on the wall of her quarters. "It is time."

***

"Madame Chairwoman, we appear before you today to present our recommendation to choose Earth as our new homeland. Tredoran and I have done due diligence and have collected a significant amount of data on all aspects of Earth life and have provided it to the council for review. It is our understanding that the council has had adequate time to review and form an opinion on this data."

Zan walked from one side of the room to the other. "Tredoran and I are here today to provide answers to any questions you may have before you reach your decision, but first, let us present the facts."

Zan projected images on the screen that she and Trey had collected while on Earth.

"Let us evaluate the pros and cons of several factors. First, the environment. Pros, it has been proven to be compatible with Vakillian life. Cons, global warming is occurring as the result of human impact on the normal cyclic nature of the climate. The humans are currently taking steps to reduce their carbon footprint to minimize their impact on climate change."

Zan advanced the presentation and Trey stepped forward. "Let us talk about natural resources next. Pros, the soil on many parts of the planet is rich in nutrients and able to support plant-based food growth. The United States, where we are currently located, supplies food not only for its own country, but also for a significant amount of the planet's population. The diversity of locally produced food includes plant based corn, soybeans, wheat, fruits and vegetables, as well as meat-based foods such as beef, pork and chicken. Many people in this country are self-sustaining based on what they can grow themselves. Cons, plant-based food growth is sometimes subject to climate and weather conditions."

Zan stepped forward. "Tredoran mentioned climate. It is true that the temperature varies significantly depending on location. Humans have learned to adapt to all types of climates and have even learned to leverage climate conditions to their advantage. As Tredoran has already mentioned, global warming has a negative effect on climate and sometimes leads to the enhancement of natural disasters. I would like to remind the council that there are many types of natural disasters on Vakillia as well."

"We will talk next about health," Trey said. "Humans do suffer from a range of health issues, some of which are brought on by lifestyle choices, some that are inherited, some that are environmental, and still others that have no known cause. If this sounds familiar to the council, it is because the same situation exists on Vakillia. The positive aspect of all this is that the medical technology of Vakillia is far more advanced compared to Earth, creating an opportunity for Vakillians to contribute to our new homeland, and to be recognized for those contributions. One distinct difference between us and the humans is that they tolerate imperfection. They value all life, regardless of defects, and they are committed to preserving and improving life for everyone, despite their primitive technology."

"Perhaps the most controversial topic we covered in our research was government and politics," Zan said. "There are several types of governments across the planet, which practice varying degrees of personal and political freedoms. Wealth and class disparity exist to some degree in all of them. Nearly everywhere on the planet, the female portions of the populations are often disadvantaged politically, socially and economically compared to the males, as are members of racial minorities. I suspect the same is true on all inhabited planets in this universe. The strong rise to the top and the people depend on them to make all their lives better. Unfortunately, that is not always the case, as the cons in this scenario include the fact that the people of this planet sometimes choose their leaders based on popularity rather than capability.

"Some of these leaders have committed crimes while in office or perpetuated near-constant states of war. On the positive side, in many parts of this planet, the leaders are elected by the people rather than appointed. Governments on this planet are somewhat authoritarian in nature and expect all citizens to follow governmental rules based on a widely accepted doctrine of rights. In other words, the laws of the government will overrule the laws of Vakillian society. Again, honored council members, I suspect the research teams on other missions similar to ours are finding the same results."

Trey stood up. "I asked Zangendar to allow me to discuss this section, humans. First, I must point out that the physical characteristics of Earth humans are much like our own, as demonstrated by Zangendar here. The primary difference is hair color and the breathing apparatus in the center of her face. The humans call this a nose. In any case, the human and Vakillian species are so similar, data indicates the Vakillians could easily adapt to living on Earth cloaked in human avatars.

"As we have pointed out in other meetings with the council, humans readily express emotion. Happiness, frustration, anger, and even love are expressed in unique ways. Each human is unique. Each human has a different personality. Each human is an individual. It has been part of Vakillian culture for generations to always be strong and to never show emotion in the event it could weaken them. I believe Zangendar would agree with me when I say we did not find them to be weak at all."

"I would like to say some final words about the urgency of this task," Zan said. "We are all aware that Vakillia is dying. The water supplies are diminishing, and those that remain are becoming toxic. For generations, we have been on these missions to find other worlds in which to procreate, only to return to Vakillia and to raise our offspring amidst a dying planet. We cannot afford to do that any longer. Settling on an inhabited planet such as Earth affords us the ability to reproduce without first having to build an infrastructure to support us. Yes, there are things we will need to adapt to in the environment and in the culture, but our species has a history of adaptation and of coming out stronger in the end. It is therefore our recommendation to choose Earth and settle in among the humans where we can coexist peacefully, and to the mutual benefit of both species. Tredoran and I thank you for your time."

The chairwoman stood. "Zangendar and Tredoran, on behalf of the council, I would like to thank you for the hard work and effort you put into this evaluation and presentation. The council will now retire to discuss your recommendations. We will convene tomorrow at the same time to discuss our decision."

"Thank you, Madame Chairwoman," Zan said.

"Thank you," Trey repeated.

Zan looked at the timekeeper on the wall and realized it was nearly five Earth time. Kenzie would be waiting for them.

***

"So, what do you think" Kenzie asked.

"About this whole alien thing? I feel like a jerk for not believing her," Charlie admitted.

"Don't beat yourself up too much. It is kind of out there."

"I know, but I still feel bad about it. I mean, I've never met anyone like her before. You are right about her being an innocent. On one hand, she is so full of wide-eyed wonder and in awe about everything around her, but on the other, she can keep up with anyone I know in a discussion about aerodynamics theory."

"Their technology surpasses anything we have on Earth. I mean, teleporting from one place to another without some sort of vehicle? That's heavy shit. If you are able to help her find employment in the aeronautical industry, imagine how she could help us advance," Kenzie said.

"I will definitely put her in touch with a few people, but all of that is a little premature. We're not even sure if they'll be able to stay on earth."

"Zan says she's staying even if the rest of her people don't. I think Trey has said the same thing."

"I hope so. I don't know what I would do if she left. Leave it to me to find the woman I want to spend the rest of my life with and then have her turn out to be an alien."

"Are you serious about that, Charlie?"

"I'm dead serious. I'd marry her today if she'd have me."

"Have you asked her?"

"I was going to. I even have a ring, but the shit hit the fan and I guess I lost my nerve."

"Have you found it again? Your nerve, I mean?"

Charlie grinned. "Actually, this feisty redhead I know kicked me in the ass and made me open my eyes, and it turns out I hadn't lost it at all. I had just pushed it into the background for a while."

"She sounds like a pretty smart redhead," Kenzie said.

"She is. She is indeed."

A static sound suddenly reached their ears.

"They're coming back," Kenzie said.

Moments later, Zan and Trey appeared in the transport area.

"That is the coolest shit!" Charlie exclaimed as he approached Trey and took her into his arms.

Kenzie walked into the circle of Zan's arms and kissed her tenderly. "Hi, love. I missed you," she said.

"I missed you, too," Zan replied.

Kenzie locked arms with Zan and the four of them walked down the trail toward the cars.

"How was the meeting?" Kenzie asked.

"I thought it went well."

"Did the council give you any indication how they might vote?"

"No, they did not. They will announce their decision by mid-day tomorrow."

"You mean they gave you no clue through their facial expressions? Nothing?"

"You must consider who we are talking about. These are eight elderly Vakillians who have spent their entire lives perfecting the art of non-emotion. Their faces gave us no clues at all."

"Well, that sucks! Now we need to wait another whole day," Kenzie complained.

"Unfortunately, it cannot be helped."

"Did you see your parents while on board?"

"I saw Belander," Zan replied.

"She caught us creating our documentation," Trey said from behind them."

Kenzie looked over her shoulder. "She did? What was her reaction? Should you be worried that she'll tell the council?"

"She will not tell the council. She promised us she would not," Zan said.

"What documentation are you talking about?" Charlie asked.

"If Zan and Trey are to stay in the U.S. and to get jobs, they'll need green cards. At some point they may also want to become citizens. To do that, they need documentation that indicates where they come from, among other things," Kenzie explained.

Charlie looked at Trey. "So, where *do* you come from?"

"Switzerland," Trey replied.

"Wow! I guess you'll have to tell us all about it during dinner. My treat," Charlie said.

The friends said their good nights in the parking lot after dinner.

"Trey, you'll need to be at the motel no later than eleven in the morning," Kenzie said. "Zan and I will pick you up and I will drop you both off at the trailhead."

"Kenzie, is there any way we can get to the trailhead sooner? I would like to meet with my parents before the council decision," Zan said.

"Sure. Tomorrow is Saturday and I don't have to work, so any time is good. Is ten o'clock better?"

"I think ten is fine. Thank you."

"I think I'll bring my yoga mat and meditate while you're gone. Maybe even get a little hiking in. That way, I'll be there when you return."

"Do you think you'll be back by one o'clock?" Charlie asked. "I have tour at two, so if you're back by one or so, I can join you on that hike."

"I see no reason why we would not be back by one," Zan said.

"Awesome! I'll meet you on the trail around ten o'clock then."

Kenzie hugged Charlie. "Thank you for dinner, my friend."

"You are welcome, feisty redhead." He squeezed her before letting her go. "Thank you, Kenz. I really appreciate you setting me straight. I am going to ask her tonight."

Kenzie just smiled and nodded her head. She turned to Zan. "Are you ready to go home, love?"

"I have been ready all day."

***

"Kenzie glanced at Zan several times during the short drive from the restaurant to the apartment. "Are you okay, Zan? You've said hardly a word since we left the restaurant."

"I have been thinking about saying goodbye to my parents tomorrow. I may never see them again, and they may never see their granddaughter."

Kenzie pulled into the driveway and turned off the ignition. "I'm sorry, Zan. I've been so absorbed in this whole council thing that I haven't even given that any thought. That was unfeeling of me."

"They have never been demonstrative, but I know they love me, as well as most Vakillians are able to, considering they do not understand what love is."

Kenzie wiped a lone tear that escaped from Zan's eye. "I'm so sorry, love."

"This thing I am feeling, Kenzie. It feels like my heart is broken. It is one of the bad things about emotions."

"Yes, it is. I wish I could take it way."

Zan looked at Kenzie. "Is this what it felt like when you left your parents behind?"

"In some ways, it was a lot like this. I was heartbroken, too, but for me, it was also a chance to heal. It was a different situation."

"But yet, you survived."

"Yes, I did. And you will, too," Zan.

"I need you to hold me, Kenzie."

"That, I can do. Let's go inside."

Chapter 35

Zan and Trey transferred to the ship after assurances from Kenzie and Charlie that they would be waiting for them to return at one. They both went directly to Belander and Molinder's quarters.

"Enter," a voice said from within when they pushed the call button.

Belander rose when Zan and Trey entered the room. "You are early, daughters."

Zan heard a slight gasp from Trey when Belander included her in the greeting. "I, *we* are here to say our farewells in the event the council decides not to settle on Earth. We feel it is best to leave immediately after the decision is rendered if that is the case."

"Zangendar, I know how difficult it is to leave someone you love," Belander said.

"Mother, please do not try to talk me out of it."

"I will do nothing of the sort. I have much to tell you, daughter, but I struggle with how to do it. I know of your internal struggle. I have lived it myself."

"Mother?"

Belander approached Zangendar and stopped within a foot of her. "Computer, return me to my natural form."

Right before her eyes, her mother transformed into a much different version of herself. When the transformation complete, Belander simply stood there and waited for her daughter's reaction.

Zangendar reached up and touched her mother's face. "Mother…you are human!"

"Yes, Zangendar. I am human."

"But…but how?"

"This is not the first visit Vakillians have made to Earth. Twenty-eight Earth-years ago, Earth was also one of the recreational choices for *my* generation of Vakillians. Twenty-eight Earth-years ago Molinder walked the path you are on right now. She was sent to explore the surface. And she met me. We fell in love. We had three glorious months together on Earth, and then she had to leave, and I was faced with the decision to choose my home, or to choose Molinder. I chose her. But it came with conditions. I had to change. I had to appear like the others before we returned to Vakillia. I had to close my mind to all emotion and tenderness.

"Molinder smuggled me onto the ship and then worked tirelessly to invent my avatar. As soon as I was cloaked, she destroyed the technology so I would never be discovered. We never dreamed you and Trey would re-invent it. Thanks to your efforts, this is the first time I have returned to human form in twenty-eight Earth years. Molinder is the only one with knowledge of this, and now you two know as well."

Zan took several steps away. "So, you have been lying to me all my life?"

Trey grabbed Zan's arm. "Zan,"

Zan shook Trey's arm off. "No, Trey. I have the right to know." She turned back to Belander. "Did you even give birth to me?"

"You were conceived on Earth. But you were not conceived by me. Molinder became pregnant before we left Earth, but she was unable to carry you, so through the miracle of Vakillian technology, you were implanted in my uterus, and I was able to carry you to term. To answer your question, yes, I gave birth to you, but you were conceived by Molinder. But that does not make you any less my daughter. You have DNA from both of us, Zangendar. You are part human."

"I am part human, and you have kept this information from me since birth? What other secrets have you kept, Mother?"

Belander took her daughter's hands in hers. "Zangendar, the decisions Molinder and I made for you were for your own protection. Please do not judge us too harshly."

Zangendar shook her hands loose. "Exactly what decisions are you talking about, Mother?" she demanded.

Belander walked a few feet away and then turned again to face Zangendar. "When you were born, you had human features that were difficult to hide. We feared our deception would be discovered, and that they would want to terminate you for what they would see as defects, so we had to take steps to protect not only you, but ourselves."

"What types of features are you talking about?"

"You had a human nose, and the gill-like structures on your neck were non-functional. We kept you out of view for several months until Molinder could use her medical skills to develop a medication that would suppress your human traits and enhance your Vakillian physiology. It was several months after that before the medication effectively erased your human features."

"The same medication I have been taking all of my life? The same medication I *stopped* taking when we arrived on Earth?" Zangendar asked.

"Yes."

Zangendar walked across the room and took Belander by the shoulders. "Look at me, Mother. Look at my face. My *human* face. Are you telling me that this is real? Is this what I would have looked like all throughout my adolescent years? Is this why the computer cannot return me to my natural form?"

Belander took Zangendar's face between her hands. "Yes. This *is* your natural form. This is your beautiful human face. By discontinuing your medication, your dominant human characteristics resurfaced."

"I am human," Zangendar said.

"You are *part* human."

Zan looked beyond Belander to Molinder, who sat in the living area of their quarters. She crossed the room and sat beside her.

"Molinder, I cannot leave Kenzie, and after seeing what it is like to live as a human, I cannot ask her to come with us and live in this sterile Vakillian environment as Belander did twenty-eight years ago. And I will not raise my daughter in a place where she is not allowed to cry, laugh or play. I cannot do it. I am sorry."

"It is doubtful the council would allow you to leave, Zangendar," Molinder said.

"This is *my* choice, Mother. I will not allow them to stop me."

"And neither will I," Trey added.

Their conversation was interrupted by three tones broadcasted on the intercom.

"It is time for the council to render their decision," Belander said. "We must go."

***

Zan and Trey stood before the council, both cloaked in their human avatars, and awaited the decision.

The chairwoman stood and addressed the assembly.

"I first want to commend Zangendar Tafadon and Tredoran Harlax for their extraordinary effort during their evaluation of the suitability of the planet Earth to sustain our species. Their data was thorough and their reporting exemplary. You have the gratitude of the Vakillian people for your efforts. I will now ask the council forewoman to read our decision."

Lorhonder stood and held a tablet before her. "It is the decision of this council not to choose the planet Earth as our new homeland."

Zan felt as though she had been punched in the stomach. Her vision became cloudy and a ringing rose within her ears. She felt Trey's arm around her, and she struggled not to cry.

The forewoman continued.

"The reasons for this decision are as follows. Whereas it has been proven that Earth's atmosphere is able to sustain Vakillian life, there are several factors which are worrisome relative to the long term survival of our species, or of any species, including that of the human race.

"Human society is rife with crime, war, and governments with too much solitary power and control. In addition, the authoritarian nature of this planet's governments would not allow the Vakillian people to rule themselves, but would in fact, expect our species to exclusively obey the rules of their governments.

"The climate is unstable, and through the human's own acknowledgement, it is degrading due to global warming.

"Despite years of protest, the female population of this planet is largely regarded as second to the male species and they are disadvantaged at every turn.

"Finally, it is the belief of the majority ruling that most of the conditions already stated here are due to the humans' inabilities to control their emotions. Atmospheric sustainability alone is not enough for the people of Vakillia to call this planet their home.

"This ends the decision of the council."

The chairwoman stood once more. "Thank you, Lorhonder." She looked around the room. "Let it be known that this decision was not unanimous, however, it does reflect the views of the majority, and as such, it is final and binding. We will leave orbit within the hour."

"Councilwoman, if I may speak," Zan said.

"Of course, Zangendar."

"During our time on the planet, Tredoran and I have built relationships, and friendships that we do not want to leave. We respectfully request permission to remain on Earth."

Zan glanced at Belander and saw a pained expression on her face.

The councilwoman raised her eyebrows. "And do you feel the same, Tredoran?" she asked.

"I do, Councilwoman. I choose to remain on Earth as well," Trey replied.

The councilwoman looked at them for what felt like an eternity to Zan. Finally, she spoke.

"I fail to see how you two remaining on Earth would help the greater good of the Vakillian people. Request denied."

"I will not go with you!" Zan shouted.

"You will do as you are told, Zangendar!" The councilwoman stated firmly.

"I will not!"

The councilwoman called to two security personnel who had been standing by the door. "Put her in confinement," she said.

The two women grabbed Zan and tried to pull her out of the room, but she resisted. One of them punched her in the ribs, and she doubled in pain.

"Stop! You will harm the child!" Trey shouted.

Every Vakillian in the room froze.

Belander was immediately on her feet and by her daughter's side.

"You are with child?" the councilwoman asked sternly.

Zan struggled to catch her breath. She nodded.

"Tell me you did not contaminate the Vakillian bloodline with human blood," the councilwoman spat out. "Who did you couple with, Zangendar?" she demanded.

"Me! She coupled with me," Trey said.

"Put them both in lockdown in Zangendar's quarters," the councilwoman ordered. "We will deal with this after we are underway."

***

Belander followed the guards as they took Trey and Zan to Zangendar's quarters and then stood outside the room to prevent them from leaving. They also blocked Belander from going into the room to see them.

"They are my daughters. I have a right to see them," Belander argued.

"Not without permission from the council," one of the guards said.

"I *am* a member of the council!" she said.

"You have been overruled by the majority. You cannot enter without proper permission."

"Then I will return with that permission."

Belander turned around and went directly to her own quarters.

"They have Zangendar and Tredoran in lockdown, Molly," she said the moment she walked into the room. "The council knows about the child."

Molinder stood and squared her shoulders. "Then, it is time," she said.

"Yes. It is time. Do you have the immobilizers?"

"I do," Molinder replied.

"Good. I need to alert Dalorthan about the change in plans, and we will need to do something about the two gorillas guarding our daughters."

"Leave that to me, Belinda."

Belinda approached Molinder and took her into her arms. "We have been planning this day for a long time, Molly, and not only has the time come to go home, but we are able to take our daughters with us. I never dreamed it would be so. Thank you for coming with me, my love."

"You have sacrificed twenty-eight years for me, Belinda. One is never too old to begin again, and I can't think of another person I'd rather do that with. You are my heart. I love you."

Belander placed a tender kiss on Molinder's lips. "And I love you, too. Now, let's go save our daughters. Engage our holographic images."

Moments later, Belander and Molinder were on their way to Zan's quarters. When they arrived, the guards were still positioned by the door.

"I have orders from the council to allow both of us entry into the room," Belander said. She handed a tablet to one of the guards while Molinder stood beside the other guard.

Belander's gaze met Molinder's and she nodded.

Before the guard realized she had been handed a blank tablet, Belander and Molinder simultaneously injected the guards with the immobilizers. They immediately crumpled to the floor.

Belander pressed the call button on Zan's room. The door slid open and Trey was standing in front of them. Zan painfully pulled herself out of the chair she was in and joined Trey.

"Help me drag these two into the room, Tredoran," Belander said.

Between the two of them, they managed to position one of the guards on the sofa and the other on the chair in Zan's room.

While they were doing this, Molinder tended to Zan. She lifted Zan's shirt and manipulated the area that was rapidly bruising. She looked into Zan's face when she winced. "I am sorry for hurting you, daughter. It does not feel like anything is broken."

"We are finished, Molly," Belander said.

Molinder pulled a scanner out of her pocket and scanned both her daughters. "Tredoran, take Zangendar into the hall. I will take care of these two," Molinder said.

She walked farther into the room and pointed the scanner at the guard on the sofa. "Computer, transform to Zangendar's human avatar." Within seconds, the guard laying unconscious on the sofa was an exact duplicate of the human Zan. She then pointed the scanner at the guard propped up in the chair. "Computer, transform to Tredoran's human avatar."

Molinder joined the others in the hall. "We must go," she said.

Belander looked into the room before the door closed and saw what appeared to be Zan and Trey sleeping. "Excellent work, Molly," she said.

The four of them made their way down the hallway toward the transference room. They entered the room and were greeted by Dalorthan, the transference technician.

Tredoran quickly keyed in a code on the access control panel to restrict entry to the room.

"Councilwoman, we must hurry. We are about to enter terminal velocity. If we do not do this immediately, it will be unsafe."

"Zangendar, Tredoran, step onto the transference pads. Molinder, cloak yourself," Belander instructed.

She turned to the technician. "Dalorthan, we will forever be in your debt. Thank you." She handed her immobilizer to Dalorthan. "Use this as soon as we are gone. I want the council to believe you were not involved in this."

"Thank you for being the mother I never had, Belander. You will always be in my heart," Dalorthan said. "Enjoy your life on Earth."

Belander stepped onto the transfer pad. "Computer, return me to human form."

Dalorthan initiated the transference sequence and watched as the images on the transfer pads slowly faded away. She carefully monitored the readings to assure her charges arrived safely on Earth. Suddenly, an alert flashed on her screen indicating an attempt to interrupt the transfer.

"No, no, no, no!" Dalorthan said as the images reappeared on the transfer pads. At the same time, a loud banging came from the transfer room door.

Dalorthan looked anxiously at Belander.

"Go to the provisional plan, Dalorthan," she called.

"But we are going into terminal velocity," Dalorthan replied. "You could be lost if we are not successful!"

"Execute the provisional plan, now!" Belander shouted again.

"Executing provisional plan!"

The images on the transfer pads again slowly faded away but returned several times before they were finally gone.

Dalorthan's hand shook as she picked up the immobilizer Belander had left on her console.

She glanced once more at the transfer room door and saw that security was in the process of manually prying the door open.

"I hope you made it. May you live a good and long life, my friends," she whispered before she injected herself and crumpled to the floor.

***

"Councilwoman, someone is initiating transference in transfer room two."

"Identify them."

"The biometrics identifies them as Belander, Molinder, Tredoran and Zangendar."

"Operations, disrupt the transfer!"

"Attempting to intercept," the operations engineer said.

After several moments, the councilwoman barked out the next order. "Status!"

"Disruption successful, Ma'am."

"Security, send a team to transfer room two."

"Councilwoman, transference is being re-initiated."

"Disrupt them again!"

"I cannot. We are entering terminal velocity."

The councilwoman stared straight ahead. "Flight control, continue on course," she said.

"But Councilwoman. If we continue, we will lose them. They will die."

"So be it. Continue on course."

"Yes, Councilwoman."

***

Kenzie glanced at her watch. "It's almost twelve-thirty. I want to be there when they get back, so maybe we should start heading in that direction."

"I agree," Charlie said.

"So, did she say yes?" Kenzie asked as they walked.

Charlie blushed.

"I'm going to take that nice pink tinge on your cheeks as a yes."

"I can't thank you enough for making me see what a jerk I was. I'm glad I listened to you."

"I'm glad you did, too. Was she excited?"

"More excited than normal."

"Wow! She must have been bouncing off the walls!"

"That's putting it mildly."

"Well, I'm happy for both of you."

"Thanks, Kenz."

"There's the transfer site. Let's sit on that rock and wait."

Charlie stopped. "Hold on. Something is happening."

A low humming and crackling sound came from the transference site.

"This is different. I've never heard that sound before," Kenzie said.

The sound persisted at varying degrees of loudness, and an uneasy feeling settled in the pit of Kenzie's stomach as grainy figures appears and then faded away again.

"No!" Kenzie shouted.

Kenzie and Charlie ran into the transference site and felt around. They were not there.

"Oh, my God, Charlie. What if they were lost in the transfer?"

"Don't say that, Kenzie. Don't say that."

Epilogue

Kenzie grabbed two corners of the blanket and spread it on the grassy field at the Crescent Moon Ranch picnic area. Charlie carried a cooler of food and drink from the car and put it down beside the blanket.

"I'm glad we decided on a picnic," Kenzie said. "It's a beautiful day for it."

"I agree." Charlie opened the cooler. "I hope you're hungry. There's a ton of food in here."

"Hey, guys!"

Kenzie and Charlie looked up to see Bree and Jimmy slowly making their way across the field. At eight months pregnant, Bree's walk was more like a waddle. Kenzie reminded herself to tease her about it.

Kenzie and Charlie met them halfway across the field for hugs and handshakes. Kenzie and Bree walked the rest of the way to the blanket with their arms interlocked.

"How are you feeling, Bree?" Kenzie asked.

"Like a whale," she replied.

"It'll pass soon. Have you settled on a name yet?"

"Macho Man wants to name him James Junior, or JR for short."

"How about you?"

"I'm thinking something cool, like Drake, or Austin, or Garth, you know, something unusual."

"Well, you're running out of time to choose."

"I know."

"Here's the blanket. Do you need help getting onto the ground?" Kenzie asked.

"Actually, we brought a lawn chair. Jimmy! Can you run back to the car for the chair?"

"Oops! Sorry, babe. I'll be right back," Jimmy said and he took off on a dead run back across the field.

"Mama!"

"There's my girl!" Kenzie said. She dropped to her knees on the blanket and opened her arms for the red-headed two-year-old to run into. The child giggled when Kenzie planted raspberries on her neck.

"Sorry, Kenz. She got away from me."

Kenzie looked up to see Trey walking slowly across the grass, holding the hand of her own daughter who was the guest of honor at this birthday picnic.

Kenzie turned her attention back to her daughter. She tried to look stern. "Izzy, I told you to hold Auntie Trey's hand until she says it's okay to let go."

"I sorry, Mama."

"It's okay, sweetie. Try to remember next time, okay?"

"Okay. Snoopy kisses!" Izzy yelled.

"Oh, no! Not Snoopy kisses!" Kenzie squealed. She allowed herself to be tackled by the two-year-old and yielded to several tongue licks on her face until she tickled the little girl into submission.

"You know that's gross, don't you?" Bree deadpanned.

"Yeah, but she enjoys it. Oh, here comes Jimmy with your chair."

Jimmy set the chair up and then headed back toward the visitors' center to find a restroom.

"I swear he's the one who's pregnant. He goes to the bathroom more often than I do," Bree said.

"You know it's just an excuse to get the football from the car. Mark my words, he'll have both Charlie and Zan involved in a touch football game before the afternoon is through," Kenzie said.

Izzy tried to climb into Bree's lap as soon as she was seated. "Up, Auntie B," she said as Bree's huge bulge left little room for the child to climb onto.

"Come on, rugrat," Bree said as she scooped the child up and sat her on the arm of the lawn chair. "Sorry, but Auntie B's belly is too big for you to sit on my lap."

Izzy pointed to her abdomen. "Baby," she said.

By this time, Charlie had caught up with Trey, scooped their daughter into his arms, and was playing airplane with her, much to the child's delight.

Izzy immediately climbed off Bree's chair and ran toward Charlie. "Airpane, Uncle Charwie!" she yelled as she ran toward them with her arms straight up in the air.

This allowed Trey the freedom to sit on the blanket and relax for a few moments. She chose a spot that allowed her to face both Kenzie and Bree at the same time. "Man, how can a one-year-old tire you out so fast?" she complained.

"Try a two-year-old," Kenzie said.

"Ah, you two are not making me feel any better about this motherhood thing," Bree added.

"Well, I'm ready to do it again," Trey said. She gently rubbed her abdomen.

Kenzie grabbed her arm. "Are you trying to tell us you're pregnant?" Kenzie asked excitedly.

Trey grinned and nodded vigorously. "Charlie doesn't know yet. I just found out yesterday. One of Kayleigh's birthday gifts is a T-shirt that says, *I'm gonna be a big sister!* I can't wait to see his face when he sees it."

Kenzie hugged her friend. "I'm so happy for you, sis," she said.

"Before you know it, we'll have enough kids between us to open our own daycare center," Bree joked. She reached down for Trey's hand. "Congratulations, kiddo. You and Charlie are great parents."

"Thank you, Bree," Trey replied.

Kenzie reached a hand toward each of her friends and they formed a closed circle of sisterhood. "I'm so glad I have the two you in my life."

"Me, too," came simultaneous replies from Trey and Bree.

"Speaking of sisters, where's Zan?" Trey asked.

"Diaper duty!" Kenzie said. "And here she comes."

Zan left the sidewalk that led to the visitors' center and headed across the grass toward the blanket. "Here, take Sophie. It looks like Charlie has his hands full."

She dropped the diaper bag next to the blanket and handed six-month-old, Sophia, to Kenzie. She kissed Kenzie on the head and then ran across the grass to pick Izzy up to play 'fighter pilot' with Charlie and his daughter Kayleigh.

Kenzie dug a bottle of formula out of the diaper bag. "Hey, sweet pea, whaddaya say we get your lunch out of the way first so the rest of us can enjoy our meal?" The little girl settled into the crook of her arm and eagerly accepted her bottle. Kenzie looked down at her daughter. Another redhead. "I am so in love," she whispered.

Trey leaned forward and looked at the baby. "You and Zan make beautiful babies, Kenzie."

"Kayleigh is just as beautiful," Kenzie responded.

Trey looked at her family playing in the field. "She *is* kind of cute. I am really happy that the human features are more prominent. The gill marks on her neck are barely noticeable, and she has the cutest button nose. She looks a lot like Charlie."

Kenzie looked at Charlie and Zan playing with the girls. "He's a good dad. It's obvious how much he loves his daughter."

"I don't know what I would have done if we had been forced to stay on that ship. I can't imagine never having this kind of life," Trey said.

Kenzie's memories flooded in as she recalled those final moments on the trail while she and Charlie waited for their loved ones to return from the ship.

The humming grew louder, and faint images alternately appeared and then faded. This happened several times before the images simply failed to return at all.

Kenzie fell to her knees and a guttural moan escaped from deep within her. Charlie knelt behind her and wrapped his arms around her while he, too, allowed his fear and anguish to flow from his eyes.

"Charlie, they're gone. My poor Zan, the baby, Trey. They're gone."

"I've got you, Kenz. I've got you," Charlie said while he tried to control his own sorrow.

Charlie was momentarily distracted by a vibration in his back pocket. He reached in, pulled out his cellphone and looked at the screen. He released Kenzie and stood up. "Trey?" he said.

Kenzie immediate climbed to her feet. "Trey? Did you say Trey?"

Charlie smiled through his tears and answered the phone. "Trey?" he said tentatively.

"Charlie, we made it," Trey said.

"Wait. Let me put you on speaker so Kenzie can hear."

"Trey," Kenzie said. "Trey, is Zan with you?" she asked through a voice choked with emotion.

"Yes, we are here. We are all here."

"Are you all right?" Kenzie asked.

"Zan is injured."

"Let me talk to her," Kenzie insisted.

"Kenzie." Zan's voice was raspy, like she was fighting for air.

"Zan. Sweetheart, what happened? Are you all right? Is the baby okay?"

"Our daughter is fine. My ribs are bruised, but otherwise I am okay."

"Where are you?" Charlie asked.

"We are on Bell Rock," Zan replied.

"Bell Rock? How did you get there?"

"I will ask Trey to explain. I need to sit down."

"I love you, Zan," Kenzie said before Trey came back on the line.

"Trey, how did you get to Bell Rock?" Charlie asked.

"We tried to transfer to Little Horse, but the ship was going into terminal velocity and the vortex wasn't strong enough to hold our signal. I am thankful Belander had a provisional plan. Bell Rock has one of the strongest vortexes in Sedona."

"Belander? Is she with you?" Kenzie asked.

"Belander and Molinder are both with us, Kenz."

Charlie took Kenzie's hand and they headed down the trail as they continued their conversation with Trey. "We are on our way, Trey. We'll be there in about twenty minutes," he said.

"I am not sure Zan is well enough to hike down to ground level," Trey said.

"Wait. You're ON Bell Rock, not AT Bell Rock?"

"Yes, the apex was the easiest and most assured point of entry," Trey explained.

Charlie glanced at Kenzie as they walked. "Okay, Trey. New plan. I will drop Kenzie off at the base of the rock so she can meet you at the top, and I will get the helicopter to transport Zan by air, and anyone else who doesn't want to hike down. I need to grab Jimmy first to help me out with the rescue basket."

"Okay. I love you, Charlie."

"I love you, too, Trey. We'll be there soon."

Charlie slipped the phone into his back pocket. "I am so glad I got her a cellphone," he said.

"Charlie, I'll drop you off at the airport and then take your truck to Bell Rock," Kenzie said. "I'm not sure all of us will fit in the helicopter. We're going to need a vehicle to get those of us who hike back down to

the urgent care center, which is where I assume we'll bring Zan."

"Good plan."

"Give me the spare water in your pack, Charlie. I think I may need it once I reach the top."

Kenzie hiked the long and winding path through the Lower Bell Rock and Upper Bell Rock trails in under an hour before she heard her name being called from the top. She looked up and saw Trey waving her arms. She took her hat off and waved it back and then drank about a half-bottle of water before continuing up the Final Ascent portion of the trail.

When Kenzie reached the top, she was sweaty and covered in a fine layer of red rock dust, deposited on her by the wind. Trey met her at the top of the trail.

"I'm kind of sweaty," she warned Trey, who pulled her in for a big hug anyway. "Where's Zan?"

"Sitting in the shade with the parents, just a little farther up the trail." Trey replied.

When they reached the top of the trail, Kenzie saw immediately that Zan was in pain as she sat on a boulder, clutching her side. "Zan!" she whispered hoarsely and then ran to her side. "Zan, sweetheart, what happened?"

"She was assaulted by a guard," Trey said.

"Bastards!" Kenzie said as she slipped her pack off her back. She unzipped it, pulled out a full of bottle of water and then handed the pack to Trey. "There's more water in here. Give it to the others."

Kenzie placed the bottle of water on the ground and then knelt on one knee in front of Zan. "Let me look at your side," she said. She lifted Zan's shirt and exposed a large angry-looking red welt, mid-torso. She ran her fingertips deftly across it.

"Ah," Zan said. She flinched and grunted several times as Kenzie's fingertips pressed into the bruise.

"I'm sorry, love. I know this hurts, but I'm trying to determine if any of your ribs are broken." Kenzie studied Zan's face. *"Are you having problems breathing, like shortness of breath or panting?"*

"No, but my side really hurts when I take a deep breath," Zan replied.

"I don't feel any obvious breaks, but I'm guessing there may be a fracture or two." She leaned in and placed several light kisses on the bruised area, and then pulled Zan's shirt back down. She looked into Zan's eyes and her heart lurched in her chest at the love she saw there.

Kenzie looked out over the landscape toward the airport mesa and spotted a helicopter headed their way. She opened the bottle of water and held it for Zan to drink from. *"Charlie's on the way, love. I'm so sorry this happened to you."*

"I wasn't going to let them keep me there, Kenzie. I needed to come home to you."

Kenzie smiled through her tears. *"Drink. You need to hydrate. You're drinking for two now."*

"Thank you, Kenzie."

"You're welcome. So, is it finished, Zan?"

"It is done. Belander and Molinder helped us to escape. I will forever be indebted to them."

"Maybe it's their way of telling you they love you, Zan."

Zan glanced at her parents. *"They have surprised me in so many ways today."* She looked back at Kenzie. *"Belander is human, Kenzie. The Vakillians came to earth twenty-eight years ago. She met Molinder and they fell in love. She went back to Vakillia with them."*

"Are you serious? She's human?" Kenzie exclaimed.

"Yes, and I am half human. That means our child will be more human than Vakillian."

Kenzie placed a gentle kiss on her lips. "I would love you just as much if you were full Vakillian, Zan. I can't imagine my life without you."

"After today, we will never have to worry about that again. I am here forever if you will have me," Zan said.

"Forever."

***

While Kenzie tended to Zan, Trey handed Belander and Molinder each a bottle of water. "Here, Kenzie brought water for all of us."

"So, that is Kenzie," Belander said.

"Yes."

"Is she a healer?" Molinder asked. "She appears to be examining Zan's wound."

"They call them nurses here on Earth," Trey said.

Belander nodded. "From my experience before I left earth, nurses are the backbone of any medical community. They tend to be more hands-on than the doctors, and in many ways, are more experienced in the treatment of injuries and illnesses."

"Well, I like her already. She knows how to take charge," Molinder said.

Moments later, Charlie hovered the helicopter above them while Bree was lowered down in the basket. She hugged Kenzie as soon as she climbed out.

"I'm so glad you came with them," Kenzie said.

"When it comes to family, there is no limit to what I'll do, Kenz. And besides, I thought you could use another nurse."

Bree and Kenzie worked together to secure Zan in the basket and then gave Jimmy the thumbs up to begin hoisting her into the helicopter while Charlie skillfully kept the helicopter as still as possible in the air above them.

"*He's really good at that,*" *Trey said as she watched the process.*

"*It's what he did during the war in the Middle East. He was a rescue pilot,*" *Bree explained.*

"*Okay, the basket is on the way down again. Who's next?*" *Bree asked.*

Trey approached Belander and Molinder. "*Which of you would like to go first?*"

"*I will go,*" *Molinder said.* "*But tell me, who is the male in the flying machine?*"

Trey looked up. "*The one you can see from the doorway is Jimmy. He is Bree's partner, and the one flying the helicopter is Charlie. He is my partner.*"

"*You have a boyfriend?*" *Belander asked.*

"*Yes, and no,*" *Trey replied.* "*It is complicated.*"

Belander nodded. "*Say no more, daughter. I understand.*"

"*What do you understand, Belinda?*" *Molinder asked.*

"*I will explain it to you later, Molly.*"

Belander took Molinder's hand and walked her over to the basket.

Bree, Trey and Kenzie watched as the basket containing Belander was hoisted upward. Once it was inside, Jimmy gave them a thumbs up signal and slid the helicopter door closed. Since Zan was not injured enough to need emergency medical attention, the plan was to return to the airport and to transport Zan and the others to the clinic by car, where Bree, Trey and Kenzie would meet them.

Kenzie turned to her friends and pulled them into a group hug. "*What would I ever do without you two?*" *she asked.*

"*Well, I for one don't plan to let you find out,*" *Bree said.*

"*Make that two of us,*" *Trey agreed.*

"So, I guess I'm stuck with you then, huh?"
Kenzie said.
"Forever," Bree replied.
"I could think of worse fates," Kenzie chuckled.
"Okay, let's hike down. They'll be waiting for us at the clinic."

Returning her thoughts to the present, Kenzie once more thanked the gods that Zan hadn't been severely injured and that the baby had been okay. When she saw that Zan was wounded, she had been terrified that the future they had planned together would never happen. It turned out Molinder was right though, her ribs were only bruised and not broken. The baby *was* fine but the angry purple hematoma that covered one side of her abdomen for weeks was testament to how hard the guard had hit her.

Zan's parents, Belander (who's original, human name was Belinda) and Molly, moved into the motel room vacated by Zan and Trey, until Zan and Kenzie found a two-bedroom apartment, big enough for their growing family. Belinda and Molly then moved into Kenzie's old apartment, and Trey moved in with Charlie.

Kenzie had grown to love Belinda and Molly. The women were stunningly beautiful, and their love for one another and their family was clearly written on their faces. Kenzie learned that they had made plans to remain on Earth even before Zan and Trey stated their intentions to do the same. Zan and Trey's plans only made their decision easier, since they would not be forced to leave their daughters behind.

Having been born on Earth, Belinda already had an established social security number and personal history so it was relatively easy for her to reestablish herself. She also helped Molinder become Molly, and to insert herself into the medical community, where she was able to contribute greatly to several medical breakthroughs.

Zan and Kenzie jointly decided to delay seeking employment for Zan until after the baby was born. Zan had since secured a position at the Arizona Department of the Interior in Flagstaff, working with environmental regulations.

With Charlie's help, Trey found employment with an aviation agency, also in Flagstaff, and Kenzie finally made the decision to resume her genetics research at the Northern Arizona University Environmental Genetics and Genome Laboratory, with Bree's encouragement, of course, but on the condition that they continued to live in Sedona.

Kenzie, Charlie and Belinda worked with the Arizona Immigration Department to secure fiancée visas for their significant others, and as required by law, they all tied the knot within the first nine months.

That all seemed like a lifetime ago to Kenzie.

Kenzie watched Zan and Charlie play with the girls.

"BaBa! MoMo!" Izzy cried suddenly.

Kenzie, Trey and Bree all sat forward. "They're here," the three of them said, almost in harmonic unison.

Izzy ran across the field and met Belinda and Molly. Belinda scooped the little girl into her arms and swung her around in a circle. "How's BaBa's little girl?" she asked.

Izzy hugged Belinda tightly around the neck and then reached out for Molly to take her.

"MoMo missed you, little one," Molly said, and was rewarded by another tight hug.

"It's Kay-Kay's birfday," Izzy said.

"Yes. Why don't we go say happy birthday to her?" Molly suggested.

Izzy wriggled herself to the ground and then took both Belinda and Molly's hands. "I bwing you, BaBa, MoMo." Izzy led her grandmothers to Zan and Charlie.

Molly immediately took Kayleigh from Charlie's arms. "Happy birthday, sweet girl."

Kenzie looked at Trey and saw the pride on her face as Belinda and Molly made a fuss about her daughter. Trey reached up to wipe a tear from her eye.

Kenzie nudged her. "Go on, sweetie. Go join them."

"I think I will."

Kenzie watched Trey join her parents and sister, Zan, and her heart swelled when both mothers hugged her tight. She was so overwhelmed with love for her family that a tear ran down her own cheek.

"Stop that or you're gonna make me cry, too," Bree said.

"Softy," Kenzie teased. "How about taking your niece off my hands so I can get lunch organized?"

"Hand her here," Bree said. She took the child from Kenzie and settled her onto her shoulder where she promptly fell asleep. "It doesn't get any better than this, Kenz."

Kenzie stood up. "No, it doesn't." She kissed Bree on the head and then opened the cooler.

"Football!" Jimmy yelled from behind them.

Zan and Charlie immediately left Trey alone with the mothers and kids and went out for the pass.

"Told ya!" Kenzie chuckled.

Never in a million years had she thought she could live such a fulfilling and loving life. She wouldn't trade this for anything in the world.

"And to think this all started with a shadow!" Bree said.

THE END

Photo Credit: Song of Myself Photography

See Karen's author page at www.karendbadger.com

About the Author

Karen D. Badger is the author of *On A Wing And A Prayer, Yesterday Once More* (a 2009 Golden Crown Literary Award winner for Speculative Fiction), *In A Family Way, Unchained Memories, Happy Campers, Collective Identity, Sweet Angel, and Relative-ly Speaking, Tailspin, Flashpoint, In The Blink of an Eye and Udder Nonsense* (Books I, II, III, IV, V, VI, VII, VIII, IX and X of the Commitment Series), *The Blue Feather, All My Tomorrows* (sequel to the 2009 award winning *Yesterday Once More*), *1140 Rue Royale, Over The Crescent Moon* (a 2019 Two-time LesFic Bard Award winner for both Historical and Action/Adventure Fiction), *In The Blink Of An Eye – A Young Adult Novel* (a 2019 LesFic Bard Award Finalist for Young Adult Fiction), *A Shadow in Love* (her first attempt at sci-fi romance), and this, her latest novel, *Udder Nonsense* (comedy). All of these works have been released by Badger Bliss Books, which Karen co-owns with her wife Barbara Sawyer (aka Bliss).

Born and raised in Vermont, Karen is the second of five children raised by a fiercely independent mother, who remains one of her best friends. Karen earned her B.A. in Theater and in Elementary Education, and later, a B.S. in mathematics.

In addition to her novels, Karen is the author of more than two dozen technical papers and journal articles on photomask manufacturing, which she has published and has presented at numerous semiconductor industry conferences. She is also the holder of several technical patents. Karen is currently in her forty-third year as a Principal Member of the Technical Staff with a prominent semiconductor manufacturer in Vermont.

Karen and her wife, Barb (a retired Lt. Colonel, U.S. Air Force) live in the beautiful state of Vermont—home of Ben and Jerry's. They spend their spare time with family as well as doing home improvement projects on both their homes in Vermont and New Mexico. They also enjoy camping, kayaking, motorcycling and singing Karaoke.

Please take a moment to visit Karen's author website at www.karendbadger.com, or the Badger Bliss Books website at www.badgerblissbooks.com. Also like us on Facebook!

TITLES BY KAREN D. BADGER
www.badgerblissbooks.com

On A Wing and A Prayer
First edition published by Blue Feather Books, Sept, 2005
Second edition published by Badger Bliss Books, Sept, 2014
Third edition published by Badger Bliss Books, August, 2016
ISBN 13: 978-1-945761-01-0, ISBN 10: 1-945761-01-6

Yesterday Once More
First edition published by Blue Feather Books, July, 2008
Second edition published by Badger Bliss Books, Sept, 2014
Third edition published by Badger Bliss Books, August, 2016
ISBN 13: 978-1-945761-02-7, ISBN 10: 1-945761-02-4
2009 Golden Crown Literary Society Award - Speculative Fiction

In A Family Way – Book One of the Commitment Series
First edition published by Blue Feather Books, March, 2010
Second edition published by Badger Bliss Books, Sept, 2014 Third
edition published by Badger Bliss Books, August, 2016
ISBN 13: 978-1-945761-05-8, ISBN 10: 1-945761-05-9

Unchained Memories – Book Two of the Commitment Series
First edition published by Blue Feather Books, Oct, 2011
Second edition published by Badger Bliss Books, Sept, 2014 Third
edition published by Badger Bliss Books, August, 2016
ISBN 13: 978-1-945761-06-5, ISBN 10: 1-945761-06-7

Happy Campers - Book Three of the Commitment Series
First edition published by Blue Feather Books, Sept, 2013
Second edition published by Badger Bliss Books, Sept, 2014 Third
edition published by Badger Bliss Books, August, 2016
ISBN 13: 978-1-945761-07-2, ISBN 10: 1-945761-07-5

The Blue Feather
First edition published by Blue Feather Books, July, 2014
Second edition published by Badger Bliss Books, Sept, 2014 Third
edition published by Badger Bliss Books, August, 2016
ISBN 13: 978-1-945761-04-1, ISBN 10: 1-945761-04-0

Collective Identity – Book Four of the Commitment Series
First edition published by Badger Bliss Books, January, 2015
Second edition published by Badger Bliss Books, August, 2016
ISBN 13: 978-1-945761-08-9, ISBN 10: 1-945761-08-3

All My Tomorrows – Sequel to Yesterday Once More
First edition published by Badger Bliss Books, May, 2015 Second
edition published by Badger Bliss Books, August, 2016
ISBN 13: 978-1-945761-03-4, ISBN 10: 1-945761-03-2

Sweet Angel – Book Five of the Commitment Series
First edition published by Badger Bliss Books, June, 2015 Second
edition published by Badger Bliss Books, August, 2016
ISBN 13: 978-1-945761-09-6, ISBN 10: 1-945-761-09-1

Relative-ly Speaking – Book Six of the Commitment Series
First edition published by Badger Bliss Books, March, 2016
Second edition published by Badger Bliss Books, August, 2016
ISBN 13: 978-1-945761-10-2, ISBN 10: 1-945-761-10-5

1140 Rue Royale
First edition published by Badger Bliss Books, Sept, 2016
ISBN 13: 978-1-945761-00-3, ISBN 10: 1-945761-00-8
2017 Golden Crown Literary Society Award – Paranormal Fiction

Tailspin- Book Seven of the Commitment Series
First edition published by Badger Bliss Books, December, 2017
ISBN 13: 978-1-945761-22-5, ISBN 10: 1-945761-22-9

Flashpoint – Book Eight of the Commitment Series
First edition published by Badger Bliss Books, December, 2018
ISBN 13: 978-1-945761-24-9, ISBN 10: 1-945761-24-5

Over The Crescent Moon
First edition published by Badger Bliss Books, June, 2019
ISBN 13: 978-1-945761-26-3, ISBN 10: 1-945761-24-5
2019 LesFic Bard Award – Historical Fiction *and*
Action/Adventure

In the Blink of an Eye – A Young Adult Novel – Book Nine of the Commitment Series
First edition published by Badger Bliss Books, December, 2019
ISBN 13: 978-1-945761-28-7, ISBN 10: 1-945761-29-4
2019 LesFic Bard Award Finalist – Young Adult

A Shadow in Love
First edition published by Badger Bliss Books, January, 2021
ISBN 13: 978-1-945761-32-4

Udder Nonsense – Book Ten of the Commitment Series
First edition published by Badger Bliss Books, March, 2021
ISBN 13: 978-1-945761-34-8

COMING SOON FROM KAREN D. BADGER AND BADGER BLISS BOOKS

www.badgerblissbooks.com

Udder Nonsense - Book X of the Billie/Cat Commitment Series
- Comedy
- Tentative release, Mid-2020

For those of you who are fans of the Billie/Cat Commitment Series, you are *really* going to enjoy *Udder Nonsense*. This book is a total departure from the rest of the series in a side-splitting, rip-roaringly funny interlude.

Normally, individual books in a series are supposed to stand alone, such that each one could be read without having to have prior knowledge of the characters. Well, folks, I'm afraid I broke the rules on this one! To truly appreciate *Udder Nonsense*, and to get the biggest bang for your buck on the laugh-meter, you really need to read the rest of the series first. Contact me at karendbadger@together.net and we can talk about how to make that happen at a fraction of the cost.

Here's a sneak preview!

Udder Nonsense

Book X of the Billie/Cat Commitment Series

CHAPTER 1

Cock-a-doodle-do! Cock-a-doodle-do!

"Billie! Billie, wake up. It's time to milk the cows." Cat nudged the woman sleeping by her side.

"Umf," came the reply.

"Billie! The cows are gonna burst if you don't get yerself outta bed!" Cat persisted.

"I don't wanna get up. I'm tired," Billie whined.

"Well, I'm tired too, but you knew what you were gettin' into when you bought this damned farm. Now get 'cher self movin', woman!"

Billie reluctantly pushed herself upright on the bed and swung her legs over the side. She placed her forearms on her thighs and rested her chin nearly on her chest so that her long dark hair fell forward to completely hide her face.

"Damned cows," she mumbled under her breath. "Why can't they milk themselves? If I wanted to pull teats all morning, I'd stay in bed with you. Them beauties of yours beat Bessie's old leathery teats any day!"

Cat had risen and was in the process of putting her housecoat on. She stopped short and placed her hands on her hips. "Billie Charland! Must you always compare me to the cows? 'You got better teats.' 'You got nicer legs.' 'Yer ass ain't as bony.' Geesh! Yer spending way too much time in the barn!" she scolded.

"Yer right," Billie flopped backward onto the bed. "I guess I should go back to sleep, then."

"Oh, no you don't." Cat picked up a pillow and threw it at the prone woman. "Get yerself out to that barn and take care of them cows. I need some milk to make breakfast. I'll go get the young'uns up to help," she ordered and then left Billie alone to fret about her exciting start to the day.

***

"Mom? Wanna tell me again why we bought this farm?" Seth shoveled a pitch fork full of soiled hay into the manure pile.

Billie sat on a three-legged stool and tried her best to squeeze enough milk from the cow for breakfast.

"We bought the farm to give you and your sisters a break from the city, Scout." Billie turned her attention back to the reluctant cow. "You fat piece of shit! Damn it! Gimme some milk or yer gonna *be* dinner!" she cursed at the animal.

"What was wrong with the city?" Seth persisted.

"Too much crime. Too dangerous. After what happened at the high school we thought this would be a safer environment for all of us. Mama and I thought we all needed a break," Billie explained.

"Eww! I don't know what crawled up inside Bessie and died, but this stuff is bad enough to gag a maggot!" Seth complained once more before he dug into the pile for another fork full. "I don't think Mama is crazy about living here," he added.

"What's not to like?" Billie asked. "We've got everything we need right here. We grow our own food, raise our own meat, collect our own eggs, and even draw our own milk—that is, when this overgrown sirloin steak decides to cooperate!" Billie's voice rose a few octaves while directly addressing the bovine in front of her. "So what makes you think Mama doesn't like it here?"

"Well, she was trying to draw water from the pump yesterday and somehow managed to soak herself from head to foot while she was at it. She cursed pretty loudly about outdoor plumbing, outhouses, barns and backwoods living. She was pretty dang mad," Seth explained.

Billie focused on the small squirts of milk that were slowly accumulating in the bottom of the bucket as she listened to her son. "Well, she's just a city girl at heart. It's quite a change for her, going from the luxury of running water, electricity and convenience stores to self reliance. She'll get used to it after a while," she replied.

"She also misses the shopping. She was saying that the general store only sells potato sacks for dresses," Seth added.

Finally satisfied that she had enough milk for breakfast, Billie pushed her stool backward and stood up. She leaned her backside against Bessie and pondered what her son had said.

"Mama has a lot to learn about living on a farm. First, she's got to stop being afraid of the animals. She's even afraid to feed the chickens! Second, the smell is something we've all got to get used to. Face it, all these animals do is eat and shit, well, you know what I mean."

"It didn't help that she stepped into a huge cow pie yesterday." Seth grinned from ear to ear.

Billie looked at the expression on her son's face and snorted loudly, which startled Bessie and caused her to jump sideways. Unable to catch her balance in time, Billie, who had been leaning against the animal, fell backward into the pile of manure-covered hay Seth was shoveling, spilling the contents of the milk bucket all over her.

Billie struggled to regain her composure and her dignity while she climbed back to her feet and shook off as much as the milk and manure as possible. She turned to stare at the bovine.

"Seth!" she shouted. "Fetch the butcher!"

***

"Billie, do you really have to wear those overalls when we come to town?" Cat caught a glimpse of their reflection in the general store's window.

Billie looked down at her clothing. "What's wrong with them?"

"Well, for starters, they're all stained with manure, chicken blood, and God knows what else...and secondly, you're a woman. Don't you even wanna to look like one?" Cat asked.

Billie stood beside Cat and looked at their reflections in the window. Cat was as beautiful as ever. Perfectly coifed hair, perfectly laundered and pressed gingham dress, brightly colored sweater, shiny pumps, sun bonnet and parasol. She was the epitome of a pampered southern belle. Billie on the other hand, wore stained bib-overalls, a flannel shirt with rolled up sleeves and shirt tails hanging out one side, work boots and her hair loosely tied with a piece of rawhide, topped by an old leather cowboy hat.

"What's wrong with the way I look?" Billie asked sincerely.

"What's wrong? What's wrong? Look at yourself! You look like a man with long hair. Ever since we bought this farm you've let yourself go. Look around, Billie. Everyone is staring at you. You're a lawyer for crying out loud. Don't you miss looking the part?" Cat ranted.

Billie did as Cat asked and looked around. Cat was right, they did seem to be drawing stares from several passersby, many of whom Billie tipped her hat to as they passed. One person in particular, who had been standing close enough to hear their conversation, warily approached them while removing his hat.

"Ah, excuse me ladies. I couldn't help but overhear your conversation." The gentleman looked directly at Cat. "Did I hear you say this fine lady here is a lawyer?"

"Yes. Yes she is, although you'd never know to look at her," Cat mumbled. "I'm sorry sir, but I didn't catch your name."

"Stafford. James T. Stafford, at your service, Ma'am. I am the Mayor of this fine town," he said.

"Nice to meet you, Mr. Stafford," Cat replied politely. "My name is Caitlain Charland, Cat for short, and this is my...this is Billie Charland."

Billie looked at her with raised eyebrows.

Mr. Stafford looked back and forth between the ladies. "Charland," he said. "Are you sisters?"

Billie grinned at the double entendre while Cat quickly replied . "Something like that."

"So, Miss Charland," he said to Billie. "You're a lawyer."

"Yes I am, but I'm kind of taking a break from it right now. You see my wif...I mean, my sister and I bought the McCoy farm a few months back and we're trying our hands at farming," she explained.

"I see. Well, I guess I won't bother you then," Mr. Stafford said, clearly disappointed. "Good day, ladies."

Cat, desperate to distract Billie from this asinine farming idea of hers, was not about to allow this opportunity to pass them by. "Mr. Stafford," Cat said, effectively halting his retreat.

"Yes?" Stafford asked.

"May I ask sir, why you are in need of a lawyer?" Cat asked.

Clearly overjoyed that he had their attention once more, Stafford quickly removed his hat. "Well, I seem to have a bit of a problem. You see, someone is blackmailing me," he stated.

"Why?" Billie asked.

"Well, I'd rather not say unless you agree to take the case, Miss Charland. You see, it's kind of personal in nature," Mayor Stafford explained.

"Well, Mr. Stafford, how can Billie consider taking the case without knowing the nature of the problem?" Cat reasoned.

"I suppose you're right," Mr. Stafford responded.

Cat listened attentively to Mr. Stafford's explanation while Billie looked around distractedly.

For the next ten minutes, the Mayor recited every detail about his case. When he was finished, Cat shook his hand enthusiastically.

"Billie, doesn't this sound like an interesting case?" Cat asked.

"Yes, very," Billie replied in a deadpan manner.

Cat frowned at Billie, obviously disappointed with her wife's lack of enthusiasm. She had hoped Billie would be more interested. This case would surely cause Billie to realize how much she missed her law practice in the city.

"So, may I count on you for your services, Miss Charland?" Stafford asked Billie.

Billie looked impatiently at the man and opened her mouth to tell him exactly what he could do with her services, but before she could speak, Cat jumped in.

"We will surely discuss it, Mr. Stafford. As Billie said, we are trying our hand at farming right now, so let me discuss this with her in private to see if she has time to fit it in," Cat suggested.

Mr. Stafford quickly accepted Cat's suggestion. He removed a billfold from his breast pocket and retrieved his business card which he handed it to Billie before shaking both hers and Cat's hands. "I can't thank you enough," Mr. Stafford said.

"You'll be hearing from us soon, Mr. Stafford," Cat said as the man bade them good day.

Billie stared at the business card as Cat watched Mr. Stafford walk away. "Hmph," she mumbled and then flipped the card into a nearby trash can.

Cat was aghast. "Billie! What are you doing?" She retrieved the card from the trash.

"Cat, we moved here to get away from stuff like this. I didn't come all this way to set up a new practice. I'm a farmer now— not a lawyer," Billie explained.

"Billie, you will always be a lawyer just like I'll always be a doctor. You can't resist a good case, and you know it," Cat admonished. "Now, I want you to consider this seriously before closing your mind to the idea. We'll talk more about it tonight."

They stopped in front of the clinic Cat had opened when they moved into the area.

Billie shoved her hands deep into her pockets and looked at Cat. "I'm a farmer now, Cat," was all she said.

"We'll talk later." Cat unlocked the clinic door and pushed it open. "I should be finished around three p.m. I'll see you then?" she asked.

"I'll be here with bells on!" Billie replied.

"Well anything's better than those shitty overalls!" Cat returned with a smile of her own.

"Hmph," Billie replied as she walked toward the saloon.

***

All activity stopped when Billie pushed the swinging doors open and stepped into the saloon. The loud roar that could be heard from outside the building died to a low murmur. All eyes in the room were on her as she sauntered up to the bar.

"What can I get cha?" the bartender asked.

"Gimme a soft drink," she replied.

"A soft drink?" the bartender commented incredulously.

"You got a hearing problem? I said a soft drink." Billie looked around the bar and saw dozens of eyes staring back at her.

Just as she reached for the drink the bartender placed in front of her, a very inebriated man chose that moment to plant himself next to her.

"Fred, gimme a whiskey." He weaved side to side and nearly bumped into Billie as he swayed.

"Haven't you had enough, Barney?" the bartender replied.

"Do I look like a friggin' camel, Fred? I need a drink!" Barney looked at Billie, who was in the process of taking a long drink of soda. "Hey, ain't you that carpet muncher?" he asked loudly

Billie sprayed soda all over the bar. She grabbed Barney by the front of his shirt and slammed him against the bar. "What did you say?" she asked. The murmur in the room suddenly rose several decibels.

"I...I...I," Barney stammered.

Suddenly, a shot was heard and all activity once more came to a halt. Billie released the drunken sop and turned to see a slight, older woman approach her. Billie guessed the woman to be close to seventy years old. She was nearly the same height as Cat and was dressed in an expensive, man's three piece suit, complete with pocket watch and top hat. A large stogie hung from the corner of her mouth. In an odd sort of way, Billie thought that this woman before her resembled an older version of Cat.

"Okay folks, the show's over," the woman declared as she returned a small handgun to her coat pocket. "Barney, go home to your wife. You've had enough to drink for one day. The rest of you, go back to your business."

The woman took Billie by the arm and directed her toward the table in the corner. "Sweetheart, come with me. Fred, bring us two whiskeys," she said.

Too shocked to resist, Billie allowed herself to be dragged to the table in the corner.

"Sit." The woman pushed Billie into a chair and extended her hand. "The name's Wycliffe...Josephine Wycliffe," she said.

"Billie Charland." Billie shook the woman's hand and consciously acknowledged the firm grasp this Wycliffe woman had for her age.

Josephine sat beside Billie and then leaned back and slid the tips of her fingers into her waistband. "You're new in town, aren't cha?" she asked just as the bartender delivered their drinks. "Thanks, Fred," she added.

"Yes. We just purchased the McCoy farm on the outskirts of town," Billie replied.

"We?" Josephine asked.

"Yes, my wif... I mean, my sister and I," Billie explained.

"Sister?" Josephine cocked an eyebrow at her and then lifted her glass to Billie. "Cheers," she said.

Billie picked up her whiskey and toasted Josephine. She downed the shot and then promptly choked as the amber liquid slid down her throat.

Josephine reached forward and patted Billie on the back. "You okay?" she asked.

Billie struggled to catch her breath. "Yeah, I'm okay. Thanks," she replied.

"So, you and your *sister* bought the McCoy farm, huh? Ever farmed before?" Josephine asked.

"Ah, no. As a matter of fact, I'm a lawyer by trade and Cat is a doctor," Billie returned.

"Cat?" Josephine quipped.

"It's short for Caitlain. She's set up a practice here in town," Billie explained.

Josephine's eyes opened wide. "The new doc is your wif...I mean, your sister?" Josephine asked. "Wow, she's a real looker!"

"You've met her?" Billie asked.

Before Josephine could answer, another murmur rose from within the room. Both women looked toward the grand staircase that graced the center of the bar. There, descending the stairs, was the most regal looking older woman Billie had ever seen. Nearly six feet tall, and dressed in a long maroon velvet gown, the woman's aging beauty was firmly in residence. Her long, grey-streaked black hair was pulled up into a loose bun on top of her head with tendrils gracing the periphery of her hairline. A cameo necklace completed the look.

Josephine immediately rose to her feet as she watched the woman descend the stairs. "Damn! She takes my breath away every time she makes an entrance like that," Josephine exclaimed.

Billie was mesmerized. "You know her?" she asked.

"Oh yeah!" Josephine exclaimed, adoration clearly reflected in her eyes.

Halfway down the stairs, the woman noticed the two ladies standing by the table in the corner. She waved and allowed a gentleman to take her hand and escort her toward them. As she approached, Josephine removed her top hat and reached her hand forward to receive the beautiful woman.

"Thank you, John," she said to the woman's escort. She turned to address Billie. "Billie, may I have the pleasure of introducing you to Alexandra Spirakas, owner of this great establishment. Alexandra, my dear, this is Billie Charland. Billie and her sister, wink, wink, just purchased the McCoy farm," Josephine explained.

Alexandra leaned forward to allow Josephine to place a kiss on her cheek before extending her hand to Billie. "Miss Charland, it's so nice to meet you," Alexandra said.

Billie was captivated by this beautiful creature, who bore an uncanny resemblance to herself. She took the lady's hand, bowed at the waist and kissed the back of it. "The pleasure is all mine...and please call me Billie," she replied.

"Billie it is. So is your sister with you, or is she off shopping somewhere?" Alexandra asked.

"Cat is actually working. She runs the local health clinic in town," Billie responded.

Alexandra looked at Josephine. "I assume she is the new doctor you've been ogling?" she asked.

"Oh, no, my dear. I only have eyes for you," Josephine said to Alexandra while winking at Billie.

Billie grinned at the obvious teasing between these ladies.

"So, dear Josephine, what time are the boys coming by?" Alexandra asked.

Josephine removed her pocket watch and checked the time. "In about three hours," she replied. She turned to address Billie once more. "The boys are a group of local ranchers who meet here at three p.m. every day for a few hours of poker before going home to the wives. They're a dim-witted group—haven't figured out yet that I'm a woman—but they don't seem to mind losing their money to me. Personally, I think they come around more for the saloon girls, but heck, no skin off my ass! Would you care to join us, Billie?" she asked.

"As much as I'd like to, Josephine, I need to collect Cat at three p.m., and I've got cows to milk this afternoon, so I'm afraid I'll have to pass," Billie explained regretfully.

"Well then, why don't you and Cat join us for the show tonight. My treat," Alexandra suggested.

"Show?" Billie asked.

"Oh, yes, dear. As you can see, this saloon doubles as a theater. The stage at the far end of the room is where most of the performances are done. We bring in only the best entertainment. The show starts at seven," Alexandra offered.

"Sounds wonderful," Billie replied. "I'll talk to Cat when I pick her up and let you know before we head home," Billie replied. "Thank you so much for the invitation."

"It's the least I can do to welcome you to town. Until later, then," Alexandra said.

"Until later." Billie watched Alexandra make the rounds of the saloon greeting each patron personally.

"She's beautiful," Billie said.

"That she is...that she is," Josephine agreed. "Well, I hate to desert you, but I promised to take the lovely lady to lunch. We hope to see you this evening." Josephine extended her hand to Billie once more, tipped her hat, and then walked away.